Hunting the Witch

A Jane Lawless Mystery

by

ELLEN HART

Bella
BOOKS

2011

Bella Books, Inc.
P.O. Box 10543
Tallahassee, FL 32302

Originally published by St. Martin's Minotaur Edition: 1999
First Bella Books Edition 2011

Printed in the United States of America on acid-free paper
First Edition

Cover designer: Kathy Kruger, Whistling Mouse Illustration & Design

ISBN: 978-1-59493-238-0

For Tim and Midge Bubany
With much love

About the Author

Ellen Hart is the author of twenty-five crime novels in two different series. She is a five-time winner of the Lambda Literary Award for Best Lesbian Mystery, a three-time winner of the Minnesota Book Award for Best Popular Fiction, a two-time winner of the Golden Crown Literary Award, a recipient of the Alice B. Medal, and was made an official GLBT Literary Saint at the Saints & Sinners Literary Festival in New Orleans in 2005. *Entertainment Weekly* named her as one of the "101 Movers and Shakers in the Gay Entertainment Industry." For the past twelve years, Ellen has taught "An Introduction to Writing the Modern Mystery" through the The Loft Literary Center, the largest independent writing community in the nation. In the spring of 2008, Ellen, William Kent Krueger and Carl Brookins (who have traveled together for 9 years promoting their individual novels as The Minnesota Crime Wave) began a monthly TV show, The Minnesota Crime Wave Presents. Segments are available on YouTube and the MCW website, www.minnesotacrimewave.org. Ellen's newest novels are *No Reservations Required*, A Sophie Greenway Mystery (Ballantine, June 2005) and *The Mirror and the Mask*, the seventeenth Jane Lawless mystery (St. Martin's/Minotaur, November 2009). She lives in Minneapolis with her partner of 31 years.

Cast of Characters

Jane Lawless: Owner of the Lyme House Restaurant in Minneapolis.

Cordelia Thorn: Artistic director of the Allen Grimby Repertory Theatre in St. Paul. Jane Lawless's closest friend.

Jeffrey Chapel: Retired Marine Corps colonel. Chief financial officer of the Haymaker Club. Husband of Brenna. Son-in-law of Andrew Dove.

Father Michael Latimer: Priest at the Cathedral of St. Paul.

Patricia Kastner: Owner of the Winter Garden Hotel in Minneapolis. Head of the marketing department at Kastner Gardens. Friend of Jane Lawless's.

Eddie Flynn: Architect.

Andrew Dove: President and CEO of Dove Aviation. President of the Haymaker Club. Father of Brenna Chapel. Father-in-law of Jeffrey Chapel.

Joe Patronelli: Pro football running back. Vice president of the Haymaker Club.

Brenna Chapel: Advertising executive. Wife of Jeffrey. Daughter of Andrew Dove.

Julia Martinsen: Medical doctor.

Loren Ives: Jeffrey Chapel's best friend. Curator of American Decorative Arts at the Comstock Opus Foundation.

Rhonda Wellman: Julia Martinsen and Cordelia Thorn's neighbor at Linden Lofts.

Sgt. Ralph Duvik: Minneapolis police officer, Criminal Investigations Division.

Burl Hedges: Former chief financial officer of the Haymaker Club.

Raymond Lawless: Criminal defense attorney. Jane's father.

Most people are other people. Their thoughts are someone else's opinions, their lives a mimicry, their passions a quotation.

—Oscar Wilde

Chapter 1

ST. PAUL, THURSDAY EVENING

It was a raw, gusty November night the last time Jeffrey Chapel walked up the broad sweep of steps to the St. Paul Cathedral. Entering through the side door, he passed into the vestibule. The two appointments that awaited him in Minneapolis weighed heavily on his mind. To stay focused, to bolster his flagging courage, he needed a few minutes of quiet reflection, and that's why he'd come. The cathedral had become a refuge of late, a place of retreat when he needed time alone.

Jeffrey had never been much of a churchgoer. Before his mother died, she'd written to him, calling him a "lukewarm Catholic"—a mighty condemnation coming from her pious lips. During his many years in the military, he'd never attended church regularly. He hadn't been to confession in years. And yet, with all the chaos surrounding him now, he'd found a kind of peace within the walls of this magnificent baroque edifice. Catholic theology meant nothing to him—less than nothing. It was the atmosphere inside the sanctuary that affected him so deeply.

Perhaps, he reasoned, it was a holdover from his childhood, a time when the Catholic God he'd been taught about was safely on his throne and his own life made sense. Black-and-white creeds were made for children. The curse of adult life was to see those clear-cut blacks and whites dissolve into millions of shades of gray. Jeffrey realized that most of the people in this building believed passionately in their image of God, and though he found their certainty bewildering, the feel of the place still appealed to him, especially since his own life had suffered terribly from a lack of personal conviction.

None of this would have been enough to placate his mother, of course, but in a strange way, Jeffrey needed to be here. He needed the tiny, flickering candles, the hushed voices echoing through the cavernous interior, the scent of polished wood, and the perfume of incense. But most importantly, he needed that reverent, meditative calm, the kind of quiet that got inside his soul and stayed there. He hoped to find strength here tonight, because for what he had to do, he'd need every ounce of strength he could muster.

Entering the nave through one of the rear doors, he saw that a few parishioners were still sitting in the pews, perhaps leftovers from the early evening mass. Directly to his left was an alcove that held Mary's shrine. Breathing in the serene atmosphere, he walked up to the votive candles and lit one, saying a silent prayer. Then, kneeling before the statue, he gazed up into Mary's youthful face. True to form, the artist had created a child, not a woman—a sweet girl who could accept simple answers without question. Jeffrey would have felt more secure confiding in a face that looked as if it had lived a little, one where innocence had been worn away by the hard realities of life. And yet, he'd come here tonight for help; he might as well ask for it.

Bowing his head, he folded his hands and pressed them to his forehead. He quickly became so lost in his own thoughts that he didn't hear the footsteps behind him until a soft voice called, "Colonel Chapel?"

Jeffrey turned to find a short, portly man with a neatly clipped gray beard leaning over him. It was Father Latimer, one of the priests.

"I'm sorry to interrupt you," said the priest apologetically, "but I haven't seen you here in weeks. I've been . . . concerned. I'm leaving in a few minutes, and I was hoping we might talk."

Jeffrey didn't feel like having a conversation just then, but since he owed this particular priest a great deal, he got up and followed him to one of the back pews. He'd been planning to call Father Latimer to thank him for the information he'd passed along almost two months ago, but with everything in his life caving in around him, he'd put it off.

After they'd settled themselves, the priest asked, "Did you see her? Was she able to help?"

Jeffrey looked down at the wedding band on his left hand. Father Latimer had officiated at his marriage five years ago. "Yes," he said, pressing his lips together and looking up at the altar. "I saw her."

"And?"

"It's not good news."

The priest gave a deep sigh, sitting back in the pew. "I was afraid of that."

"Listen, Father, I've done a lot of thinking in the past month. I'm going to ask my wife for a divorce tonight. She deserves much better than me."

The priest looked shocked. "Shouldn't she be the judge of that?"

"No. And I want to take it a step further. Once the divorce is final, I want the church to grant us an annulment. Brenna *must* be able to marry again." As much as he needed to protect his wife from what was bound to happen, he knew he couldn't. The best he could do was cut her loose—give her a second chance—and hope like hell that one day she could forgive him.

"But the sacrament was celebrated. You took vows. It's not as simple as you might think, Colonel."

"Please, I'm retired from the military. You promised to call me Jeffrey."

"Yes, right . . . but . . . you . . . you consummated the marriage, yes? You've slept together?"

"Of course. That's not an issue."

"But it is. I mean—" Latimer paused, then looked off into space.

Jeffrey felt a moment of intense guilt for the pathetic lies he'd told the man during their last meeting. At the time, he had seen no other way.

Returning his attention to Jeffrey, the priest seemed very sad. "God loves you, my son. If you want to talk further—"

"Thanks—but no thanks."

"You say you're going to speak with Brenna tonight?"

3

Jeffrey nodded.

"She doesn't know?"

"She knows something's been wrong for a long time; she just doesn't know what."

"And your father-in-law?"

"He's part of the problem."

"I see." He scratched his beard, looking confused. "Well, actually, I don't see. But . . . have you informed him of your plans?"

Sure, thought Jeffrey. The priest had to be concerned about how one of the parish's most influential members would take the news. "Andrew and I haven't . . . Well, let's just say, we need to sit down and talk. Work some things out."

"You make it sound serious."

"It is."

"But the two of you were always so close—such good friends. I know for a fact that Andrew loves you like his own son."

Jeffrey wasn't sure how to respond.

"If I can be of any help—"

"Nobody can help."

"I think you're wrong there."

But Jeffrey knew he wasn't. He also wasn't interested in debating the subject. "You've been very kind to me. I don't know what I would have done if you hadn't put me onto Julia Martinsen. I've made a mess of everything, Father, and now I have to live with the consequences. I'm not particularly optimistic, but I'll let you know what happens— that is, if you don't read it in the papers first."

The priest grimaced, but offered nothing more.

With one last glance over his shoulder at the statue of Mary, Jeffrey eased out of the pew, nodded good-bye, and then headed for the rear door. It was getting late. A glut of rush-hour traffic would undoubtedly slow him down, and the parking near the hotel would be the usual nightmare. He didn't have a minute to spare.

Trotting down the steps to his car, Jeffrey was struck by the fact that crossing the river tonight meant far more than just driving from St. Paul to Minneapolis. In a way, it was a metaphor. Once he made it to the other side, there'd be no turning back. All bridges would be burned. That's how he'd set it up. And come hell or high water, that's just how he intended to play it.

4

Chapter 2

Patricia Kastner stood underneath the rounded stone arch, the once elegant entrance to the Winter Garden Hotel in downtown Minneapolis, and watched a white limo pull up to the curb. She waited, her excitement growing, as two men got out, both of them eyeing the dilapidated Romanesque building with serious expressions. She wondered where the third member of the group was, but assumed he'd be along shortly.

So, this was it. The moment she'd been waiting for. Two weeks ago she'd presented her proposal to the entire membership of the Haymaker Club, a group comprised of wealthy individuals who donated five percent of their very substantial net incomes to a charitable work each year. The group had hustled Patricia to join almost as hard as she'd hustled them to back her plan to turn the vacant and decaying Winter Garden into the Twin Cities' newest assisted-living home.

At the initial meeting, Patricia had explained in great detail her primary motivations. First, ever since she was a child, she'd loved the decaying grandeur of the Winter Garden. As an adult, she'd come to the conclusion that it should be preserved at all costs, not torn down to make room for another inner-city parking lot, as several developers had proposed. Secondly, last spring when she'd visited New York on a business trip, she'd been introduced to a new kind of assisted-living environment, one targeted at the fastest-growing segment of the population—the aging baby boomer.

The theory was simple. Take an old hotel, preferably one with charm, class, and historic significance, and turn it into luxury apartments for older men and women—those who, for various health reasons, can't live independently any longer, but who also don't want to give up their privileged lifestyle. Add to the mix an à la carte menu of services—a gourmet restaurant on the premises for personal use or for entertaining guests, one that also delivers meals directly to the apartments; a staff of home health care aides; medication reminders; cleaning assistance; even someone to make beds and do laundry—all accomplished with taste and professionalism. Patricia believed that she had the makings of a gold mine.

Quite simply, boomers had bucks. As the time came for them to check out of their homes, they still wanted the good life. And Patricia was planning to give it to them. What was currently available for the aging population's declining years was not only limited, but often depressing. But set the boomers up in the middle of a thriving metropolis, with theatre, sports facilities, and tons of exclusive shops just a stone's throw away, and Patricia bet people would be lining up to get in. It was a gamble, of course, as most new ideas were, but she knew she could make it work. She simply needed a one-time infusion of capital. That's what the Haymaker Club would provide.

Three months ago, Patricia had purchased the building. She came from a family of wealthy boomers herself, and had milked her trust fund for all it was worth. The Winter Garden had been vacant for several years and was viewed by most city planners as a white elephant—too expensive to restore just to keep history alive. She intended to show them a new way to preserve history and, ultimately, to prove them wrong.

While she'd assembled enough money to cover the purchase, Patricia needed a silent partner to back both the restoration and the renovation—and the Haymaker Club fit the bill perfectly. Even though this wasn't a strictly charitable undertaking, Patricia had agreed to provide a fixed number of low-income apartments complete with housing subsidies for those who couldn't afford to pay full price. She could tell by the excited looks on the faces of the Haymaker Club's general membership that this was an idea that appealed to them—personally.

Tonight, the three members of the executive board were scheduled to meet her at the hotel. Eddie Flynn, her architect, was also in attendance. It was his job to explain the proposal firsthand. Because the building had been erected in 1896, Eddie was working with the State Historic Preservation Office to have it placed on the National Register of Historic Places. That would not only ensure the opportunity to take advantage of federal tax credits for capital investments in rental property, but bestow on the building something less tangible and yet equally important—the status of being listed in the National Register. Eddie had worked with the SHPO office before, and he was certain that all the renovations he and his firm were proposing would be considered "sympathetic" alterations and would not in any way endanger the historic nature of the building. The jewel was to be the complete restoration of the main lobby and the first-floor restaurant, the Palmetto Room.

Waiting as the two men walked up the steps to the entrance, Patricia took a moment to study them again. She'd done a thorough investigation of the club before she made her approach, but her face-to-face meeting with Andrew Dove, founding member and the current president of the organization, had told her more in five minutes than had all her research.

Dove was smart, wily, and believed firmly in the good old capitalist ideal. Just her kind of man. He was in his early sixties, tall, elegant, silver-haired. The perfectly clipped beard and the English tweeds he wore gave him a professorial air, although underneath he was really just a hustler in a designer suit. Before purchasing Sterling Air, which he quickly renamed after himself, Dove had been both an entrepreneur and a developer. Shopping centers were his particular specialty. Dove Airlines had appeared on the scene five years ago to challenge Northwest on its home turf, boasting cut-rate fares to most of the larger airlines' priciest destinations. At first, it had seemed to be not only a brilliant idea, but a lucrative one. And yet, in the last six months, Northwest had begun to engage the smaller airline in a fare war. Labor unrest also seemed to dog the new airline. Still, if anyone could make it work, Patricia had confidence that Andrew Dove could.

The younger man, Joe Patronelli, was a running back for the Minnesota Vikings. Patricia assumed he'd been named vice president to add to the group's visibility—something Andrew Dove appeared to covet. In fact, Patronelli was a one-man walking event. Wherever he went, reporters soon followed. He was blue-eyed, dark-haired, hunky, and handsome and, unfortunately, as Patricia had already found out, seemed to know it. He'd been married for many years, but that didn't stop him from making passes at attractive women. In the short time she'd known him, he'd come on to her twice. If he wasn't careful, she just might take him up on his offer. She didn't mind mixing business with pleasure—as long as it was just fun and games.

As Andrew got to the top step, he thrust out his hand. "Good to see you're on time, Ms. Kastner." His smile and his enthusiasm reminded her of a game-show host.

"Where's the third member of your party?" she asked, holding the door open as the two men entered. Joe Patronelli gave her a conspiratorial wink as he walked past.

Frowning, Dove checked his watch. "I'll have Jeffrey's hide if he's not here in the next five minutes."

Jeffrey Chapel, the chief financial officer, was married to Andrew Dove's only daughter. To Patricia's way of thinking, he was the key member of tonight's group because he remained the only potential opposition. Patronelli would do anything Dove said, but not Chapel. After her presentation two weeks earlier, she'd taken some extra time to get to know him. The more they talked, the more she realized she liked him, especially his "can-do" attitude, which would make working with him a pleasure. He appeared to be the kind of man who got things done—and done right.

After his retirement from the marines, Jeffrey had joined Dove Airlines as a senior flight executive. He explained to Patricia that by the end of his twenty-year military career, he'd reached the level of wing commander. She wasn't sure what that meant, but tried to look impressed. He seemed particularly proud of the fact that he'd flown the Harrier, the Marine Corps special jet fighter. Even in retirement, he still served on the board of directors of the Marine Corps League in Quantico, Virginia. And because he seemed to have his own special charisma and following at the club, she'd taken a great deal of care to walk him through the entire project. She hoped it was enough to sway him in her direction.

Patricia led the two men into a small office behind the reception desk where Eddie Flynn had already laid out his architectural plans. Dove instructed the architect to get right down to business. The missing member of their group could be brought up to speed later. By the sarcastic tone of his voice, Patricia could tell something was up between the two men. She wondered what it was, hoping it had nothing to do with the Winter Garden.

Eddie, an attractive young man with ginger hair and a permanently amused expression, immediately took over, explaining how the ten-story structure currently had twenty-four units per floor. These would be combined and made into luxury apartments—some one-bedroom suites, some two-bedroom, and some with the addition of a den or study. He handed the two men the proposed floor plans; then he slipped several renderings of the restored lobby and restaurant out of his portfolio.

As he talked, Patricia stood to the side. She had great confidence in the architect she'd chosen to do the renovation. He was unusually gifted, and therefore in great demand locally. He also had an enthusiasm for his work that he seemed able to pass along to others. Since they were about the same age—late twenties—Eddie's relative youth was hardly a liability in Patricia's eyes. As it turned out, his specialty and passion was for historic restorations. She felt lucky to be working with him.

Sensing that he had the first part of the meeting well in hand, Patricia slipped out and returned to the front entrance to wait for Colonel Chapel. Just as she made it to the door, she saw him bounding up the front steps, two at a time. Ever since their first meeting, she'd been trying to decide who he reminded her of. She'd finally settled on Richard Gere. He had the same sexy movements and animal attractiveness. His bearing was still all marine—but underneath, she could almost feel his pulse. He wasn't as overtly gorgeous as Patronelli, but if *he'd* made a pass at her, he wouldn't have needed to make a second.

"Sorry I'm late," he said, giving her a frustrated smile as he pulled off his leather gloves and stuck them into his pockets.

"You may need those," she said, nodding to the gloves. "We haven't got much heat in here. It's just enough so that the pipes don't freeze."

9

Chapel followed her into the lobby.

"You haven't missed much," she assured him. They stood for a moment while he visually inspected the space. "We're just getting started."

"Then everyone else is here?" His gaze moved to the water damage and the gang graffiti on the walls. "This place really is a mess."

"I'm told most of the problems are cosmetic. The structure is solid as a rock."

He eyed a bank of elevators. "Hey, look at that. Those make me feel like I'm back in Paris. You don't see many open cages in the U.S. anymore."

"They don't work," said Patricia, pulling her leather jacket more snugly around her body. "They're something we may have to replace."

"But they're so . . . rare. All that ornate ironwork. It seems a shame." He walked nearer, pulling back one of the sliding grates. "Maybe the mechanism can be repaired and brought up to code. Even if our group doesn't end up helping you with the renovation, I'd get a second opinion from a structural engineer." Chapel peered down into the dark hole.

She didn't like the sound of his last comment. "Be careful, Colonel. That shaft is open all the way to the basement."

He turned around. "You were going to call me Jeffrey, remember?"

"Oh . . . right." God, he had a sexy smile.

"Come on. Let's find the others."

She would have preferred to talk to Jeffrey privately—to ask him what his sticking points were—but he seemed so intent on being part of the meeting that she led him directly into the back room where Eddie was just finishing his initial run-through.

When Dove heard them come in, he turned around. "How nice that you could join us, Jeffrey." His tone oozed sarcasm.

Chapel didn't respond. Instead, he glanced at Patronelli, then at Eddie.

"You remember Eddie Flynn," said Patricia, trying to ease the tension in the room with an unnecessary introduction.

"Of course," said Chapel, stepping forward to look at the architectural plans.

Something was going on, thought Patricia. She wished she had a better fix on what it was. Even Patronelli looked uncomfortable, and he rarely ever lost his swagger.

"Shall we take a short tour of the building?" said Eddie, moving toward the door. "I'd like to show you some of the more interesting features of the hotel. You can ask whatever questions you want, and then I'll give you some time to look the place over on your own. I feel confident that what you'll see here tonight will not only convince you that our ideas for the Winter Garden are feasible, but also truly exciting."

Patricia brought up the rear as the group left the office.

"The architect who designed the building," continued Eddie, moving slowly through the two-story arcade that served as the main lobby, "was none other than Leroy Buffington." A colonnade of carved marble pillars flanked the space, each pillar topped with a different animal head. "Buffington was famous for his Romanesque designs, but with the Winter Garden, he combined all the classic details—the massive red sandstone exterior, the rounded stone arches, the ornate ironwork—with an even more exuberant examination of the style. This hotel, once restored, will allow us a rare glimpse of our past—the Gay Nineties, with all its brash effervescence."

Eddie allowed that to sink in for a moment. Then he continued, "If you'll all follow me to the end of the arcade, I'd like to show you the famous Palmetto Room. This restaurant was one of the finest in its day—and certainly one of the most architecturally unique."

Patricia was particularly interested in this aspect of the restoration. She had a friend, Jane Lawless, who owned one of the hottest restaurants in town. Patricia was hoping she'd be able to talk her into consulting on this part of the renovation. It would undoubtedly mean some private dinner meetings, even some late night consultations, which was all part of her plan.

The truth was, Patricia had been attracted to Jane ever since they'd first met last fall. This wasn't the first woman she'd been attracted to. Her first love in high school had been another girl. Patricia wanted to pursue a relationship with Jane to see where it might lead, but unfortunately, Jane was currently involved with someone else, a woman Patricia loathed. This might just be the "in" she'd been looking for—a way to spend more time together. If the girlfriend got jealous, hey, it was just business, right? In Patricia's experience, late-night business meetings often led to more pleasurable kinds of negotiations. She figured Jane was already interested in her. All she had to do was apply the right pressure at the right moment.

As Eddie led the way into the restaurant, Patricia heard her cell phone give a beep. Walking away from the group, she removed it from her coat pocket and clicked it on, surprised to find Kate, her secretary, on the line. She sounded upset.

"Slow down," said Patricia, covering her other ear with her hand. Since she was head of marketing at Kastner Gardens, a family-owned home-and-garden store, she knew she had to deal with whatever emergency situation had come up. Returning to the room behind the reception desk, she shut the door. The top half of the door was glass, so if this took more than a few minutes, at least she'd be able to see when the tour ended. She wanted to talk to each member of the board before he left and get a feel for how he was leaning—especially Jeffrey Chapel.

"All right, Kate, what's up?"

"It's that poster—the one you commissioned for the Thanksgiving mum show? The one we do every year at Manderbach's department store?"

"I know where it's held, Kate. What about it?" Wearily, Patricia sat down at the shabby desk.

"Remember how they went back and forth about the date? Well, I'm not clear on how it happened, but the film with the wrong date went to the printer."

"Didn't anyone do a press check?"

"Apparently not. It had been proofed here in the art department by four different people. Actually, I think you saw it too. No one noticed it."

This was a catastrophe. "Give me the bottom line."

"Well . . . it looks like it will be another thirty-five thousand dollars to have it reprinted."

Patricia groaned, covering her eyes with her free hand.

"It was a four-color poster."

"I know that. Isn't there any way to fix this without reprinting the entire thing?"

"Well, I suppose we could print some sort of sticker to put over the date to alter it."

Patricia began to massage her temples. "Is that the best you can do?"

"Well, maybe we could mail an 'oops' note with it. You know, something about the date being changed?"

Thirty-five thousand dollars, thought Patricia. And it was her ass on the line. "How long will it take to redo the film and then reprint?"

"Well, they could make the computer changes in no time. Then three days I suppose for the film and proofs. Then another week for the press to run the new ones off."

The more they talked, the worse it got. Patricia became so consumed by the disaster that she lost track of time. She started making notes on the back of one of her proposal statements. While she was adding up some figures, she heard a soft knock on the door. Looking up, she saw that it was Eddie. He gave her a triumphant grin and a thumbs-up. "We got'em."

She shot to her feet. "Where are they now?"

"Leaving."

"Can't you make them wait?"

"I don't think so. Dove was in a real rush to get home. He said he'd call you in a few days."

Damn. "What about Chapel? He didn't seem all that positive."

"You know what? You worry too much." He folded his arms and leaned casually against the door frame.

Easy for him to say. He hadn't milked his trust fund to within an inch of its life to buy the place. "Can you stay?" she asked, holding her hand over the receiver. "I've got a crisis here, but I should be done in a few minutes."

"Hey, sorry, but I've got a hot date. You understand. We can talk tomorrow. I'll call you first thing in the morning. Will you be at your office?"

"Yes—unless I'm standing in front of a firing squad." Good thing she was the daughter of the owner. "Tell me the truth . . . you really think they were *all* convinced the restoration is a good idea?"

"We've got Dove in our pocket, Patricia. That's all we need. I'll give you the full details tomorrow." He backed out of the doorway with a quick wave.

Half an hour later, Patricia was still on the phone with her secretary trying to run damage control. The longer they talked, the more apparent it became that she wasn't going to find a solution. "Listen, leave the head of graphics a message that I want him in my office at nine sharp tomorrow morning. No excuses."

13

"Will do," said Kate.

As Patricia hung up, she realized her toes were going numb. Nylons and stiletto heels didn't do much to insulate a woman from the cold. Pushing out of the chair, she picked up her briefcase and then started for the door. She was just about to switch off the overhead light when she thought she saw something move out in the lobby. Sure enough, as she came out of the back room, she found a woman standing at the base of the central stairs.

"Can I help you?" she asked, wondering how she got in. Surely Eddie had locked the front door on his way out.

The woman seemed startled by Patricia's abrupt entrance, but quickly recovered, giving her an appraising look. She was thirtyish and attractive, expensively dressed in a full-length fur coat and designer boots. Her long hair, twisted into an elegant bun at the back of her neck, was the color of straw. "I hope so. I'm looking for my husband. Jeffrey Chapel?"

"Oh, sure. Mrs. Chapel. We haven't met yet, but I'm Patricia Kastner. I assume you knew about the meeting here tonight. I'm afraid your husband left about half an hour ago."

"I see." She lowered her eyes, then raised them again. "I don't suppose you know where he went."

"I didn't talk to him before he left."

The woman walked a few paces closer. "We were supposed to meet for dinner at a restaurant just down the street. When he didn't show up, I thought perhaps he'd been delayed here."

"No, sorry." Even though she hid it well, Patricia could tell Mrs. Chapel was upset. "I'm sure there's a simple explanation for why he's late."

She nodded, then bit her lower lip and looked back up the stairs.

"If you'd like, we can take a walk around the building. I can't imagine why he'd stick around, but—"

"That seems like a lot of trouble. Maybe I should just go back to the restaurant and wait."

"That might be the best idea."

"I'm sorry I bothered you." With one last look around, Jeffrey Chapel's wife turned and headed for the front door. Perhaps she was rushing to get back to the restaurant before her husband arrived, but whatever the case, she sure seemed to be in a hurry.

After she'd gone, Patricia crossed to the front door and felt the

14

handle. Sure enough, it turned easily in her hand. Eddie probably thought she was leaving any minute, so why bother to lock up?

Feeling uneasy, Patricia threw the bolt, securing the door. Then she returned to the back room and grabbed a flashlight from one of the lower desk drawers. Something about Mrs. Chapel's demeanor had unsettled her. She needed to make a quick sweep of the building before she left for the night.

Beginning her search on the top floor, she worked her way down. Everything seemed quiet enough as she passed through the dimly lit hallways, shining her flashlight into the rooms. Finally, returning to the main floor, she realized her search was not only pointless, but silly. Yet she knew she had to finish it before she could leave for the night.

On her way down the narrow stone steps to the basement, Patricia thought she heard a noise, a kind of scraping, but assumed it was just traffic sounds coming in from the street. She switched on the light in the laundry room, but found that everything was quiet. That's when she heard it again. Another scraping noise—and then a thump.

Her instincts told her to run and yet she felt an irresistible urge to find the source of the noise. She walked slowly, quietly, toward the west end of the building. As she came around a corner, she felt a breeze. Shining her flashlight on the far wall, she saw that one of the high windows leading to the back alley was open. Beneath the window were a filthy-looking knapsack and a shopping bag filled to overflowing with empty soda cans. This was the second time she'd seen evidence that a homeless man was using the hotel as a place to crash. She'd probably scared him when she came downstairs, and he'd beat it as fast as he could.

First thing tomorrow, she would get a workman in to put some bars on the windows. She didn't want the place trashed any more than it already was.

Well, she thought to herself as she walked back down the hall, Jeffrey Chapel clearly isn't here. By now, he had probably made it to the restaurant and was apologizing to his wife over a glass of merlot.

As Patricia trudged past the elevators on her way back to the stairs, she noticed that one of the iron doors was open. She wondered if the recent street guest had been doing something inside. Making a fire to warm himself. Or shooting up.

Turning her flashlight into the dark hole, she noticed immediately that there was a shiny spot on the floor. As she bent down to examine it, she felt something drip onto her hand. Aiming the flashlight upward, her breath caught in her throat.

"Oh my God!" she gasped, standing up, her eyes transfixed by the sight.

The body of a man was suspended above her in the elevator shaft, hanging upside down, both arms flung outward, one leg caught in the cables. The coat was also tangled in the lines; part of it had fallen forward, covering the man's head. Blood was dripping from some part of the body, but Patricia didn't take time to analyze the source. Wiping the sticky liquid off her skin as if it were burning acid, she felt herself begin to panic. She had to get to her cell phone right away. She might not be able to see the face, but she recognized the clothes.

Jeffrey Chapel wouldn't be joining his wife for dinner.

Chapter 3

GRAND RAPIDS, THURSDAY EVENING

Jane sat on the couch in front of the fire, finishing a letter to her Aunt Beryl that she'd started several days ago. Her little dog Bean was snuggled next to her, chewing halfheartedly on a tennis ball. Ever since she'd been released from the hospital, she'd found it hard to concentrate. The dizziness still bothered her every now and then, and the headaches often sent her to bed in blinding pain. Medication helped some, although she didn't like taking pills. For the past few days, she'd been wondering if she should stop them altogether.

Her doctors maintained that it was just a matter of time before she'd be back to her old self. She knew she needed to hold that thought, though sometimes—like tonight—it was hard. She was lonely and at loose ends, and didn't feel well enough to do much more than sit by the fire. She had noticed an improvement in her overall strength—she could occasionally walk now without the cane. The numbness on the left side of her body had also improved. Most importantly, she was able to drive a car again—that had been a big hurdle. She hated being at the mercy of others. Before her injury, she had no idea how danger-ous being hit on the head could be.

The worst part was, Jane loathed the whole invalid trap. After she got out of the hospital, she'd stayed with her best friend, Cordelia Thorn, for a couple of weeks. She simply couldn't go home, not after what had happened there. She couldn't face the quiet house—or perhaps more precisely, her own sense of vulnerability. Her life had changed since the night she was attacked. She was just now beginning to understand some of the physical as well as psychological ramifica-tions. She had no real notion of what would be permanent and what would go away in time, but one thing she did know for sure: the con-fidence she'd once felt, the sense that she could weather any storm, had been severely damaged.

Just before the attack, Jane had broken up with Julia Martinsen, the woman she'd been dating for nearly a year. Yet somehow, during her stay at the hospital, she and Julia had reconnected. Julia had begged for a second chance—and had promised that when Jane felt stronger, she'd explain to her why she'd lied about so many aspects of her life.

For the first week after Jane had regained consciousness, Julia barely left the hospital room. She said that, because she was a doctor, she wanted to make sure Jane got the best medical care possible. Jane figured all the checking of charts and private consultations with the staff were just ploys to allow Julia to stick around, though Jane was touched by her concern. She didn't want to admit how much she needed Julia's strength as well as her professional judgment. At times she felt inordinately grateful for something as simple as the offer of a cup of tea. Her reactions were completely out of proportion and she knew it, and yet she couldn't stop herself. She was scared, and Julia's reassuring presence helped.

And then later, after Jane had moved into Cordelia's loft, Julia kept at her with invitations to come up north and spend some time at her house on Pokegama Lake. She insisted that the country air would do her good. She could go for walks in the woods. The sauna and hot tub would be great physical therapy. And yet even though Julia painted an inviting picture, Jane wasn't sure she was ready to renew every aspect of their former relationship. Eventually, however, her desire to get away from the city won out over her better judgment.

And that's where she was now: sitting on Julia's couch, writing a letter, and waiting for Julia to come home from the clinic in Earlton.

18

Julia had called around seven to say she'd be late. She'd had an emergency. Such was a doctor's life, as Jane was beginning to find out. She'd been here for three days. So far, Julia had made no demands on her. They kept separate bedrooms, and for now, until they could clear the air with the talk Julia had promised, that's how Jane wanted it to stay.

To be fair, Julia had brought up the subject several times, intending to come clean, to tell it all, but Jane had cut her off. She just couldn't stand any more stress in her life right now. The secret Julia had been keeping from her was bound to be difficult to handle—otherwise, why had she lied or misled Jane so many times about what was going on in her life? No, Jane needed peace and quiet, for the world to be sane, normal, predictable, if only for a little while until she felt better. Passion had to be put on hold too—though, increasingly, she was finding it hard to live this way. She wanted Julia, perhaps more than she ever had, and yet she wasn't sure how much of that "wanting" was pure neediness. Her weakness repelled her, and probably repelled Julia too. She couldn't stand the idea of a relationship built on weakness. No, she had to regain her strength, both mental and physical, before she would feel right making love again. That's just how it had to be.

As she resumed the letter to her aunt, the phone next to her on the end table gave two rings, alerting her to the fact that this was Julia's private line—one she wasn't supposed to answer. The phone had been ringing two or three times an hour for most of the day and had become a growing source of irritation. Getting up from the couch, she grabbed her cane and walked into the study.

Julia had turned off the sound on the answering machine, probably so that Jane couldn't hear what message, if any, was being left. But she'd just about had it with the barrage of phone calls. Turning up the sound, she leaned against the desk and listened.

It was a male voice. Nobody she recognized. *"You know who this is, Doctor, so I'll cut to the chase. I got your message this afternoon. I'm not very happy about it."* The voice seemed to grow angrier. *"If any of this information gets into the wrong hands, you know what could happen. In many ways, I wish to God I'd never heard of you! And now what am I supposed to do? Huh? Any sage advice from the good doctor?"* The line clicked.

Jane felt a familiar ache begin to throb behind her eyes, but she couldn't give in to it. She rewound the tape, sat down behind the desk, and listened to all the messages. Julia would have objected, but then she wasn't home. Besides, in many ways, Jane was past the point of caring about a lot of things these days—a gift from her recent knock on the head. It took almost fifteen minutes to get through all the messages. Most were just like the first—an unfamiliar male voice that ran the gamut of emotions from worried to frustrated to angry. Several pleaded with Julia to change her mind. One was from a man named Loren, or Florian. Jane couldn't quite make it out. He was the only one to actually identify himself. He also didn't seem as angry as the others, but did make it clear that he needed to talk to Julia right away. One of the callers even threatened her. Clearly, these men were all upset. Jane couldn't help but wonder if it didn't have something to do with the secret Julia had been keeping from her ever since they'd first met. Jane had been able to put Julia off up until now, but she couldn't ignore this.

In a kind of confused fog, Jane got up from the chair and made her way slowly back to the living room. The fire was starting to die, but she was too tired to throw more logs on it. Everything took so much effort these days. At this moment she felt very fragile. What did it all mean? Who were these people? How serious was that one man's threat? Jane pressed her hand hard against her temple, trying to calm the pounding behind her eyes. Without giving it much thought, she walked into the kitchen, removed a bottle of brandy from the cupboard, and poured herself a drink.

Julia arrived home shortly after nine. She'd been hoping to get back sooner, but one of her patients had gone into cardiac arrest right in her office, something that had never happened before at the clinic. After attempting to get him stabilized, he'd been taken to St. Gervais in an ambulance. The man was incredibly lucky. If he'd been alone when it happened, he would have died. As it was, his condition was serious. Julia had stayed at the hospital for almost an hour, but since he was now under the care of a highly competent cardiologist, there was nothing more she could do.

Entering her house through the kitchen, she set her bag on the table and then removed her coat. The room was dark, as was the rest of the house, but a dim light came from the living room. Assuming that Jane might have fallen asleep, Julia crept quietly through the open doorway. Sure enough, there she was, lying on the leather sofa, her eyes closed. Bean immediately jumped off a pillow on the floor and ran over to give her a welcome-home lick.

Tiptoeing up to the couch, Julia looked down at the sleeping woman, feeling an overwhelming sense of tenderness. Jane's long chestnut hair, usually kept so neat in a bun or a French braid, was a tangle around her face. She'd lost a lot of weight since the injury. Julia couldn't help but wonder what she'd had to eat today. She saw no evidence of food anywhere—just an open bottle of brandy and a glass on the coffee table. The glass was empty, and the bottle was about two-thirds full. Julia had opened it herself the other night, feeling the need for a nightcap, so she didn't think Jane had taken more than a couple of drinks before she fell asleep.

Sitting down next to her, Julia brushed a lock of hair away from Jane's cheek. The movement caused Jane to stir. Opening her eyes, she glanced over at the fire's dying embers, then reached up and touched Julia's face. Closing her eyes again, she let her hand drop back on her stomach.

"How are you feeling?" asked Julia softly.

Jane cleared her throat. "About the same."

"Have you been taking your medication?"

"Yes, Doctor."

She glanced at the bottle of brandy. "Didn't anyone tell you that it's not okay to mix alcohol with painkillers?"

"Not . . . that I recall."

"Well, I'm telling you now."

"I'm tired, Julia. I don't want a lecture."

Julia stared at her for a moment, then out of frustration leaned down and kissed her. For the first time since she'd arrived, Jane seemed to respond. She kissed Julia back, slipping her arms around her shoulders and drawing her close. "I miss you *so* much," she whispered, caressing Julia's golden hair.

"I miss you too," said Julia. She kissed her again, but for some reason, Jane pulled away and sat up.

"Oh, God," she groaned, holding her head.

"Are you dizzy?"

She nodded, then tried to stand.

"Let me help you."

"No, I can do it myself."

"I know you can, sweetheart." Julia took a deep breath, giving herself a moment to figure out how to handle this. She never knew what kind of mood Jane would be in when she got home. Tonight's was the blackest so far—and at the same time, the most promising. "Since I'm here now, can't you lean on me a little?" She sat on the couch and watched Jane move unsteadily across the room.

"I'm fine." She stumbled, but caught herself on the edge of a chair and sat down.

"That's another reason not to drink. You don't have your normal sense of balance."

"Tell me about it."

It seemed that everything these days was a double entendre. Julia was finding it a bit hard to take. Not that they wouldn't get through it. They had to. She refused to entertain any other outcome. "You'll feel better in the morning."

"Is that your medical opinion, or just another pep talk?"

"Look," said Julia, unable to hide her frustration, "did I do something to upset you? I mean, I walked in here, we kissed, and now all I get is sarcasm."

Jane covered her eyes with her hand. "I'm sorry. Really. It's been a bad day."

"And I'm sorry I couldn't get home earlier."

"It's not your fault. I understand that you have a job."

But Julia could tell something really *was* wrong. "Jane, let me in. Tell me what you're thinking. I get crazy when I feel like you're holding everything inside."

"I'm not. Running a hand through her hair, she gave herself a minute, then said, "If you want the truth: I've been thinking about you, about *us*. What we had. What we've lost. And whether we've got a chance in hell to get any of it back."

"You've got to give it time."

"Time," she repeated. "And me, such a paragon of patience."

"Well . . . then, we'll work on it. Together." Julia tried a smile, though it felt too strained to be anything other than fake. "You know, we've never had that talk. Don't you think it's about time—"

Jane held up her hand, cutting her off. "Yes, it's past due. But not tonight. I'm so tired I can hardly keep my eyes open."

"You're still recovering. You can't expect to get out of the hospital and have instant health."

"It's been five weeks, Julia. *Five weeks.*"

"And look at all the progress you've made."

She shook her head. Pushing out of her chair, she said, "Will you help me up to my bedroom?"

"Of course," said Julia, glad that for once Jane was making an attempt to rein in some of her stupid independence.

Putting her arm around Jane's waist, they started up the stairs.

Halfway up, Jane looked over at her and said, "You better go listen to your phone messages—the ones on your personal line. You must have gotten twenty calls today."

Julia felt her pulse quicken. "Oh?"

"I listened to all of them. About an hour ago. I just sat down in your office and played the tape until it was done."

"You what?" She was aghast. She'd asked Jane not to answer that line. It never entered her mind that she'd listen to her messages.

"They all sounded pretty upset. One of them even threatened your life."

Julia swallowed hard. She was truly at a loss for words. "Jane, I—"

"Are you in trouble?"

She didn't respond.

"Just give me a simple yes or no. It's about all I can handle tonight."

Very slowly, Julia replied, "I don't know, Jane. Maybe."

"Spoken like a true diplomat."

"I'm not trying to put you off."

"No, of course not."

Julia could tell Jane didn't believe her. And why should she? Julia had lied to her more than once. It was all her fault. She'd set the situation up and now she had to live with it.

Continuing on up the stairs, neither one spoke until they reached Jane's bedroom.

"Do you need any help getting undressed?" asked Julia, helping her sit down on the bed.

"No," she said, kicking off her slippers. "I think I'll just sleep in my clothes tonight."

"Whatever you say, sweetheart." Julia could tell Jane was exhausted. It was so hard watching her struggle with the aftermath of this insidious injury. And it was even harder facing the fact that her own problems were leaking into Jane's life. Perhaps she'd made a mistake inviting her up to the lake.

After covering her with several warm blankets, Julia switched off the light and sat down next to her on the edge of the bed. She stroked her forehead soothingly.

"That feels good," whispered Jane, closing her eyes.

"I'm here for you, sweetheart. Always." She wished desperately that it could be true.

They sat like that for several minutes. When Julia felt pretty certain that Jane had fallen asleep, she kissed her on the cheek and then got up. Before she made it to the door, she heard a soft voice call, "Julia?"

She turned around. "What, Janey? I'm still here."

"Be sure all the doors and windows are locked tonight, okay?"

At that moment, Julia felt such an intense wave of guilt, the sensation almost knocked her over. What had she done, allowing Jane to get mixed up in her crazy life? "I will, sweetheart. Rest now. Everything's going to be fine."

Hurrying down the stairs, Julia went straight to her office. She needed to get to those voice messages right away. She didn't want to worry Jane unnecessarily, but she *was* in trouble. Perhaps the worst trouble of her life.

Chapter 4

FRIDAY

Feeling any better today?" asked Julia, looking up from the stove and smiling at Jane as she entered the kitchen.

Jane had been drawn by the smell of frying bacon and freshly brewed coffee. It was the first morning in weeks that she could truly say she felt hungry. "Yes, I guess I am." She ran a hand through her long hair, noticing that the table was set with Julia's best china.

"I thought I'd fix us something to eat before I headed off to the clinic." She checked the contents of the oven, then returned her attention to the bacon.

"What's baking?"

"A coffee cake. The same one you made for me when I stayed with you last summer. I think it's fair to say your cooking expertise is rubbing off." She opened the refrigerator and took out a bowl of eggs. "Scrambled okay?"

"Fine," said Jane, pulling out a chair and sitting down at the glass-topped table. She was always happy when someone cooked for her.

"Why the old-fashioned damn-the-fat-and-cholesterol breakfast?"

"Oh, well, I guess I like to live dangerously."

After yesterday's barrage of phone calls, the irony wasn't lost on either of them.

"I was hoping you'd be up in time to join me." Once Julia had poured the beaten eggs into a pan, she turned around with another bright smile on her face. "Actually, if you hadn't, I would have brought everything up on a tray."

"You're in a good mood this morning." Jane wondered if some of the cheerfulness wasn't a cover. Surely she'd listened to her messages last night. "You know, Julia, I think it's about time we had that talk."

"I agree." She stood motionless for a moment; then she turned the heat off under the bacon and removed the slices to a paper towel. "We will. Tonight."

Jane was relieved that Julia wasn't trying to stonewall her, as she'd done so many times before. "What time will you be home?"

"No later than seven. That is, unless I have another emergency." All of her cheerfulness seemed to have faded. In its place Jane saw a kind of grim determination. Julia quickly scrambled the eggs, and then dished up the plates and removed the coffee cake from the oven.

Her own feelings about the impending conversation were about as mixed as Julia's, and yet after what she'd heard last night, she knew they couldn't put it off any longer. For whatever reason, Jane was feeling a bit better this morning. Instead of spending the day on the couch sleeping or reading a book, she planned to hit Julia's exercise room for a workout. The physical therapy she'd been given in the hospital had taken her only so far. It was about time she started getting serious about her own program. She'd been moping around, feeling sorry for herself for too long.

Once Julia had cut the coffee cake into wedges, she set the plates on the table, poured the coffee, and then sat down. "Dig in," she said, trying to rekindle some of her former cheerfulness.

Jane reached for Julia's hand, squeezing it gently. "I do love you, you know. There was never any question about that."

"I know."

"If we try hard enough, maybe we can work through this."

Julia nodded, though she didn't look all that confident.

The fact was, Jane wasn't either.

For the next few minutes, they ate their food in silence. Jane wasn't quite sure how much more to say about yesterday's phone calls. Deciding to stick to more neutral subjects, at least for the duration of the breakfast, she nodded to the morning paper. "Have you read any of that yet?"

Julia kept abreast of Twin Cities news with a subscription to the *Minneapolis Star Tribune*. "I glanced at the front page. I guess there was another murder yesterday. I didn't read the article."

Jane pulled the paper in front of her. Taking her glasses out of her robe pocket, she skimmed the far left column. "It says here that it happened at the old Winter Garden Hotel. Hey, that's the one Patricia wants to restore."

"Well then," muttered Julia, "it doesn't surprise me. Anything that woman touches turns to—what's the opposite of gold?"

"That's a little harsh, don't you think?"

The truth was, Jane knew that Julia was leery—and perhaps even a little jealous—of her friendship with Patricia Kastner. Julia was keenly aware that Patricia had been pursuing Jane for months. She also knew that when Jane thought her relationship with Julia was over, she had entertained the idea of going out with Patricia.

Jane liked Patricia. She was drawn to the younger woman's energy and feistiness. And the fact that Patricia was more than a little attractive wasn't lost on her either. And yet, after Jane had been attacked, Patricia had backed off. Jane hadn't seen or heard from her in weeks, which made her think that Patricia had finally seen the light, given up her fruitless pursuit, and headed for greener pastures. Patricia Kastner was hardly the kind of woman who'd stick around where she wasn't wanted. She didn't seem to be the romantic type either, believing in fated love. She did, however, believe in sexual attraction, though Jane was never quite sure why such a young woman would be interested in her. Not that forty was over the hill, but it was a far cry from twenty-eight.

Jane continued to read. After a moment, she said, "A guy named Jeffrey Chapel was stabbed and then pushed down an elevator shaft at the Winter Garden. It says Patricia found him tangled in the elevator cables. Jeez, that must have been gruesome." She looked up to see Julia's response. Instead of revulsion, Julia seemed stunned. "What's wrong?" asked Jane.

"You say the man's name was Chapel?"

Jane glanced back at the paper. "Right." She continued to read, this time out loud: "'Chapel was a senior flight executive at Dove Airlines, as well as the new chief financial officer of the Haymaker Club, the philanthropic organization that is currently considering a request to back the renovation of the hotel.'" Again, Jane stopped. "Come on, Julia, why do you have that startled look on your face?"

Julia put her fork down. Very slowly she responded, "I knew him."

It was Jane's turn to be surprised. "That's awful. Did you know him well?"

"No."

"How did you meet?"

"It's . . . a long story."

Jane didn't need to ask the next question, but she did anyway. "Is it part of what you're going to tell me tonight?"

She gave a guarded nod.

"Come on, Julia. I can't wait that long—especially if you've got some inside information about a recent homicide."

"I don't."

Julia clearly expected Jane to believe her, but where Julia was concerned, Jane was hardly the same credulous person she used to be. "Come on, give."

"I can't."

"You mean you won't."

"I have to think about this first." She pushed her plate away and then slid the paper over to her side of the table. After reading through the article herself, she said, "He's survived by a wife. No children. That's it. They don't say anything more."

Jane watched her set the paper down, wondering what she was thinking. "Are you suggesting they left something out?"

Rising from the table, Julia scraped her half-eaten plate of food into the garbage. "I don't know anything about his murder, Jane. You've got to believe me. I wouldn't lie about something like that."

"I'm not accusing you of anything."

Julia leaned against the counter. Her strong, Nordic features were composed, but Jane could tell that it took an effort of will to keep them that way. Julia might not know anything about Jeffrey Chapel's murder, but she did know *something*.

Glancing at her watch, Julia moved away from the counter. "I've got to get going. I don't want to be late for my first appointment."

Lifting her coat from a rack by the back door, she slipped it on, then walked over and gave Jane a kiss on the top of her head. "You'll be okay today, right?"

"Don't worry about me."

"I do," said Julia, her voice regaining its warmth. "More than you know. Don't forget to take your medication."

"I won't."

"And be sure to take a couple of naps. Your body needs the rest."

"I fall asleep at the drop of a hat, Julia. It won't be a problem."

"And there's lots of food in the fridge."

"Do I look like I'm starving?"

"You look thin, Jane. Too thin. I'll bring home some Chinese take-out for dinner." She sighed. "Just eat something, okay? And call if you need anything."

"Yes, Doctor."

As she got to the door, Julia turned around and tried a smile, though it never quite reached her eyes. "Don't forget to keep all the doors locked today—just as a precaution. I'm not trying to scare you, I'm just saying . . . it's better to be safe than sorry. And if someone stops by, just—"

"I won't answer the door, Julia. And I'll brush my teeth and comb my hair—and I promise I won't talk with my mouth full."

Julia shook her head. "I'm insufferable, right?"

"At times."

"Okay, okay. But I just want you to know that everything's going to be fine. We'll talk tonight."

Underneath Julia's positive act, Jane could sense a deeply nervous woman. Thankfully, in just a few short hours, she'd finally hear the secret Julia had been keeping ever since they first met. What Jane feared most was that Julia had actually become involved in something illegal. She wasn't sure how she'd handle that. If worse came to worst, well . . . at least she had her dad. Sometimes, having a criminal defense attorney in the family came in handy. Not that she really believed Julia had committed a crime, but until she knew the whole story, her uneasiness wouldn't go away.

After cleaning up the breakfast dishes, she sat down on the couch. Just about everything tired her out these days. She ended up dozing for a good hour before Bean plopped down in her lap and jolted her awake. He wanted his morning scratch. She snuggled with him for a few minutes, ruffling his fur and telling him he was a good dog. Then, like clockwork, he fell asleep on a floor pillow. He was getting old, and his hearing was so bad that when she got up, he didn't even stir.

For the next hour, Jane walked on the treadmill, did some slow stretches, and then finished up with some relatively easy weight-bearing exercises. As she slipped into the hot tub shortly after one, she wasn't sure she felt any better physically, but her mental attitude was more confident. If she could just continue with this regimen for the next few weeks, she was sure her strength would improve. She desperately wanted her old life back. Health was something she'd always taken for granted, but never again.

Julia's private line continued to ring every so often throughout the day, though not as often as yesterday. Jane listened to the messages if she happened to be near the answering machine, but she made no attempt to hear them all. They were simply a repeat performance of yesterday.

After making herself some lunch, she spent the afternoon reading and napping. Around four, as the light was just beginning to fade over Pokegama Lake, she and Bean went for a short walk along the shore. The November chill felt like a tonic after the closed-up heat of the house. She needed her cane outside for extra stability, especially where there were patches of ice. A tumble out here could be dangerous. Then again, if she never took any risks, even small ones, she'd never get better.

Returning to the second-story deck shortly after five, she and Bean watched the sun set over the lake. She tried to put the coming evening out of her mind and just enjoy the moment, but her Zen skills had never been very good. All she could think about was Julia. How close they'd once been. How much she still loved her. And how they'd reconnected in the hospital only to have that rapprochement poisoned by the secrets that still remained between them.

Once back inside, Jane built a fire and then sat down to phone Cordelia. She had an hour or so before Julia would return from the clinic, and she needed to hear a friendly voice. She also wanted to ask Cordelia if she'd heard anything more about the murder of Jeffrey Chapel—other than what had been printed in the newspaper. Cordelia was the artistic director of a repertory theatre in St. Paul, which didn't necessarily suggest that she'd have any inside information into a homicide investigation, but she was also exceedingly well-connected in the larger community, and that made her an absolute font of local gossip. Occasionally, she even learned things before the nightly news reported them.

The phone rang a good six times before Cordelia's answering machine picked up. Since Jane didn't feel like talking to an inanimate object, she hung up. She tried her father's house next, but he and Marilyn also seemed to be out. She could call Peter and Sigrid, her brother and sister-in-law, but they were having some serious marital problems, and she didn't want to get into the middle of anything—especially not tonight, when she had her own personal drama to face. So, picking up her book again, she decided to read until Julia came home.

By a quarter of seven, she was getting restless. She'd looked at her watch at least a dozen times in the last five minutes. Time seemed to be slowing down in an effort to annoy her. She had to *do* something. Move around. She felt like pouring herself a drink, but knew that Julia would disapprove.

Ending up in the kitchen, she looked around for something to occupy her time. She decided she might as well make some green tea, since Julia said she would bring home Chinese food for dinner. While she was filling the kettle with water, she glanced over and saw that the door leading to the basement was open. It was just a crack, but it struck her as odd because she couldn't recall it being open earlier. Julia always kept it locked, especially since she had an office, files, medical supplies, and an examination room downstairs. She'd explained to Jane that she did private consulting occasionally, and it was just easier to do it from her house.

For a moment, Jane wondered if Julia had come home while she was outside walking along the shore. She moved to the window over-looking the driveway, but saw no car. Maybe Julia had put the Audi in the garage. Walking over to the basement door, she drew it back, but saw that it was pitch dark downstairs.

"Julia?" she called, flipping on the light. "Are you back?"

No answer.

Gripping the side railing with both hands, she started down. She still had trouble negotiating stairs, so she moved slowly. When she reached the bottom, her eyes swept the long central hall. All the doors to the various rooms were closed. She'd only been downstairs once

31

before, but had no trouble remembering which rooms were which. She knocked on Julia's office door first.

"Julia? Trick or treat?"

When she didn't get a response, she tried the knob. It wasn't locked. As she pushed the door open, the overhead light suddenly snapped off, momentarily disorienting her. She realized that the upstairs kitchen light was off too, and that meant someone had flipped the master circuit breaker, cutting the power to the house. In a flash, her thoughts returned to that one threatening phone message. Her stomach clutched. How dumb could she be? All alone in the house, she was a sitting duck. The medication she was taking might help the pain, but it made her thick as a brick.

With her adrenaline kicking into high gear, she felt her way along the wall back toward the stairs. Suddenly, out of nowhere a hand gripped her shoulder, forcing her roughly to the cement floor. Pain shot through her leg as her knee hit with a thud. She let out a groan, then desperately tried to scramble away, all the while searching the darkness for her attacker.

Just as she reached the stairway, a voice whispered, "I'm running out of patience, Doctor. Your files. Where are they?"

So that was it. Someone was after those damn files. "No, you've got it wrong. I'm not the doctor. I'm just a houseguest."

At the same moment, she heard the back door open and Julia's voice call: "Hey, what's going on? Did we blow a fuse?"

Jane heard the unmistakable sound of a gun's hammer being drawn back. Without stopping to consider the consequences, she screamed, "Julia, get out! Now!"

A second later, Jane saw a bright explosion. She also saw clearly for the first time where the intruder was standing. Lunging at his feet, she knocked him down, hearing the gun skitter across the cement.

"Damn you!" he snarled.

She could hear him flailing, groping for his weapon. She tried to slide away, but it was no use. Before she could get up, a hard blow caught her in the side, flipping her onto her back and leaving her gasping for breath.

"Give the doctor a message from me," the voice whispered again. "Tell her that she'd better cooperate. If she doesn't, she won't live long. I'll be in touch."

Jane was only half listening now. In the distance, glass shattered, and then there was silence. She lay on the floor in her cocoon of pain, her knees drawn up to her body, her arms around her stomach, wondering if the guy was really gone. Closing her eyes, she waited to see what would happen next. She was too weak to do anything else.

"I examined the lock on the back door," said Julia, returning from the second floor carrying a blanket. "I think he picked it. And the inside door to the basement wasn't locked."

Jane was lying on the living room couch shivering, and at the same time watching Julia rush around the house, closing curtains and blinds. As Julia covered her with the blanket, she heard the private line ring again. This was intolerable. They had to get out.

"I thought you always kept the basement door locked."

"Not anymore."

The ringing stopped. Several seconds later, it began again.

In utter exasperation, Jane kicked off her covers and started to get up.

"Hey, where do you think you're going?"

"We can't stay, Julia. We've got to pack."

"Not before I check you over." She covered Jane with the blanket again, then sat down on the side of the couch. "No broken ribs," she said, pressing different spots and asking if it hurt.

"Lucky me." Jane's hand found the bruise just above her waist.

"Do you hurt anywhere else?"

"My knee."

She rolled Jane's pant leg up. Touching it a moment, she said, "You've got a nasty bump, but no serious injury. God, but I'm glad I got home when I did."

"Yeah, and almost got your head blown off." She stared at the gun resting in her lap. She'd found it on the floor after Julia had switched the main breaker back on. She didn't know a lot about guns, but she knew this one was a single-action revolver. She also noticed that the identification number had been filed off. "We've got to call the police. And then we should get the hell out. No—scratch that. We should get the hell out first, then call the police."

"Absolutely not. No police."

"But—"

Julia's eyes surveyed the living room. "With the lights off, I don't suppose you got a good look at the guy."

She shook her head.

"But you're sure it was a man, right?"

"I think so. He whispered. He wanted to know where your files were. I know you have a file room downstairs."

"I used to. I moved it."

"Where to?"

Instead of answering, Julia got up and walked to the windows overlooking the deck. Closing a crack in the curtains, she kept her back to Jane.

"The intruder wanted me to give you a message," Jane said. "Another threat. He said you'd better cooperate—or else. He said he'd be in touch."

As Julia turned around, a slight tremor passed across her face. "We're not safe here, Julia."

"I know."

"So what are we going to do?"

"I've been thinking about that all day."

"And?"

More hesitation. She was about to say something when a knock on the front door startled them both into silence.

Jane sat up straight. "Are you going to answer that?"

She hurried across the room and looked out through the peephole. "It's a woman," she whispered. "I've never seen her before."

"Let her in."

"What?"

"Two visitors in one night, especially way out here in the boonies . . . It's a little too much of a coincidence. We need to know why she's here—and what she wants."

"But what if it's the same person?"

Their eyes locked.

Holding up the gun, Jane said, "At least our odds are better this time."

Chapter 5

The woman was tall, blond, attractive, and dressed all in gray. Jane put her age at somewhere in the mid-thirties. Her clothes were expensive—wool slacks, leather boots with an abbreviated high heel, a short fur coat that came down just below her waist, and a matching fur hat. If she had a purse, she'd left it in her car.

"Yes?" said Julia, holding the door open.

The woman's expression was pure ice. "Are you Julia Martinsen?"

"That's right."

"May I come in?"

"What's this about?"

"My husband. I believe he was a friend of yours. I need some information."

Julia seemed hesitant, but finally stepped back, allowing her to enter.

Slipping off her gloves as she came inside, the woman took in the room with one quick appraising glance, her gaze coming to rest on Jane. "Oh," she said, swiveling back to Julia. "I was hoping we could talk privately. This is . . . a personal matter. I'm Brenna Chapel. I believe you know the name?"

Julia glanced at Jane. "I do," she said, shutting the door. "I was very sorry about what happened to your husband."

Bean took that moment to trot down the stairs from the second floor. As soon as he saw Brenna, he galloped over to her, wagging his tail energetically and sniffing her boots.

Brenna glared at him, staying put until he'd finished his examination and had hopped up on the couch next to Jane.

"You know, Mrs. Chapel," said Julia, her frustration beginning to show, "this hasn't been a very good evening for me. Perhaps we could schedule this for another night."

"I've driven all the way from Minneapolis. I don't intend to leave without some answers."

Julia held her gaze, then conceded the point with a shrug. "All right. But anything you've got to say, you can say in front of my friend."

The woman seemed annoyed by Julia's ground rules, but resigned herself to the situation. Sitting down in one of the armchairs, she glanced at Jane and said, "May I at least know who you are?"

"My name's Jane Lawless."

She thought about it for a moment. "I don't suppose you're any relation to Raymond Lawless, the defense attorney."

"He's my father."

The ice melted just a little. "I hear he's a fine lawyer."

"Yeah," said Jane. "Perry Mason in the flesh." So far, Brenna Chapel hadn't impressed her. She didn't think she'd need the gun, but she was pretty sure this woman hadn't come for a friendly chat.

"And you own a restaurant, don't you? I can't recall the name, but someone gave me your cookbook last Christmas."

Jane didn't really feel like making small talk. She wished the woman would get to the point. "Yes. It's called the Lyme House."

"That's it."

Julia sat down on the end of the couch. "So, Mrs. Chapel, what can I do for you?"

Switching her attention back to Julia, Brenna said, "I'm not going to beat around the bush, Doctor. I want to know if you were sleeping with my husband."

If Jane had been chewing gum, she would have swallowed it.

Julia looked dumbfounded. "Whatever gave you that idea?"

"A simple no would answer my question."

"No, Mrs. Chapel."

"But he stayed here overnight."

"How do you know that?"

"I hired a private investigator." Brenna shifted in her chair. She obviously felt uneasy about her actions, but not sufficiently so to hide what she'd done. "My husband and I were having some . . . problems. When he wouldn't talk about it, I went a little crazy. I know he was here twice. If you weren't lovers, then why did he come? He had a perfectly good set of doctors in Minneapolis. He'd hardly need to drive all the way up to Grand Rapids to see you."

Julia sat politely and listened, but made no effort to comment.

"So what was it? Did he get someone pregnant? Do you perform abortions—or broker babies?"

"No, Mrs. Chapel. I don't."

"Then what? Was he hooked on something? Something illegal. Something you were only too willing to supply?"

"I resent—"

"I don't care *what* you resent, lady. I want an answer!"

Julia hesitated, obviously trying to rein in her own anger. "Your husband wasn't addicted to anything I'm aware of."

Her eyes narrowed, subjecting Julia to a penetrating gaze. "I've had a lot of time to think about this, Doctor. I've come up with dozens of different scenarios, each one worse than the last. Was he dying, is that it?"

"No," said Julia.

"Does that mean you examined him?"

Julia crossed her legs and leaned back against the couch cushions. "I'm afraid all I can tell you is that your husband did come to see me. I'm not at liberty to talk about the specifics because he wanted our conversations kept private."

"I'm his wife!"

"I realize that."

"Can't you at least reassure me that what you talked about had nothing to do with his death?"

"I'm sorry, Mrs. Chapel."

"Damn you!" said Brenna, her face flushing in anger. She thrust herself out of the chair. "I'm not going to get a thing out of you, am

I? This was a complete waste of time."

"Again, I'm sorry."

"No you're not. You're an arrogant bitch just like a lot of other doctors."

"What your husband and I discussed is privileged information, Mrs. Chapel. In good conscience, I can't tell you what you want to know."

"Privileged information?" she spit back.

"Yes."

"Then he *was* your patient!"

Julia's expression hardened.

"The man is dead, for god's sake! Murdered!"

"I'm aware of that."

"How do I know you're not responsible?"

Rising from the couch, Julia stood eye to eye with her. "I've had just about enough of your accusations. I had nothing to do with your husband's death. I wasn't even in Minneapolis when he died."

"But you could still be behind it. Or know who is."

"I don't. Look, your husband seemed like a fine man to me, so I understand what a great loss this must be for you, and why you're so upset. I wish I could help you, but I can't."

"That's bullshit, lady. You know what? I may just ask my private investigator to investigate *you*. It may be the only way I ever learn the truth."

"You do what you have to," said Julia, her mouth set in a grim line.

"You're damn right I will," said Brenna. "Maybe I'll even hire a lawyer to subpoena your medical files."

At the mention of files, Jane's ears pricked up.

"Good night, Mrs. Chapel." Julia's words were spoken with a chilly correctness.

Brenna stared at her, her expression full of venom. Finally, turning on her heel, she crossed to the door. "You'll be hearing from my lawyer."

Once she'd slammed the door, Julia walked over to the window overlooking the driveway. "She's backing out," she said, waiting another minute before pronouncing, "She's gone." Turning to Jane, she asked, "So what do you think? Was she the same one you saw downstairs?"

Jane shook her head. "I don't know. She has kind of a low voice. I suppose, if she whispered, I might think it was a guy." She was hoping Julia would come back to the couch, but instead she started to pace.

"I've got to think this through." She paused next to the stairs, rubbing her temples.

"Think what through?" asked Jane. "You've got to help me here. I didn't like that woman much, but you wouldn't give an inch. Couldn't you at least have told her *something* that would have put her mind at rest?"

"It wasn't possible."

" Why?"

Julia's eyes drifted back to the windows. "God, this is a nightmare." After a few more seconds, she seemed to reach a decision. "I'm going to pack your suitcase for you. Do you think you can drive home?"

"Sure, but—"

"We're leaving. Both of us."

"Then you can drive."

"We have to take separate cars."

"Slow down, Julia. You've lost me."

"There are some things I need to do. But I can't stay here. It's not safe."

"Wherever you go, I'll go with you," said Jane.

"You can't." She returned to the couch and removed the blanket from Jane's legs. "You can take the Audi. It's comfortable, and it just about drives itself. I'll keep the Jeep for my use. If you get tired, or you have one of your headaches, just pull off the road—or get a motel room."

"I'm not a baby, Julia. I know how to take care of myself."

Julia's expression softened. "I realize that. But you're not entirely healthy either. I'm going to give you a different pain medication. Hopefully, this one won't make you as sleepy. I'd never ask you to leave if I didn't feel you were in danger staying with me here."

"I agree. But . . . what about our talk?"

"Jane, be serious. We can't deal with that now. We've got to get out of here."

She was probably right, but that didn't mean Jane wasn't frustrated by the change in plans. "When will I see you again?"

"I'll be in the cities on Sunday. I'll meet you at my loft, okay? Seven o'clock. Will you go back and stay with Cordelia until then?"

Jane felt as if she were in the middle of a whirlwind. "Yes, I guess so."

"Good. At least you'll be safe there."

She grabbed Julia's arm. "Just tell me this much. How bad is the trouble you're in?"

"It's more serious than I first suspected," said Julia. "But I'm going to try to handle it. I think I can—given a little time. I'll tell you more on Sunday night."

Jane didn't see that she had any choice. "What about your cell phone? Can't I contact you that way?"

Julia hesitated. "I got rid of it this morning. I may get another one later, but as of tomorrow, my private line at the house is the only way to reach me. I'd prefer you didn't use it, but if there's an emergency, you can always leave a message."

Jane didn't like the sound of that.

"I'll help you upstairs," said Julia. "You can put on some warm clothes. And I'll pack you some sandwiches and hot coffee."

"Maybe you should keep the gun.

"No. You take it. I hate guns."

Reluctantly, Jane got up. She didn't like guns any better than Julia did, but she didn't want to just leave it here either. It was evidence of a crime. Somewhere down the line, it might help prove who'd broken into the house.

Once the two of them had reached the top of the stairs, Julia stopped, turned, and held Jane by her shoulders. "You know I love you, don't you?"

"Sure."

"The idea that we can put our relationship back together is the only thing keeping me going right now." She took Jane in her arms and held her tight; then she kissed her eyes, her cheeks, and finally her lips. "I'm doing this for us—for you. So you can be proud of me." Tears glittered in her eyes.

"Julia, you're not making any sense."

"I know, but just be patient a little while longer. I'll explain everything on Sunday night."

Chapter 6

On the way back to Minneapolis, Jane had to pull off the road only once to rest. The new pain medication Julia had given her was far less sedating. She hadn't realized how goofy she felt simply because of a little pill. It made her want to throw all the pills away—and maybe she would, but she supposed she should talk to Julia about it first.

Sunday night seemed a long way off, but staying at the house on the lake was no longer an option, not after what had happened. Jane didn't much care for Julia's disappearing act, but for now, that's the way it had to be.

It felt good being out on the open road again, her little dog snoring away contentedly on the seat next to her. Julia's car was like a sleek silver bullet, hurtling through the darkness, the soft lights of the dash mingling with the Irish music she'd slipped into the CD player, creating an inner world of warmth and comfort in sharp contrast to the frozen, potentially threatening world outside. The coffee tasted great, and so did the sandwiches. Jane felt almost happy, heading for home on the spur of the moment, living her life again instead of accepting all the limitations her body imposed. The happiness faded a little when she realized that she wasn't going back to her house—or her normal life. At least, not yet.

The closer she got to Minneapolis, the less she felt like staying with Cordelia. She'd had keepers—nurses, doctors, and friends—for the past five weeks, but now that she'd had a taste of freedom, she didn't want to give it up. It felt good to be on her own, even if she wasn't completely well.

It would be almost two A.M. by the time she hit the outskirts of downtown Minneapolis. At two in the morning, Cordelia would just be hitting her stride. She loved the night, and usually stayed up late after a performance at the Allen Grimby. Wineglass in hand, she'd be ready to talk until the wee hours. She'd demand all the details: What had Julia said? Had they slept together? Had Jane learned anything more about Julia's secret? Jane couldn't stand the thought of being interrogated. No, she had another idea in mind for temporary housing—one that, for the time being, would suit her much better.

When she stopped for gas in Hinkley, she got out and stretched, breathing in the chilly night air. Her stomach was starting to feel a little queasy, but she passed it off as just a momentary phase, paid the bill, and headed back to the freeway. As she was pulling out of the gas station, she noticed a dark minivan on the side of the road. It pulled into her lane as soon as she passed by and followed her to the on-ramp. She watched it in the rearview mirror for a few minutes, wondering if it was following her, but as it dropped back into the darkness, she decided she was being unnecessarily paranoid and eventually forgot about it.

Two hours later, the downtown Minneapolis skyline appeared in the distance, the tall spires and bright lights a beacon, calling her back home. She took the 35W turnoff and headed straight for tonight's bed—and tomorrow's breakfast.

When she'd first opened the Lyme House back in the early eighties, she was the head chef for over a year, until she found a woman who seemed to intuitively understand the kind of cuisine she was after. And even after that, she spent a great deal of time in the kitchen. In those early days, she put in long hours—sometimes spending as much as eighty hours a week on the job. Thankfully, she'd had the foresight to design her office as a small home away from home. She'd included a bathroom complete with shower and dressing area, a large closet where she could keep her street clothes and her chef's whites, a fireplace, a comfortable couch for sleeping, and finally, a comfy chair for reading. This was where she planned to spend the next few nights. Her one problem was Bean, but tomorrow she'd drop him off with Evelyn Bratrude, her next-door neighbor. Evelyn was always delighted to take care of him when Jane was out of town—or otherwise occupied.

The Lyme House's downstairs pub closed at one, so Jane doubted anyone on the staff would still be around, which was fine with her. She was exhausted, and her stomach was starting to act up again. She'd taken another pain pill an hour earlier, and she was beginning to wonder if that wasn't the cause of her nausea. The other pain pill made her tired, but at least it didn't make her sick.

After tapping in the security code, Jane entered through the door next to the delivery dock. Bean trotted along beside her as she moved through the darkened kitchen into the main dining room. She set her suitcase down near the large windows overlooking Lake Harriet and then pulled out a chair. Bean hopped up into her lap, and she hugged him, scratching his fur idly as she savored her first moments back. She hadn't set foot in the restaurant since her injury. She'd kept in touch with her manager by phone, but she'd been too weak to resume a normal work schedule. It would still be a while before she could return to work full-time, but just being here again made her feel better—more whole. She loved this place. It was such a huge part of who she was. And with the new, state-of-the art security system she'd installed last summer, she felt safe, even though she was all alone.

As she sat gazing at the moonlight shimmering across the still unfrozen water, she wondered where Julia was, and what she would have to say for herself on Sunday night when they finally got together again. Jane was sick to death thinking about what Julia's "secret" might be. And yet the part she hadn't considered before was the idea that Julia might be in danger. Wherever she was, Jane hoped she was safe.

"Well, Beany," she said, holding him up and giving him a kiss on his furry muzzle. "I guess we better hit the sack." Wearily, they made their way down the stairs to the ground floor. The pub, the banquet rooms, and her office were on this level. After unlocking her office, she switched on a light, let her suitcase thump to the floor, and then sat down behind her desk. Bean curled up on the rug in front of the cold fireplace and quickly fell asleep.

Jane was so tired, she could barely move, but her stomach wasn't going to let her rest—at least not well. She contemplated walking down to the pub so she could get herself a glass of ginger ale, but decided it was too much trouble. Out of habit, she checked her voice messages. For the past couple of weeks, she'd felt well enough to handle a little business, so she'd been calling in every few days to retrieve her messages. The longer she'd been gone from the restaurant, the fewer calls she'd got—until the past few days, when she'd received none at all. So much for being indispensable.

Tonight, however, she did have a call. After a couple of seconds, Patricia Kastner's voice came on the line.

"Jane, hi. It's Patricia. Remember me? Look, I just wanted you to know that I'm not the complete jerk you probably think I am. I came up to the hospital lots of times while you were sick, but both Cordelia and Julia let me know—in no uncertain terms—that I wasn't welcome. I found out through a friend that after you were released, you moved in with Cordelia, so I didn't even try to contact you. And then, yesterday, when I finally did call her and ask to speak with you, she said you weren't staying with her any longer. She wouldn't give me any more information. That's when I phoned your house. But since I just got your answering machine, I thought maybe you'd gone to stay with Julia."

She paused, then continued. "I just wanted you to know that I've been thinking about you. Actually, I haven't *stopped* thinking about you. We never did have that talk. Maybe you and Julia are back together now, but . . . I just thought you should know that I was still hoping we could get together sometime. My life's taken a few bizarre twists recently. Believe it or not, I'm a suspect in a freaking murder investigation! It's no big deal, though. I'm innocent."

Patricia laughed. "Not a word you'd normally associate with me, right? Between you and me, I think the guy's wife did it. I can't prove it, of course. It's just a feeling. Anyway, it's kind of a long story—how this all happened. If you remember, I was trying to find some funding to renovate the old Winter Garden hotel in downtown Minneapolis. Well, I think I've got it. Actually, that's one of the main reasons I called. I was hoping you could take a look at the restaurant. It's a mess now, but I'm told it was once a pretty classy spot. You could be a big help if you'd consider consulting on the renovation—and it might even be fun. If you've got a few minutes sometime, maybe you could give me a call. Surely your jailers will let you make a simple phone call. Sorry—don't mean to be snide. The *hell I* don't. I mean, what do they think I'm going to do to you? Hypnotize you and then drag you off to my cabin in the woods? Hey, come to think of it, that's not a bad idea."

Another pause. "Frankly, Jane, I could use a friendly ear right now. This murder thing has upset me more than I care to admit. I'm the one who found the body, in case you didn't know. It's not the kind of stuff you talk about with just anyone—but I know you'd understand. You were there for me, Jane, when I needed you. I never forget my friends. Anyway, by the time you get this message—if you ever do—I hope you're feeling better. You can reach me at my home, or my office at Kastner Gardens. I . . . I miss you. Maybe I'm wrong, but I think you miss me a little, too. I hope we can talk soon. Bye."

Jane placed the receiver back on the hook and then leaned back in her chair and closed her eyes. She was thoroughly disgusted with the way Julia and Cordelia had behaved. Patricia was right—they'd acted more like jailers than friends. They had no right to prevent Patricia from seeing her. Jane *had* missed her. She'd even picked up the phone to call her more than once, but each time she'd stopped herself, thinking that if Patricia wanted to keep in touch, she would. By not calling or making any attempt to stop by the hospital, Jane assumed Patricia was sending a clear message—she wanted nothing more to do with Jane. Only now did she realize what had been happening behind her back.

Patricia was right about something else, too. By never having that talk, they'd left a lot unresolved between them. Jane was in a somewhat different place now than she'd been on that night back in mid-October when she was positive her relationship with Julia was over. But as much as Julia was still an unanswered question, so was Patricia. Tomorrow was Saturday. First thing in the morning, Jane intended to give her a call and invite her to the restaurant for dinner. And then? Only time would tell.

Chapter 7

MINNEAPOLIS, SATURDAY AFTERNOON

Where were you yesterday?" demanded Andrew Dove, hands rising to his hips. "I called your condo four times. I even drove over. Your car was gone."

Brenna glanced up at her father. She was in the midst of lunch at the Haymaker Club and didn't want to have this discussion right now. She'd arrived around noon, hoping to begin the process of cleaning out her husband's office, but found the door locked up tight, with yellow police tape stretched across it. She'd asked the receptionist for an explanation and was told that the room was considered a crime scene. Her husband's desk calendar had disappeared the same night he'd died.

"I was out," she said, breaking off a piece of her popover.

"With Loren?"

Loren Ives was Jeffrey's best friend. He'd been the first person she'd called on Thursday night after the police had come to her condo with the news of her husband's murder. She knew her father didn't like Loren. He'd made it clear that he thought of him as the smug intellectual type, not the sort of man she or Jeffrey should ever want for a friend. Loren had stayed the rest of the night with her. She didn't care how it looked—she simply couldn't be alone. She'd called her father around midnight to tell him what had happened. She'd been nearly hysterical, choking back her tears, almost unable to talk. When she mentioned that Loren was with her, her father had grown sullen, saying he should be the one there to comfort her.

"No, Dad. I wasn't with Loren yesterday."

"I'm worried about you!"

"I know. But I have to grieve in my own way, in my own time. I left a message with your secretary saying that I wouldn't be back at my own office for several weeks. You'll have to reach me at home."

"Exactly. And I tried, but you weren't there. Where did you go, Brenna?"

She didn't like his demanding tone. "If you must know, I drove up north to see . . . a friend."

"What friend?"

"Why are you interrogating me?"

"I'm your father, honey. I want to help you through this awful time."

She waited until he'd seated himself across from her. Then she said, "You can't. No one can." Her eyes began to tear, but she fought back her emotions. Since Thursday, she'd cried enough tears for ten lifetimes, and still she was no closer to understanding what had happened. She had a feeling that that horrible Dr. Martinsen held the key, but how was she supposed to make her talk?

She'd gone over and over in her mind every detail of the last few days before Jeffrey's death, but she still couldn't understand his behavior. Their marriage might not have been everything she'd ever hoped for or dreamed of, but then, whose was? She'd waited a long time to find the right man—well into her thirties—and when she married, it was forever. She thought Jeffrey felt the same way. Not that they both didn't spend a lot of time working on their careers, but then that's the way the world was today. Workaholism was the norm for upwardly mobile couples. Lately, Jeffrey had grown strange. He'd made her almost hate him, and that's why she'd lashed out. And yet now, she would give anything to take it back, to turn down the heat and try instead for more understanding.

"Honey? What are you thinking?"

She tossed her napkin on the table. It wasn't her fault—at least not *all* her fault. "I'm just trying to make sense of what happened."

Andrew gave a guarded nod.

"Jeffrey seemed so . . . out of sorts lately."

"You have no idea what was upsetting him?"

"None." With a hint of hope in her voice, she asked, "Did he tell you anything? Maybe you know something I don't."

"I'm as much in the dark as you are, honey."

She slumped despondently in her chair.

"Have the police contacted you again?"

"Not since Thursday night."

"I'm sure they will. You've got the name of my lawyer, right?"

The injustice of it all tasted sour in her mouth. "Yes."

Andrew leaned his arms on the table and spoke more confidentially. "After the funeral tomorrow, I thought maybe you'd like to come out to the house and stay with me for a few days. Let me take care of you."

She smiled at him, grateful for his concern. "Thanks, Dad, but I'll be okay."

"Of course you will. But . . . think about it, hon. You'll be all alone in that condo. You won't have any work to occupy your time. What will you do?"

"Try to find a way to put my life back together, even though right now it seems hopeless."

He stopped and thought a little before going on. "It's no good, honey. You're used to activity, to accomplishment. I understand why you don't want to go back to work yet. But just listen to me for a second. I've got another idea, something that might work wonders at getting you back on track."

"Dad, I appreciate—"

Andrew held up his hand. "Hear me out first, please. If your answer is no, I'll accept it. I'm just asking you to give this some thought." A waiter walked by and offered him coffee, but he waved him away. "I'd like you to take over Jeffrey's position here at the club."

"As financial director?"

"It's not a full-time job, honey. At most, it would get you out of the house a few times a week. But it would be something—some focus for your energy. Otherwise, I'm afraid you're going to eat yourself alive.

We're a lot alike, Brenna. We need to be in motion. When we're not busy, we don't know what to do with ourselves."

She had to admit, he had a point. It was probably why she'd come over to the Haymaker Club today, even though she had no real reason to clean out her husband's office—certainly not this soon.

"I feel terrible about Jeffrey's death, but I think it would be a fitting memorial to him if you helped the club go on with his work. Just say you want the job, Brenna, and you'd be a shoo-in. Nobody would challenge your right to take over where your husband left off. You'd still have plenty of time to yourself, time to heal, to grieve."

Sipping her coffee, Brenna ran the pros and cons over in her mind. "Look, I can't give you a decision right now."

"Fine, honey. But don't take too long, okay? We need to get back to Patricia Kastner with our decision in the next couple of weeks. We can't proceed with a final vote on the Winter Garden until we find someone to fill Jeffrey's position. Of course, you'd want to familiarize yourself a bit more with the project. See what you think about it."

"If it was okay with Jeffrey, I'm sure it will be okay with me."

"That's wonderful, honey. Then, the next order of business would be for you to meet with the architect—he's a very talented young man. I could arrange it anytime. And then Patronelli—"

"What's *he* got to do with it?" asked Brenna. "I thought you just paraded him around as a marketing ploy to get other people to join."

Andrew cocked his head. "Do I detect a note of dislike?"

"Not just a note, an entire chord." She hadn't mentioned her feelings to her father before because it hadn't seemed pertinent. When it came to famous football jocks, Andrew Dove was a man with stars in his eyes. But the truth was, Brenna found Joe Patronelli beyond obnoxious. He'd never made a pass at her, but she'd seen him working the crowds at various charity events. He was like a heat-seeking missile. Any women under the age of thirty was a prime target.

"Well, Joe's the other member of the executive committee. Don't you keep up with club news?"

"I guess not."

"For your information, he's been invaluable."

She groaned.

"You know, honey, you wouldn't have to work with him directly. He'd be more of a liaison between the architect, Patricia Kastner—the owner of the hotel—and the club."

Brenna nodded, taking the last bite of her salad.

"You could even move right into Jeffrey's office."

At least she wouldn't have to clean it out. Going through his things at home was hard enough. So hard, in fact, that every time she opened his closet to look at his suits and ties, she started to cry. It was too soon to deal with his personal belongings, and yet her father was right. She had trouble just sitting around. Erasing Jeffrey from her life wasn't the way to keep busy. "I'll give you an answer Monday, after the funeral."

"Fine, honey." Andrew pushed away from the table, then stopped himself. "Say, do you need help with anything? I mean, have all the arrangements been made at the cathedral?"

"Everything's taken care of, Dad. Loren's been by my side through the entire ordeal. He's handled it all."

"It's hard to believe he could tear himself away from his precious antiques."

Loren was the curator for eighteenth- and nineteenth-century American decorative arts at the Comstock Opus Foundation. He and Jeffrey had roomed together at the University of Minnesota until graduation, when Jeffrey headed off to officer candidate school in Quantico, Virginia and Loren went on to receive his doctorate at Princeton.

"Be nice to him at the funeral, Dad. He's my friend too."

Looking disgruntled, Andrew said, "I'll see you on Monday."

Brenna sat at the table and watched her father walk away, glad that he'd finally gone, and at the same time lonely for the company of another human being. Before her marriage, she'd been so good at being alone. It was a skill that had atrophied in the last five years.

Waving at the waiter for her bill, her gaze drifted around the crowded restaurant. On Saturday afternoons, the club was a popular place. It probably hadn't been the best choice to have lunch here. A few club members had come up to her, extending their sympathies, but mostly she'd been left to eat in peace—for which she was grateful. She didn't have much of an appetite, but knew she had to eat something. The restaurant was bright with afternoon sunlight—open, airy, with lots of greenery.

As she waited for the check, she decided that perhaps her dad's idea wasn't such a bad one after all. The Haymaker Club was familiar and, in its own way, comforting. Her father had designed the club to blend the modern with the traditional. Everything, from the furnishings to the food, was first class. It was located in the IGS Tower, one of the largest and most prestigious skyscrapers in the Twin Cities, and took up three full floors.

The restaurant, bar, and main offices were on the twenty-fourth floor. Up one flight were conference rooms; a library containing recent periodicals and most of the daily papers from around the country; a dark, oak-paneled smoking room complete with coffee bar; and a business center where members could send a fax, browse the Internet via state-of-the-art computers; or use one of the many private phone-conferencing rooms. On the twenty-sixth floor were eight luxury apartments maintained for the members' private use. Some might be reserved for a night or two, while others might be booked for a month or more, depending on a member's needs. There was also a gym on that level, though it was small.

After paying her bill, Brenna left immediately for home. Loren was coming by later in the afternoon to discuss the last-minute details for the funeral, and she wanted to take a nap before he arrived. She was still tired from her trip up north yesterday. It had been a long drive—and a depressing one.

Entering her downtown condo half an hour later, Brenna tossed her coat over a chair and switched on the TV. For now, silence was the enemy. She turned the volume down so that it served as background noise, and then grabbed a blanket and stretched out on the couch. She was almost asleep when the fax line rang. Annoyed at the interruption, but curious what it might be about, she got up and crossed into the study where the machine was hooked up next to the computer. She lifted the paper from the tray and read the typewritten words.

Fax Transmission
Page 1 of 1
Date: November 23
To: Brenna Chapel
From: ?
Dear Brenna:
In case you didn't know, your husband was a faggot. I have the proof. If you would like to keep his little secret safe from the prying eyes of the public, I will contact you soon with my

proposition. If you speak to the police about this, the deal is off, and the details of your husband's secret life will appear in the local papers in a matter of days. If you do not want to risk this, wait for my next communication.

Brenna was stunned. More than stunned. She was dumbfounded. She sank into the desk chair and reread the message several times. Finally, she looked at the top of the sheet to see where the fax had come from. "The Haymaker Club," she whispered, letting the significance sink in. Was it possible the message came from someone she knew?

Her first inclination was to show the fax to Sgt. Duvik, the homicide investigator in charge of her husband's case, but she quickly nixed the idea, deciding that she didn't want anyone to get wind of it until she knew more herself. But what about Loren? He'd be arriving in a few minutes. It didn't seem fair to just drop this kind of news on him—especially not two days before he buried a man he'd known and loved for over twenty years. How could she let this slander ruin that moment? She didn't for an instant believe it was true, but knew that once a rumor got started, it developed a life of its own. She owed it to Jeffrey to preserve his good name.

As the doorbell sounded, announcing Loren's arrival, Brenna folded the sheet of paper and slipped it into the pocket of her sweater. For now, at least, she'd decided to do what the message suggested. She would keep it to herself and wait for further instructions. She had a sinking feeling that she wouldn't have to wait long.

Chapter 8

"Get in here, girl. You had me worried sick." Cordelia opened the door of her loft and yanked Jane inside.

"It's nice to see you, too," said Jane, rubbing her arm.

"Don't give me that *nice* crap." Cordelia stomped into the kitchen and turned down the heat under a tall pot; then she returned to the living room. "I got a call from Julia a little over an hour ago. She wanted to talk to you. I, being a rational human being, thought she'd lost her mind. I mean, last I heard, you were staying with *her*. If she'd misplaced you, it was her fault, not mine. So I told her that in no uncertain terms, and that's when she explained that you'd driven back to Minneapolis last night all by yourself. Well! That gave me a brief heart tremor, but it passed, no thanks to you. Then she said you were supposed to come directly to my loft. When I told her I hadn't seen or heard from you, we both had a meltdown—a *major* meltdown, Janey. Where the hell were you?" She waved air into her face with a black and gold oriental fan—one that matched the glitzy chopsticks in her hair—but didn't stop talking long enough for Jane to answer. "After I got off the phone, I called your house, Julia's upstairs loft, and every other place I could think of. I had visions of you being blown away by some deranged highway pervert and your body ending up in a wood chipper. I saw *Fargo*, you know. *Four* times. I know what dangers lurk out there on the open road. Besides, you had no business driving by yourself. You're still sick."

"Amazingly enough, I seem to have made it," said Jane, sniffing the air. Cordelia was cooking a Russian beef stew. It was one of Jane's recipes, and it smelled wonderful.

"So where did you spend the night? Julia thought maybe the driving had tired you out and you decided to stop at a motel. That gave us both a brief moment of peace—until I got to thinking about Norman Bates."

"Cordelia, I stayed at the restaurant. In my office. By the way, did Julia happen to say when she'd be getting into town?"

"By the way? *By the way!* Here I am, worried sick about you for the past hour, and you stand there with that Noel Coward insouciance of yours and ask a casual question!"

"I'm sorry, Cordelia. I apologize. I should have called you when I got in."

"Damn straight."

"It was terribly late."

"Oh, pull-ease. Since when has my beauty sleep been any concern of yours?"

Jane walked over to the couch and eased herself down. She hadn't taken any pain medication since last night, and her left leg was killing her. Thankfully, her normal afternoon headache wasn't too bad.

Noticing that Jane was in pain, Cordelia rushed over to the couch. "Are you all right? Can I get you anything?"

"I'm fine, Cordelia. Just a little sore. And I really *am* sorry I caused you to worry. I thought I'd have plenty of time to get hold of you today to tell you what happened."

Cordelia cocked an eyebrow. "What did happen?"

"First tell me if Julia left me a message."

"No message, Janey. She was rushing—on her way to catch a plane."

"A plane? To where?"

"She didn't say. But she'll call again tonight. She assumed you'd be back staying with me by then."

"Actually, I won't."

"No?" Cordelia moved her shiplike frame over to her favorite comfy chair and dropped anchor. "And pray tell, where will you be?"

"I'm going to stay at the restaurant for a while."

"Can't stand my cooking, huh?"

Jane smiled. "No, of course not. You're a great cook."

"Maybe there's not enough room for you here?"

Again, she smiled. Cordelia's loft was huge. Eighty feet long by thirty feet wide, with fourteen-foot-high ceilings. All six lofts in the Linden Building—including Julia's, which was located directly above Cordelia's—were the same size, but appointed differently. Some were open, like Cordelia's, and some had walls dividing the space into more traditional rooms. Julia had inherited the building after her mother's death last year. Since moving to northern Minnesota, she'd rarely used her loft, but tomorrow night, that's where she and Jane would meet. "I just want to try being on my own for a while."

"I see," said Cordelia, steepling her fingers together in front of her. "Well, at least you can stay for dinner. Fill me in on what happened while you were up north visiting Dr. Kildare."

"Sorry, but I can't." Jane glanced up at the fresco Cordelia had commissioned a friend, a set designer at the theatre, to paint on the ceiling. It was finally complete, all the gold leaf having been added. One half of the mural was a rip-off of Michelangelo's *Creation*—the finger of God touching the finger of Man. Except, in Cordelia's version, God was touching the white-gloved finger of Minnie Mouse. Where the hands met, Renaissance gave way to pure Peter Max. The rest of the apartment was equally eccentric. At the far end, Cordelia had built a stage. Jane wasn't quite sure what she planned to use it for, but as Cordelia said, "All life's mysteries will be made clear in time."

"And why can't you stay?" asked Cordelia, tapping her foot impatiently.

"I have a dinner date."

"Dare I ask with whom?"

Jane knew the answer wasn't going to please her, so she braced herself for another explosion. "Patricia Kastner. I called her this afternoon, and she happened to be free."

"Well! Now I can see why you couldn't possibly stay. You're having dinner with God's gift to bar gropers." She leveled her gaze.

"You might try to be a little nicer. Her mother may have some influence on your future career at the Grimby. Patricia could put in a good word for you."

"I'd rather drag my tongue through ground glass than ask that woman for a favor."

"Has anyone ever told you you need to work on expressing yourself more clearly?"

She gave a disgruntled harumph. "That little twit is bad news, Jane. Take the advice of someone who's been around the block a few times. Stay away from her."

"She's hardly a *twit*. She's being groomed to take over Kastner Gardens, one of the largest home-and-garden stores in the Midwest, and she just bought a multimillion-dollar hotel."

"I'm speaking of her private life, Janey. Twit is as twit does. It's an ancient axiom. Forget it at your peril."

"You know, since we're on the subject of Patricia, I think we need to clear the air. As I understand it, you prevented her from seeing me at the hospital. I just found out about it last night."

"No doubt from the horse's ass—excuse me, I mean *mouth.* "

Jane shook her head. "And then later, when I was staying here, you wouldn't take her calls."

"She only called once."

"You're splitting hairs."

"Possibly. What's your point?"

"That I'm angry! You have no right to control who I see or don't see."

"I had every right!"

"And how do you figure that?"

"Janey, just think back. Before you were attacked, you were literally falling apart. You thought your relationship with Julia was over. You weren't sleeping. You were drinking too much. And because of all the stress you didn't have the wit to see the kind of person Patricia Kastner really is."

"Meaning?"

"Janey, she could have *prevented* what happened to you if she'd wanted to."

Jane shook her head. "That's not true."

"It is! Open your eyes."

"They *are* open."

"But you're still not yourself. You're ill. Give yourself some time. Stay away from her until you're stronger—until you're back to being the sane, sensible woman you've always been."

Jane was fed up with Cordelia's dim view of her mental state—both prior to her injury and now. "I'm fine, Cordelia. And I resent your insinuation that I'm not."

In utter exasperation, Cordelia flung her arms in the air. "Then why are you dating a psychopath?"

"I'm not *dating* her," said Jane, trying to keep her voice even. "I'm merely having dinner with her."

"Now who's splitting hairs?"

Jane stood. Her head was beginning to throb. "I've got to go."

"But you just got here."

"I can't have this argument right now."

Cordelia got up too, putting a hand on Jane's arm as she passed by, stopping her. "I'm sorry, Janey. Really, I'll stop."

"You can't, Cordelia. We just see things differently."

"But . . . stay a little while longer. You haven't even told me why you left Julia's house. Did the two of you have a fight?"

She pressed her fingers to her right temple. With each passing second, the tension inside her head coiled tighter. "No. It wasn't that simple."

"You know, dearheart, I really came to respect Julia while you were in the hospital. I might have doubted her feelings for you before, but she never left your side. I think she truly cares about you."

"I think so, too."

"So," said Cordelia, wiggling her eyebrows suggestively. "Did you . . . you know? Have some fun together?"

"No, Cordelia." Anger edged back into her voice. "We didn't sleep together, if that's what you're asking. And no, I still don't know what her secret is. I do know that she's in danger. Last night, I was attacked in the basement of her home by someone with a gun. That's why I left in such a hurry. Julia left too. It was too dangerous for either of us to stay there any longer."

"Heavens!" Cordelia's hand flew to her chest.

"So when she phones tonight, tell her to call the restaurant's main number. They'll find me, wherever I am." She pushed her way past Cordelia and headed for the door.

"Janey?"

"What?" She stopped, but kept her back to Cordelia.

"I can see that I've hurt you, and for that I'm sorry. You're my best friend. If I've done something to damage that friendship, you have to understand—I did it out of love and concern."

Jane did understand. And yet, at this moment, she felt a cold, confusing distance between them.

"Don't go. Stay and talk to me a while longer. I've missed you."

Jane lowered her head. "I'll call you tomorrow."

Cordelia was silent for several seconds. Finally, in a soft, defeated voice, she said, "All right."

Jane felt terrible about leaving on such a negative note, but she couldn't stay. After she had that talk with Julia tomorrow night, she had faith that her life would finally come back into some kind of focus. And then, she'd make it right with Cordelia.

Chapter 9

At nine sharp, Jane stood in the shadows near the entrance to the pub and watched Patricia Kastner talk briefly to a bartender. Jane hadn't seen her in over a month. In that time, her punk shag had been replaced by a new cut. Her black hair wasn't quite shoulder-length, but it was longer, and she'd grown bangs. Her *Pulp Fiction* look was further enhanced by a tight leather miniskirt, matching vest, black nylons, heels, and a red silk blouse. She looked terrific.

The bartender pointed Patricia to the more intimate, dimly lit back room, where a fire glowed softly in the stone hearth. Jane had reserved the same table they'd sat at several times before, hoping Patricia didn't mind that they weren't eating in the main dining room upstairs. Jane simply felt more comfortable right now in the semidarkness.

Since she'd lost quite a bit of weight in the past five weeks, most of her clothes hung limply on her body. So, wanting to look her best tonight—she viewed it as her first night back in the real world—she'd gone shopping earlier in the day. She'd bought a couple of pairs of new jeans, two new ski sweaters, and for more formal occasions, a pair of gray wool slacks, a black turtleneck, and a dark green blazer. The trip had tired her out, so much so that she felt the need for her cane tonight. She didn't want her leg to buckle at the wrong moment and send her crashing into one of her customers.

Approaching the pub's back room, she saw that Patricia had taken a seat and was studying the menu. When she looked up and saw Jane in the doorway, she smiled, but as her eyes locked on the cane, the smile dimmed.

Jane tried not to limp as she made her way to the table, but it was hopeless. As she got closer, she couldn't stand the look in Patricia's eyes. Pity was the last emotion she wanted to engender. "You made it," she said, sitting down with some difficulty. "The weather's pretty nasty tonight."

Patricia's smile returned to high beam. "God but you look great."

"You're lying."

"I never lie," she said indignantly.

"Come on, Patricia. I look like I've been through the Crimean War."

"Hey, you think I'm all weirded out because of the cane? Canes don't bother me. They suggest a sort of classy eccentricity. Besides, they come in handy when you want to club someone."

Jane couldn't help but laugh.

"You've lost weight."

"One of the perks of severe head trauma."

Patricia frowned and looked down. "I'm sorry about what happened."

"Let's make a deal, okay? I don't want to talk about any of that tonight. It's over and done with, and I need to get on with my life."

Glancing back up, she searched Jane's face. "All right," she said finally, breaking into another grin. "Deal."

"Would you like a drink? Some wine?"

"Wine would be great." She couldn't seem to take her eyes off Jane. "I mean it. You look fabulous."

"I don't look sick? Pitiful? Damaged, both physically and mentally?"

"*You?* Hardly. You're one of the strongest women I've ever met."

"Thanks. I think I needed to hear that." She waved a waiter over and ordered a bottle of Cote Rotie Mordoree. She hadn't taken any of her pain pills, so she figured Julia couldn't be upset if she had some wine with dinner.

"So," said Patricia, laying down the menu. "Are you and Julia an item again?"

"You sure don't waste any time getting to the point."

"Why should I? You know how I feel about you. As far as I'm concerned, it's the burning question of the hour. Once I get an answer, I'll know how to play my hand."

"Life isn't a card game, Patricia."

"Sure it is. And you're way the hell too serious about it. Comes from spending too much time with certain doctor types."

"Is that a fact?"

"It's a diagnosis." She smirked.

The wine arrived. Jane waited while the waiter poured her a glass. After taking a sip, she smiled at Patricia and said, "You'll like this. I don't know what you're going to order, but it goes with just about anything."

Taking out his pad, the waiter said, "We have a wonderful mulligatawny soup on the menu tonight."

Patricia flipped quickly through the menu. "I want a burger. Rare. Put the works on it—whatever you've got."

"Well, we have—"

Patricia held up her hand, flashing him a grin. "Surprise me. It's more fun."

The waiter grinned back. "Okay."

Jane knew that Patricia flirted with just about everyone—it was her preferred method of communication—but tonight, Jane found herself responding a little too viscerally. She didn't like it. "I'll have the soup," she said, looking up at the waiter.

"Sure thing, Jane. Anything else?"

"No, that'll do it."

Patricia watched him walk away, her eyes traveling up and down his body. "So—I'm still waiting," she said, returning her attention to Jane. "You didn't answer my question. Are you and Julia back together?"

Jane didn't know how to answer the question because she wasn't sure herself. "I don't know," she said, lifting the glass to her lips. "Maybe. I mean, we're working on it."

Patricia gave a playful shiver. "Sounds pretty dreary to me. What you need is a little fun in your life."

"You know, lately, everyone's awfully quick to tell me what I *need.*"

"Ah. You mean, you're getting the full invalid treatment? We love you, Jane dear, but you can't be trusted right now because you're sick, so we're going to tell you how to run your life until you recover."

"Something like that. I guess it's partially my own fault. It's how I see myself a good part of the time."

"You've been through a lot of physical pain, Lawless. I can see it in your face. Your old zest for life is missing. But that's temporary stuff. It'll come back. On the other hand, I can tell you're bothered by something more immediate—something that has nothing to do with your health. My guess is, it's Julia. There's trouble in paradise if I'm not mistaken."

"You can skip the sarcasm."

"But I'm right—yes?"

"You're transparent. It's wishful thinking."

"Maybe."

How could Jane tell her she was dead-on? She knew she needed to talk about what was happening in her life, but Patricia was hardly an unbiased ear. Jane was starting to feel ill at ease with all this talk about her personal life. Fortifying herself with another sip of wine, she said, "And what about you?" She glanced over her shoulder at the waiter. "You still seem to be checking out everything that lives and breathes."

"A girl can look, can't she?"

"You do a whole lot more than look."

"That's just fun and games. You, on the other hand, represent something far more intriguing."

"Like what?"

"I'm not sure."

"That's decisive."

"Okay, how about this? You fascinate me, Lawless. You're smart—almost as smart as me. And your dark side is almost as dark as my own. Sure, you try to reject it, but it won't go away—trust me on that one. I'm not saying we're mirror images, but I am betting that we could actually understand each other. In today's world, even with people who swear undying devotion on a stack of Bibles, that's a rare commodity."

"Understanding, huh. Let's say you're right. How long do you think this fascination of yours will last?"

"You mean after we sleep together?"

Jane rolled her eyes.

She shrugged. "A week. A year. A lifetime. Who knows? But I'm willing to give it a try if you are."

"I think," said Jane, feeling the temperature in the room zoom up a good twenty degrees, "that we're getting a little ahead of ourselves."

"Fine. We can discuss anything you like—as long as you understand my interest isn't going away."

"I got that part."

Again, Patricia grinned. Picking up her glass of wine, she studied the color.

Jane took advantage of the lull in the conversation to ask, "What's happening with that homicide investigation? I've been reading about it in the papers. Sounds pretty nasty."

Patricia's expression turned serious. "It is."

"Look, if you don't want to talk about it—"

"No, it's okay."

She hesitated a moment, then asked, "How well did you know Jeffrey Chapel?"

"Not well. His father-in-law, Andrew Dove, is the president of the Haymaker Club. He's *very* interested in the renovation of the Winter Garden. Just between you and me, I think I can say that the financial backing we were looking for is in the bag."

"You said in your phone message that you thought Chapel's wife had committed the murder."

"Oh, who knows? It's just . . . I caught her in the lobby after everyone had left—or I should say, after I *thought* everyone had left. I didn't know then that Chapel was hanging upside down from the elevator cables. There was just something about her. She seemed so . . . jumpy, so distracted. I know she said she was looking for her husband, but I got the distinct impression she couldn't wait to get out of there."

Jane thought about it, tried to square Patricia's impression with the Brenna Chapel she'd met last night. "And the police seem to think that one of the people at that meeting might be responsible for his death?"

"As long as you add his wife to the mix, that's right."

"Who else was at the meeting?"

"Well, Andrew Dove. And me. Then there was Joe Patronelli, the famous football jock. And my architect—Eddie Flynn. That was about it."

63

"Could someone else have entered the building while you weren't looking? I mean, the wife got in somehow."

"Yeah, apparently Eddie didn't lock the door when he left. He thought I was leaving right after him, but I was on the phone with my secretary, in the midst of a work crisis."

"So, someone could have come in. Someone other than Brenna."

"I suppose. You know, Lawless, you're good. The police asked me the exact same questions."

Jane tried not to look pleased. "Do the police have any ideas about a possible motive?"

"None that they've shared with me. The problem is, with Dove tied up in a murder investigation, I'm not sure what effect it will have on the Haymaker Club's vote. For now, the Winter Garden project is on hold."

Jane hoped that when she talked to Julia tomorrow night, she'd come clean about what she knew. Maybe her information about Chapel would help the police find his murderer, and also, get Patricia's project back on track.

"You know, Lawless, there's a famous old restaurant in that hotel."

"Yes, you mentioned your plans to restore it. I assume you mean the Palmetto Room. I haven't been in there since I was a kid."

"It's been closed for the past three years, and before that, it was a dive."

"Not when I was there."

"Oh, that's right. Sometimes I forget how old you are."

Jane saw the humor in her eyes. Patricia loved needling her about their age difference.

"Well, shortly after you had dinner there in your hoopskirt and bonnet, it turned into Art's Eatery. Art specialized in grease. The walls in the kitchen are still covered with it. But I intend to recreate the original Palmetto Room. In our case, posh, but reasonably affordable. The kitchen will also do meals for the assisted-living clients, but I'm hoping the restaurant will bring in its own revenue.

"That's very possible," said Jane. "If you handle the food intelligently and promote it right. You've got a great location, and that wrought-iron and leaded-glass dome over the main dining room is a stunner. There's no way you could afford to reproduce it today—unless you were Donald Trump."

"I'm not The Donald yet, but I'm still young," said Patricia, her eyes glittering with excitement. "Eddie found some menus from the turn of the century. I plan to have them framed and put up in the lobby. He also dug up some photos of the way it appeared back in the Roaring Twenties. That's the look we're aiming for." She paused as the waiter set her hamburger down in front of her. "Maybe you can show me some of your flapper dresses, Lawless. You've probably got lots of them packed away in old steamer trunks."

"Cute. But watch it."

"Actually, I was hoping you'd consider working with us as a consultant."

Jane took a taste of her soup. It needed a little more apple. "It sounds fascinating, and really, I'd love to be part of developing something like that, but I haven't felt well enough to come back to work here yet."

"You look pretty healthy to me," said Patricia. Once again, her smile turned seductive. "It won't be long before you're back to full steam."

It was a happy thought, one Jane held onto as they ate their dinner. Over the next hour, they talked about specific menu ideas for the new restaurant, as well as Patricia's plans for the general renovation of the hotel. Jane found herself laughing more than she had in months. The silliness felt good. So did the wine. And the catalyst for it all seemed to be Patricia.

"You know," said Patricia finally, wiping her mouth on a napkin and then picking up her glass. "What are you doing for exercise these days?"

"Well, I had some physical therapy in the hospital, but I haven't really continued with the exercises. I used Julia's exercise room once. I suppose I'll have to renew my membership at the Y."

"Hey, why drive all the way uptown when there's a great gym just up the street?"

"And what gym would that be?" asked Jane, pouring the last few drops of the Cote Rotie into their glasses.

Patricia reached into her vest pocket, drew out a set of keys, and then pushed them across the table. "The one at my house."

Jane's eyebrow raised. "You just happened to have an extra set of keys to your house with you?"

"Will wonders never cease?"

"Come on, Patricia. I can't bother you with—"

"It's no bother," she said, touching Jane's hand lightly, then leaning back in her chair, retreating to a more neutral corner. "I'm never home in the day. You'd have the house all to yourself. You've seen my exercise room. It has everything you'd ever want or need to help get yourself back in shape. Not that your shape isn't already pretty damn good."

"You're hopeless, you know that?"

"No. I'm hopeful. And I'm going to stay that way. You and Julia aren't good for each other."

"Oh, and now you're telling me you believe in fated love."

"Do you?" asked Patricia.

She hesitated. "Maybe."

"And you think *I'm* indecisive."

"It's about as decisive as I'm going to get after one too many glasses of wine." She drew her glass in front of her, but stopped before she took a last sip. "Answer your own question. Do you believe in fated love?"

"Of course not." She laughed. "I'm not an idiot."

Jane found herself laughing, too. She was about to ask another pointless, philosophical question when she felt a tap on her shoulder.

"Ms. Lawless?" said the bartender.

She turned around and looked up. "Yes?"

"There's someone here who wants to speak to you."

"Now?" She looked at her watch. It was ten after eleven. "Did you tell them I was having dinner?"

"She said she'd wait until you were done. I got the impression she isn't going to leave until she talks to you."

"What's her name?" asked Jane, annoyed by the interruption.

"She wouldn't give one. But she did say it was urgent."

"What does she look like?" asked Patricia.

He thought for a minute. "Blond. Attractive. I'm never very good at judging people's ages."

Oh my God, thought Jane. There was only one person that could be. "Where is she now?"

"I put her in your office. I hope you don't mind."

"No, that's fine." She eased away from the table, trying not to look too eager. "Patricia, I'm sorry, but I've got to deal with this."

"Sure, I understand." She nodded to the keys. "Take them. You'll regret it if you don't."

Jane stared at them a second, then picked them up and put them in her pocket. "I'll call you."

Patricia stood. Moving over to where Jane was still seated, she touched Jane's cheek, then leaned down and whispered in her ear, "You'd better." Proceeding out the door, she called over her shoulder, "Oh, and tell Julia from me that she has lousy timing."

Chapter 10

When Jane opened the door to her office, instead of Julia, she found Brenna Chapel pacing in front of her couch. Jane tried to hide her disappointment behind an insincere smile. "Mrs. Chapel. This is . . . a surprise."

With no sop to social niceties, Brenna launched into her attack. "You've got to help me, Jane. Where can I reach that friend of yours—Dr. Martinsen?"

It didn't take the sensitivity of Mother Teresa to notice that Brenna was wound tighter than a watch spring. "Did you try calling the business number at her home?"

"Sure I did, but as of this morning, all phone service to the house was cut."

This was news to Jane. Sitting down behind her desk, she glanced at her answering machine to see if she had any messages. There were none.

"Tell me the truth. Is she some sort of quack?"

"Absolutely not," said Jane, surprised by the question.

"You seem very sure of yourself. Do you know for a fact that she even has a license to practice medicine?"

"Of course she does."

"Then why did she disconnect her phone? Has she moved?"

"I . . . I don't think so."

"You know, for a good friend, you certainly don't know much about her."

That stung, perhaps because some part of it was true. "She was supposed to call me this evening."

"Let me guess. She didn't."

Jane shook her head.

"What am I going to do?" muttered Brenna, continuing to pace. Finally, stepping up to the desk, she placed her hands on the edge and leaned forward aggressively. "I went to the library this afternoon."

Jane wasn't sure how she was supposed to respond. "Looking for a good book?"

"No, looking for some information on you."

"Me? Why?"

"I thought I remembered reading something in the local papers—articles about how you helped solve a couple of recent crimes. I suppose you were assisting your father with his cases.

It was a common misconception. "No," said Jane. "I was just at the wrong place at the right time."

Brenna subjected her to a penetrating gaze. "I doubt that. If what I read was correct, you seem to have a knack for private investigation."

"I'm a restaurateur, Mrs. Chapel. I don't have a PI license."

"But that doesn't stop you from helping people. On a personal basis, of course."

"I thought you were already employing a private detective."

Brenna sighed. "A guy followed my husband around for a while. He may have tracked him to Martinsen's house, but frankly, I don't have confidence he could find his own car in a parking lot. We parted company weeks ago."

"I'm sorry to hear that. I'm sure there are other people you could contact if you feel you need to look for Dr. Martinsen."

Brenna drew back. "That's only part of the reason I came to see you tonight. Here," she said, reaching into her purse and taking out an envelope. She tossed it on Jane's desk.

When Jane opened it, she found a stack of hundred-dollar bills inside. "What's this for?"

"1 want to hire you. If it's not enough, just tell me, and I'll get you more. Money isn't a problem."

"What is?" asked Jane, noticing that the amount must be close to two thousand dollars.

Removing a folded sheet of paper from her purse, she handed it to Jane. "This should explain things."

Jane put on her reading glasses and read through it briefly; then she looked up. "You got this fax today?"

"This afternoon."

She hesitated, reading through it a second time. "Is it true?"

"That's what I need to find out." Once again, she began to pace. "I don't believe for a minute my husband was gay. I mean, I would know, wouldn't I?" She stopped in front of the fireplace, placing her hands on the mantel. After a long moment, she turned around, facing Jane squarely. "You're gay, right?"

"That's right."

"So you're familiar with the gay community in this town. You're the perfect person to find out what I need to know."

"Look, Mrs. Chapel—"

"Call me Brenna."

"Okay . . . Brenna. If your husband was gay, he was probably in the closet—hiding his sexuality. It may be difficult to prove.

"But if this blackmailer has evidence, that means there's something out there—something you could find too. If that's the case, I have to know what it is. I'm betting that it's all a ploy to extort money from me, but I have to find out for sure. If the blackmailer has trumped something up, then whatever phony evidence he has *must* be destroyed before it does any permanent damage."

"I don't understand why someone would go to that kind of trouble."

"I told you! For money!"

Jane still wasn't convinced.

"Believe me, I have every confidence you're the right person for the job."

"Because I'm gay."

"And because you're friends with a woman who knows far more about my husband's murder than she's willing to tell. All that mumbo jumbo last night about doctor-patient privilege. It was enough to turn my stomach."

Jane didn't understand Julia's motives or actions any better than Brenna did. Without knowing it, Brenna had pushed exactly the right button. If anything was going to convince Jane to get involved in a homicide investigation, it was the presumption that Julia might somehow be involved. "Why don't you sit down, and we can talk about this a little more. Maybe I can help you—although I can't accept your money."

Brenna sank into a chair on the other side of the desk. "Sure you can. If you don't want it for your services, give it to your favorite charity."

Jane stared at her a moment, tapping the envelope with her index finger.

"Besides, you may have some expenses you don't anticipate right now. Remember, if you need more, just let me know."

Jane put the envelope away in the top drawer. Whatever she decided, she could deal with it later.

Tipping her head back, Brenna closed her eyes and let out a deep sigh. "God, how could he do this to me? How could he marry me if he was gay?"

Jane cocked her head. "But . . . I thought you said you were sure he wasn't."

"I am. At least, most of the time." Pressing a finger and thumb to her eyelids, she continued, "Maybe I'm naive, but it never occurred to me that a gay man would want to get married."

"It happens," said Jane, gently. "More often than you might realize. Actually, I can think of a number of reasons why someone who is gay might want to marry. It's certainly an effective place to hide. And with society out there telling you you're sick and sinful just for being who you are, it's often a whole lot easier to deny reality, even lie to yourself. I'm not saying that was the case with your husband."

Brenna glanced away. After several moments, she raised her palms in a gesture of surrender, looking as if she were about to cry. "I know it sounds pathetic, but there's no one in my life I can talk to about this. And I really *need* to talk."

Jane was feeling the effects of the wine. She wasn't only tired, but her head was beginning to ache. Still, even though she hadn't made an absolute commitment to help, it might be interesting to hear what Brenna had to say. "Why don't you give me a little background?"

Brenna's nod was full of gratitude. Attempting to regain some of her composure, she sniffed a few times, then began. "Jeffrey and I met shortly after he came to work for Dove Airlines. For the past fifteen years, I've worked as an ad executive. Two years ago, I started my own company. Chapel & Wolcott has become one of the hottest ad agencies in the Midwest. Anyway, when I was still working for the Rainbow Group in downtown St. Paul, I'd occasionally drive over to Dad's office to have lunch with him. I'd bring sandwiches or bagels. Something light. One day, Jeffrey happened to be there, so Dad invited him to stay. I liked him immediately. I suppose you could say one thing led to another, and we eventually started getting together after work. All strictly as friends, you understand, but my feelings for him just seemed to grow. One night, when he was dropping me off at my door, he kissed me. It didn't go beyond that, but I knew right then where we were headed, and I'll be honest with you. I was thrilled. I was already head over heels in love with the guy. He invited me to his staff Christmas party a few months later. I got a little tipsy, maybe even a little crazy, and on the way home, asked him to marry me. I mean, I was thirty-two years old. I knew a good man when I saw one, and I thought we were in love with each other."

"Did he accept?" asked Jane.

"Well, we both treated it like it was a joke at first, but then later we got to talking. We were spending most of our evenings together. Sure, there was an eighteen-year difference in our ages, but that didn't matter to me. I didn't want children, and neither did he. We both liked to ski, to hike; both of us were devoted to our careers. In so many ways, we seemed the perfect match. I don't remember exactly how it happened, but we just sort of drifted toward marriage."

"Was it a long engagement?"

"We were married exactly two years after Jeffrey came to work for Dove Airlines."

Jane's polite attention had turned to real interest. "And . . . was your marriage happy?"

"Yes," she said, biting down hard on her lower lip. "Jeffrey was kind and considerate. Neat to a fault—I suppose from all those years in the marines. He was away a lot lecturing on college campuses. He loved the Marine Corps—felt honored to be able to serve his country. And, as he liked to point out, being a flier was the most exciting job in the world. He wanted to pass his enthusiasm on to other young people. He was a good speaker—funny, casual—and he knew how to grab an audience and really move them. Dad couldn't have been happier when we announced our engagement."

"But there must have been some problems in your marriage. Otherwise, you wouldn't have hired that private investigator."

Her expression sobered. "You're right. I've lied to others so long, it almost comes naturally. The truth is, for the past year, Jeffrey's been gone far more than he was home. Sure, there were some difficult problems at the airline that needed his attention, but I think he was using it as an excuse. Personally, I would have preferred to spend less time at my own office, but there was no reason to sit around an empty condo. I've made a great deal of money in my life, Jane, and I guess I just used the time to make more. Colleagues of mine thought I was becoming a workaholic, but the truth is, it was mainly loneliness. Every now and then, Jeffrey and I would talk about spending more time together, but nothing ever changed.

"Last August, Jeffrey started staying away later and later in the evenings. When he'd come in, he'd tell me he'd been in a meeting, but I didn't buy it. I jumped to the conclusion that he was seeing another woman. But when I confronted him, he laughed and said I was being ridiculous. After we'd cleared the air, a strange thing happened. He began to drift even further away, though he was home almost every night by seven. He seemed preoccupied. After a while, I noticed that he'd completely stopped talking about his work. We always talked in great detail about our daily lives. Something was wrong, Jane, but I couldn't get him to tell me what it was."

Again, she looked down, but this time her eyes swelled with tears. "I was so confused. For weeks, I berated myself. I assumed it was something I'd done, something he couldn't bring himself to talk to me about. Then the thought struck me that maybe he was ill. It would be just like Jeffrey to want to spare me that kind of pain. So I called his doctor. He'd had a physical recently, but the doctor informed me that he was in perfect health. And *that's* when I hired the private detective. I was angry and hurt. I had to have answers."

"How long ago was that?"

"September. Jeffrey visited your friend, Dr. Martinsen, the last week of September and then again the second week in October. I thought for a while he'd lied to me—that *this* was the woman he was seeing behind my back. But now I'm not so sure. I don't suppose you have an opinion."

"They weren't involved," said Jane. It was the only thing she did know for sure.

"Where *is* that woman?" She whipped her head up and fixed Jane with a fierce look. After a long moment, she removed a snapshot from her purse and pushed it across the desk. "Here's a photo of Jeffrey."

Jane studied it, then asked, "Who's the other guy in the picture? The gray-haired man with the beard. The one with his arm around your husband."

"Oh, that's my father. It was taken last Christmas. Maybe you could show it around at your . . . places. You know, your bars. Bathhouses. Whatever. See what you come up with."

"I rarely go to bars, and there hasn't been a bathhouse in town for years. But I'll do some checking."

Brenna gave her a quizzical look. "If you don't go to bars, where do you find people to . . . you know . . . have sex with?"

Jane took a deep, cleansing breath. It was hard being courteous to someone with such dingy ideas. "You know, Mrs. Chapel, your concept of what it means to be gay is pretty limited and insulting. Sure, pickup bars are a part of gay culture—just like they are in straight culture—but not everyone lives that way. The gay community isn't a monolith. We don't all wear the same shoes, read the same books, or have the same political opinions. There's no one 'lifestyle.' There are lots of ways to live a life, Mrs. Chapel, even a gay life. I was in a committed relationship with a woman for ten years, until she died of cancer. I didn't date much after that . . . until recently. To be honest with you, I feel like my sexuality is just one part of my life—important, but no more or less important than other aspects. I don't define myself by my sexuality—society does that." She paused. "Do you understand what I'm saying?"

"Of course I do. I'm not homophobic."

Jane looked at her a moment, then decided what she needed was a good night's sleep.

"But what about the blackmail?" asked Brenna. "We haven't discussed that yet. Do you think I should pay to keep my husband's name out of the mud?"

The woman was *not* a wealth of sensitivity. "I don't know. Why don't you call me if you get another fax? Maybe this was just a prank."

"Yes, that's possible." As she stood to go, she seemed a little more positive. "Thanks for agreeing to work for me, Jane. You'll find that I can be a very appreciative woman when someone is on my team. I'll keep you posted."

Jane wasn't sure she'd agreed to anything, but she was suddenly too weary to argue about it. As she got up to walk Brenna to the door, Brenna noticed she was limping.

"Are you okay?" she asked, looking concerned.

"It's nothing," said Jane. "Just one of those cases of being at the wrong place at the right time."

Brenna eyed her a moment, then said, "There's something else you'll need." She took a business card out of her pocket. "It has my number at work and my home phone. I'll be at home for the next few weeks, so if you find out anything about Jeffrey—"

"I'll let you know," said Jane, eager for the woman to leave.

"These have been the worst few days of my entire life. It's good to know I've got someone to talk to, someone who understands the gay lifestyle better than I do." She shook Jane's hand and then left.

As Jane closed the door, she was pretty sure that Brenna Chapel hadn't heard a word she'd said.

Chapter 11

SUNDAY MORNING

Jane slept until close to noon. After a leisurely brunch in the dining room, she took a walk by the lake, feeling the need for some fresh air before she tackled the stack of work on her desk.

As she walked along the shore, watching the sun play hide-and-seek with the clouds, the only conclusion she could come to about Brenna's surprise visit last night was that she needed to wait until she'd met with Julia later today. After their talk, she'd decide whether or not to help. As for what was potentially brewing between Patricia Kastner and herself, Jane had no choice but to put that subject on hold.

Returning to her office shortly after two, she sat down behind her desk and switched on the light. The stack of mail looked daunting, particularly to someone who hadn't worked a lick in over a month. She was about to send an SOS up to the kitchen for a carafe of strong, black coffee when the phone rang.

Sensing a reprieve, she answered it.

"Don't hang up!" It was Cordelia.

"Of course I won't hang up," said Jane.

"Well . . . after yesterday, I wasn't so sure you ever wanted to hear from me again."

"I'm sorry I was so short with you."

"I'm sorry too, Janey. Are we still pals?"

"Always."

"Because if that sofa gets too uncomfortable in your office, you can always come back to my loft. That is, unless you're planning to move back home."

"I am," said Jane, realizing as she said the words that she hadn't given it any thought. "But not quite yet. I need a little more time." She was pathetic. Sooner or later, she had to face that house—and what had happened there—but not just yet. "What about Julia? Did she call your place last night?"

"She did, and I passed on your message. Didn't she phone you at the restaurant?"

"Afraid not."

"Well, she was in a rush. Between planes somewhere. She was glad to hear you were all right, but disappointed that you weren't staying with me."

"Did she say anything else?"

"Just that she'd see you tonight."

Jane breathed a sigh of relief. Wherever Julia was, at least she planned on keeping their date.

"So, if I may be so bold as to change the subject, how did your dinner go last night with the neighborhood sociopath?"

"Cordelia!"

"I'm biting my tongue, Jane."

"Not hard enough. If you're really interested, Patricia's fine. As a matter of fact, she's invited me to use her home gym so I can work out, improve my mobility."

"How . . . selfless. She has ulterior motives, Janey. Maybe even hidden cameras."

"Oh, *come on*."

Cordelia gave an exasperated grunt. "She's like a tractor, Janey, crushing clods of dirt, chewing up mother earth and spitting her out."

Jane couldn't help herself. She began to laugh. "When you resort to farm images, I can tell you're really desperate."

"Why are you treating this so lightly?"

"Because you've got no business telling me who I can or can't see. I thought I made that clear yesterday. And anyway, I can use all the help I can get."

"Right," said Cordelia snidely. Under her breath, she added, "It takes a village."

"What?"

"Look, Janey, indulge me for one minute, and then, I promise, I'll shut up. But I want you to really listen. Deal?"

"Just get it off your chest once and for all."

"Okay." She took a deep breath. "Patricia Kastner wants what she wants *passionately* until she gets it. Then she doesn't want it anymore."

"And you know this . . . how?"

"I have eyes."

"The chase is all that matters."

"Precisely."

"And she has no feelings except those of a predator."

"Now you're getting the idea."

Jane shook her head. "You're wrong."

Silence. "All right, Janey. I tried. You've been warned. I shall forever remain silent on the subject."

"I doubt that."

She snapped her gum. "What time are you meeting Julia tonight?"

"Seven."

"I have my *Mildred Pierce* cell meeting at six. You and Julia are invited, of course, though I doubt you'd want to come."

"I think we'll pass."

Five years ago, Cordelia had formed a group based on the movie classic, *Mildred Pierce*, starring Joan Crawford. Everyone in the group acted the part of a specific character in the movie. When they got together, they *became* that person. Cordelia, of course, was the long-suffering Mildred, a role she was born for. Her friend Michael, a set designer at the Allen Grimby, had taken the role of Vida, Mildred's spoiled-rotten, older daughter. Everyone agreed he had the most charming pout, even though he did have a beard.

"We're having appetizers at the Greek restaurant downstairs first," continued Cordelia, "and then we're going to watch an old

Greer Garson flick on my new huge-o-vision TV. I know that thing is pathetically suburban, but what can I say? At least I don't watch football games in my underwear. Anyway, remember, if you need me tonight, my humble loft is right downstairs."

"Thanks, but I'm sure Julia and I will be fine."

"Whatever you say, dearheart. Well, I'm off to the Grimby for an afternoon of fun and frolic."

"Sounds dreadful."

"It is. Another fund-raiser, and I'm in charge of the event. Say, speaking of beer kegs and jockstraps, the guest of honor is none other than the illustrious Joe Patronelli. Joseph, believe it or not, has become a dear friend."

Jane knew she'd heard the name, but couldn't quite place it. "Who is he?"

"Patronelli? The Vikings' number one running back?"

"Sorry. I don't follow football. How do you know him?"

"As the reigning queen of this town's social whirl, I know all the glitterati—even the ones with excessive muscles. Joe's a real crowd pleaser, and a true supporter of the arts. Just between you and me, I think it's because someone once told him he looks like Michelangelo's *David*."

Now Jane remembered where she'd heard the name. "Do you know he's considered a suspect in the Chapel homicide?"

"Yes, and it's positively ridiculous."

"He's too sweet and gentle, right?"

"Actually, he is. But we'll have to talk about it some other time. I gotta boogie, dearheart. I'm not even dressed yet, and for this event, Cordelia Thorn has to *sizzle*."

"I'm glad you called."

"Yeah, me too. Later, Janey."

Chapter 12

It took Jane the next several hours to make even a dent in her mail, and by then she felt ragged. Recognizing that she might be in trouble later in the day if she didn't take it easy, she napped until the main dining room opened for dinner at five. She hadn't greeted customers in so long, she almost felt as if she'd lost her touch. But after speaking with a few of her regulars, she started to get into the swing of things again and began enjoying herself, just as she always had. As of tonight, she was back, and she intended to stay.

Shortly before seven, she arrived at the Linden Building. She parked Julia's Audi across the street and entered through Athena's Garden, the popular Greek restaurant on the first floor. Seeing Cordelia and the rest of her *Mildred Pierce* cell sitting at a prominent table in the center of the room—everyone dressed in full forties retro drag—she gave a wave but kept on going to the back hall where the old freight elevator was located.

The Linden Building had been constructed back in the late eighteen hundreds as a livery, a place that cared for and housed both horses and delivery wagons. Later, in the early nineteen hundreds, the owner had built three additional floors. Today, the second and third levels were rented to a printing company. Only the top three floors had been made into apartments, two lofts per floor. Cordelia's loft was on the fifth level, and Julia's sat directly above it on the sixth.

The security in the building was pretty good. To get up to one of the apartments, you either had to have a key to the stairway or the elevator, or you needed to be buzzed in. Sometimes people buzzed up callers indiscriminately, not knowing who they were. There was a bank of pay phones next to the stairway door that allowed people to announce their visit, but since Jane had her own key, she had no trouble getting in.

The battered elevator rumbled its way toward the sixth floor as Jane stood silently, wondering what the evening would bring. Once the elevator stopped, she opened the wood grate and stepped off into a long, unadorned hallway. As she walked past the laundry room, a woman sauntered out and smiled at her. It was Julia's neighbor, Rhonda Wellman. Rhonda owned a popular uptown bar, one that catered to the Minneapolis theatre crowd. She'd become one of Cordelia's favorite loft mates.

"Hey, Lawless. Long time no see." She leaned her heavy frame against the door, sipping from a can of Dr Pepper. Rhonda was in her early sixties, but with the tons of makeup she usually wore—and the dyed red hair—she definitely had no plans to grow old gracefully.

"It's been a while."

"You feeling any better?"

"I am. Thanks."

"Still using the cane, though."

"On and off."

She nodded toward Julia's door. "I see the good doctor is back. We had a brief powwow this afternoon. Mostly we talked about hot subjects like the sixth-floor washing machine—the spin cycle doesn't always work, so sometimes I have to use the one on fifth."

"I'm sure she'll have the management company take care of it."

"Yeah, that's what she said. She also mentioned that she was fixing you two some sort of fancy dinner tonight."

Jane's expression brightened. Julia didn't like to cook, so that meant she was trying to make it a special evening. A good sign. "I thought maybe we'd just order some food from downstairs."

"I guess you lucked out, hon. Well," Rhonda said, stretching and then taking a last sip from her can, "I don't wanna keep you. See ya around."

Jane walked the rest of the way to Julia's door, anticipation and excitement churning together inside her. Her pulse always quickened when she knew she was about to see Julia—which probably signaled something important, though she didn't feel like analyzing it tonight.

Giving the door a couple of firm raps, she waited. After knocking twice more, she decided that Julia was probably in the shower and couldn't hear her. At this rate, she could be standing around forever.

Since she had a key, she used it. Stepping inside, she was surprised to find the loft dark—and absolutely quiet. No sound of running water, no candles lit, no soft music, and no smell of dinner in the oven.

She flipped on the switch next to the door, and track lights went on from one end of the room to the other.

"Julia?" she called, her eyes searching for some simple explanation. Did she have the date or the time wrong? Surely her brain wasn't so addled that she'd remembered it incorrectly. No, Rhonda had verified it just a few minutes ago. Checking her watch, she saw that it was seven on the dot. So what was going on?

Jane headed up the steps to the loft's only bedroom. Maybe Julia had fallen asleep and hadn't realized the time. But when Jane found the bed empty—without so much as a wrinkle in the bedspread—she knew her guess was wrong.

Switching on the bedside lamp, she searched the room. There was no sign that Julia had arrived—no reading material next to the bed, no slippers on the floor or clothing tossed over a chair.

Opening the closet door, she saw that it was empty. If Julia had returned, as Rhonda said she had, her visit gave new meaning to the concept of "traveling light."

Next, Jane entered the bathroom. She touched one of the towels hanging on the wall and found that it was damp. Finally, some proof that Julia had been here—and not long ago either.

Again, she called, "Julia? It's Jane. Are we playing hide-and-seek?"

Turning the light back off, she returned to the main floor and entered the study. Julia's usual traveling miscellany—medical journals, personal notebooks, her address book—was missing. No briefcase rested next to the chair, and the desktop was cleared of papers. With the exception of the kitchen at the far end, the loft was completely open. Jane made a physical sweep of the long room. Finally, frustrated by her inability to make sense of the situation, she entered the kitchen. She looked into the refrigerator and found that it was stocked with food—another indication that Julia had been here and was at least planning to make a meal. But if that was the case, where was she now?

Returning to the living room, Jane stood in front of a long bank of windows overlooking downtown Minneapolis. It was a wintry November night. Frost obscured some of the panes. In the past ten minutes, the anxious knot in her stomach had tightened into a fist. If Julia had to go out, why hadn't she left a note? Had something happened to her? Or . . . could it be that Jane had been stood up again? More than once, Julia had promised they'd get together only to back out at the last minute. Later, she'd offer a plausible excuse. In a couple of instances, Jane had even caught her in an outright lie. But why would she tell Rhonda she was making dinner for them tonight and then pack her things and leave?

Feeling totally confused, Jane dimmed the track lighting and sat down on the couch to think. By seven-thirty, she'd come up with dozens of reasons why Julia might have taken off, and the longer she obsessed over it, the more reasons she knew she'd find.

Okay, she thought. If for some reason Julia had to get away on the spur of the moment and didn't want to leave behind a written message, what would she do? The answer seemed simple. She'd contact Cordelia.

Jane returned to the study, sat down behind Julia's desk, and punched in Cordelia's number. After several rings, the line picked up.

In a voice that projected the nobility of heartbreak, Cordelia said, "You have reached Mildred Pierce. Yes, what you've heard is all true. I am a busy woman—running my restaurant, falling in love with a good-for-nothing playboy, rejecting my long-suffering yet boring husband, and creating a monster out of my eldest daughter—so make it quick."

"Cordelia, it's Jane."

"Hey, Janey. How's tricks?"

In the background, she could hear laughter mixed with forties jazz. "Have you heard from Julia this afternoon?"

"No. Why?"

"Rhonda Wellman said she saw her. That she was back, and she was making dinner for the two of us tonight."

"Lucky you. I know how much you love burned chicken."

Jane tapped her nails impatiently on the desktop. "You heard from her yesterday, right?"

"Twice. Once in the afternoon, and once in the evening. Is something wrong, Janey? You sound worried."

She hesitated. "I'm upstairs in Julia's loft, and she's not here."

"She probably just ran out for some last-minute truffles."

"The apartment was dark, Cordelia. There's no dinner, and all her clothes are gone."

"Oh. That's different. Do you want me to come up? I'm good at hand-holding."

"No," said Jane, leaning her head against her palm. "I guess I'll just wait a while longer."

"Hey, don't sound so down in the dumps. And don't worry. She'll turn up. Doesn't she always? And with some great reason why she couldn't make it at the appointed time."

She had a point, albeit an infuriating one.

"Let me know what happens." Cordelia was rushing now to get off. "The movie's about to begin. And nothing can start without Mildred. I need to be there to *suffer*, Janey. The old black-and-white classics *require* it."

"I'll catch you later."

"Anytime, babe."

As Julia's grandfather clock struck nine, Jane was still sitting on the couch, wondering what to do. She'd been toying with the idea of calling the police, but wasn't sure what she'd say. Thinking that a pot of tea might help, she pushed on her cane to help her get up and then headed into the kitchen. Halfway there, she heard the sound of a key in the lock.

She stopped midstride and turned around, walking slowly toward the door. She wanted to catch the look on Julia's face when she entered. She figured it might tell her something important, though she wasn't quite sure what that would be. It was simply an instinct—one she had to obey. And yet the longer she stood waiting, the clearer it became that what she was hearing wasn't a key at all. Someone was attempting to pick the lock. If they were any good at all, they'd be inside in a matter of seconds.

That's when she noticed the yellow Post-it on the rug next to the door. Scooping it off the floor, she hit the wall switch, killing the lights. She wanted to read the note, but knew she had to find a place to hide first. The glow from downtown Minneapolis allowed more light into the loft than she might have liked, but she couldn't do anything about it now.

Panic gripped her as her eyes shot in every direction. There was another door to the apartment, but the lock was a double dead bolt, and Julia had the only key. She was trapped inside with nowhere to go. She had no idea who was outside, but as she hurried into the kitchen, her mind flashed to the basement of Julia's northern Minnesota home. It seemed not only possible, but likely, that it was the same person who had attacked her once before.

Easing into the narrow broom closet, she closed the door, but then reopened it just a crack so she could see what was happening. The front door was a good sixty feet away. Watching for a few seconds, it occurred to Jane that she should have found a weapon of some kind—just in case. Knowing she had mere seconds to make a decision, she pushed out of the narrow space and grabbed a boning knife from a woodblock on the counter. A second later, she was back in her hiding place, clutching it for dear life.

It was almost a full minute before the front door finally opened, and a man entered. Jane looked for his gun, but saw only a flashlight in his right hand. The intruder was wearing a baggy coat, dark slacks, dark, heavy-soled shoes, and a ski mask. This time, she was positive it was a man.

Pausing for a moment to listen, he ran the beam of light carefully over the loft's interior, and then began his search in the study.

Now that her vision was blocked by several tall Chinese screens, Jane couldn't see him, but she could hear desk drawers being pulled out and emptied. The same with Julia's filing cabinets. After a few minutes, he emerged into the living room. Now she could watch him again. He opened every drawer and examined the contents; then he turned his attention to the couch, dumping the cushions on the floor. Taking out a small pocketknife, he ripped the cushions open. It was hard to watch Julia's beautiful loft being systematically trashed, but Jane had no way to stop it. Her only chance was to stay quiet and hope he'd leave without checking the broom closet.

Next, he disappeared upstairs. She could only imagine what kind of havoc he was causing up there. If it was the same person she'd encountered the other night, he was undoubtedly still looking for Julia's files. Whoever the guy was, he didn't give up easily.

After a few more seconds, Jane opened the closet door a little wider and tried to determine if she'd have enough time to make it to the front door before he came back down. If both of her legs had been working normally, she might have risked it, but the strain of the evening had taken its toll, making her even more shaky than usual. A few moments later, the question became moot as the intruder bounded down the stairs.

This time, he turned his attention to the kitchen. Jane held her breath as he passed the broom closet and began opening drawers and cupboard doors. He hadn't missed a thing so far—which meant the closet wouldn't be spared. She gripped the knife, feeling her insides begin to tremble. She had the element of surprise on her side. It wasn't much, but it was something.

After toppling the spice rack to the floor, he leaned against the counter and rested for a moment, surveying the carnage. Shining his light down the row of cupboards, he seemed to be thinking. As he started to move toward the closet, the phone gave a sudden, jarring ring.

The intruder stopped dead, apparently unsure whether he should answer it or not. On the fifth ring, he picked it up, but said nothing. He listened for a few moments, looking more confused with each passing second. Finally, holding the receiver away from his ear, he cocked his head and stared at it; then he set the phone back down on the counter without hanging it up. Jane had no idea what it all meant, but she knew she was next on his agenda.

Placing his hand on the closet door, he opened it several inches, then seemed to grow curious about a wastebasket on the other side of the room. He trained his flashlight on it, then walked over, bent down, and dumped the contents on the floor. Jane watched through a tiny crack as he sifted through a bunch of papers. Nothing seemed to interest him very much, although he examined a couple of envelopes quite carefully. After straightening up, he turned back to the closet. Jane raised the knife, clutching it with both hands. Seconds later, she was startled to hear someone banging on the front door.

Whizzing past the closet, the intruder burst into the living room, and then came to an abrupt halt near the door, his body language suggesting he didn't know what to do. As the shouting and banging grew louder, he backed up several steps. He no doubt hoped the person would get tired of making such a racket and go away.

Jane finally recognized the voice. It was Cordelia. Thank God, she thought to herself silently—the marines had landed.

It now occurred to Jane that maybe the man hadn't locked the door when he first came in. She didn't remember seeing him do it, so that meant that if Cordelia tried the lock, she could get in. A second later, that's just what happened.

Cordelia lunged into the room shouting, "Janey, are you all right?" Before Cordelia knew what hit her, the man blasted past her into the hall, knocking her down.

With some difficulty, Jane extricated herself from the closet. It took a great deal of strength to knock the wind out of a two hundred-pound-plus, six-foot-tall woman, or perhaps it just took fear, but Cordelia was flat on her back in the hall, gasping for air when Jane reached her. As she helped her to a sitting position, Jane could hear the thud of footsteps on the metal stairs leading down to the street. With each passing second, the sound grew more faint.

"What the hell was *that?*" asked Cordelia, waving air into her face.

"Are you all right?"

The forties-style wig Cordelia was wearing had been knocked sideways. Her bright red lipstick was smeared, but the dress with its foot-wide shoulder pads showed no signs of damage. "No, I'm *not* all right." She gave a weak cough, then sat forward. "I called up here a few minutes ago, but all I heard was heavy breathing. Not your kind of humor, Janey. I knew something was up."

"Thanks. I think." She rubbed Cordelia's back until she seemed to recover a bit. "The guy that just decked you was the one who answered the phone. What did you say to him?"

She yanked her wig on straight. "Well, I thought *you'd* answer. So I said that it was Mildred Pierce and that I'd just shot my playboy lover. He deserved it, the sniveling little runt. I explained that he'd been sleeping with my daughter, Vida, and I couldn't let it go on any longer. Then I invited you down for pizza and beer."

Jane burst out laughing.

"Well, I mean, we only had appetizers at the Greek restaurant downstairs. It was intermission, and we all felt like having another snack. I thought you might like to join us. You haven't had dinner, have you?"

After all that had happened, here was Cordelia talking about pizza. It boggled the mind. "No."

"I didn't think so. You're wasting away, Janey. You need fat grams."

Jane eased down against the wall until the two of them were sitting side by side. "Cordelia, you're too much."

"Thank you, Janey. You're too much, too."

They both sat in dazed silence, considering what had just happened.

Finally, Jane said, "You know, Cordelia, you saved my life."

"Well, of course I did." Doing a double take, she said, "I did?"

Jane remembered the Post-it she'd found on the floor by the door. Pulling it out of her pocket, she held it up to the light.

"What's that?"

"A note from Julia."

"What's it say?"

Jane read out loud, "Sweetheart, I called your restaurant, but the manager said you'd left. Sorry we can't get together tonight, but it's out of my control. Someone's been watching the apartment ever since I got back. When I went out for groceries, I was followed. It's too dangerous for me to stay, even for a few more hours. As soon as you get this, I want you to leave—and don't come back. I'll contact you soon. I'll be fine—don't worry. Just be patient a little while longer. I love you. Julia." Jane passed the note across to Cordelia.

"What the hell is all this about?"

"If you've got a couple of hours, I'll explain."

"Damn straight you will."

Jane helped her friend get up. "The guy who knocked you down broke into Julia's apartment looking for her files. I've been hiding in the broom closet hoping he wouldn't find me."

"Heavens!"

She was about to explain more when she felt suddenly dizzy. Steadying herself against the wall, she noticed a look of horror pass across Cordelia's face.

"Janey, you need to lie down."

"I guess . . . maybe I do."

"You're doing too much. You put yourself into too many strenuous situations."

"I didn't know Julia's loft was going to get ransacked tonight, Cordelia. I just need to rest for a second."

"You know, Janey, I realize I threaten this all the time, but one of these days I really *am* going to lock you in a trunk!" She shut the door to Julia's apartment, then put her arm around Jane's waist and walked her toward the elevator. "You're staying with me tonight. I won't take no for an answer."

Jane wasn't going to argue the point.

"And if the cell meeting's too much for you, I'll tell them you need peace and quiet and send them packing."

"That won't be necessary." She didn't feel like driving all the way back to the Lyme House anyway. When it came to internal reserves, she didn't have much to rely on these days. Cordelia's loft sounded great, with or without the Mildred Pierce crowd.

"You need some TLC."

"And some pizza and beer."

"Now you've got the idea. Hey, where's Bean?"

"You say the word 'pizza' and you immediately think of my dog?"

"Well, he likes a little nibble every now and then."

"Not when I'm around."

Cordelia stuck out her tongue. "Meanie."

"He's staying at Evelyn Bratrude's."

"Good. Then he's probably OD'ing on popcorn. He deserves some fun in his life."

Jane shook her head.

As they approached the elevator, Cordelia pressed the down button. Giving Jane a sideways look, she added, "You know, dearheart, you may think I'm being melodramatic, but one of these days, you really are going to be the death of me."

Chapter 13

"Thanks for bringing me home, Loren. I don't know what I would have done without you today." Brenna stood zombielike in the middle of her living room and allowed him to take off her coat.

As she gazed around the silent condo, a strange thing occurred. She felt almost as if she were seeing it for the first time: her two favorite wedding photos, the ones she always kept on the mantel; the Mission-style furniture she and Jeffrey had picked out so carefully at Gabberts; the silly turtle puppet he'd bought for her at the state fair two summers ago; the pillows they'd brought back from their honeymoon trip to Spain. But Jeffrey was gone now. The funeral was over, and the reality of his loss was sinking in. How could she ever move forward with her life when the past was still such a question mark? Who *was* the man she'd married? And was she being disloyal to his memory by even asking the question?

Loren hung her fur in the front closet and then draped his own coat over a chair. Taking her hands in his, he said, "I watched you at the church. You didn't eat a thing. At least let me make you some coffee. You're chilled to the bone, Brenna. If you don't mind the opinion of a non-Catholic, that priest went on way too long at the grave site. You people sure know how to make a production of things."

It had been a running joke between them for years. "So do you Lutherans, though you lack our fundamental class." She looked up into his eyes. "You don't have to stay."

"I know I don't." If a smile could be sad, his was. "But how could I be anywhere else?"

Loren was an attractive man, and yet physically he was the opposite of Jeffrey in almost every way. Where Jeffrey was an outdoorsman with athletic interests, Loren was thin, elegant, bookish. Jeffrey was dark: black hair beginning to gray, warm brown eyes, and a weathered complexion. Loren was fair: fair skin, sandy blond hair, and icy blue eyes. His eyes were too hard sometimes—not the kind that suffered fools gladly.

Their personalities were also very different. Jeffrey was an extrovert: rough-and-tumble, mischievous, always ready for a good fight or a loud party. Loren, on the other hand, was more of an introvert: temperamental, intellectual, a man who liked his solitude. The only real interests he and Jeffrey had shared—other than a deep respect and love for each other—were chess and the theatre. Loren was a confirmed bachelor who rarely dated, and with the exception of Brenna and Jeffrey, he had few friends. Jeffrey was the kind of man who drew people to him. Not many, she suspected, cared for Loren Ives.

For the past six years, Brenna had watched these two very different men interact. She saw how they drew on each other's strengths, how they supported each other, and how they often disagreed. All during the funeral, she was buoyed by the fact that Loren would miss his best friend almost as much as she would miss her husband. They were truly partners in misery today, and that made him seem even more special.

Making herself comfortable on the living-room couch, she listened to the familiar sounds of a man preparing coffee in the kitchen. Unlike Jeffrey, Loren loved to cook. He usually invited them over for a gourmet meal at least once a month. She was going to miss their evenings together, but if she started to take stock of everything she'd lost, she would drive herself crazy. For now, she simply needed to be glad Loren had decided to stay. He would help take the edge off some of her loneliness, even if it was for only a couple of hours. And . . .

perhaps this was as good a time as any to ask him some of the questions she'd had on her mind.

The teakettle whistled, and a few minutes later Loren appeared carrying a tray. It was an antique, a gift he'd brought back from one of his buying trips to Vermont. He'd made a fresh pot of coffee, and put some shortbread cookies on a plate. Pouring the steaming liquid into two mugs, he handed one to Brenna. Then he sat down in an easy chair on the other side of the coffee table. "Do you want a blanket?" he asked, giving her a concerned look.

She shook her head, wrapping her fingers gratefully around the warm mug. "This is wonderful."

"I wish it could be more."

"You've done nothing but help me ever since—" She abandoned the end of the sentence, but knew Loren understood her meaning.

"Everything I've done was as much for me as it was for you. Jeff was my dearest friend. As long as I live, I'll never know anyone like him again."

For a moment, Brenna considered showing him the fax, but again changed her mind. The subject of her husband's sexuality was best approached cautiously. Maybe Loren knew more than he'd let on. It would be so simple if he could just confirm or deny it for her.

After taking a couple of sips of coffee, she screwed up her courage and said, "Loren, I know this question may seem like it's coming out of left field, but you've known Jeffrey since you were what—sixteen?"

"Fifteen. We met in ninth grade." The corners of his mouth turned down. "God, but that makes me feel old. I'm fifty-two now. That means I've known him for—" He did the mental calculation. "Thirty-seven years. Unbelievable." As he held the mug to his lips, he asked, "What's the question?"

Brenna fidgeted with her diamond bracelet, then set her mug down and leaned forward. "Did Jeffrey ever talk to you about having feelings for . . . another man?" She watched his face carefully.

Loren blinked at her a couple of times. "You're right, that is a strange question—especially coming from you. What's up, Brenna? Why would you even ask such a thing?"

She was keenly aware that he hadn't answered her. "Just give it to me straight. I can take it. I *need* to know."

His brow furrowed, but he didn't hesitate this time. "Jeff was as heterosexual as any guy I've ever known. *I'm* the one who's never dated much. I would think if you've got doubts about anyone's sexuality, it would be mine. For the record, I'm straight, Brenna, just in case that was going to be your next question." Folding his arms over his chest, he added, "For chrissake, Jeff was a decorated marine. A hero."

"And the two are mutually exclusive?"

"Well, no," he said, looking annoyed. He seemed to be struggling to find the right words. "I'm just trying to reassure you."

"So you point to something that isn't really proof?"

"I try to be sensitive and P.C. and you attack me for it." He was growing impatient. "Okay, so maybe I'm making a mess of this, but it's because I didn't expect the question. Jeffrey liked women—you in particular. End of story."

She wished she could believe him. "He never spoke about an attraction to another man?"

"At the risk of quoting a liar, *read my lips*, Brenna. Jeff was *not* gay."

"Because you'd tell me if he was."

"I don't know how many more ways I can say it. And since we're on the subject, Jeff once asked me to take care of you if anything ever happened to him. I want to do that, Brenna—if you'll let me."

That was a strange response. She couldn't see what it had to do with her initial question. "And when did you have that conversation?"

"I guess it was a few months after you were married. He cared for you deeply, Brenna. He wanted to spend the rest of his life with you. I'll admit . . . up until the time you two met, he never considered himself the marrying type, but he wasn't stupid. He couldn't let you get away."

All right, so now she was left with a dilemma. Did she believe him, or did she believe the blackmailer? In the absence of conclusive proof, everything depended on whose story she accepted.

Loren got up from his chair and sat down next to her on the couch. Taking her hands in his, he said, "I always told Jeff that he got lucky when he met you. If he hadn't grabbed you when he did, I would have been forced to propose myself."

Brenna smiled at him. He was trying to make her feel better, and in a way, he had. If only for a few moments, he'd given her back the husband she thought she knew.

"What brought all this on?" he asked, his eyes focused completely on hers. He'd always been a good listener.

She hesitated before answering, mostly because she wasn't sure how much she should say. Shifting her gaze to the photos on the mantel, she said, "Jeffrey and I were having some problems before he died."

Loren gave an uneasy nod.

"We hadn't slept together . . . for a while. I thought maybe he'd found someone else and couldn't bring himself to tell me. He'd been so preoccupied lately." She paused, looking back at him. "He didn't confide in you, did he?"

"No, Brenna. I'm sorry."

"Because—" She stopped herself. She didn't really want to bring this next part up, but she had to have some answers. "Sgt. Duvik, the police officer who took my statement, said he'd received information from Jeffrey's secretary that the two of you had a pretty heated argument in his office late last Thursday afternoon—right before he left for the day. They asked me about it. Wanted to know if I knew what it was about."

"The fight had nothing to do with you." As he said the words, his body stiffened.

Even though he was clearly uncomfortable, she wasn't about to let the subject drop. "The officer made it sound like you were terribly angry at Jeffrey."

"I was."

She waited for Loren to elaborate. When he didn't, she said, "I know the police talked to you. They must have asked you what the fight was about. Surely you can tell me what you told them."

He got up and walked over to an end table, picking up an ashtray. "Do you mind if I smoke?" he asked, removing a package and a matchbook from his pocket.

"Have I ever minded before?"

After returning to his chair, he wedged the cigarette between his lips and bent to light it. "I probably didn't notice that Jeff was preoccupied because I've been somewhat preoccupied myself lately." Looking down, he added, "It's personal, Brenna. Not something I want to talk about."

"But you talked to Jeffrey about it?"

"I wish I hadn't."

"And that's what you were arguing about?"

Studying her face through the smoke, he nodded.

"You can't just leave me hanging, Loren."

"No," he said, sighing deeply. "I suppose I can't." He flicked some ash into the ashtray. "The truth is . . . I've been audited. The government insists I owe them an astronomical amount of money."

His revelation took her by surprise. "Loren, that's awful."

"If I don't start making some fairly large payments on the debt soon, I could go to jail." Giving an oddly casual shrug, he added, "This could very easily ruin my life."

"You've got to get a lawyer or an accountant and fight it!"

"I already have. You don't argue with the IRS, Brenna; otherwise, they come and take everything but your false teeth—assuming you have the presence of mind to hide them."

"Then pay them."

"I can't. I freely admit that when it comes to money, I'm hopeless. Besides, a curator doesn't earn all that much."

"So . . . how did you get into such a bind?"

Another sigh. "My antique collection. They say I've been dealing in antiques—buying and selling—without reporting it to the government."

"And have you?"

"Much like our esteemed former president, Ronald Reagan, my memory fails me at the oddest moments."

"But your personal collection must be worth a small fortune. You could sell that and—"

"Never."

He said the word mildly, even with a slight smile, but Brenna could sense the determination behind it.

"Besides, if I couldn't wait for the right buyer, I'd have to sell at a fraction of the real value. I refuse to do that. It wouldn't get me out of debt, but it would destroy the work of a lifetime."

"This is insane. I'm not going to let you go to jail."

"Jeff said the same thing, and I'll tell you what I told him. I can handle my own problems. I don't need handouts."

Brenna was appalled. This was no time to get hardheaded. "But Loren—"

He took a quick drag on his cigarette. "I don't want to talk about it anymore, Brenna. If you persist, I'll have to leave."

He was terribly upset, but too proud to show it. Perhaps he was right. Now wasn't the time to pursue the issue. Later, when they were both less emotional, she'd get him to accept her help. What were friends for? "All right. I just want you to know that I'm here for you."

"Thank you. And I'm here for you. At least we'll always know where we are."

The humor was just a cover for his wounded pride. Men were all alike. It took her the better part of the next hour to get him to thaw out. He wasn't an easy man to understand. He was far too intelligent to simply charm, and too complex to manipulate. Eventually, however, as they fell into reminiscing about Jeffrey, his mood lightened. It felt good to talk about the man she knew—the man she loved, not the one she'd glimpsed through the eyes of a blackmailer. She was starting to feel a little more positive by the time they'd finished their coffee and Loren had smoked his last cigarette.

Checking his watch, Loren said, "Hey, look at the time. I'm afraid I've got to get going. The Institute of Arts has asked to feature some of the foundation's furniture collection in its winter exhibit, and that means I'm buried in paperwork."

"Did anyone ever tell you you work too hard?"

"No, but I'll pass your comment on to that smarmy little rodent at the IRS."

Rising together, she walked him to the door.

"I'd like to have dinner with you soon, Brenna. You pick the place."

She smiled up at him, straightening his bow tie. "You're a kind man, Loren. And a good friend."

He held her gaze, then kissed her lightly on her forehead. "I'm not kind, but I'm glad someone thinks so."

She could tell his IRS problems hadn't left his mind. "Why don't we make it the Haymaker Club? You name the night."

He grimaced. "You know, they're going to throw me out of there when they find out about my coming financial debacle."

Brenna never did understand why Loren had wanted to join. Jeffrey had probably launched into one of his "responsible wealth" speeches, and Loren had bought the idea because, among other things, Jeffrey was a good salesman.

"How about tomorrow night?"

"All right." She didn't feel much like going out, but it was probably good not to be alone all the time. As she opened the door, she was startled to see her father standing outside in the hallway, about to ring the bell.

"Mr. Dove," said Loren. His smile grew sardonic.

Andrew's expression was also less than friendly. "Thanks for bringing my daughter home."

"It was my pleasure." Lifting his coat from the chair, he gave Brenna another good-bye kiss. "I'll see you tomorrow night."

"I'll look forward to it."

Nodding to Andrew, he brushed past him into the hallway and headed straight for the elevators.

Brenna had no sooner closed the door when her father said, "Has he been here long?"

"A few hours. We had some coffee."

He took off his hat and coat and handed them to her.

Brenna loved her father, though she didn't care for his imperial treatment of women—herself included. She was hardly a hatcheck girl.

While Brenna cleaned up the dishes in the living room, Andrew went into the kitchen, removed a bottle of Chivas Regal from a lower cupboard, and poured himself a stiff drink. "You want to join me?" he asked.

"No thanks." Alcohol was the last thing she needed after such an emotionally draining day. She'd completely come apart at the funeral, soaking every tissue she'd brought with her. Since then, the tears had come in waves. She'd been fine for the past few hours, but she had a long night ahead of her.

Instead of returning to the living room, Andrew walked into the study. When Brenna was finished in the kitchen, she found him sitting behind Jeffrey's desk, sipping his scotch. His red face told her he'd started drinking well before arriving on her doorstep.

"Sit down, honey. I want to talk to you."

She felt more like taking a hot bath, trying to relax the tense muscles in her neck and shoulders, but her father had come for a reason, and she knew what it was. Taking the chair on the other side of the desk, she waited for him to bring up the subject.

"First of all, honey, how are you doing? I didn't get a chance to talk to you much at the church."

The crowd at Jeffrey's funeral had been much larger than she'd ever imagined it would be. It had filled the St. Paul Cathedral to overflowing. "I'm doing about as well as you might expect. Not great, but I made it through the day."

He acknowledged her comment by saluting her with his glass, then taking another hefty sip. "You looked so solemn and distant in that black dress today. You still do." He gazed at her with a mixture of sadness and uneasiness. Loosening his tie, he leaned back in the chair, still studying her, though now his eyes had grown red and puffy with tears. "Not like my daughter at all, but like some woman I hardly know. A *grown* woman. I'm guilty, I guess. Sometimes I still think of you as a child."

She didn't know how to respond, so she just sat there, looking down at the wedding ring on her left hand.

"I'm so sorry this happened."

"I know that, Dad." She could feel herself start to crumble. He didn't have to say how sorry he was every time they talked. It was almost as if he were apologizing for Jeffrey's death, and that was ridiculous.

"I'd give anything if we could have him back."

"Me too," she whispered, wiping the tears from her cheeks.

He tilted the drink back and finished it. This time his hand was unsteady as he set the glass back down on the desk. "I just came from the police station. As far as I can tell, that Sgt. Duvik is simply chasing his tail. I don't think he's any closer to finding Jeffrey's murderer today than he was last week. And you know what they say. The longer the police go without nailing down a suspect, the less likely it is they'll solve the crime." He glanced somewhat cautiously at his daughter, then added, "We may never know the truth."

Brenna shook her head and looked away.

Andrew continued, "I know this is bad timing, but . . . you did promise you'd tell me today whether or not you're going to take over Jeffrey's position at the club. I need someone to fill that vacancy, honey. It can't wait." He hesitated for a moment, then went on. "Think of it this way, Brenna. You'd be carrying on his charitable work. The renovation of the Winter Garden could even become a memorial of sorts to your husband's belief in the value of the entrepreneurial spirit. And, like I said before, it would help you to get out of the house, focus some of your talent and energy on something important. What do you say? Is it a deal?"

She'd given it some thought, though perhaps not as much as she should have. All her instincts told her to say no, but if she did, she knew her dad would be terribly disappointed. For some reason, he had a bee in his bonnet that she was the best person for the job. As far as she was concerned, all this business about getting her out of the house was just plain silly. She was hardly going to take to her bed and waste away, like some fictional Victorian heroine—especially not with a blackmailer on the loose. Then again, the idea that the renovation of the Winter Garden would become a memorial to Jeffrey appealed to her, too. And if there was a blackmailer at the club, it might be a perfect chance for her to do some snooping and find out who the bastard was. "All right, Dad. I'll do it. But on one condition."

"Name it."

"If it gets to be too much work, if it takes up too much of my time, I want you to find someone else."

His smile was triumphant. "I promise."

"You're also going to have to walk me through my duties. I'm not exactly a trained financial expert."

"It's just a title, honey. Basically, you just carry out my decisions and sign the checks." The smile dimmed as he added, "As your father, Brenna, I must point out that you don't want to spend all your time with Loren Ives. It doesn't look right."

Now he'd gone too far. "Loren is my friend, and I'll see him whenever I want."

The argument was about to escalate when the fax line rang.

Oh no! thought Brenna, her mind moving into panic mode. What if the call was from the blackmailer? She couldn't have her father getting wind of that—not until she knew what it all meant. Rising quickly, she said, "I'm exhausted, Dad. I don't want to fight with you; I just want to take a hot bath and go to bed."

Andrew swiveled around and glanced at the machine as the fax started to come through.

"Come on. It's time to go." She knew she was rushing him, but didn't care.

Giving her a disgruntled look, he got up, but continued to watch the paper as it rolled into the tray. "It's for you."

"It's just some agency business. Leave it, okay? I can't think about any of that now."

She could tell he wasn't going to go until he'd read the entire thing. She just prayed it *was* business and not another note from the blackmailer.

"Brenna, what *is* this?" He ripped it out of the tray. Handing it to her, he waited.

She read silently:

Fax Transmission

Page 1 of 1
Date: November 25
To: Brenna Chapel
From: ?

I assume you got my last fax. I hope you thought long and hard about what I said. I am watching you, Brenna. If you go to the police, I will know. Unless you want the world to learn your husband was a faggot, you will give me $100,000 in unmarked, small-denomination bills. I will let you have until the day after Thanksgiving to get the money. You will be contacted later with the location of the drop-off point. Do not think you can outsmart me, Brenna, unless you want to see your husband's reputation ruined.

Just as before, the fax had been sent from the Haymaker Club. Brenna wondered if her father had caught that part.

Andrew Dove's eyes now sparkled from both alcohol and what looked like revulsion. "Is . . . is this true? Was Jeffrey—"

"I don't know."

He stared at her a moment, then looked away. Brenna could see he was struggling hard to understand. He was a Catholic, and he'd been brought up to believe that homosexual acts were mortal sins. She'd been taught the same thing, though in general she'd adopted a live-and-let-live attitude. That attitude, however, didn't extend to the man she'd married.

"Have you heard from this blackmailer before?"

"Once."

"You didn't tell me!"

"How could I?"

He walked around the desk and grabbed the fax sheet back from her, reading it through one more time. His face had grown deeply flushed. "Where's the other note?"

"I threw it away." It was a lie. Maybe she was just being obstinate, but she didn't think it was any of his business.

Raising a trembling hand to his forehead, he said, "You've got to do what the note says. You've got to pay the man."

Brenna was amazed that her father would cave in to a blackmailer, though she knew he was shocked, and that he'd had too much to drink.

Once he'd had a chance to think it through in a more reasoned, sober light, his reaction might be different.

"I'll think about it."

"Does anyone else know? Have you told anyone else about these faxes?"

She wasn't sure how much to say. "Yes, one person."

"Ives?"

"No, a woman named Jane Lawless. She's Raymond Lawless's daughter." She hesitated. "She's gay, Dad. And discreet. I thought she could help me find out whether or not it was true."

"You mean . . . you hired her?"

"More or less."

"Well, get rid of her! Tonight. We have to keep this quiet. The last thing this family needs is a scandal." Turning away from her, he dropped the fax on the desk and stomped out of the room. Brenna didn't quite understand his reaction.

Feeling utterly alone, she realized that the first fax had altered her sense of reality and had made her deeply afraid. This fax elicited a far different reaction. She was furious—at the blackmailer, at herself, at Jeffrey, and at her father.

When she reached the living room, she saw that her dad had put on his hat and coat and was about to leave. "Listen to me for a second. We don't even know if it's true. The whole thing could be a scam." When he didn't respond, but kept on walking out the door into the hallway, she followed. "Are you sure you should drive? How much have you had to drink?"

"Don't worry about me." He yanked on his gloves. "Worry about the person who sent that fax."

"Where are you going?"

"To see a friend."

"No police. I mean it."

He gave her a peck on the cheek. "Your father will take care of everything."

"Dad, no!" She watched him weave his way down the hallway. "Stay out of it. I don't need your help. I don't want you messing things up for me."

"They're already messed up."

Before she could respond, the elevator doors closed.

"Damn," she said, turning and slamming her fist into the wall.

Chapter 14

Jane eyed the treadmill in Patricia's exercise room with little enthusiasm. She'd stayed up way too late last night talking to Cordelia, and then, because she didn't want to take either of her pain medications, her night's sleep, if you could call it that, was fitful. All morning she'd expected a phone call from Julia, but none had come.

Feeling her mind ache with too many unanswered questions, Jane switched on some music, then stepped onto the machine and adjusted the speed control until she was walking at a comfortable pace. Mindless exercise was what she needed. Thanks to Patricia, she didn't have to drive to the Uptown Y. Her left arm was still weak, but it was her left leg that continued to give her the most problems. She hoped it wouldn't take long before she would see some dramatic improvement, especially if she walked regularly. As long as she exercised during the day, she wouldn't run into Patricia—and that's how she wanted it. She needed to keep her relationship with the young Ms. Kastner as simple as possible until she and Julia could sort everything out.

Checking her watch, she saw that it was just after three. She'd spent the morning on the phone at Cordelia's loft, making business calls. She'd also contacted Norm Tescallia, her father's paralegal, to ask if he could get her a copy of the police report on Jeffrey Chapel's murder. Norm occasionally did her favors. He'd been her father's assistant for over fifteen years, and because Raymond Lawless was so high-profile, Norm was also well known in local legal and law-enforcement circles. He was also just a nice guy who happened to like helping out his boss's daughter.

Once her calls were completed, Jane invited Cordelia to lunch at the Lyme House. Later, after stuffing themselves on a roasted vegetable strudel, a fall specialty at the restaurant, they'd driven around town, stopping at some of the local gay hangouts to show Jeffrey Chapel's photo to bartenders, restaurant owners, coffeehouse managers, and even a few patrons. Just as Jane had suspected, nobody had ever seen him before. By the time Cordelia dropped her off at Patricia's house, Jane had come to the conclusion that if Chapel was gay, he had hidden it. That didn't surprise her, though she knew Brenna was hoping for something more concrete than mere speculation.

As Jane continued to walk, she realized that getting a look at that police report had less to do with Brenna Chapel's questions than it did with her own. When it came to Julia, Jane was concerned and frustrated, and frankly, just plain angry. The least she could do was call and say where she was.

Stop it! she ordered herself, turning up the speed on the treadmill. She was supposed to be using this time to empty her mind and de-stress. Glancing at the indicator lights, she saw that she'd walked only a quarter of a mile. If she didn't stop brooding and start getting serious about this exercise business, she might as well go read a book.

Willing herself to think about something else, it occurred to her that Thursday was Thanksgiving. Unlike other years, this year's get-together was a dreary prospect. Aunt Beryl and her new husband, Edgar, were away in England on their honeymoon. Her father and Marilyn were taking a much-needed four-day vacation to Hawaii. Her brother Peter and his wife, Sigrid, were in the midst of terrible marital problems. They'd made it clear they weren't up for entertaining or even going out. And since Jane wasn't completely recovered from her injury—and wasn't even living at her own house—that meant the Thanksgiving dinner would fall to Cordelia.

Jane didn't relish the idea of spending the day with a bunch of Cordelia's theatrical pals. The food would be good and the conversation intelligent, but in Jane's mind, Thanksgiving should be a family day. Normally, it was, but this year it seemed nothing was normal. She had hoped to spend the day with Julia—whether at Cordelia's, or privately up in Julia's loft. Cordelia no doubt assumed that Jane would be coming for dinner, but Jane wasn't so sure she'd actually show up. The restaurant would be closed, and that meant an entire day of peace and quiet. Right now, it was a tempting thought.

Forty-five minutes later, she turned off the treadmill and stepped down onto the carpet, wiping the sweat from her neck with a towel. She'd walked a mile and a half—nothing much by her old standards, but it was the farthest she'd gone since her injury. Every day she wanted to walk a little farther and a little faster. Her leg ached from the exercise, but she'd made some real progress today, and it felt good.

After showering and changing into clean clothes, she sat down in the exercise room and pulled on a fresh pair of wool socks. She felt pleasantly tired for a change, not the dreary fatigue she'd experienced for so many weeks. Stretching out on the couch, she closed her eyes and allowed her mind to drift to a Rachmaninoff concerto she'd found in Patricia's CD collection. She was just going to relax for a few minutes and listen to the first movement, but before she knew it, the soothing second movement had put her to sleep.

When Jane woke, it was dark outside. The music had been switched off, and only one dim light burned in the room. Surprised to find that she was covered with a quilt, she rubbed the sleep out of her eyes and then eased into a sitting position. Her watch told her it was ten past seven. Damn. How could she have let this happen?

She tried to get up, but felt a shooting pain in her damaged leg, sending her a clear message that she'd overdone it this afternoon. She was afraid to put too much weight on it now for fear that it would buckle. Hopping on her right foot over to the chair where she'd left her cane, she leaned against the sturdy stick and tried a few baby steps. So far, so good. She could smell coffee, so she assumed that Patricia was downstairs, probably having dinner. Jane's plan was simple. She'd say a brief thank you, order a cab to take her back to the Lyme House, and be on her way.

After zipping the top of her gym bag shut, she limped out of the room. As she reached the stairway leading down to the front foyer, she heard voices. Patricia was in the living room talking to a man, a voice

Jane didn't recognize.

Pausing at the top of the stairs, she listened for a moment. She hated to interrupt them. She was embarrassed that she was still there, especially since she'd promised herself—and Patricia—that she'd only use the gym during the day, when no one was around. As she tried to form an apology, something Patricia said caught her attention:

"I think a small celebration is in order. Maybe we should open a bottle of champagne, drink a toast."

"To what?" asked the man. He had a pleasant voice. It wasn't terribly deep, but he sounded educated. "Fate?"

"Chapel's death was hardly that."

"No, but it *was* a tragedy. Then again, I suppose it's all in how you look at it."

Jane found it an unusually cold remark. Quietly descending a few steps, she could now see that the man was sitting in one of the leather armchairs near the archway into the foyer. He appeared to be about the same age as Patricia. Curly, ginger hair. A ruddy complexion, and a trim body. He was dressed casually in tan corduroy slacks and a dark brown leather jacket.

Patricia was silent for a moment. "Let's just say . . . it was a lucky turn of events."

"I can live with that." He flicked a piece of lint off his slacks.

"On the other hand, if you recall, I assured you Dove was in our camp.

"Then why haven't we heard from him?"

"We will. Just give it some time." He paused, then added, "You know, Patricia. Jeffrey was never a foolish man. He would have come around sooner or later. He had to."

Jane's ears pricked up. Was this guy actually saying that Chapel might not have been going to vote to spend the Haymaker Club funds on the hotel's restoration? If that was true, it was the first she'd heard of it. It was hardly a motive for murder, but it did explain some of their earlier comments. With Jeffrey out of the picture, and Andrew Dove backing the Winter Garden proposal, Patricia was virtually assured the vote would go her way. No wonder she wanted to break out the champagne.

Patricia laughed. "It sort of torpedoes the club's idea of 'responsible wealth.'"

"So much for rampant idealism."

Finally stepping into view, Patricia perched on the edge of the couch. She was wearing a tailored navy blazer, a miniskirt, and heels, so Jane figured she probably hadn't been home long. "Trust me, Eddie. This is just the beginning. With me as the developer and you as the architect, we can't lose. We may need a little financial push to get us over the first hurdle, but as soon as the Winter Garden is up and running, we can use the profits to finance the rest of our plans. It's a sweet deal, and only a matter of time before we can both quit our jobs and form a partnership. Then, the sky's the limit."

He smiled at her. Using a southern accent, he said, "You *are* ambitious, Miss Scarlett."

She returned the smile. "I get what I want."

"No matter what the cost?"

Matching his southern drawl, she answered, "Why fiddle-dede, Mr. Flynn. You know cost is a relative concept."

He laughed. "You don't lack confidence."

"And you don't lack talent. I think we make a great team." His response was a slow grin. "Speaking of teams, Miss Scarlett, I've got tickets to a Vikings' game next week. You interested?"

Clearing her throat, Jane made as much racket as she could coming down the rest of the stairs.

"Hey there, sleepyhead," said Patricia, getting up from her perch. "You finally decided to join the land of the living."

Jane put her gym bag by the front door and then, using her cane, limped down the step into the sunken living room. "I thought I'd be out of here hours ago. I never expected to fall asleep."

"No problem. My couch is always available. *Day or night,*" she added, her smile pregnant with meaning. "Jane, I'd like you to meet Eddie Flynn. He's the architect who's going to restore the Winter Garden."

Eddie rose from his chair.

Up close, Jane found him quite attractive. He had striking blue eyes, a few freckles left over from childhood, and an easy smile. "It's nice to meet you."

"Jane owns the Lyme House," continued Patricia.

Now he focused his full attention on her. "I love that place! It's the only really authentic modern log structure in the Twin Cities. Lars Peterssen was your architect, right?"

She nodded.

His enthusiasm seemed to be real. "He's one of our finest contemporary designers. Believe me, he'll go down as one of the greats."

106

"Actually," said Jane, "he lives around here. He comes to the restaurant occasionally for dinner."

"No kidding. I'd really be in your debt if you'd introduce me to him sometime."

"I'm sure that could be arranged," said Patricia, slipping her arm through Jane's. "By the way, Eddie was just leaving, but. . . why don't you stick around and have some dinner with me?"

Jane could have predicted this would happen. "I think I should get back to the restaurant. I worked out a little too hard today, and my leg is killing me. I'd like to take a long, hot shower."

At Eddie's questioning look, Patricia said, "She's living in her office right now. But don't feel sorry for her. It's got all the comforts of home."

He nodded and then smiled. "I'd be happy to give you a lift. It's right on my way."

"If you stayed," said Patricia, her tone growing even more seductive, "we could use my hot tub, complete with Jacuzzi. That would do wonders for your leg . . . among other things. Before you say no, think about it. I could open a bottle of wine. We could nibble on some Brie and crackers."

It did sound good. "I . . . don't know."

"I'll even throw in a free Swedish massage. My masseuse is coming by later tonight. She could do you instead of me."

"Jesus, lady," said Eddie, grinning, "if you don't say yes, I will."

Jane knew she was an idiot for turning down the offer, but she just couldn't stay. Not tonight. "Can I have a rain check?"

Patricia seemed disappointed. "Anytime," she said, her voice uncharacteristically gentle.

On the way out the door, Jane said, "Thanks again for letting me use your exercise room."

"My pleasure. I liked coming home and finding you crashed on my couch. I hope you'll do it more often."

Patricia was hardly the floating Ebola virus Cordelia always made her out to be. By all rights, Jane should change her mind and stay, and yet . . . she couldn't. She needed to settle the situation with Julia before she would feel free to date someone else. She owed Julia that much. On the other hand, if Jane didn't hear from Julia soon, that debt was going to start feeling like a burden—one she wasn't willing to carry around forever.

Chapter 15

On the way back to the restaurant, Eddie gave Jane an architectural minitour of the Linden Hills area, commenting on the most notable houses as they drove slowly down Sheridan Avenue. Many of them were period revivals: Dutch Colonial, Victorian, Tudor, and French Colonial. His favorite was a large Georgian toward the end of the block. Turning toward the lake, he explained that he'd been lucky to find a row house on Grand Avenue in St. Paul. It was genuinely historic, but he hoped that one day soon he'd be able to design and build his own home. He already had the land picked out.

Jane found their conversation fascinating. She'd always been interested in architecture, and was especially glad to learn more details about her neighborhood. Eddie was a wealth of arcane facts and tidbits of local history. By the time they reached the Lyme House, she'd invited him in for a drink. In the back of her mind, she had an ulterior motive. She couldn't quite get the conversation she'd overheard at Patricia's house out of her mind. Something Eddie said had given her the impression that he and Jeffrey Chapel had been more than just passing acquaintances.

Jane stopped at the bar and ordered a couple of red lagers. As she was waiting for the beer to be pulled, she used the bar phone to check her messages—both at the restaurant and at Cordelia's loft. There was still no word from Julia. Feeling disappointed but not surprised, Jane took the pints and led the way to a table in the back room.

After making himself comfortable, Eddie continued to look around, studying the exposed beams and the brick-and-mortar walls. "I know there's no one prototype of an English pub. Were you trying to make this look like some place in particular?"

She took a sip of beer. "All I was aiming for was a building that looked like it fit in with its surroundings."

"The woods and the lake."

"That's right. Lars understood exactly what I wanted. He also knew that I liked to play with contrasts. I'm especially drawn to the rustic elements as they mix with the more formal elegance of the main dining room upstairs. To me, it all works beautifully together."

"It does," said Eddie, eyeing her with curiosity. "Where did you come up with the name? The Lyme House."

"My mother was English. I lived in England until I was nine. My parents met in a little village on the southwestern coast of England, Lyme Regis. I remember it so vividly that I guess I wanted to honor that very happy time in my life by naming the restaurant after it."

"And what do your parents think of it?"

"My mother died when I was thirteen, so she never saw it."

He sat forward, folding his hands over his pint. "We have something in common then. My mother died when I was eleven." Keeping his eyes fixed on her, he added, "It's hard, isn't it?"

She looked down. She didn't feel comfortable talking about that time in her life. "Yeah. Very."

"Not many people understand what it's like having a parent die at such a formative period in your life. I'm afraid I didn't handle it very well."

She searched his eyes, wondering how much more she wanted to say. He was a good conversationalist, not just because he talked easily, but because he asked intelligent questions that seemed to truly interest him, and then he listened. The listening part was a rare quality in Jane's opinion, and it made her like him even more. Hesitating for just a second, she continued, "I didn't handle it well either. It's a long story, but my mother's death and my subsequent actions caused a rift in my family that's only recently begun to heal."

"We belong to a special club."

"I think maybe you're right."

He looked her square in the eye, then smiled. "Your mother would have been proud of what you've created, Jane."

"Thanks. I think so too." She leaned back as a waiter set a bowl of popcorn between them. "Since we're discussing personal history, are you from the Twin Cities?"

"I was born in North Dakota." Grinning at her, he added, "Wipe that smirk off your face, woman. It's a great place to grow up."

"I'm sure it is."

"No, you're not. Everyone jokes about the Dakotas."

"Well, I *have* heard that if you stand at the border and shout hello, you're most likely to get a response from a buffalo."

Eddie's indignation was full of good humor. "Some of my best friends are buffalo. And it's very antienvironmentalist of you to make fun of them."

"I apologize."

"Apology accepted." He tipped his glass back and drained a good quarter of the beer. "My dad still lives in Grand Forks. Works for a plumbing-supply company—always made dirt wages. We lived in a small, dreary post—World War II piece of ticky-tacky, as the song goes. I guess you could say that his life was extremely motivating to me. At a very early age, I knew I wanted more than a shitty job with TV and cheap bourbon as my only rewards."

"Were you always interested in architecture?"

"Always. I got my undergraduate degree on full scholarship at UCLA, and then went on to architecture school at the U of M. I was fortunate to be offered a job with a great firm even before I graduated."

"You must be good at what you do."

"I am. Someday I'm going to be an exceedingly rich man."

"Is that important to you?"

He seemed thrown by the question. "Of course it is."

He and Patricia were more alike than she'd first suspected. Their backgrounds were different: he'd come from little money, and Patricia had come from wealth, but they both wanted to make it big. So far, Patricia had been amenable to working for her mother's business, especially since it paid well and she was learning firsthand what it

110

took to run a large company. But Jane always suspected she had other ideas in mind for her future.

"Well," Jane said, taking a handful of popcorn, "I hope the renovation of the Winter Garden goes well."

"Thanks. I think it will." He took another sip of beer, then rested his elbows on the table. "As soon as we get the okay from Andrew Dove, I've got people lined up to move in and start work."

"What happens if the vote doesn't go your way?" She was interested in how deeply invested he was in the project.

"Well, I guess we're back to square one then. But we've got a good idea, and we'll find the financing somewhere—of that I have little doubt."

"You know, as I was coming down the stairs at Patricia's house, I overheard a little of what you two were saying. I got the impression Jeffrey Chapel didn't think the Haymaker Club should back your renovation with a charitable contribution."

At the mention of Chapel's name, Eddie's expression grew more guarded. "You're right, he didn't."

"Do you know why?"

"I believe he had another project in mind: the development of a low-income apartment complex up in Duluth. Some ex-marine buddy of his was looking for financial backing."

So that was it. "How much money are we talking about here?"

"Well, currently, the club has about two hundred and thirty members. The yearly charitable contribution is close to five million, though some of it goes for the general maintenance of the club's facilities."

Jane's eyes opened wide. "I had no idea it was that much."

"These are wealthy people, Jane. *Lots* of them. The same people, I might add, who might want to take advantage of a place like the Winter Garden at some point in their future."

No wonder the idea appealed to the membership. She finally asked the question she'd been wanting to ask ever since they first sat down. "How well did you know Jeffrey Chapel?"

He pushed back slightly from the table. "We met at a political fund-raiser about a year ago. After that, I'd run into him every now and then at the Lakeside Athletic Club—we were both members. I guess you could say we struck up a friendship while sweating away our job stress. Eventually, he gave me his pitch about joining the club. I wasn't all that interested, but he kept pressing the point. You know, *responsible wealth.* The private sector showing that it truly cares about society by helping others in the private sector deal with issues such as poverty, unemployment, housing—and not waiting for government to do its usual half-assed job. In essence, Jeffrey felt that it was important to support the entrepreneur *as* that entrepreneur made those less fortunate part of his or her priority. It's all very Republican political chic right now. A lot of hot air if you ask me. The bottom line for any capitalist will always be profit, no matter how much lip service gets paid to helping the unfortunate."

"Do you consider yourself a capitalist?"

"God, yes. Don't you? You run a restaurant for lots of reasons, but if you don't make money, you're history. The Lyme House is hardly a philanthropic organization."

He had a point. "So did you join the Haymaker Club?"

He shook his head. "I just wasn't convinced I wanted a large organization making my decisions for me. It felt a little too *governmental*, if you catch my drift. But Jeffrey persisted. He finally issued me a temporary membership when he became the new financial adviser a few months back, just so that I could see what it was like. When I mentioned the club to Patricia, she saw right away how valuable it might be to our plans. She took the ball from there, although I was supposed to convince old Jeffrey that our idea of bringing an assisted-living home to downtown Minneapolis was not only a sound one, but would provide housing for the low-income elderly, as well as a lot of new jobs for inner-city workers."

From what Jane had been able to glean from her earlier conversation with Patricia, low-income housing was definitely not where she was headed. "Do you think he would have come around?"

Eddie shrugged. "It really didn't matter if he did or he didn't. Andrew Dove is the founder and prime mover over there. What he wants, rules. We'll get our money, I have little doubt about that." Leaning closer into the table, he added, "Just between you and me, Jeffrey had been so busy with his personal problems, I don't think he would have had the steam to mount a campaign against the Winter Garden's renovation. In case you didn't know, he was in the middle of some big-time marital difficulties."

Jane decided to play dumb. "I'm sorry to hear that."

"Yeah, he wanted out of his marriage. I don't suppose you've ever met Brenna Chapel."

"Actually, I have. We're not friends, but she seems like a nice enough woman."

"Well she's not. She's a shrew. Brenna made his life miserable with her constant demands, almost from day one. Lately, he couldn't even stand going home at night. She has a horrible temper. I think he got sick of having plates thrown at him."

"Did he tell you that?"

"Sure. And a lot more. He thought she was crazy. Literally. One minute she'd be all loving and sweet; the next she'd fly into a rage. And then recently, she somehow figured out that he was sleeping with someone behind her back, and she went ballistic. Jeffrey didn't want to hurt her. Somewhere, down deep, I think he still loved her. He even said he thought the failure of the marriage was his fault. But the bottom line was, he wanted out."

"Do you have any idea who the new person in Jeffrey's life was?"

"Someone he'd met on one of his speaking tours. I never actually met her myself, but he'd talk about her occasionally."

He seemed to have little doubt about the gender of Chapel's newest love.

Lowering his voice and speaking more confidentially, he continued, "If you ask me, I think Brenna could easily have been responsible for his death. Jealousy is a pretty lethal motive. And she was there at the hotel, you know. After I left, Patricia caught her in the lobby."

It was an interesting theory, one she'd heard before—from Patricia. She wondered if there was a reason why both of them were advancing it. With so much innuendo in the air, it was hard to make sense of what was really true. She was about to ask another question when she heard someone call her name. Turning around, she saw Brenna charging toward the table.

"Jane, I've got to talk to you." She was wearing a full-length black mink over jeans and a fluffy pink angora sweater.

Eddie stood. "Mrs. Chapel. How are you?" He managed to sound concerned, though knowing what she now knew, Jane could see it took some effort.

Brenna looked out of breath as she unhooked her purse from her shoulder. "Eddie. What are you doing here?"

He didn't answer the question. "I'm sorry I couldn't make it to Jeffrey's funeral this afternoon. I hope the cathedral received my flowers."

"I'm sure they did." She said it dismissively, returning her attention to Jane. "I got another fax this afternoon."

Eddie quickly stepped away from his chair, nodding for Brenna to sit down. "This sounds like business—and my cue to leave." At Jane's apologetic look, he added, "Don't worry. It's past my bedtime. I'm not getting any younger, and we all have to think about our beauty sleep."

She laughed, grateful that he understood. "This has been a lot of fun. I hope we can do it again soon."

"I hope so too. In the meantime, think about coming down to the Winter Garden to look at the restaurant. I could use your input—and I know Patricia would be grateful for any help you could give us." He drew his wallet out of his back pocket and handed her a card. "Call me anytime. If I'm unavailable, just leave a message."

"Thanks. I may do that."

Even before he'd said good-bye, Brenna had dropped a folded sheet of paper on the table in front of her. By the determined look in her eyes, Jane could tell that she had no intention of leaving, even if it meant interrupting Jane's evening. Eddie was right about one thing. Brenna Chapel was demanding.

"Read it," said Brenna.

In the dim light, Jane couldn't hope to see such small print. Slipping on her reading glasses, she got up and took the page over to the fire. Sure enough, it was another note from the blackmailer—this one, she noted, also sent from the Haymaker Club. After studying it for a good minute, she returned to the table and handed it back to Brenna. "Are you going to pay the money?"

"Certainly not."

That surprised her.

"I've been thinking about it all evening, ever since I received the second fax. I don't believe for a minute that this person, whoever he is, has any proof. It's just a scam to squeeze money out of me."

"So you're going to sit tight? Not do anything?"

"That's right. Do you think I'm not taking this seriously enough?"

Jane held up her hand. "It's your call. I have no advice to offer because I have no idea what the truth of the matter is."

"Well I do. No more second-guessing my husband. He loved me and that's the end of the story."

"I'm happy you're so confident."

"I am." Her unblinking eyes held Jane's. "Have you had a chance to do any checking around yet?"

"Yes, but I came up empty. If he was gay, he wasn't out about it."

"I knew it," said Brenna, crossing her legs and relaxing into her chair. "You just proved it all over again. My husband wasn't gay.

Jane didn't feel as if she'd proved a thing. "You weren't so sure about that on Saturday night."

"That was during my panic phase. After the funeral today, I had a long talk with Loren Ives. Loren was Jeffrey's best friend. If anyone would know the truth about my husband, Loren would, and he insisted that Jeffrey loved me and wanted to spend the rest of his life with me."

Since Jane had received some rather conflicting stories tonight, she assumed somebody was lying. "So, do we call off the investigation?"

"About Jeffrey, yes. But I still need to know who's behind the blackmail."

"But . . . what about your husband's murder? Maybe I should widen my search to include that. After all, there may be a connection."

Brenna's response seemed a little too quick. "Keep your focus on the blackmail, Jane. I think we should let the police handle the rest of it. They don't know anything about the faxes, nor will they—that's what I'm paying you for."

Jane wasn't sure she could separate the two.

"I just wish this whole, nasty business would go away." Opening her purse, Brenna stuffed the fax back inside. "By the way, I'm taking over Jeffrey's position at the Haymaker Club. I'll be working with Eddie and Patricia Kastner on the renovation."

This was news to Jane. "Is it going through then?"

"We'll be voting on it soon, but yes, it is."

"You think it's a good idea?"

"Sure. Why not?"

Jane was hardly in a position to argue the point. "How does the voting work?"

"Well, the membership at large gives a general vote of interest, and then, after a closer examination, the executive board either votes to affirm or deny the request for charitable funds."

"How many people are on the board?"

"Three. My father—he's the president. And then Joe Patronelli, the VP of the organization, and finally the chief financial officer—myself in this case."

"Does the vote have to be unanimous?"

"Yes. It's in the bylaws."

"So if one person were to feel the project wasn't, shall we say, proper—for whatever reason—he or she could veto it?"

"They'd have to present some very compelling reasons, but yes, that's the way it's set up."

Jane wondered what Chapel had been planning. "Did you know your husband had reservations about the project? He was interested in backing a low-income housing complex in Duluth."

"Oh, I think you're wrong about that, Jane. He never said anything to me about it. And my father would certainly have told me if that had been the case. As a matter of fact, I'm going to insist that the hotel be designated as a memorial to my husband. Maybe we'll have a plaque in the lobby. Or name one of the meeting rooms after him. Come to think of it, maybe I should endow a yearly charity event there."

Jane found the ideas revolting. After all, it was where the man had died. Why memorialize *that?*

"The good thing about my appointment to the board is, since I'll be spending some extra time at the club, maybe I'll get lucky and discover who's sending me those horrible faxes."

Unless Jane was sorely mistaken, the only good thing about Brenna's appointment to the board was that Andrew Dove had just assured himself that his wishes would be carried out. Jane understood why it was so important to Patricia and Eddie, but wondered why it was so important to Dove. She also wondered if Dove had Joe Patronelli in his pocket or if, like Chapel, Patronelli had his own reservations. The whole situation left Jane feeling uneasy.

"I'd be careful, Brenna. Really, this blackmailer, whoever he is, could be dangerous."

"Oh, I'll be discreet. Don't worry."

Brenna seemed to be a woman who was about to ignore any facts that didn't fit her theory and, at the same time, believe what she wanted to believe, come hell or high water. Jane had pegged her as a much smarter woman. But then, denial was a powerful emotion.

As Brenna started to get up, Jane said, "Will you keep me posted? I'm concerned about you. You realize, of course, that if you don't send the money, you're calling the blackmailer's bluff."

"Exactly. I'm convinced that, since he has no real proof, he'll slink back under a rock where he came from."

"For your sake, I hope that's true."

Brenna stood, gazing down at Jane with a distant look on her face. "Thanks. You know, you've turned out to be a good friend. It's weird, isn't it, how life throws such different people together?"

Jane couldn't help herself. She had to ask. "You mean, I'm a restaurant owner and you're the owner of an ad agency?"

"Well that, of course—but also the fact that you're gay and I'm straight."

"Yeah," said Jane, draining her pint. "That is weird, Brenna. Really very . . . very weird."

Chapter 16

TUESDAY AFTERNOON

You *do* remove the feathers don't you? And the beak?" Cordelia put her hand over the receiver and whispered to Jane, "For our Thanksgiving dinner, I'm ordering a natural turkey from one of the co-ops." Looking smug, she returned to the conversation. "Well, pardon me, but how the hell should I know what state the bird will be in? 'Natural' could mean anything—and believe me, Cordelia Thorn does not *pluck.*"

Jane sat on the other side of Cordelia's large mahogany desk. She'd arrived at the Allen Grimby shortly before two, knowing her friend often took an afternoon break between two and three. Cordelia called it her "meditative hour," though Jane doubted she did much meditating. She did, however, darken her office by pulling the blinds, and then she'd light a stick of incense and a few candles. Sometimes she even put on some sitar music while she sat on the floor in the lotus position. Cordelia knew how to create the right image, she just wasn't very good at the inner-peace part.

"You can keep the feet and anything above the neck. What? No, I don't want that either." Again, she put her hand over the phone. "What's the 'gobble,' Janey?"

Jane could tell the person on the other end of the line was playing with Cordelia. "Tell them we definitely want that. It's essential to making a good gravy."

Cordelia gave a knowing nod. "I take that back. We need the gobble. Just wrap it up with the *thoroughly* plucked bird, and I'll pick the whole mess up tonight on my way home from the theatre. Yes, Thorn. T-H-O-R-N." Her expression grew annoyed. "I assume you think that's funny. No, I have never been a *thorn* in anyone's side. My personality is pure sweetness and light. And now, my good man, you may return to hacking up cows, and I shall return to creating theatrical history." She slammed the receiver down, muttering, "The nerve of some people." She blustered for a few more seconds, arranging papers on her desk; then she fixed Jane with a glare that would have done a fifteenth-century inquisitor proud. "You have that look in your eye, Janey."

"What look?"

"You want something."

"Just to talk."

"Said the spider to the fly." One eyebrow inched upward. "About what?"

Jane took some papers out of the pocket of her pea coat. "This was messengered over to me this morning from Norm Tescallia."

"Ah. Your dad's paralegal."

"It's the police report on the Chapel homicide."

Cordelia stared at her a moment, then blew out the candles and opened the blinds. "I'm not wasting good karma on this." Leaning back in her chair, she closed her eyes and waved a dismissive hand. "All right, continue. Dazzle me with the gory details."

Jane often bounced ideas off Cordelia. Occasionally, Cordelia even came up with a theory or two of her own. "I'll start at the beginning," she said, slipping on her reading glasses. She intended to paraphrase the report, hitting only the high points. "Chapel died sometime between seven and eight last Thursday night, November seventeenth. The body was discovered shortly after eight, tangled in the elevator cables at the Winter Garden Hotel."

"By Patricia Kastner."

"Right."

"How convenient."

Jane flicked her eyes to Cordelia, then went on. "He died from two stab wounds to the back—one puncturing his right lung, the other his heart. Death was immediate."

"I'd say he turned his back on the wrong person."

"Which makes me think that he either trusted the person who murdered him, or at the very least, didn't realize he was in such imminent danger."

"Since he probably knew every martial art known to man, he no doubt figured he could handle anything. Did they find a murder weapon? I haven't seen anything about it in the papers."

"Actually, they did, but it's been kept under wraps. Initially, they thought it was a knife, but during a search of the building, one of the officers found a bunch of tools in a room near the fourth-floor elevator. Apparently, an electrician who'd been working in the building left them behind. Turns out Chapel was stabbed with a screwdriver. It had been wiped clean of fingerprints, but whoever committed the murder was in a hurry. Some of Chapel's blood was still on it."

Cordelia gave an involuntary shudder.

"After Chapel was stabbed, he was pushed down the elevator shaft. Hiding the body that way gave the murderer valuable time to leave the building before the murder was discovered. Bloodstains were found on the fourth-floor carpet about six feet from the elevator opening. That's where the police think the attack occurred. Since deadweight is pretty heavy, they're leaning toward a male suspect."

"Which lets Patricia Kastner and Brenna Chapel off the hook. Hey, didn't you tell me once that Patricia works out with weights?"

"Cordelia."

She held up her hand. "Just asking." Clearing her throat, she continued, "If it *was* a woman, maybe she had an accomplice."

"You mean two people were involved in the murder?"

"Why not?"

Jane thought about it for a few seconds. "I suppose it's possible."

"Did forensic investigators find any clothing fibers, hair samples—anything that would lead them to a specific person or persons?"

"It's all pretty inconclusive. The fact that Brenna's hair was on her husband's topcoat means nothing, and all the main suspects were on the fourth floor at one time or another in the past few weeks, and they were all physically near Chapel that night. Oh, there is one other interesting point. Both Eddie Flynn, the architect, and Patricia mentioned that they thought they saw evidence that a homeless person had been sleeping in the hotel. The police found corroborating evidence in the basement as well as in several of the upstairs rooms. It appears to be a man."

"Hey, maybe *he* murdered Chapel."

Jane assumed the police had considered it. "The fact that Chapel's wallet and keys were missing might indicate that his death was part of a robbery attempt, so your point is well taken. But, if that's the case, why did someone steal his desk calendars that same night? They were missing the following morning from both of his offices."

"Fascinating," said Cordelia under her breath.

"And his briefcase was missing from the trunk of his car, but not the car itself. Why would a street person, someone totally unknown to Chapel, attack him viciously, take his keys and his wallet, figure out where the car was parked, and snatch the briefcase, but leave the vehicle still parked on the street? It doesn't make sense."

"What if the guy couldn't drive?"

"That's possible. But we're still left with the mystery of the calendars. After reading through this entire report, it sounds to me like Chapel used his desk calendars not only for appointments, but to write down his thoughts."

"And you're betting he wrote something that someone else didn't want anyone to see?"

"Exactly."

"Then why not just remove those pages?"

"Maybe there were too many—or there wasn't enough time. The thief couldn't take the chance that he'd miss something, so he just takes the entire calendar."

Cordelia digested that for a few moments. "I suppose they've both been tossed in a dumpster by now. Has anyone tried to use Chapel's credit cards?"

Jane paged through the report. "If they have, it's not in here."

"You mentioned statements. Who did the police question?"

Jane consulted the list on the front page. "So far, Connie Brogaard, Chapel's secretary at Dove Aviation. Betty Hanson, his secretary at the Haymaker Club. Then, Andrew Dove. Eddie Flynn. Loren Ives. Patricia Kastner. Brenna Chapel. And Joe Patronelli."

"Joe had nothing to do with it," said Cordelia flatly.

"Because he's your friend?"

"Tell me his motive?"

He did seem to be a truly innocent bystander—which, of course, made Jane wonder about him all the more. "I can't."

"Just as I suspected. Now, who's Loren Ives?"

"Jeffrey's best friend. Except, according to Chapel's secretary at Dove Aviation, he and Ives got into a heated argument last Thursday afternoon, and Ives ended up threatening his life."

"Really. I just love twisted friend stories—almost as much as I love a good twisted family saga. What were they arguing about?"

"According to Ives's official statement, he'd recently been audited. He owes the government a ton of money. Chapel told him that he'd help pay off the debt if Ives agreed to sell off his extensive antique collection. Ives refused, said he didn't need Chapel's help. Chapel called him a fool. The argument escalated. The only thing is, it doesn't jibe with what the secretary said she overheard. I've got her statement right here."

"Which says—?"

"Ives said he could, 'kill Jeffrey for what he'd done.' And then Jeffrey called him a 'poor sap' and said Ives had 'never been very lucky in love.'"

"Curiouser and curiouser," mused Cordelia, tapping a finger to her chin.

"Whatever the argument was about, it was pretty intense. But if Ives did murder Chapel, there's no evidence that he was at the Winter Garden that night."

"He could have slipped in—just like Brenna."

"That's true. Since the door was unlocked, I suppose anyone could have gotten in."

Cordelia stretched her arms high into the air, then clasped her hands behind her head. "So, what do the police say about motive?"

"Actually, at this point, I think we may know more than they do."

"Because of the fax Brenna Chapel received?"

"Fax*es*."

Cordelia's eyebrows shot upward. "She got another one?"

"Last night." Jane quickly explained what it said.

"Is she going to pay the money?"

"She thinks the blackmailer is full of hot air—that he has no proof.

On the basis of a conversation she had with Ives, she's decided it's all bunk. Ives assured her that Jeffrey was head over heels in love with her. So she's going to call the blackmailer's bluff."

Cordelia shrugged. "Maybe that's the best move."

"She's about to find out. The thing is, in the last couple of days, I've been given such conflicting stories. Ives says Chapel loved his wife. Eddie Flynn says Chapel thought she was a demanding shrew and wanted out of the marriage. The blackmailer says Chapel was gay, but both Eddie and Ives insist he was straight—Eddie even said Chapel was about to leave his wife for another woman. And Brenna and her father insist that Chapel was all for supporting the renovation of the Winter Garden with Haymaker funds, but Eddie and Patricia feel he was against it. Eddie even suggested that Chapel had another project in mind."

Cordelia's chin sank to her chest. "Where's Deep Throat when you really need him?"

"Now, the second fax was also sent from the Haymaker Club. Brenna said that since she'll be over there more regularly—she's temporarily taken over her husband's position as financial director—maybe she'll get lucky and catch the guy in the act."

"Does that woman have rocks for brains? Why does she want to put herself in that kind of danger? If you ask me, it sounds like something *you'd* do."

"I beg your pardon?"

"Well, doesn't it?"

Grudgingly, Jane had to admit it did. "Tell me this, Cordelia. Do you think the blackmailer and the murderer are one and the same person?"

"Sure, don't you?"

"I don't know. They could be completely separate issues. Somebody gets wind of Chapel's involvement with a man and decides to make a little extra cash. It might be that simple."

"So the blackmailer isn't dangerous?"

"I didn't say that."

Patiently, Cordelia leaned forward and folded her hands on the desk. "Look, Janey, I can tell something about this really gets to you. You wouldn't have agreed to help Brenna, a total stranger, if it didn't. What is it? The fact that we have a well-known marine who might have spent his life in the closet? If it's true, it would make a fascinating headline—blow some people's preconceptions right out of the water, but what's it got to do with you?"

Jane lowered her head. "It's Julia. She's involved in it somehow; I just know it. Remember I told you about all those phone calls she received while I was staying with her? And that someone broke into her house—and later, her loft—looking for her files? I don't know what's in them, but it's got to be pretty explosive stuff. Chapel met with Julia before he died. I'll bet any amount of money that he confided in her and that somehow, it's all connected."

"Why did he go see her in the first place? Was he sick?"

"According to Brenna, he'd just had a full physical and was pronounced the picture of health."

"Maybe he was HIV positive."

Jane wondered about that too.

"Did they test for AIDS? It's not done routinely."

"I don't know—and no doctor is going to give out that kind of information." She had so many questions, but unlike the police, she couldn't just march in and demand answers.

"Why would he drive all the way up to northern Minnesota to see Julia?" asked Cordelia, tapping her fingernails on the desktop.

Jane shook her head.

"It had to be something medical. She is a doctor, after all. I don't suppose you've heard from her."

"Not unless she's called in the last hour."

Cordelia gave a deep sigh. "I'm really sorry, dearheart. She's totally jerking you around. I don't understand, because I know she cares about you."

All her reassurances were starting to sound pathetically empty.

"I'm sure she'll call soon."

"I'm not."

"You know," said Cordelia, her expression full of exasperation, "you really need this kind of stress in your life right now—especially when you're trying to recover from a serious injury."

Jane conceded the point with a shrug.

"So how *are* you feeling?"

"Frustrated. Angry. Impatient. Disgusted. Even, I suppose, a little scared." She wasn't about to tell Cordelia that she'd thrown away her pain medication.

"Did you exercise at Patricia's yesterday?"

"Yes. And I'm driving over there now when I leave the theatre. I figure it's the only way I'm going to get my strength back."

"Well," said Cordelia, getting up from her chair and then perching on the edge of her desk in front of Jane, "Thanksgiving's just around the corner. We'll have a great time. I guarantee the food and witty repartee will be just what the doctor ordered. Oops." She covered her mouth with her hand. "Freudian slip."

Jane glowered.

"Admit it, Janey. You're just in a lousy mood. But Auntie Cordelia will fix that right up on Thursday. Say, speaking of turkeys—"

Jane stiffened. "If this is another comment about Patricia, I refuse to listen."

Cordelia raised an innocent hand. "Just a simple culinary question."

"Like what?"

"How long do you bake a turkey?"

Jane was relieved to move to a more comfortable subject. "Depends on the size. The rule is, twenty minutes per pound—in a 325-degree oven."

Cordelia grinned. "You are *such* a storehouse of culinary wisdom."

"Thanks. At least my damaged brain still works."

"Generally, yes."

"You really know how to build up a person's self-confidence." Behind Jane's eyes, the deep rumble of a headache was revving up again. She was angry at herself for responding so viscerally to Cordelia's comments. "Thanks for your trust."

"It's not that, Janey. I'm just worried about you."

Jane plastered on a fake smile, then used her cane to help herself get up. "Well, don't. Every day, in every way, I'm getting better and better."

Cordelia studied her a moment. "I'll expect you at one o'clock on Thursday afternoon. If you come early, you can help me decorate the place with all the jingoistic, sentimental Thanksgiving Day crap I've collected—I call it "Pilgrim Vulgaris." And don't forget, it's going to be a real feast, enough to feed nine hungry thespians—and then you and me."

To Jane, it sounded like spending an afternoon in lower hell. The more she thought about it, the more a day of complete peace and quiet appealed to her. Not that she was going to tell Cordelia. She wouldn't get out of the office alive.

She was about to ask Cordelia to do her a small favor when the phone rang.

"Just a sec and I'll walk you out," said Cordelia, propping the receiver between her ear and shoulder. "Thorn here." She listened for a moment and then said, "Hang on." Holding her hand over the receiver, she said, "It's for you, Jane. Andrew Dove."

Jane had given the Lyme House Cordelia's number, just in case someone—specifically Julia—needed to reach her. Stepping around the side of the desk, she took the receiver and said, "This is Jane."

"I need to speak with you this afternoon," rumbled a deep voice. "You're at the Allen Grimby now, and I'm on 94 heading for St. Paul. Perhaps we can meet at the Maxfield Plaza's bar? Do you know Scotties?"

"Sure." It was only a few blocks away. "What time?"

"Right away. I should be there in ten minutes."

"Fine." She wanted to ask him what it was about, but felt it was best to talk face to face. This was actually perfect timing. She'd been wanting to meet him, get a feel for the kind of man he was.

As she hung up, she saw that Cordelia was staring at her. "What?"

"You're now getting personal phone calls from airline moguls?"

Jane let the question slide past her. "Listen, I want you to do something for me."

"How unusual."

"It's no big deal."

"Then why do I have an intense yearning to crawl under my desk and insist that Cordelia Thorn has left for the day?"

"I just want you to call your friend Joe Patronelli and set up a time for the three of us to meet. Preferably tonight—say, at the Haymaker Club bar. If we're his guests, we can get in."

"Dare I ask why?"

"I need to ask him a few questions."

"About Chapel's murder?"

"Among other things. Just leave a message at the restaurant, and let me know whether he'll do it—and what time. I'll meet you at the club."

"You know, Janey, I have an extremely busy schedule. My dance card is *always* full."

126

"But it's flexible enough to accommodate your best friend."

"You think so, huh?"

Jane was on her way out the door. "You're a peach, Cordelia."

"Yeah," she grumbled. "Softheaded and ripe for the picking."

Chapter 17

Before entering the historic art deco bar at the Maxfield Plaza, Jane stopped in the lobby to make a quick call. She wanted to clarify something Brenna had said to her just the other night. After tapping in the phone number, she unbuttoned her pea coat and waited, hoping Brenna was home. A few seconds later, she heard a click.

"Hello?" It was Brenna's voice.

"Hi. It's Jane Lawless."

"Jane. What's up?" She sounded eager. "Have you learned anything new?"

"No," she said. "Nothing yet. But I need to ask you a question. The night you hired me, you mentioned that in the past few months, your husband had stopped talking to you about his work."

Hesitantly, Brenna replied, "That's right."

"What about his position at the Haymaker Club? Did he stop talking about that too?"

Silence. Then, "Yes, as I think about it, he did. Why do you ask?"

"I'm not sure yet. But it could be important."

"You mean because that's where the faxes have been sent from?"

"Um . . . right. And you never discussed the renovation of the Winter Garden with him?"

"Well, I did bring it up once, but he just put me off, gave me some general nonanswer—pretty much the way he did with the ongoing labor problems at the airline. He used to value my opinion, Jane. We talked about everything under the sun. I can't tell you how much it hurt when he began to shut me out."

"When was that exactly? Did it coincide with anything else that happened in his life?"

More silence. "Well, in a way, I guess it did. About a month after he'd become the club's financial director, I noticed that we weren't talking as much. I remember thinking there was a connection. He seemed so tired that I suggested he give up the position, maybe even take some time off for a vacation. To be honest, Dad had pretty much forced the job on him. Jeffrey was a natural at many things, but financial matters weren't his forte. I'm not saying he was inept, but I knew he was struggling. He eventually cut back on his hours at the airline to accommodate his new duties. He said it was only temporary, just until he got a better handle on things, but it didn't help. By then, our dinners had become unbearably silent. I didn't know what to do. It seemed pretty clear to me that our problems had gone way beyond his general fatigue."

Jane had suspected as much. Before Chapel died, two major issues appeared to dominate his life. One had to do with his marriage and his sexuality. Was he straight and seeing another woman, or was he gay and perhaps involved with a man? The other had to do with the Haymaker Club—and the restoration of the Winter Garden. Was he for it, as Andrew Dove insisted, or was he against it, as Eddie suggested? And if he was against it, did it have some sort of larger meaning? Jane hoped that if she followed both of these threads, one of them would lead her to the truth behind his murder. "Thanks, Brenna. You've been a big help."

"I have?"

"Sorry, but I've got to run now. I'll catch you later."

As she hung up, she realized she'd only seen a small snapshot of Andrew Dove. She wasn't sure she'd recognize him in person.

Entering Scotties, her eyes swept the darkened room, searching for a gray-haired man with a beard. She found him sitting at a side booth, staring intently into a highball glass. Since he probably didn't know what she looked like, she had a momentary advantage. Watching him from one of the bar stools as a bartender poured her a cup of coffee, she noticed that he seemed to be deep in thought. Something important was on his mind, all right, and she assumed that whatever it was, she was part of it.

"Excuse me," she said, approaching the booth, cup in hand. "Are you Andrew Dove?"

He looked up, his serious expression quickly replaced by an insincere smile. "Jane. I'm delighted you could join me."

She eased into the other side of the booth. Since this was his idea, she decided to let him fire the first shot.

"I saw you walk in, but I wasn't sure it was you." He glanced at the cane.

"A small accident," she said, answering his questioning look. "It's nothing."

He nodded, fixing her with his rather formidable gaze, the one he no doubt reserved for recalcitrant junior executives. "I see you found yourself something to drink."

Jane wished he'd dump the prologue and just get to the point, but in Minnesota, social niceties were mandatory.

Examining her a moment longer, he said, "You know, you look a lot like your father."

"Do you know my dad?"

"We've met. I was impressed with his honesty and his intelligence."

"Yeah, Dad's a pip all right."

"Excuse me?"

"It's a word my mother always used when she wanted to annoy him." Jane had no idea why it had jumped into her mind right then, but there it was. "It's sort of English slang—for somebody special."

"A pip." He laughed. "I'll have to remember that."

She was sure he'd already forgotten it.

"I'm told you own a local restaurant. The one on Lake Harriet?"

"That's right."

"You know, you should stop by the Haymaker Club and pick up some of our brochures and membership information. You might want to consider joining."

"I may do that."

"Good. Good." Again, the slick smile.

Jane decided to introduce a subject of her own. "I was sorry to hear about your son-in-law. I understand he was the club's financial director."

The smile dimmed ever so slightly. "Yes, that's right."

"Actually, Patricia Kastner is a good friend of mine. I may be doing some consulting on the renovation of the Palmetto Room."

"Really. I had no idea. It's a small world, Jane."

"Yes, it is, Andrew." She didn't want to be accused of jumping to conclusions—the way Cordelia always did—but she didn't like him. "Patricia thought that perhaps Mr. Chapel wasn't all that sold on the idea of restoring the hotel."

"That's not true," said Dove, frowning at the very idea. "We all want to see that project receive the funding it deserves. My daughter has just agreed to take over Jeffrey's position as financial director. We'll be voting on the matter in a couple of days. It's a worthy cause, Jane, and a damn fine piece of entrepreneurial leadership. Your friend Patricia will go far."

"I'm sure she will," agreed Jane, taking a sip of her coffee. In an effort to move things along, she asked, "I assume there's a reason you wanted to get together?"

He nodded, stirring his drink with the swizzle stick. "I understand Brenna hired you to do some . . . research for her."

That was an interesting way of putting it. She'd have to use it herself in the future. "Yes, she did."

"May I ask what you've found out?"

"Nothing concrete."

"Then you have no idea who the blackmailer is?"

"Not yet."

"But you do have . . . theories?"

"Yes, a few."

"Would you care to share them with me?"

She wondered what Brenna would think of this little meeting. "I'm sorry, but since Brenna hired me, I feel that any information I have should go to her first."

"I see." He tried not to scowl, but his face wouldn't cooperate. "Well, then, Jane, I'm sorry to be the bearer of bad tidings. Brenna will no longer be needing your services. I'd take it as a personal favor if you kept what you do know about the blackmail notes to yourself."

She wasn't sure what to say. "I just spoke to your daughter a few minutes ago. She didn't mention anything about giving me the boot."

"Brenna doesn't like to hurt people's feelings."

"She seems like a very direct woman to me."

"Are you saying you know my daughter better than I do?"

Jane wondered why this had escalated so quickly into an adversarial conversation. "I'm saying, Andrew, that I'd like to talk to your daughter before I give up my . . . research." Once again, she was amused by the word.

"You're making a mistake, Jane. Believe me, you don't want me for an enemy."

"Why would continuing to help your daughter make you my enemy?"

"You'd be doing it against my wishes."

"Pardon me, but I think that's her call to make."

"This is a family matter, and it must remain within the family."

"Your son-in-law was murdered. If the blackmail notes are for real, that could mean his death was a hate crime—and that's not the kind of thing you just sit on."

He glared at her. "I'm taking care of this in my own time and in my own way."

"Does Brenna know that?"

"Why the hell did she contact you in the first place? There are plenty of reputable private agencies in this town."

"We have a mutual friend. A doctor, someone Jeffrey saw a couple of times before he died. Also, I'm gay. She thought I might have an inside track when it came to finding out whether or not her husband was also gay."

Finishing his drink, Dove set the glass down on the table, and then took his wallet out of his inner coat pocket. "How much?"

"Pardon me?"

"Come on, Jane. Let's not play games. How much money is it going to take to make you go away?"

"I don't want your money."

"Whatever Brenna paid you, I'll double it."

She couldn't believe her ears. No one had ever tried to buy her off before.

"Okay, so you don't want cash. What *do* you like?" He paused, watching her face. "Drugs? Girls? I could make you a very happy woman, Jane. How I do it doesn't make any difference to me."

She wanted to leave. "I think this conversation is over."

"You're making a big mistake."

"I doubt it."

Now he was offended. "I suggest you take what I said to heart. Stay out of my business. Do I make myself clear?"

"Perfectly."

If she'd ever had second thoughts about continuing to look into Jeffrey Chapel's murder, Andrew Dove had just settled it for her. Perhaps it wasn't a flattering personal trait, but nothing spurred her on like opposition. She wouldn't give up her "research" now for anything.

Chapter 18

Brenna had just started reorganizing the desk in her husband's office at the Haymaker Club when she heard a knock on the door. It was shortly after six on Tuesday night, and as far as she knew, all of the regular business staff had gone home for the day. She'd come by after hours so she could have some privacy. If she started crying as she sifted through Jeffrey's papers, she didn't want an audience.

Her first inclination was to sit totally still and not make a sound, hoping that whoever it was would go away. But when the second knock came less than a minute later, this time louder and more insistent, she knew she couldn't hide.

Rising from the desk chair, she approached the door. The man who finally faced her was the last person she expected to see.

"Hi," said Joe Patronelli, his expression tentative. He was dressed in gray sweatpants and a tight, black muscle T-shirt, which suggested to Brenna that he might be headed up to the gym on the twenty-sixth floor. Or perhaps he was just out impressing the natives. He stood back and for a moment looked at the door. "I see they finally removed the police tape."

If he wanted to make small talk, this wasn't the time. "Look, Joe—"

"I'm sorry to bother you, Brenna, but—" He glanced over her shoulder into the office. She assumed he was making sure they were alone. "I've got something I need to give you."

She couldn't imagine that Joe Patronelli had *anything* she needed—and if this was a ploy to put the hustle on a poor, grieving widow, he'd come to the wrong place. He might not know how much she disliked him—his arrogance, his assumption that any woman he wanted was his for the taking merely because he carried a small ball around a field—but he was about to find out. "Joe, I'm busy right now."

"This won't take long." He pushed his way past her into the room.

She'd barely recovered from his forced entry when she saw that he'd been holding a briefcase behind his back. She recognized it at once. "Where did you get that?" she demanded, grabbing it out of his hand. "The police have been looking for it for days!"

"I know," he said, massaging the back of his neck.

"It was stolen from Jeffrey's car the night he died. Did you take it?"

Looking flustered, he said, "No! No way. Look, Brenna, can I sit down for a sec? I'm kinda sore from last night's game—and this could take a minute to explain."

She wasn't comfortable being alone with him, but she wanted that explanation. Her curiosity finally won out over her reticence. "I suppose. But I've got work to do, so make it fast." She hesitated. "As I think about it, maybe I'm making a mistake. Maybe I should call the police right now."

"Just hear me out, okay? Then if you want, we'll both call." He lowered himself onto the leather loveseat, stretching his legs and then rubbing his right calf.

"Is that an order?"

"Brenna, please. I know you don't like me, but I do have an explanation, not that I entirely understand it myself."

Now he had her intrigued. And surprised. How did he know she didn't like him? She'd never said one word to him about her negative opinions. She doubted her father could have said anything because, to be honest, he assumed everybody adored the Vikings' illustrious golden boy. And Patronelli hardly seemed like the sensitive type to her.

Eyeing her warily, he continued, "See, I've been living at the club—up in one of the guest suits—for a couple of months now."

"I thought you were married?"

"I am." He looked down at a bruise on the back of his right hand. "But my wife and I are having problems. I'm not sure we're going to make it."

That came as no surprise, knowing all the skirt chasing he did.

"I miss my kids pretty bad."

"I didn't know you had children."

His face brightened. "Yeah, two boys. They're the best. Dylan is seven—and already an athlete. And Avery is nine. He's the artistic one. I'm so proud of him—he can draw anything. I don't have my wallet with me, or I'd show you pictures."

"Maybe another time."

"Right. Sure." It was his turn to look uncomfortable. "Well, anyway, I was leaving my apartment this afternoon to go have lunch when I noticed the briefcase sitting on the floor next to my door. I recognized right off that it belonged to Jeff. I took it inside and opened it up, but it was empty. Not even a paper clip was left inside. That's it, Brenna. That's why I have it. I know it sounds strange, but it's the truth." His eyes traveled around the room. "You know, it feels funny being in here, now that Jeff's gone."

It was hardly a subject she wanted to discuss with him. But again, her curiosity got the better of her. "Did you come here often?"

"No, not really. We had a few late-night meetings. Once in a while, I'd stop by to ask him a question. I liked your husband, Brenna. I thought he was a real heads-up guy."

"Thanks," she said, noticing that his face had grown sad.

He scraped a hand across an unshaven cheek. His hair was so thick and dark that his five o'clock shadow could easily have been the beginnings of a beard. "Anyway, maybe if the police go over the briefcase, it will give them some clue about who took it. I suppose I could have driven it down to the station and talked to Sgt. Duvik, but when your father told me you were coming over this evening to organize Jeff's office so you can use it yourself, I thought it should go to you. After all, all his stuff belongs to you now. I'll be happy to talk to the police—I just wish I had more to say."

She wasn't sure she believed him. "You didn't see anyone in the hallway when the briefcase was dropped off?"

He shrugged. "Nope."

"Or hear anything strange?"

He shook his head.

Brenna couldn't help but wonder what it all meant. Why would someone give the briefcase back to Patronelli instead of her? Silly as it was, she realized she was jealous. She wondered if the blackmailer could have done it—the phantom of the Haymaker Club who used the facilities to send his notes.

"Well," said Joe, glancing at her and then away, "I guess I've taken up enough of your time."

He seemed so sad that she thought she should say something more. "I'm sorry to hear about the troubles with your marriage. That can be rough."

"Hey, thanks. We'll figure it out, one way or the other."

As she continued to watch him, she noticed for the first time what large, easy eyes he had. And there was a certain self-deprecating gentleness in his manner that appealed to her. Not that *he* appealed to her. In her book, he was still an asshole of major proportions. But perhaps, as one lonely person to another, they could be friends. They'd be working together on the Winter Garden renovation, so maybe it was best to start out on a positive note.

Taking one last look around the office, Joe got up. "I guess I better hit the bricks—unless you want me to stay while you call the police."

Brenna had no interest in talking to Sgt. Duvik tonight. "Have you had dinner yet?"

He seemed startled by the question. "Me? No. Have you?"

"I'm not even sure I had lunch."

For the first time, he smiled, revealing a set of perfect, immaculately white teeth. "Well, maybe we'd better do something about that. I have a standing reservation in the dining room for dinner. You might as well share the table with me—that is, if you feel like a little company tonight."

He did look like a movie star, thought Brenna. Thick, dark hair. Ruggedly handsome face. Hunky body. Some women might be attracted to all that, but Brenna considered herself far more interested in the content of a man's character. And that left Joe Patronelli out in the cold.

"You're not exactly dressed for the main dining room," she observed.

Glancing down at his sweats, he smiled sheepishly. "You've got a point. But since my reservation isn't until seven, I've got plenty of time to shower and change. What do you say? Will you join me?"

She hesitated. In her wool slacks and cashmere sweater, Brenna was only barely presentable herself. Thank God she'd worn a strand of pearls. After a moment's reflection, she decided that, since it was a weeknight, her casual look would do. "Sure. Why not?"

"Great. And afterward, if you want to come back up to Jeff's office, I'd be happy to help you clean out anything you don't want. I'm good at muscling things around. Moving furniture. Taking boxes to the garbage. I do have to meet someone at nine, but we should have plenty of time."

Brenna assumed he had a bimbo on his agenda for later in the evening. "We'll see," she said, realizing her reticence made her sound coy.

"I'll meet you in the dining room at seven." As he headed out the door, he gave her a smile that would have melted an iceberg.

Dinner, as always, was delicious. Brenna had the duck á la Martinique—duck served in a special pineapple coconut sauce, with fresh peaches, oranges, and plums. Joe had a Greek ragout of lamb. The conversation ranged from a discussion of their respective child-hoods, to his love of football and her love of hiking. The longer they talked, the more Brenna realized she liked him. Not once did he even come close to putting his famous moves on her. She began to wonder if there was something wrong with her—if he didn't find her attractive.

"Since I invited you, dinner is on me tonight," said Joe, taking a last sip of his wine. He looked incredibly handsome in his dark suit, white shirt, and striped silk tie.

"That's very kind of you."

"Nothing to do with kindness, ma'am. It's just nice not to have to eat alone. Extroverts have trouble being by themselves, and I guess I fit that category."

What a strange comment coming from the original ladies' man. Perhaps the situation with his wife had taken some of the starch out of his collar, as her grandmother used to say. Whatever the case, he seemed very human tonight—not at all the swaggering sexual preda-tor she'd observed at parties. She was about to take a risk and ask him to explain the dichotomy when she felt a hand on her shoulder.

Looking up, she saw Loren Ives staring down at her. "Hey. Hi!" Only then did she realize he was glowering.

"I thought *we* had a date for dinner tonight, Brenna."

My God, she'd forgotten! "Loren, I'm so embarrassed. Really. You have to forgive me. I'm not functioning very well right now." She turned around and took hold of his hand.

"Seems like you're doing okay to me." He glared at Joe.

"Oh . . . let me introduce you to Joe Patronelli."

"I know who he is."

"Well, Joe doesn't know who you are. Joe, this is Loren Ives, Jeffrey's best friend, and a dear friend of mine as well."

Joe stood and stuck out his hand, but Loren wouldn't shake it.

Brenna could tell now that he really was hurt. She didn't know what to do. Should she invite him to sit down? She hardly knew Joe, but Loren's friendship meant the world to her. The choice seemed obvious. "Why don't you join us?"

"No thanks. I'd only be a third wheel."

Not at all," said Joe. "We'd love the company. I've already bored Brenna with my life story; your presence will give me a chance to bore someone new. I find myself endlessly fascinating, in case you didn't know." He grinned, apparently hoping that a little humor might ease the tension.

It didn't work. Loren continued to glower.

"Loren, please," pleaded Brenna. "Say you forgive me. We can have dinner tomorrow night."

"I have to work late."

"Then any night you want. I promise, I won't forget again."

"Right." Staring at her a moment longer, he shifted his gaze to Joe. "Nice meeting you." His voice was full of sarcasm. Taking one last look at Brenna, he turned and snaked his way through the tables, finally disappearing out the front entrance.

After he was gone, she covered her face with her hands. "Damn."

Joe waited a few moments before speaking. "That was kind of sticky. And I'm afraid I didn't help with the stupid comment."

"No, it's not your fault. It's mine. I'm the one who forgot our date."

"Does he have a thing for you?"

"What?" Her head snapped up. "No, of course not."

"Could've fooled me. You want some dessert?"

She couldn't eat anything after what had just happened. "Thanks, but I better head home. Maybe I can reach Loren by phone and try to apologize again. I hate to leave such bad feelings hanging in the air."

"Sure, I understand." He seemed disappointed that she wanted to leave.

All evening, Brenna had a strong sense that Joe wanted to tell her something. She didn't want to press him on it, just in case she was wrong. She also didn't want to jump to conclusions. Even so, she couldn't help but wonder if this "something" had to do with her husband.

Motioning the waiter over to the table, Joe said, "I'm sorry the evening had to end on such a sour note. I've enjoyed talking to you. Maybe we can do it again. Oh, and don't forget. That offer to help you clean out Jeff's office still stands. Unless I'm out of town for a game, you can reach me here. Apartment seven."

"Thanks."

After paying the bill, he walked her to the elevator. "Your friend Loren will cool off. Trust me. Guys get hot, but if you're as important to him, as I suspect you are, he'll be back."

She wasn't quite sure what to say, so she just said good night.

Half an hour later, Brenna opened the door to her condo and stepped inside. After switching on a few lamps, she took off her coat and hung it in the front hall closet. She decided to pour herself a drink before she called Loren. It might help calm her down.

Once she'd mixed the manhattan, she took it into the den and sat down behind the desk. That's when she noticed the fax machine. Another fax had come through.

Removing the single sheet from the plastic tray, she held it under the desk lamp. This one was shorter than the others. It said, simply:

I have changed my mind. Instead of $100,000, I want $200,000. I doubt it will even make a dent in your bank account. I will give you two extra days. Put the money in a brown garbage sack, and leave it in the Dumpster behind the minimall on Nicollet and 46th at exactly 5 P.M. on Sunday night. I will be watching. If I see anyone loitering around, the information I have on your husband goes straight to the press.

Brenna read through it twice. Of all the notes, this one sounded the most angry. She wondered why. Placing it carefully on the desk, her eyes strayed to a framed photo of her husband, the one that rested next to the phone. After a long, painful moment, she whispered, "You know I'm sorry, Jeffrey. You hurt me, so I hurt you back. But right now you've got to help. Give me a sign. The blackmailer's lying—isn't he? *Isn't he?*"

Chapter 19

After her workout at Patricia's house, Jane drove to Evelyn Bratrude's to check on Bean. He seemed happy to see her, but content with his temporary digs. She assumed that he was "doing" a little too much cat food, as Cordelia always put it. Evelyn had three cats. But what the hell? Jane figured he might as well enjoy himself. He was on vacation.

Passing her own house on the way back to the restaurant, she thought of her Trooper sitting inside the garage. She knew she should exchange Julia's car for her own one of these days, but didn't figure there was any hurry.

Once back at the Lyme House, the first order of business was to check her messages. As usual, Julia hadn't called. Cordelia, however, had. They were on for drinks tonight with Joe Patronelli. Nine o'clock in the club's bar. Jane was delighted Cordelia had been able to reach him, and that he was willing to get together on such short notice. She wondered idly what reason Cordelia had given him for the meeting.

The next item on her agenda was to call the Haymaker Club. She needed information on a specific aspect of the club's financial history.

After talking to a receptionist, she was put on hold. A man's voice finally answered.

"Hi," he said, sounding apologetic for the long wait. "I'm Jim Nyvold, director of operations. Perhaps I can help you."

"I hope so," said Jane. "I've been thinking of joining your club, but before I do, I'd like a list of the organizations or individuals you've given charitable donations to in the last, oh, say, six or seven years."

"No problem," said the man. "Just give me your address, and I'll be happy to mail you the details."

"Could you fax me the list instead? I'd like to take a look at it as soon as possible." She gave him the restaurant's fax number. After thanking him for his help, she opened the day's mail, then headed upstairs. It was nearly dinnertime, and she wanted to work the reception desk until it was time to leave for the club.

The bar at the Haymaker Club was a slick, modern space, filled with glass and chrome, and dominated by a brightly colored neon sculpture of dancing dollar bills. The east wall, a series of windows, allowed a particularly dramatic view of downtown Minneapolis. The bar's lavish ambience combined with the panoramic view gave Jane the impression that its patrons felt they owned what the triple-insulated glass allowed them to survey.

Spotting Cordelia at a table near the windows, Jane was glad to see that she was alone. She wanted a few minutes to talk privately before Patronelli arrived. Ordering a brandy from one of the waiters, she approached the table.

"You didn't get my message," said Cordelia, frowning in disappointment as Jane sat down.

"Sure I did. You said to meet you here at nine."

"No, the *other* message."

"And that was?"

"Well, I mean, I had to give him *some* excuse for getting together tonight, so I said you were his biggest fan. You had photos of him all over your house. You'd even memorized all his stats, ever since he won the Heisman Trophy. And you never took off your Vikings' sweatshirt. You even slept in it."

"Jeez, Cordelia, he's going to think I'm some sort of pervert."

"No, just another groupie geek."

"Oh. That's supposed to make me feel better?"

"I told you to buy a Vikings' sweatshirt. Now he's going to think I was exaggerating."

"When he finds out I know nothing about football, he's going to think you were doing something a lot worse."

"But . . . you *do* know about football, Janey. Everyone does. It's part of the American psyche. Touchdowns and extra innings . . . and . . . and—"

"And what?"

"Well, how the hell should I know! Just tell him he's fabulous. You especially like the way he . . . handles the ball."

"And how would that be?"

Exchanging her irritated look for one of absolute dignity, Cordelia replied, "With finesse, Jane. With absolute finesse."

"That's supposed to mean something?"

"If you'd just worn that damn sweatshirt, we wouldn't have to prove your loyalty!"

"My *loyalty?*"

"Just cooperate for once."

"Okay. I'll tell him he's a great . . . What position does he play?"

"How should I know? I'm a *theatrical* diva."

"Well then, I'm a culinary diva."

"You are not. There aren't that many of us around these days. That's what makes us special." She smoothed her right eyebrow with the tip of her little finger. "I think the sweatshirt is purple—at least it would have been a nice color."

"I hate purple, and I wouldn't be caught dead in a Vikings' sweatshirt."

"You're just being obstinate."

"So what if I am? Couldn't you have told him something less embarrassing?"

"How about this? My friend Jane likes to chase murderers around."

"Great, Cordelia. Just great."

"I could have said you thought you were the reincarnation of Miss Marple."

"Jane Marple is a fictitious character. She can't be reincarnated."

"Why are we even *having* this conversation!" Before Jane could respond, Cordelia's head jerked to the side. "There he is."

"Where?"

Her voice dropped to a whisper. Crouching close to the table, she pointed. "Coming through the door."

"What are you doing?"

"Assuming my invisible posture."

"A six-foot-tall woman—dressed in a slinky, red-sequined evening dress with a red feather boa draped around her shoulders like Mae West about to seduce the first cowboy who walks into the saloon—is hardly invisible."

"Cowgirl, Jane. When I go out in public, I have to consider my image. Glamour is back—and Cordelia M. Thorn is leading the battle charge." She put a finger to her lips as Patronelli approached. "Trust me on this, Janey. Just act . . . enraptured."

Stepping up to the table, Joe nodded to Cordelia, then took her hand in his and kissed it. "You look . . . lovely this evening." His hesitation and the broad grin suggested that *lovely* wasn't the first word to come to mind.

"Why thank you, Joseph. You look lovely yourself. I'd like you to meet my friend—your *biggest* fan—Jane Lawless."

"Nice to meet you," said Joe, taking a chair next to her.

Jane was relieved he didn't kiss her hand, but he did seem to be scrutinizing her face awfully closely, which made her uncomfortable. He was as good-looking as everyone said—almost too perfect, if there was such a thing. She would have preferred to get right down to business, but didn't want Cordelia to look like a total fool. So, instead of asking the questions she'd prepared, she said, "Have you been playing football all your life?" She felt it was an innocuous enough opening.

"Well, not when I was a baby, but yeah, most of my life." He waved the waiter over. After placing an order for a draft beer, he added, "But somehow, I have the feeling you didn't come here to talk about that."

"Hey," asked Cordelia, twisting the boa around her finger. "You aren't psychic are you? After a recent, shall we say, disastrous experience"—she glared at Jane—"I've sworn them off."

"No," he said, smiling. "But you laid it on awfully thick when you told me about your special friend, Cordelia. Somehow, I can't imagine you with a best friend who eats, sleeps, and breathes pro football."

"Oh." She let the boa unwind all by itself and fall across her rather robust décolletage. "Well, maybe I did exaggerate . . . just a little."

"A little?"

"She was doing me a favor," interjected Jane. "Please, don't be upset." Actually, she was so relieved to have the truth on the table, she could have cheered.

"So, why *are* we here?" asked Joe, crossing his arms and looking from face to face.

He was direct. It was a quality Jane appreciated. She wished she could be equally direct, but felt the situation called for more subtlety. "I, ah . . . well, I've been thinking about joining the club."

"Really."

"Yes, it seems like a pretty great place."

"It is. But everything you need to know is in our brochure. If you want a tour, you can arrange that with the woman at the front desk."

"I've already read the brochure. I was hoping to get . . . a more personal view."

He watched her a moment, his face blank, his eyes steady. Finally, he said, "Why don't we cut to the chase?"

"Excuse me?"

"I read the newspapers. I know your father is a defense attorney and that you help him occasionally. Who's his client this time? Dove? Patricia Kastner? This is about Jeffrey Chapel's murder, right? Some sort of fishing expedition to see what I know. Maybe you think I murdered him myself."

"Joseph!" said Cordelia. "Stop it. You're being ridiculous."

"Am I?" As his beer was set in front of him, he kept his eyes on Jane.

Jane's brandy arrived at the same time. "Look," she said, taking a sip to fortify herself. "You're right. I am investigating Jeffrey Chapel's death. I thought if you knew that up front, you might not talk to me."

"Because the police consider me a suspect."

She nodded.

"I've got nothing to hide, Jane."

"And I've got no reason to believe you do." For the moment, that was true. "But I was hoping you might be able to shed some light on a theory that's been going around."

"Theory?" he repeated, making a tiny rip in the napkin under his glass. "And what would that be?"

"That Jeffrey Chapel was gay."

Downing several swallows of beer, Joe wiped a heavy hand across his mouth. "I find that hard to believe."

"He never confided in you about his marriage—his personal problems?"

"Why would he?"

"Because you were friends. You worked together. Sometimes things get said."

"Not to me."

"Okay," said Jane, disappointed that if he did know something, he wouldn't open up about it. "But . . . maybe you could clarify a couple of other issues."

"Like what?"

"Well, when exactly did you and Jeffrey become officers of the club?"

He leaned back in his chair, making himself more comfortable. "I took over the VP position last July. Jeff signed on as financial director in August."

"Who was the financial director before Jeffrey?"

He thought for a moment. "His name was Hedges. Burl Hedges. I've only been a member here for a little over a year. I didn't know him real well."

"So what happened to him?" asked Jane. "Why did he quit?"

Joe shrugged. "I think he got sick of the work. He's pretty old. Must be in his late sixties, early seventies."

"How many years had he been in the position?"

"Since the club started back in eighty-four, I think. He was an old pal of Andrew's."

"Was he fairly wealthy?"

Joe scratched his cheek. "I guess. I was at his house once for a party. He lives in this huge old place out in Minnetonka. It's right on the lake, close to the Lafayette Club. Very ritzy."

"What did he do for a living?"

"Beats me. I think he had a lot of personal investments. I never heard him mention a specific job. He sure didn't get rich on what they pay you here."

"Do you have to be wealthy to join?"

"Reasonably well off, and you have to agree to pay five percent of your net income to the club's coffers each year. That buys you a membership, with the majority of the contribution going to a good cause."

Jane already had a list of these good causes—compliments of the director of operations, Jim Nyvold. They did all seem to be worthy of help.

"Hell," he continued, "I thought *I* was rich when I joined. Look at me now. My wife is about to take me to the cleaners, and my career is mere inches from the dumper."

"But you're so young and muscular," said Cordelia, visually measuring his biceps.

He laughed. "When you've been an NFL running back as long as I have, you get pretty beat up. I wanted to make this my best season ever because it's probably going to be my last. Problem is, I got hurt two weekends ago. Really freaked me out. My knee," he said, his hand dipping under the table. "It's always given me trouble, but if I get hurt again, it's possible that I'll have to kiss the season good-bye."

"But surely you've saved big bucks in your time," said Cordelia, trying to cheer him up. "You can buy a health-club franchise! Or sell your own brand of exercise equipment with one of those tacky infomercials. I'd even help. I can see it all now, Joseph. I'd go on and say I lost a hundred pounds with your torture machine."

He grinned at her. "I like that."

"We could make millions?"

"We?" Looking down into his drink, his expression sobered. "Unfortunately, my wife and I spent money like I was gonna be a pro running back forever. The truth is, I'm strapped. There's no health-club franchise in my future. Not even a snow-cone stand. But . . . if I can just have a really great last year, I'm guaranteed a bunch more endorsements. I might even be named a spokesperson for some product. You know—Joe Montana advertising dog food—or whatever the hell he does. And," he added, growing more confident, "this is all hush-hush, but I think I may have a chance at a commentator spot on one of the major networks. If that comes through, I'll be *the man!*"

Cordelia slapped his palm. "Go for it, Joseph."

"Damn straight."

"Getting back to Jeffrey Chapel," said Jane, knowing this wasn't his favorite topic. "Cordelia tells me the two of you used to play a lot of racquetball."

His back visibly stiffened. "So?"

"Brenna Chapel mentioned that, during the last few months of Jeffrey's life, he'd become quite preoccupied. I wondered if you knew what it was about."

148

"He was a stress junkie."

"Did his stress come from his new position at the club?"

He cupped his large hand around the base of his beer glass. "Why would you think that?"

"Because I've been told two different stories about his commitment to the renovation of the Winter Garden Hotel. Andrew Dove insists Jeffrey was behind it. Other people have told me he was against it." She paused, watching his reaction. "Did he ever mention any reservations to you?"

After finishing his beer, Joe said, "Look, I don't want to get in the middle of this."

"Then you do know something?"

"Let's just say Jeff was . . . concerned about some of the club's past financial dealings, although he never gave me any specifics."

"Concerned in what way?"

"I guess maybe he thought something was a little shady. I could be wrong. Like I said, he never gave me details. I figured that since he was pretty new at this financial director business, he just didn't understand some stuff. And as far as the Winter Garden goes, I think your friends are right. I don't think he was going to vote for it."

Jane had assumed as much. "You know Andrew Dove better than I do. How would he have reacted?"

"He would have hit the ceiling. Nobody challenges him around here and lives to tell about it. But I don't think Jeff had said anything to him yet, at least not directly. He told me he intended to have a private meeting with Andrew in the next couple of weeks. He hoped Andrew could shed some light on his questions and that that would clear everything up. There'd been a lot of tension between them recently. Sometimes I felt like I was in the middle. I mean, it seemed pretty clear to me that both men wanted me in their camp, although neither of them would take me into their confidence."

"That must have been difficult for you," said Cordelia, patting his hand sympathetically.

"It was," said Joe, amused by her concern. Glancing over her shoulder, he smiled at a woman sitting at the bar.

"And Jeffrey never mentioned another man to you—someone he was dating?"

"Jesus, no." He clearly didn't want to talk about it. "I have no idea how this 'gay' rumor got started, but I don't believe it."

"No?"

"No."

"Did you see Jeffrey much socially?"

"What are you implying?"

"Nothing. I just wondered if you got together much."

"I'm not gay, Jane."

"Don't be so touchy," said Cordelia, whapping him with her feather boa. "Your red neck is showing."

"That's me. Rednecked and proud." Pushing away from the table, he said, "It was nice meeting you, Jane. I'm sorry I couldn't help you more." Looking at Cordelia, he smiled. "I'll catch you later."

"Are you leaving? So soon?"

"The night is young," he said, continuing to eye the blonde at the bar. "And this is one fella who doesn't intend to sleep alone. That is," he said, winking at Cordelia, "unless you're free."

"Get real."

"Just checking."

"You better find someone who appreciates your charms more than I do."

"That's the plan," he said, nodding to Jane. After tossing some cash on the table, he sauntered off.

"Me thinks the man doth protest too much," said Jane under her breath.

"What?" said Cordelia, watching him whisper in the blonde's ear. A moment later, they were headed toward the exit.

"Just a thought," replied Jane. "I'm probably way off base."

"You can stop with the football metaphors now." She tossed the end of her boa over her shoulder. "Elvis has left the building."

Chapter 20

It was just after eleven when Jane returned to the Lyme House. Since she'd promised Cordelia half a case of wine for the Thanksgiving dinner—her contribution to the meal—she decided to spend a few minutes in the restaurant's wine cellar. She wouldn't be there to enjoy the feast, but she didn't want to skimp on her part of the bargain. She'd have someone on her staff drive the box over tomorrow. That way, she wouldn't have to dance around the subject of a party she had no intention of attending.

Once she was done, having selected all American wines for the occasion—with a bottle of brandy thrown in for good measure—she closed and locked the cellar door, then returned to her office. She leaned her cane next to the desk and then sat down to check her phone messages. She didn't really expect to find a call from Julia—and she wasn't disappointed.

Feeling too keyed up to go to bed, she took out a notebook and began jotting down some thoughts about her meeting with Joe Patronelli earlier in the evening. He hadn't been the font of information she'd hoped for, but she had learned a few things—most importantly, that Jeffrey Chapel *had* discovered some financial improprieties at the Haymaker Club. It was a shame he hadn't confided more specifics to Patronelli. Then again . . . maybe he had. Maybe Joe had lied about it tonight—and about other matters too. Jane wasn't as convinced of his innocence as Cordelia was. If it turned out he *was* part of Dove's scheme, he might have his own stake in the outcome of Jeffrey's financial inquiries.

Whatever the case, thought Jane, tossing her pen on top of the notebook, at least she had the name of the old financial officer now: Burl Hedges. She'd have to pay him a visit. But before she did, she had some phone calls she needed to make. Based on the conversation she'd overheard between Eddie Flynn and Patricia the other night, Jane had formed a theory, one that involved under-the-table dealings between Andrew Dove and his chosen charities. If Patricia was willing to come clean about it, getting at the truth might not be that difficult. But without any concrete evidence, Jane didn't feel she could approach Patricia. She had no idea whether Dove's financial machinations had anything to do with Chapel's murder, but if embezzlement was Dove's—and perhaps Patronelli's—game and Chapel had found out about it, it might very well have led to his death. And if Patronelli was gay—or, as wild as it might seem, if Andrew Dove was in the closet—there might have been other, more personal motives at work. Unless she was badly mistaken, one of these two threads would lead to a killer.

Once she was done making her notes, her thoughts, as usual, turned to Julia. It was Tuesday, and nobody, not a soul, had heard from her since Sunday. To get her mind off Julia's disappearance, Jane considered getting out Chapel's homicide report and going over it again, but before she could locate it, an idea struck her.

For two days, she'd been racking her brains, trying to figure out where Julia had gone. Now, a name popped into her head. Leo. Mr. Mustache, the so-called best friend who lived in D.C. The night Jane had first met Julia, Julia had excused herself to go call Leo. Though Jane had never actually met the man, she knew he was a fixture in Julia's life. If anybody would know where she was, he would. Somewhere, Jane had written his last name down; she just had to figure out where.

Starting with the *A*'s in her personal phone book, she began flipping through the pages. She found the listing almost right away: Leo Curtis. A D.C. phone number was scratched underneath. It was an hour later on the East Coast, but she was willing to be rude to get the information she wanted. If it was a home number, she might catch him tonight. If it was an office number, she'd probably have to wait until tomorrow. Either way, she intended to demand some answers.

After punching in the eleven digits, she leaned back in her chair and waited. Two rings. Three. Four. Finally, the line picked up. "Hello?"

It was a man's voice, and it sounded gravelly, like he'd been asleep. Unfortunately, Jane hadn't thought this out very well. "Is this Leo Curtis?"

"Yeah?"

"My name's Jane Lawless. I believe we have a friend in common. Julia Martinsen?"

Silence. Then, "Sure. I know who you are." He cleared his throat. "Is . . . something wrong? Is Julia all right?"

"I thought you'd tell me."

"Me?" He paused. "I don't understand."

"I don't either. Julia and I were supposed to meet at her loft in Minneapolis last Sunday night, but by the time I got there, she'd packed her bags and left. In case you didn't know, she was forced out of her home on Pokegama Lake after someone broke in with a gun."

More silence. "God, I tried to talk her out of this."

"Out of what?"

"She hasn't told you?"

Jane felt her anger surge. "No. I'm completely in the dark." Everyone seemed to know what was going on but her. "I don't know where Julia is. I don't understand why she hasn't called. I've been told nothing about the secret she's been hiding. And I'm not sure how much danger she's in. For all I know, she could be dead."

"Don't be ridiculous." He tried to sound reassuring but only succeeded in sounding anxious.

"Maybe you'd like to tell me what's going on."

A long pause. "I can't do that."

"Why not?"

"Because . . . it's Julia's call. I'd be breaking a long-standing promise if I talked to you."

It was just about what she'd expected, and yet his nonanswer made her feel like breaking dishes, screaming at the top of her lungs that he had no right to know something she didn't. Instead, Jane tried to stay calm, realizing her anger would only put him off. "Julia told me once that you were the one who got her mixed up in 'it'—whatever 'it' is."

"I hardly think—"

"Is it true?"

"Look, Jane, I needed a favor. She was more than willing to help. I didn't force her to do anything."

"Is she involved in something illegal?"

"Absolutely not. It's nothing like that."

"But somebody would sure like to get his hands on her medical files. I wonder why?"

Another long silence. "How do you know that?"

At last! Something she knew that he didn't. "I just know, Leo. I can't tell you any more because it would break a longstanding promise."

"Are you being sarcastic?"

"Why would I resort to sarcasm when everyone's so up front with me?"

"Jane, please. Be reasonable. This is serious."

"Since we're on the subject of medical files, I'll tell you something else. If I had to guess, I'd say Julia is running away from the guy who's trying to get his hands on those files. I don't suppose you'd know who that man is?"

"I'm not your enemy."

As far as she was concerned, that remained to be seen. "That's not an answer."

"No, I have no idea who might be after the files."

"Tell me, Leo. What do you do for a living?"

More hesitation. "I work on Capitol Hill."

"Doing what?"

"I'm not sure why that should be important."

"If you're not my enemy, Leo, just try answering a simple question."

He gave himself a moment. "All right. I'm Senator Patrick O'Connor's top aide."

"O'Connor? Charming." Patrick O'Connor and Ted Kennedy were both Irish Catholics, but their philosophies were light-years apart. O'Connor was so far right that if the political spectrum were viewed as a sphere, he and Kennedy could hold hands. Not that they'd ever willingly get that close. "Lovely job."

"It has its moments." More hesitation. "Jane, cut me some slack, okay? I'm not a bad guy. And I'm as worried about Julia as you are."

"Then promise me something. If she phones you, or tries to contact you in any way, tell her she *has* to get in touch with me. I'm staying at my restaurant—indefinitely. She's got the number."

"Sure. No problem."

"And Leo, if something happens to her, I want you to know that I hold you personally responsible."

"Jane, she's going to be okay. Believe me. She's smart, and she's covered her bases. Nobody's going to challenge her—it would be suicide."

"I don't even know what you're talking about."

"Just trust me. She'll be fine."

It sounded like more empty reassurances to Jane. "Good night, Leo. I hope you sleep well, although I'm not sure how you can sleep at all with what must be on your conscience."

Before he could put in his own two cents, she cut the line. She couldn't take any more of his tactful evasions or smarmy pats on the back. In the last few months, she'd been fed enough bull to feed an army.

Chapter 21

Late Tuesday night, Father Latimer opened the door to the confessional and took his seat. After blowing on his hands to bring some warmth back into them, he said a silent prayer, asking that whatever this crisis was, he'd be able to help. He'd been reading quietly in his room at the rectory when the call had come for him. He had to admit to a certain curiosity about why the man was so adamant that he be the priest to hear the confession. Thankfully, he didn't have far to walk in the bitter cold to satisfy his curiosity, or the man's spiritual need.

After waiting less than a minute, the door to the other side of the booth opened and then shut. Through the curtain, the priest could now see the dark outline of a man's face. He must have been in the nave when the priest had entered, but no doubt he wanted to remain anonymous. That wasn't unusual.

After a moment of heavy silence, the man said, "Bless me, Father, for I have sinned."

Leaning closer to the curtain, the priest said, "Bless you, my son. I pray that tonight you may make a good reconciliation with our Lord. What is it you've done?"

The man hesitated. "So many things, Father. I don't know where to begin."

Was the voice familiar? The priest wasn't sure. If the man hadn't made his confession in a long time, perhaps he needed reassurance—or just some simple direction. "I had the feeling that you had something specific on your mind when you called me a few minutes ago. Maybe you should start with that."

"Yes . . . all right." The voice deepened and grew more composed. "Actually, I was thinking of a friend of mine when I phoned. A friend of yours too. Jeffrey Chapel?"

The priest was surprised by the mention of Colonel Chapel's name and didn't quite know how to respond. "Were you good friends?"

"Oh, yes. So much so that before he died, he confided in me that you helped him in a very particular way."

The priest became suddenly wary. "And what would that be?"

"You gave him the name of a doctor, someone who helped him. I need to talk to her, too. It can't wait. That's why I came to you."

Father Latimer was silent for a moment. The turn in the conversation had thrown him, and he knew he had to proceed cautiously. When the man had phoned him earlier, he could tell it wasn't going to be a typical confession—but he hadn't counted on this. "You say Colonel Chapel told you about her?"

"Yes. He even gave me her name and address. I tried to contact her, but she's taken a leave of absence from her practice in Earlton. No one knows where she's gone or when she'll be back. But it's vital that I find her. You could almost say it's a matter of life and death."

"I see." Haltingly, the priest asked, "*Your* . . . life and death?"

"Oh no, Father. Not mine. Others. Innocent people—people we should all want to protect."

The priest leaned away from the curtain. Something about the man's demeanor had put him off. "I don't see how I can help you."

"Don't you know where she's gone? Jeffrey said you knew her personally. You've got to tell me where she's hiding!"

Father Latimer was struck silent by the man's words. Surely the colonel had understood that the information he was given was highly confidential. "I can't help you, sir."

"You mean you won't."

"I *can't*. I don't know where she is. I had no idea she'd left her home until you told me. Now, if there's something you need to confess—"

"She's made no effort to contact you?"

"Of course not. Why would she? We're not friends. I've only talked to her twice in my entire life."

"You have no other way to reach her? No other phone numbers? Does she own homes in other states? Are there other doctors she's connected to?"

The man's voice had grown not only demanding, but menacing. "Why are you so desperate to find her?"

"You don't recognize me?"

The priest turned slowly toward the man's shadow. "Pardon me?"

"I'm the Inquisitor, Father. A Catholic priest should recognize one of his own. It won't be long now before the witch-hunt starts in earnest."

"Witch-hunt? You're not making any sense."

"Of course I am. Just think about it. You've got all the pieces—just put them together."

But the priest couldn't think. Never before had he felt so trapped in the confessional box. The walls pressed in on him, making him feel as if he couldn't breathe. He felt certain that the man on the other side of the wall was sick—or evil. Or both. Every sense within him was sounding an alarm, telling him to get away.

"Will you hear my confession now?"

"I . . . I'm suddenly not feeling very well."

"I'm sorry to hear that, Father. Perhaps you caught a chill on the way over from the rectory. Maybe we should continue this another time."

The priest took a deep breath, trying to calm his pounding heart. "No, I mustn't send you away without absolution."

"Well, I suppose that could be a problem then. See, I don't really think you can absolve me tonight, because, the more I think about it, the more I'm convinced I've done nothing wrong. You, on the other hand, are standing at the edge of a moral precipice."

Again, the priest was at a loss for words.

"Some deaths are necessary, don't you agree? Burning a witch is no sin."

"Mother of God, you're insane," he whispered.

The man laughed. "Can't you tell when a poor parishioner is pulling your leg?"

"This is a joke?"

"If it makes you feel better."

The man was playing with him. "You're serious, aren't you?"

The laughter in his voice faded slightly, but didn't go away completely. "This is no time to wax philosophical, but the truth is, I'm of many minds about it, Father. There are lots of ways to look at it."

The priest took a chance. "What do you know about Colonel Chapel's death?"

"Do you really want an answer?"

"I—I want to hear whatever it is you feel you need to tell me."

"How diplomatic, but I think I'll skip it. It's obvious I'm wasting my time."

Before the priest could say another word, he heard the door to the opposite stall open and then shut. He waited several seconds and then cracked his own door so he could see into the sanctuary, hoping beyond hope that the man was too far away to hear the slight creak of the hinges. Sure enough, there he was, walking away down the central aisle. As he passed through the rear door, he turned just for a moment, allowing the priest a good look at him. "Mother of God," he whispered, clamping a hand over his mouth. It wasn't a face he'd ever forget.

On the way back to the rectory, Father Latimer pulled the collar of his coat up around his neck and held it closed with one bare hand. If possible, the wind had grown even more bitter during the time he'd been in the cathedral. A winter storm was brewing. Inside his soul, a storm had already broken.

How could he stop this monster? He'd confessed to nothing, but the priest knew beyond the shadow of a doubt that he'd murdered the colonel. Since the man hadn't come in good faith to confess, did that mean the bond between confessor and penitent had never formed? Was he free to talk about what the man had said? Maybe somebody would listen—especially since he'd seen him with his own two eyes. If nothing else, the police might be willing to check it out, see where it led.

As the priest rounded the corner and headed up the stone walk to the rectory, he felt a hand grab his shoulder like a vise-grip. Before he knew what was happening, the cold metal of a gun barrel had been shoved against his jaw. A second later, he felt himself being dragged behind a tall shrub.

"Shut up," hissed the familiar voice.

The priest's eyes flew wildly around in the dark.

"You shouldn't have looked at me. Why did you do that?"

"I don't know."

"You *do* know!"

He winced with pain as the man twisted his arm behind his back. "I . . . I just had to see your face."

"I wanted to keep my identity a secret—that's why I set it up this way. I could have spoken to you in person, but I wanted to protect you. Now look what you've done! You broke your own fucking code!"

"I . . . I didn't mean to."

"You priests are a pathetic bunch. So what do I do with you now? You know who I am."

Father Latimer felt like his arm was about to break off. "I don't know anything. You've told me nothing."

"Come on, Father. You know I murdered Jeffrey. And you know what I look like. You've given me no other choice."

"Please!" pleaded the priest, struggling with all his might to get away. "I won't say a word. I swear by all that's holy—" Before he could finish, he heard a click next to his ear, then felt a pressure against his head.

The explosion was deafening, but the pain didn't last long.

Chapter 22

Jane slipped in the back door of her restaurant, carrying Bean in her arms. She skirted her way around the edge of the kitchen, past the walk-in freezer, and down the back stairs. She'd covered Bean in a blanket because of the winter storm. He was so old now, she didn't want him to catch a chill. She'd already prepared the logs in the fireplace in her office, and she fully intended to spend a quiet evening sitting by the fire with her little dog snuggled in her lap.

After Bean was done sniffing her office, checking all his favorite spots, he settled on the couch and began licking his right paw, an activity that could keep him occupied for hours. Jane sat at her desk, finishing up some paperwork. It had been a productive day, the best one she'd had since she'd been back. Somehow, she'd managed to put Julia and the Chapel murder out of her mind for a few hours, and it had paid off. Before she'd landed in the hospital, Jane had begun a reading series on the pub's small stage, but while she was gone, it had pretty much petered out. Nothing would be scheduled over the holidays, but as of this afternoon, she'd set up a full roster of Wednesday night readings starting the second week in January. There were so many local authors and poets she loved and wanted to feature. And as the owner of the restaurant, she was always looking for new ways to bring in business. As far as she was concerned, it was a perfect marriage.

Around seven, she kissed Bean and told him to be a good boy— she'd be back in a few minutes with their dinner. Heading up the back stairs, she entered the kitchen to find the usual uproar. One of the sous-chefs nearly tackled her, explaining with a note of hysteria in his voice that a problem had developed with the new Swiss fryer. The man was so furious, he suggested to anyone who would listen that they toss the piece of junk out in the snow, douse it with gasoline, and then take turns flipping matches at it. After consulting with the head chef, Jane decided to eighty-six two of the evening's entrees. She made a mental note to contact the rep who'd sold them the unit first thing next week.

Once the crisis had been handled, Jane set off to gather a plate of beef scraps and cooked carrots for Bean—his favorites. For her own dinner, she dished up a bowl of potato-leek soup and several thick slices of Irish soda bread. That, and a thermal pot of decaffeinated coffee, and she was set for the evening. She spent a few minutes walking the line, making sure everything was running smoothly, and then returned to her office.

No sooner had she and Bean begun eating their dinners than the door to her office flew open and Cordelia entered—eyes blazing and jewelry jangling, her entire presence a walking exclamation point.

Hands rising to her hips, Cordelia tossed back her wild auburn curls and nailed Jane with her eyes. "You're not coming tomorrow, are you?" It wasn't a question, but an accusation.

Bean looked up at her briefly, but his food seemed to hold more immediate interest.

"Well?" Cordelia tapped her foot, glaring at Jane.

"Sit down, and we'll talk about it. You look cold."

"I'm upset!" She stared down her nose. "With good reason. I get home from work tonight. I'm in my usual sanguine mood. My cats welcome me home with their adoring little mews. And what do I find?"

"Do I get more than one guess?"

"A box of wine sitting inside my door, Janey. *That's* what I find."

"You didn't like the vintages?"

"Your humor is sophomoric. And you didn't answer my question."

"That's because you didn't sit down."

With a disgruntled huff, Cordelia lowered her ample frame into a chair. "There. Are you happy?"

"More on the order of content."

"How nice. Is this a Zen moment, or should we celebrate with a cup of flavored coffee?"

Jane's soup was getting cold. It was hard to be Zen about that. "Actually, I was just eating dinner."

"Well! Don't let *me* interrupt you—just because I'm here on a mission of mercy." She unbuttoned her cape, crossed her legs, and fixed Jane with a fierce look. "You shouldn't be alone tomorrow, Janey."

"I won't be. Bean is here."

"You know that's not what I mean. You're not in a good place. You're . . . overwrought about Julia, and you're not well. You'll sit here and brood. *That way lies madness*, Janey. Trust me. I know what I'm talking about."

"Don't you think you're being a little melodramatic?"

"No. You need to get out, be with people—have some fun and forget about your problems. For god's sake, Janey, why don't you just move back to my loft and let me take care of you?"

"Funny," said Jane, her mouth tightening. "I seem to be doing just fine on my own. I get my teeth brushed every morning. I manage to eat without drooling. Even in my *damaged* state, I get a little work done around here, amazing as that may seem to you."

"But you're not sleeping. Anybody can see that. And you're on edge—emotionally. You're mere inches from . . . from—"

"From what?" asked Jane, exaggerating her patient expression.

Cordelia's face flushed with frustration. "How the hell should I know? But it's not good."

"Tell me," said Jane, tossing her napkin on the desk, "why it is that lately, every time I come away from talking to you, I feel like I belong in a padded cell?"

"You're missing my point."

"I'm sure missing something."

"You're pushing me away."

"Just because I'm not coming to Thanksgiving dinner?"

163

"Yes."

Jane had hoped to circumvent this conversation, but it seemed inevitable. "Cordelia, listen to me for a second, and try to understand. I need some peace and quiet—and tomorrow will be the perfect day. Maybe you can't see it, but I feel like I'm getting healthier and stronger all the time. I can't do it overnight. But even more importantly, I can't do it with you constantly looking over my shoulder."

"You think I'm a busybody?"

Jane could see the beginnings of a pout. "No, of course not. I know you're just concerned. And I welcome that. But you've got to give me some space. Part of that is allowing me to stay here tomorrow without reading me the riot act."

She gave a tiny sniff. "Cordelia Thorn does not *browbeat*. I merely make my point, and then . . . I *leap* onto my camel and silently steal away."

"How poetic."

"Thank you."

"You know, Cordelia. Correct me if I'm wrong, but I get the feeling that some of this frustration of yours has nothing to do with me."

Cordelia acknowledged Jane's point with a shrug. "Sometimes . . . I don't know. Things just get to me." Gripping both hands together in her lap, Cordelia turned serious. "Maybe you haven't heard, but there was a murder last night at the rectory right next to the St. Paul Cathedral. That's less than two blocks from the theatre! *My* theatre! The streets in this town aren't safe anymore, Janey. And here you are, willingly chasing a murderer around."

"Who was murdered?"

"Some priest. I think his name was Latimer."

"How did it happen?"

"A gunshot to the head. It made the front page of both papers."

Jane jotted down the name and a note to herself to locate a paper and read the article. "Do the police have any idea who did it?"

"Hey? Why all the questions?" She narrowed an eye. "Don't you have enough current mayhem on your plate to keep you occupied?"

"You don't need to be snide. I was just curious."

She heaved a deep sigh. "No, the police don't have a suspect. I mean, who would want to kill a priest?" Her gaze shifted to the cold fireplace. "I guess the poor guy won't be having his Thanksgiving dinner tomorrow—or ever again. That's another reason why I need you to be at my loft. Life is so short, Janey. We never know what's going to happen. I mean, that idiot who broke into Julia's apartment on Sunday night could just as easily have come after you. If he's looking for something, he may think you've got it—or that you know where it is."

"But Cordelia, can you imagine a safer place for me than this restaurant? We have a high-tech security system. During the day, there are lots of people around. Really, I don't think you should give it another thought."

"But . . . but—" She just couldn't seem to drop it. "What will you do for food tomorrow?"

Jane laughed. "This is a restaurant, remember? I was the head chef here for many years. I can fix myself anything I want."

She straightened up and sat erect in her chair. "Okay, fine. But it just won't be the same without you."

Very gently, Jane replied, "Nothing feels quite normal this year. I think we simply have to accept it."

Cordelia seemed to consider that for a moment; then she nodded. "All right. If I can't change your mind, then so be it. At least we can drink a toast to you."

"And I'll drink one to you." Jane had no sooner said the word than she noticed an odd expression pass across Cordelia's face. "Is something wrong?"

"No," she said, offhandedly. "What could be wrong?"

Jane had the feeling that she was once again missing something, but shrugged it off. "Good. Now that it's all settled, would you like some dinner?"

"Can't. I've got too much work to do before the big day tomorrow. Not only do I have oodles of food to prepare, but I've got to figure out where to put up all those smarmy decorations."

"I'm sure everything will be wonderful."

"It would be more wonderful if you were there to help. Life is so fragile, Janey."

"Cordelia, relax, *please*. I'm going to be fine. Next year we'll have Thanksgiving together. I promise."

Cordelia closed her eyes and lifted her chin. "I did my best. I know when to throw in the towel." As she rose to leave, she held up her hand to prevent Jane from following her. "I've interrupted your dinner long enough. I can find my way out."

Now she was going to play the long-suffering martyr.

"Thanks for coming. And for the concern."

Halfway to the door, she stopped, turned around, and raised an eyebrow. "I don't suppose you're planning to spend the day with Patricia Kastner."

"No, Cordelia. I'm not."

"Because, that would *really* hurt my feelings."

"She's probably spending the day with her family."

Cordelia shivered. "That almost makes me feel sorry for her. Almost, but not quite."

"You have a big heart."

"Yes, I do. It's my cross."

"Good night, Cordelia."

Another sigh. "Call me if you need anything."

"I will."

She continued to hesitate.

"Is there something else?"

"No, not . . . really." She turned to go, but once again stopped herself, then thought better of it—and finally left.

After Jane took the dirty dishes upstairs to the kitchen, she and Bean snuggled on the couch together while she started a new biography of Edith Sitwell. Around ten, she switched off the lights, and lit a fire under the logs, and the two of them watched it burn until there was nothing left but glowing embers. Bean was such a sweet little animal, and his presence made all the difference in her mood. Around eleven, she got up and took a shower, made the couch up for the night, and then crawled under the covers. Bean took up his guard-dog position on the rug in front of the fireplace. Not that he was much of a guard dog these days, especially without his hearing, but old habits died hard.

Jane tossed and turned for a while, trying to empty her mind and relax her aching leg. Cordelia was right. She hadn't been sleeping well. She knew it was taking a toll, but she didn't regret throwing away her pain medication.

Shortly after two, her private line rang. She was dozing by then, but not fully asleep. Getting up with some difficulty, she hobbled over to the desk and picked up the receiver. She felt a bit disoriented, but rubbed the side of her face for a moment to help her focus. After saying hello, she sat down. No one responded. She said hello again several more times, but when she heard nothing but silence, she figured some jerk was playing games. "Look, if this is a prank call—"

"Don't hang up. It's me. Julia."

Jane felt her heart skip a beat. "Julia? My God, are you all right? Where are you?"

"I'm fine. I'm at a motel outside Santa Fe."

"What the hell are you doing there? And why haven't you called before this? I've been worried sick."

"I wanted to call, but . . . I wasn't sure what to do—what was best."

"What's that supposed to mean?" She had so many questions, she didn't know where to begin. "Couldn't you have stayed long enough on Sunday night just to say hello?"

"I desperately wanted to, but I had to get away quickly."

"Because that man in the ski mask was following you?"

Silence. "How do you know he wore a ski mask?"

"I didn't find your note right away; it must have fallen off the door. So I waited in your apartment thinking you might show. He picked the lock and broke in."

"While you were there?"

"Afraid so. I hid in the broom closet and watched him ransack the place."

"Oh, God," she groaned. "I should have been more careful." Her voice rose anxiously. "Did he find you? Are you okay?"

"Thanks to Cordelia, I'm fine. I was just a little shaken up."

She let out a sigh of relief. "Don't go back there. Promise me."

Jane had lost all patience with this cloak-and-dagger crap. She wanted answers. "Julia, what's going on?"

More silence. Finally, "First, tell me how you are. How are the headaches? Is your leg getting any stronger?"

"I refuse to let you change the subject."

"Please, just answer me. I've been so concerned. Why aren't you staying with Cordelia? The message on her machine just said that you could be reached at the restaurant."

"I don't need a keeper, Julia."

"You are so hardheaded sometimes."

"Why? Because I want to resume some semblance of a normal life? I'm exercising every day. Patricia's letting me use the gym at her house."

"Really." She hesitated. "That's . . . that's nice of her."

"I thought so too. My leg seems a little stronger, but I know I'm going to have to take it slow. The headaches come and go; some are bad, some just annoying. Otherwise, I'm fine. There, you've got the full report, Doctor. Now tell me why you're in Santa Fe. And why you decided to call me at two in the morning."

"God, it's so great to hear your voice—even if you are furious with me."

"I'm not just furious, Julia; I'm scared. What's happening? Who is that man who's stalking you, and why is he so interested in your files? And who were all those people phoning you at your house?"

The silence lasted longer this time.

"Are you still there?" asked Jane. For a moment, she thought she'd lost the connection.

"Yes," whispered Julia finally. "I'm here."

"So answer my questions."

"I can't. That's what I called to talk to you about."

"What do you mean you can't?"

"I mean . . . I've decided that the only way I can protect you is to keep you in the dark—and to stay away from you until this all blows over."

"Stay away from me? You mean you're not coming back to Minnesota?"

"Not anytime soon."

"But Julia . . . what if it doesn't blow over?"

"I have to believe it will. I'm doing everything in my power to see that it does."

"But . . . this doesn't make any sense. How long am I supposed to wait? Days? Weeks? Months?"

"I don't have an answer yet."

"Then, how will I know you're all right? Before I left Grand Rapids, you said you were in trouble. Are you really asking me to live in limbo indefinitely? Not knowing what's happening to you? Not knowing if you're alive or . . . or—?"

"Jane, please. I have no other choice. If I come back, I risk both our lives."

"I can handle the danger; I've done it before. But trust me when I tell you that I can't live with uncertainty and silence. Maybe it's just the way I am, but it will literally drive me crazy."

"Janey, please," pleaded Julia. "I've been thinking about this for days, and I know I've made the best decision for both of us."

Now Jane really was furious. How could Julia make a choice that affected her life so dramatically without even consulting her? "How could things have gone so wrong for us?"

"Don't talk like that. We'll be together again. One day I'll explain everything to you. You may hate me for what I've done, but I'll make you understand. I have to. You mean the world to me, Jane. You're the glue that's holding me together."

Jane had to wonder what glue was holding *her* together. "Right. Well, I guess that's it, then. We should probably say good night."

"Don't go. Not just yet. I need to hear your voice for a few more minutes. This has been hard for me too, sweetheart."

"I'm sure it has."

"Are you back to work? I hope you're taking it easy."

"I am."

"And Cordelia? Are you getting together with her for Thanksgiving dinner tomorrow? I sure wish I could be there to celebrate with you."

"That's right," said Jane. She didn't have the energy to explain anything more.

"What else is new?"

"Nothing, really." Then a thought occurred to her. "Well, that's not entirely true. You might be interested to know that I've been helping Brenna Chapel figure out if her husband was gay. She was sent some blackmail notes this week, faxes to be exact. The blackmailer says he wants money or he'll send proof that her husband was gay to the local papers. *Was* Jeffrey Chapel gay, Julia?"

The question hung heavily in the air between them. After several silent seconds, Julia said, "I can't talk about it, remember?"

"I'll take that as a yes. You know who murdered him, don't you?"

"No, Jane, I don't. That's the truth."

"The truth? How novel. How come he came to see you all the way up in Grand Rapids? Did a doctor down here refer him?"

"You never let up, do you?"

"It's one of my better qualities."

More hesitation. "All right," she said finally. "I'll give you that much. It can't hurt. A friend of his, a priest, recommended me."

Jane sobered suddenly. Switching on the desk lamp, she glanced down at the name of the clergymen who'd just been murdered. "What was the priest's name?"

"I can't tell you that."

"Was it Latimer? He was murdered yesterday, Julia. Shot in the head."

Julia gasped. Her reaction said it all.

"Everything's connected, isn't it? Chapel's murder, the priest's death. You. The blackmail notes. The secret you've been hiding. The phone calls. The man who's searching for your files. For God's sake, Julia, stop shutting me out. I can help you!"

"Jane, please." Her voice was desperate. "You've got to stay out of this."

"If you refuse to talk to me—if you disappear—the only way I can get to the bottom of whatever's wrong is to figure it out on my own. Don't you understand? My life's in total turmoil. I can't eat or sleep without thinking about you—about the danger you're in—about what's going to happen to us. I can't live this way."

"Look, if I promise to call you every day and tell you I'm fine, will you back off then?"

"I'm not sure I can."

"But would you just try! For me?"

Jane felt the conversation was becoming more and more surreal. Could simple romance have done this to boring old stable Jane? Sure, she might take some risks for a good cause, but her personal life had always been solid and sensible. "When would you call?"

"Well, tomorrow is Thanksgiving. What time will you be home from Cordelia's?"

"Call me at *six—my* time. She's planning an early meal." A lie. Jane didn't have a clue what Cordelia was planning. "I'll be back to the restaurant by then."

"Six it is. I promise, I'll call you every day, Jane. It's no sacrifice on my part; I want to talk to you. It was just . . . I thought it might be better if you knew nothing about my activities right now."

"Let me take that chance. As long as we're communicating daily, I won't be so worried. Maybe I can wait this thing out."

There was a smile in Julia's voice now. "I know we can get through this. It might not take that long, sweetheart. I've still got some travel-ing to do, but I'm almost finished with that. Remember, I have your

170

absolute promise that you'll stay away from anything to do with the Chapel murder investigation."

She took a deep breath. "Yes. It's a deal."

"God, it's so hard to say good-bye. I wish we could go on talking all night, but I can't. I've got to get some sleep because I've got a big day tomorrow."

Jane wondered what that meant. "We'll talk again at six tomorrow evening, my time." Jane didn't want to leave any room for error.

"On the dot, sweetheart. And don't ever forget—I love you."

Chapter 23

THANKSGIVING DAY

Brenna was sitting in her father's living room when she heard the front doorbell chime. Rising from the couch, she was determined to get rid of whoever it was fast; otherwise, she and her father would be late for their eleven o'clock reservations at the Nicollet Island Inn. Thanksgiving wasn't going to be much of a celebration this year, but her father had insisted they spend it together, and she didn't have the heart to say no.

Swinging back the door, she felt a moment of alarm when she saw who it was.

"Good morning, Mrs. Chapel," said Sgt. Duvik, smiling amiably. Sgt. Ross, the taller and younger of the two homicide investigators, stood next to him. Two uniformed patrolmen brought up the rear. "I'm sorry to bother you on a holiday, but I've got a search warrant here which I intend to execute at this time." He held up the papers.

Before Brenna could respond, her father rushed down the central stairs and hurried into the front hall. He was wearing a white terrycloth bathrobe, his silver hair still wet from his shower.

"Search warrant?" he repeated, his eyes colliding with his daughter's. "What's going on?"

Duvik motioned for the officers to enter.

Brenna was so stunned, she simply backed up and stood dumbly, watching the men disburse throughout the house.

"Let me look at that thing," demanded Andrew, tossing the towel he was holding over his shoulder. He grabbed the sheets out of the sergeant's hand. Squinting and holding them at arm's length, he said, "This is ridiculous. What do you expect to find?" When the sergeant didn't respond, Andrew glanced furtively at his daughter.

Brenna was surprised to see her father looking so anxious, which in turn, only frightened her all the more.

"I'm going to call my lawyer!" announced Andrew.

"Go ahead," said Duvik. "He can't stop a lawful search." As the detective moved silently into the living room, Brenna watched his shrewd eyes pass over the expensive paintings, the oriental rugs, the long wall of mullioned windows overlooking the back garden, and finally, her father's pride and joy, a lighted cabinet filled with Steuben glass.

"How long is this going to take?" asked Andrew.

"That depends on what we find."

"But my daughter and I have plans for Thanksgiving dinner."

"Don't let me stop you."

"You mean . . . we can go?"

"You're not under arrest."

"But . . . I'd have to leave you here all alone."

"Look at it this way. At least we won't steal anything."

"Is that supposed to be funny?" Pressing his lips together angrily, Andrew nodded to his daughter. "Go call Craywell. Tell him to get over here on the double—and don't let him give you any excuses."

Milton Craywell was her father's lawyer. Retreating to the kitchen, Brenna found his number in the yellow pages and quickly tapped it into the wall phone. Since it was Thanksgiving, his service picked up. "Hi," she said, leaning her hip against the butcher-block table. "This is Andrew Dove's daughter. I need to speak with Mr. Craywell. It's an emergency."

A woman's voice responded, "I'm sorry, but Mr. Craywell is out of town. I could have one of his partners call you back."

Brenna knew her father would never stand for that. "Where's Milton?"

"On vacation in Switzerland."

"Can you give me the hotel number?"

"I'm sorry, I can't do that. But I'd be happy to have one of the other—"

"I'll have to call you back."

Brenna returned to the living room. Her father was sitting on the couch, looking both worried and impatient. Duvik had shed his topcoat and was seated on the piano bench, gazing up at the mantel, checking out some of her wedding photos. Seeing him dressed in something other than the jeans, work boots, flannel shirt, and red-and-black checked jacket—the clothes he'd been wearing the night he'd shown up at her door with the news of her husband's death—she was struck by the transformation. Gone was every trace of blue-collar crude. In his Hugo Boss suit, Duvik was a study in sartorial elegance. Everything about the man seemed more official, more commanding—and more dangerous.

Joining her father on the couch, she whispered, "Craywell's in Switzerland."

"It's just like him to be gone when I need him," he whispered back.

"Do you want me to call someone else?"

He shook his head. Looking over at Duvik, he said, more audibly this time, "Your search is just an exercise in futility."

Duvik's expression remained pleasant. "Did you reach your lawyer?"

"Not yet. Aren't you going to help your partner?"

"Well, I could. Or the three of us could talk for a few minutes."

His relaxed attitude was just a manipulation, thought Brenna.

"Talk about what?" asked Andrew.

Removing an envelope from his inner pocket, Duvik tossed it on the coffee table. "I thought you might like to look at that, Mr. Dove."

"What is it?"

"I understand you contacted one of our medical examiners earlier in the week."

Brenna was taken aback by the comment.

"That's right," said Andrew, trying to sound casual. "Dr. Stan

174

Waller is an old friend. I *thought* I could rely on his discretion."

"You asked him to run an HIV test on your deceased son-in-law using the blood sample that was taken during the autopsy."

"You did what?" Now Brenna was shocked.

"I don't see any crime in that," replied Andrew.

Duvik pointed to the envelope. "Those are the results. I assume you understand—nothing like this could be done without my knowledge."

"I had no intention of hiding anything from the police." Grabbing the towel around his neck with both hands, he asked, "So, what were the results?"

"Positive, Mr. Dove. Your son-in-law was infected with the AIDS virus."

Brenna felt as if someone had just whacked her across the back with a two-by-four. For a moment, she wasn't sure she could even breathe.

"He was completely asymptomatic, according to Dr. Waller, so the infection was probably recent. A year, maybe less."

"I . . . see." Andrew's eyes shifted to an indeterminate point in space. "I see," he said again, his voice dropping to a whisper.

"Why did you ask for the test to be run, Mr. Dove?"

Andrew looked up, then glanced at Brenna. "Well . . . I . . . you see . . . my daughter mentioned to me recently that . . . well, that she and Jeffrey had been having some . . . marital difficulties before he died. This is all very personal, you understand . . . and hard for me to talk about."

Duvik turned to Brenna. "In your official statement, Mrs. Chapel, you mentioned nothing about marital problems."

Before she could respond, her father interjected, "She loved Jeffrey, don't misunderstand. But she was confused by his behavior. Frankly, I was too. If she didn't say anything about it before, I'm sure it was simply her misplaced pride."

"Pride," repeated Duvik, inspecting the word for its true meaning. "Is that accurate?"

Brenna had been careful to keep her marital problems off the table when she'd been interrogated by Duvik. Now, since her father had opened the door by blundering in where he didn't belong, she'd have to address the issue. "Well . . . yes," she said, shifting in her seat. "I suppose pride was part of it."

"What's the other part?"

She shrugged. "I didn't think it was any of your business. Our problems had nothing to do with Jeffrey's murder."

"Well then, if they're not relevant, perhaps you wouldn't mind telling me just what kind of problems we're talking about."

It was a question she didn't want to answer. At this moment, she hated her father for the mess he'd made. Why had he gone against her wishes and insinuated himself into her affairs? "Well . . . Jeffrey had been . . . pulling away from me for some time. It was confusing. I didn't understand why."

"So when you lied to us, stating that your marriage was happy—"

"It was happy!" insisted Brenna. "Every couple has good times and bad times. We'd just hit a rough patch."

Duvik nodded. Shifting his gaze back to Andrew, he continued, "Then, let me get this straight." He was still sitting on the piano bench, his legs stretched out in front of him. "On the basis of your daughter's recent revelation, you jumped to the conclusion that Colonel Chapel was *gay?* That's quite a leap, Mr. Dove."

"Gay?" repeated Andrew, his tone indignant. "Certainly not. If Jeffrey contracted the virus, it must have been from a woman. A tragic one-night stand, perhaps. Or a call girl."

"And . . . what? A little bird told you he might be HIV positive?"

"I knew he was promiscuous. I thought it should be checked out. If it turned out he was negative, then I wouldn't have to worry my daughter with it."

"Did your son-in-law regularly visit prostitutes?" Duvik returned his attention to Brenna.

"Of course not." She shot her father a nasty look.

"We saw no evidence of IV drug use during the autopsy."

"Jeffrey never used drugs!"

"Were you angry at your husband, Mrs. Chapel? Because of his . . . promiscuity?"

"I'm not sure he was promiscuous. But yes, I was hurt by his behavior. Surely you can understand that."

"It seems to me that anger would be a natural enough emotion if you thought your husband might be sleeping around. Did you know Col. Chapel was HIV positive before he died?"

"Absolutely not," said Brenna.

"You're sure about that?"

"My daughter answered the question," snapped Andrew. "Leave her alone."

"What about you, Mr. Dove? Did you know?"

"Certainly not."

"Because if either of you did, and Mrs. Chapel here was infected, you both had a very strong motive for murder."

"Brenna knew nothing about it! If she had, she would have said something to me."

"But she never said anything about her marital problems—up until recently."

"That's different. Look, Sergeant, before Jeffrey's death, Brenna hoped that things could turn around for them—that their marriage would get back on track. She loved him. She wanted to make things work. She would never have hurt him."

"I'm not saying she did."

Well then, what the hell *was* he saying? thought Brenna.

"You have to understand, Mr. Dove. This new piece of information about Colonel Chapel opens up a whole new range of possibilities, especially if it turns out he was gay. Murders are rarely random. People usually know the person who kills them. In this case, it might have been someone the colonel infected with the virus. Or maybe, the person who murdered him did so to cover up the fact that *he* was gay and HIV positive. However you slice it, I now have to look very carefully at the sexuality of every man who knew Jeffrey Chapel, especially those who were with him the night he died."

"He wasn't gay!" insisted Andrew.

"That remains to be seen."

Andrew was obviously disgusted by the comment. "You're telling me you're going to turn this investigation into a sexual witch-hunt?"

Duvik shrugged. "Your words, not mine."

When the sergeant stood, Brenna assumed the conversation was over. She watched him pass by the cabinet and glance for a moment at the contents. Turning around, Duvik slipped his hands casually into his pants pockets. "Did either of you know Father Michael Latimer?"

Another curveball. "Of course we did," said Brenna. "He officiated at my wedding."

"Did you know he was murdered on Tuesday night?"

"Yes," she answered slowly. "I heard it on the news."

When the sergeant didn't continue, Andrew asked, "What does

177

Father Latimer's murder have to do with my son-in-law?"

"I don't know. Maybe nothing. Maybe everything." He moved over to examine one of the paintings more closely. With his back to Andrew, he added, "Father Latimer was a gay priest. Most people in his parish didn't know it, but his friends did, and so did the church hierarchy."

Andrew narrowed his eyes. "I wasn't aware of that."

"In her statement, your son-in-law's secretary told us that he planned to drive to the St. Paul Cathedral directly after work on the night he died. We now have an eyewitness that says he sat in one of the back pews and spoke with Father Latimer for about ten minutes. I don't suppose either of you know what their meeting was about."

"No, of course not," said Andrew.

Brenna didn't respond.

"Because, Mr. Dove, when two gay men—friends, perhaps even confidants—are murdered within days of each other, it sets off a whole bunch of my alarm bells."

"I repeat. My son-in-law wasn't gay."

Duvik turned around. "Have you ever been tested for the AIDS virus, Mr. Dove?"

Andrew blinked "Me? Of course not."

"What about you, Mrs. Chapel?"

Feeling sick inside, she shook her head.

"Hey, Duvik," called a voice from one of the back rooms. "Come back here a sec."

Immediately, the sergeant excused himself and disappeared into one of the side hallways.

Brenna couldn't wait to talk to her father privately, but as soon as Duvik was gone, he darted into the kitchen. He was probably trying to contact another lawyer, anyone who could help them out of this quicksand.

Did her father know more about Jeffrey than he was letting on? And why was he so quick to insist she pay off the blackmailer? He said it was because he wanted to avoid a family scandal, but was that the only reason? Brenna felt muddled, unable to focus. Too many things had hit her all at once.

A few moments later, Duvik reentered the room. "Mr. Dove," he called, turning toward the kitchen, "please come out here."

As Brenna stood, she noticed that he was holding a large, red plastic box.

"I believe you know what this is," said Duvik, carefully watching the expression on Andrew's face as he came out of the kitchen.

Seeing the box, Andrew stopped dead in his tracks. He passed a trembling hand over the back of his hair, then cleared his throat. "I . . . ah—"

"Yes. Please explain."

Moving back into the living room, Andrew glanced helplessly at his daughter. "Yes, well. You see . . . I found them. I didn't tell anyone because I wanted to look at them myself first, see what all the fuss was about. I would have turned them over to you—but I've been so busy, I guess . . . I forgot I had them."

"What's in the box?" asked Brenna. She couldn't stand to be the only one in the room who didn't know what was going on.

"Your husband's desk calendars," said Duvik.

"You mean the ones that were stolen?"

He nodded.

Andrew retied the knot on his bathrobe, attempting to regain his composure. "I asked some of my staff to go through the garbage at Dove Aviation the day after Jeffrey was murdered. Somebody—God knows who—had put them in a plastic bag and thrown them in a Dumpster outside the building."

"We checked all the Dumpsters, Mr. Dove."

"The bag was probably thrown in after you checked."

"You didn't take them from your son-in-law's office yourself?"

"No! And I resent your implication." He turned as Sgt. Ross walked out of the dining room.

"Mr. Dove," said Ross, picking up the interrogation. "Late last night, I confiscated a videotape taken by security in the IGS tower the night Colonel Chapel died. On it, we can see you entering your son-in-law's office at the Haymaker Club. It was shortly after two A.M.—approximately six hours after he was murdered. You didn't leave until nearly three."

Andrew's face suddenly lost all its color. "Yes . . . well—"

"Dad, is this true?" Brenna couldn't believe what she was hearing.

"You were seen leaving with the desk calendar," continued Ross.

This time, Andrew said nothing. He just stared straight ahead.

"We don't have absolute proof that you took Colonel Chapel's calendar from his office at Dove Airlines, but since it's in your possession now, it seems a reasonable assumption."

"I—" He cleared his throat. "You see—" Andrew was momentarily distracted as the two uniformed patrolmen entered the room.

"There are pages missing from both of the calendars, Mr. Dove. Most are from this past month. Some go as far back as August. Can you explain that?"

Andrew bit his lower lip, but didn't respond.

Duvik asked the next question. "Did your affair with your son-in-law begin in August? Or was that when he tried to extricate himself?"

"Affair?" Brenna was so surprised, her mouth dropped open. All she could do was stare at her father.

"Did you feel jilted, Mr. Dove? Or—were you afraid he might tell your daughter the truth? You couldn't have that."

"That's ridiculous," insisted Andrew. "Jeffrey and I were never lovers."

"No? Those missing pages—don't they record the dates and times of your trysts?"

Andrew looked from face to face. "I'm not gay! I couldn't be! It's against everything I believe. And I didn't murder my son-in-law!"

"Why should I believe you?" demanded Duvik. "You lied about taking the calendars. You refuse to tell us what was so important on those missing pages that you had to find and destroy them within hours of your son-in-law's death. You were at the Winter Garden the night Colonel Chapel died. Others there that night said the two of you weren't on the best of terms. You had a test run on your son-in-law to determine if he had the AIDS virus. I can see no reason you'd even think of doing that—unless you were afraid that *if* he had the disease, so did you—and so did your daughter."

Brenna suddenly felt dizzy. This couldn't be happening. How could she have misjudged two men in her life so badly? "No more, Sergeant. My dad refuses to answer another question until we've talked to a lawyer."

"That's a good idea, Mrs. Chapel, because I'm arresting your father for the murder of your husband." He nodded to Ross. "Read him his rights, and then take him downtown and book him."

Chapter 24

By five-thirty on Thanksgiving afternoon, Jane had returned Bean to Evelyn Bratrude's home and was back in the main dining room at the Lyme House, sitting at a table by the windows, watching the deep purple light fade over the lake.

In honor of the occasion, she'd opened a bottle of pinot noir and was sipping contentedly from a glass, waiting for Julia's phone call. Her private line could be answered from the phone on the reception desk, although the cord didn't quite reach all the way into the dining room. She'd turned off the answering machine downstairs in order to allow herself extra time to get from where she was seated to the comfortable chair she'd set up next to the desk. Until Julia called, she wanted to enjoy the wintry view. Small votive candles were burning all over the room, setting the mood for what she hoped would be an intimate talk.

Contrary to Cordelia's prediction of doom and gloom, Jane hadn't spent one moment of the day brooding. Julia's phone call last night had made all the difference. Jane wasn't a Pollyanna. She knew they had a long way to go if they were ever going to make their damaged relationship work. But if they could just stay in contact—and eventually get to the bottom of what was going on in Julia's life—then they had a chance. That thought alone had lifted her spirits immeasurably, so much so that the day had flown by.

Pouring herself a second glass of wine, she glanced at her watch. It was almost six. For the past hour, she'd felt her excitement building. It was silly, really. She was acting like a teenager. At forty, she should be well past such adolescent behavior. The fact that she wasn't caused her a moment of acute embarrassment. Getting up from the table, she walked over to the chair next to the phone. She might as well be ready when the call came in.

As the last few minutes ticked by, Jane made a toast to Cordelia and all her Thanksgiving Day guests back at the loft. Then she made one to her brother and sister-in-law, another to her Aunt Beryl and Edgar in England, and finally one to her father and Marilyn vacationing in Hawaii. She hoped they were all having a great holiday, as good as the one she was having right now. She'd call Cordelia tomorrow and tell her the good news. Julia was safe. Nothing had been settled between them, but at least they were talking.

One minute to six.

Jane glanced at the phone; then she shifted her attention back to the dining room and the softly glowing candles. Taking the last sip of wine from her glass, she looked up at the clock on the wall and saw that it was six on the dot. Her stomach tightened.

The next time she looked up it was five after six.

Nothing to worry about. Not all clocks were synchronized. Maybe the one she was looking at was fast, or maybe Julia's watch was off. She just had to be patient. Julia would call.

Six-twenty.

Now Jane was beginning to get a little uncomfortable. There were lots of reasons why Julia might not be able to call right at the stroke of six; it was clearly too early to push the panic button. So, instead of sitting and stewing, Jane rose and returned to the table where the nearly full bottle of wine was still resting. She poured herself a third glass, then stood and looked out at the deck. The Christmas lights and the pine boughs would be tacked up on the railings next week. It was something she usually did herself, but this year she'd need help.

When she finally checked the clock again, she saw that it was six-forty. She couldn't help it—now she was worried. She'd been very

182

clear last night about the time Julia was supposed to call. There couldn't be any misunderstanding because Julia had repeated the time to her more than once. So what had happened?

Moving back to the table, Jane sipped her wine and struggled to keep her impatience under control. As seven o'clock approached, she rose and began to pace. Sante Fe was an hour earlier than Minneapolis. That meant, if Julia had become mixed up, she'd call at seven, not six. Feeling her excitement return, Jane poured herself another glass of wine.

By nine, she was slumped in her chair, the wine bottle empty. For the past half hour, she'd been staring out the window, barely moving. The depression that had once again settled over her permitted no motion. She might as well face it: Julia had stood her up again. She was fairly certain that if she waited long enough, she'd be treated to another *grand excuse*. That was Julia Martinsen in a nutshell. Endless excuses. And Jane, no matter how hurt or angry she was, always seemed to forgive her. Idly, she wondered what tonight's excuse would be.

But then, right on cue, the fear returned. Had something happened to Julia this time? Was she hurt, or trapped, unable to get to a phone? Walking herself one more time through the endless possibilities, Jane realized she was exhausted by the process. No matter how hard she tried to stay centered on Julia and the potential danger she was in, she was sick to death of this unrelenting dance.

A sudden rap on the window brought her tumbling back to the moment. Focusing her eyes with some difficulty, she saw Patricia Kastner standing outside on the deck. She was motioning for Jane to let her in. Jane was about to tell her she couldn't, that she'd have to go around to the back door; then she remembered that in her haste to get everything set up in the dining room, she hadn't reset the security code after returning from Evelyn Bratrude's house. That meant that if she unlocked the door to the deck, no alarms would go off. So, rising from her chair, that's just what she did.

Patricia was all bundled up in a down parka. In the moonlight, her hair looked like shiny black ribbons, one wisp escaping across her cheek. Jane wanted to reach out and smooth it back, but even in her current state, she knew it wasn't appropriate. And Jane Lawless was nothing, if not appropriate.

"What's wrong?" asked Patricia, looking concerned. She pushed her way inside, shutting the door behind her.

Feeling the room sway, Jane sat back down. "Wrong?"

"You've been crying."

"I have?" She touched her cheeks.

Patricia picked up the wine bottle. "Did you drink this all by yourself?"

"I seem to be the only one here, so, using my famous powers of deduction, it must have been me."

Patricia gave her a pained look. "I saw the candles burning so I figured you were here. Except . . . I thought you were spending the day at Cordelia's place."

"There was a last-minute change in plans."

"So I see." She glanced around the room, then back at Jane. "You know, Lawless, you look awful."

"Thanks."

"Something happen?"

"I suppose that's a matter of interpretation."

"Right. You always sit around and get wasted all by yourself for no particular reason."

"I am not wasted."

"No, of course you're not."

Jane wiped the tears off her cheeks. "It's been kind of a . . . bad evening."

As Patricia scrutinized her face, the light appeared to dawn. "Hey, I get it. You were expecting Julia to show, and she never did."

"Not . . . precisely correct."

"Nobody gets under your skin the way that woman does. I thought we'd gone through this months ago. You should have dumped her then like you intended."

Closing her eyes and pressing her fingers against her temples, Jane realized she didn't have the steam to put up a good front, not even for Patricia. "Maybe," she mumbled. "I don't know anymore."

Patricia moved closer, stroking Jane's hair. "When was the last time you had something to eat?"

"I had some breakfast around nine. I tried to sleep in, but I couldn't."

"What time did you get to bed?"

"Around four."

"Oh, just great, Lawless. I thought you were trying to build your health back, not give yourself a nervous breakdown."

"All I get from people these days is melodrama."

Patricia shook her head.

"Look, it's nice of you to be concerned, but—"

"But what? You want to stay here and spend the rest of the evening crying yourself to sleep? With Julia for a lover, it's nothing but fun and games, right Lawless?"

"Leave Julia out of it."

"Sure. Defend her to the last."

Jane bowed her head. "No. I won't do that. Not anymore."

"Good. That's the first sensible thing you've said. Now, what you really need is some dinner. And then you need to talk about what's bothering you. What's *really* bothering you."

"I just want to forget this evening ever happened."

"Give me some time, and maybe we can change that attitude."

Jane looked up at her, wishing she'd go away and leave her alone. She didn't want to be with anyone right now.

"Where's your coat?"

"Patricia, I appreciate—"

"Bag it. I'm taking you home and feeding you. No more arguments."

After placing their omelets on a tray, Patricia entered the living room.

"Damn, *damn*," she muttered, seeing that Jane had stretched out on the couch and fallen asleep. "Just my freaking luck."

She set the tray down, then sat on the arm of a chair. Jane's cheeks were still mottled from all the tears, but the tension in her face had eased. Whatever had happened tonight, it must have been rough. Strange, but Patricia found herself wanting to do something to make it all better. She certainly wasn't in love, but she had come to care about Jane in a way she hadn't cared about anyone in a long time. She didn't have much use for monogamy or undying devotion, but she did feel she was experiencing something new, something she wanted time to explore.

Thinking that for now, at least, sleep was more important than food, Patricia went upstairs and removed a couple of wool blankets from the linen closet; then she returned downstairs and covered Jane with them. The living room was drafty, but the couch was comfortable. She'd slept on it herself more than once. Bending over, she kissed Jane

185

on the forehead. That simple action made her feel strangely content, not an emotion she'd experienced much of in her young life.

Once she'd dimmed the lights, she took the plates back to the kitchen and scraped the omelets into the garbage. She wasn't hungry, and she wasn't sleepy. After lighting a joint and achieving a certain mellow buzz, she sauntered back into the living room and sat down in a chair to watch Jane sleep. She looked so vulnerable—and so very beautiful.

Even though Patricia had no specific information about why Jane was so upset, she knew it had to involve Julia Martinsen. She wished that woman would evaporate off the planet. Jane would be ten times better off if she never saw her again. And once Julia was out of the picture, Patricia had a clear shot. As far as she was concerned, doctors were dreary people. Jane needed someone younger, more alive. Someone willing to live closer to the edge. Jane liked that herself, although she wouldn't admit it. She'd spent too many years carefully crafting her squeaky-clean image. But that was all right. She could keep the image, as long as Patricia got a crack at the real woman underneath.

Even though the all-knowing Cordelia had insisted that Patricia was no good for Jane, the truth was, if Jane didn't cut Julia loose and soon, that woman was going to give her a coronary. Their so-called relationship was nothing but frustration and heartbreak. Jane deserved a little fun in her life.

"She deserves me," whispered Patricia, holding the smoke in her lungs for several seconds, then releasing it. By now, Jane was probably dreaming. Patricia had some dreams of her own. And after tonight, she had a feeling they were all going to come true.

Chapter 25

FRIDAY MORNING

I'd forgotten how truly beautiful this hotel once was," said Jane, moving slowly down the long colonnade in the Winter Garden's central lobby, taking it all in: the chandelier, now missing bulbs and bits of crystal; the elegantly carved marble pillars; the faded, almost unrecognizable murals; and finally the ornate ironwork. Some of it was damaged from water, some from neglect—but all was covered with the grime of decades.

"It's dramatic," said Patricia, correcting her.

"Yes, it is. Almost like a stage set. Ibsen, maybe. No, more . . . Chekhov."

"Whatever."

"It does need a little work, though."

"Your diplomacy is unnecessary. I know the place is a dump. But that's why I've got Eddie. His architectural plans for the hotel are nothing short of inspired. And he's lining up a group of restoration artisans that will turn this disaster into a showpiece. The seniors in this town will be falling over themselves to rent an apartment here. Just being inside the walls of the Winter Garden will make them feel rich and famous."

"And Russian and doomed," muttered Jane.

"What?"

"Nothing. It sounds like you've got it all planned."

"I do. Everything but the financing."

Jane had spent the night on Patricia's couch. A distant siren had awakened her around one, but the idea of returning to the Lyme House—to her empty office with its phone that refused to ring—was too awful to contemplate. Besides, it was freezing cold outside, and she was snug and warm under Patricia's blankets. For a brief moment, she was overwhelmed by self-disgust for becoming the kind of woman who would even consider waiting by a phone for her lover to call. But then, still groggy from the wine, she turned over and fell back asleep.

When she finally rose, shortly after nine, Patricia was in the kitchen, already dressed and making them breakfast. Over fresh melon, yogurt, and toast, she'd invited Jane to come downtown with her for a short tour of the hotel. Since Jane didn't have anything pressing on her schedule, and her headache was the size of the Grand Canyon—a fact that made the idea of work seem even less appealing—she decided to accept the offer. She was curious about the place, the scene of the crime, especially since she was no longer bound by her promise to stay away from her "research" into Jeffrey Chapel's death. As far as she was concerned, all bets were off now that Julia was once again pulling her disappearing act. And as of this morning, she wouldn't be waiting by any more phones. Nothing and nobody were worth her health—and that's what was at stake if she didn't distance herself from her romantic entanglement with Julia.

In the cold light of day, the decision seemed an easy one, though Jane could almost bet she'd have second thoughts about it later. That seemed to be her pattern. But as of this morning, she was resolute. And it felt good. Now that the aspirin she'd taken earlier had begun to work, her head felt better, too.

On the drive downtown, Patricia had commented on the change in Jane's mood, even asked her what it was about. All Jane would say was that she'd made an important decision, one she intended to stick with. That seemed to satisfy Patricia, though Jane wasn't sure why she seemed so happy about it. The problem was, Jane had very little memory of what had been said last night. She remembered Patricia knocking on the window at the Lyme House. And she remembered sitting on Patricia's couch staring at a cup of coffee. But that was about it. At breakfast, Patricia mentioned that Jane had fallen asleep almost as soon as she'd walked in the door, so apparently they hadn't had time to do much talking—which was fine with Jane. Patricia had already picked up enough pieces after Jane had been stood up by Julia. It wasn't fair to continue to use her that way.

"Next stop on our tour is the restaurant," said Patricia with a distinct twinkle in her eye. As they entered through the lobby doors, Patricia added, "Unfortunately, it looks like our financial backing just fell through."

"The Haymaker Club isn't going to back the restoration after all?"

"Afraid not."

This was news to Jane. "But you and Eddie were so positive that Andrew Dove could swing the vote."

"True. But Dove was arrested yesterday. It was all in this morning's paper."

"*Arrested?*" Jane came to an abrupt halt. "Why?"

"He's being charged with Chapel's murder. According to the *Star Trib*, Dove and Chapel may have been lovers. Dove was the one who removed the desk calendars from Chapel's office after the murder."

"For what reason?"

Patricia shrugged. "The article didn't say."

"Amazing," whispered Jane. If Dove was gay, he certainly hadn't set off her "gay-dar." She'd have to call Norm, her dad's paralegal, and see if she could get the full story.

"I will admit," continued Patricia, "this does sort of trash our timeline. But, I'm optimistic. We'll find another backer. And as far as Dove is concerned, the cops have been dragging their feet long enough. It's about time they made an arrest."

The police might have arrested the right man, thought Jane, but she wasn't sure they had the right motive. According to Patronelli, Chapel had found evidence of financial improprieties at the Haymaker Club. Jane didn't understand it all yet, but based on comments made by both Patricia and Eddie Flynn, she'd formed a theory. Both of them seemed certain that the Haymaker Club vote was in their pocket. The question was, how could they be so positive, especially with Chapel's potential opposition? The most obvious answer was that they'd cut some sort of under-the-table deal with Andrew Dove. If Chapel *had* caught his father-in-law with his hand in the cookie jar, so to speak—taking kickbacks from charities in payment for assuring them that the club's vote would go their way—it would answer a lot of questions. Dove might very well have gone to great lengths to shut his son-in-law up. Murder didn't seem out of the question.

"Enough about all that," said Patricia, walking around the dank kitchen, making sure none of her expensive clothing touched the filthy surfaces. "What do you think of the place?"

Jane felt the topic had been switched rather abruptly, but decided not to pursue it—for now. Stepping over to the grill, she glanced up at the hood, still caked with grease. "The square footage is pretty big by modern standards. But you're going to have to gut it—all of it." In her opinion, nothing in the kitchen was salvageable.

"Yeah, I know. This is the most depressing part of the hotel." Her cell phone gave a sudden beep. "I better get that. We're in the middle of a small crisis at work. Patricia Kastner," she said, listening for a few seconds. "No, that's *not* what I authorized. You tell Frank that I want to see him in my office right after lunch." Covering the receiver with her hand, she nodded to Jane. "I've got to deal with this—shouldn't take too long. Why don't you wander around the hotel a little? Get a feel for the place."

Jane followed her out of the kitchen, through the once grand dining room, and finally reentered the lobby. As Patricia disappeared into a small back office, Jane paused for a moment to get her bearings, then headed up the central stairs. Since she'd read the police report, she knew Jeffrey Chapel's murder had occurred on the fourth floor. She was actually glad for the interruption. She'd been hoping for a chance to roam around the old hotel by herself. She didn't expect to find anything, especially since the police had already gone over the place with a fine-tooth comb, but she still wanted to get a firsthand look at the scene of the crime.

Four flights was a long trek for someone with a bad leg, but once she'd reached the fourth floor, she moved down the dimly lit hallway, assaulted by the smell of mildew, dirt, and decay. The yellow police tape had been removed from the elevator—the one with the missing door—and dumped in a small heap on the floor next to it. Stepping carefully up to the threshold, Jane noticed that only a few feet down, darkness swallowed up the shaft. Chapel had probably been unconscious when his body had been pushed over the edge—at least, she hoped that was the case. She felt her stomach grow queasy at the thought of his free fall.

Hearing the floor creak suddenly behind her, Jane grabbed for the wall to steady herself. The sound had startled her, making her feel as if someone were about to push her over the edge. Stepping carefully away from the dark shaft, she turned around and surveyed the hall, her eyes stopping at each door, looking for signs of movement. A few of the doors were open, but most were shut. She had no way of knowing what had made the sound or where it had come from. Not that it mattered. The noise had frightened her. She was alone and vulnerable, and her first response was to run. But running wasn't an option these days. Hobbling was more her style. Whatever she did, she had to do it slowly.

On her way back to the stairs, the first door she passed was closed. So was the second. But the third was open. She moved cautiously in front of it, but stopped when she saw a pillow and a blanket at the far end of the room. The window directly above it was open. A filthy, partially ripped shade was blowing in the bitter November breeze. She knew she should just ignore it and keep going, but she couldn't help herself. Inching inside the room, she checked behind the door; then she stepped into the bathroom. No one seemed to be around.

Stepping over to the window, Jane was now able to hear the clank of footsteps descending the metal fire escape. She stuck her head out of the window and saw a man fleeing as fast as his legs would carry him. By the gray in his ponytail and beard, she could tell he wasn't young, but she couldn't get a good look at his face. From this distance, his jeans looked pretty new—and so did his jacket—both denim. She didn't think she was jumping to conclusions to assume he'd been sleeping in the hotel room. It wasn't exactly warm inside the building, but compared to outside, it was a summer day.

Crouching down, she quickly examined the blanket and pillow. Again, both seemed new. If he was a street person, he must have come into a recent windfall. A bottle of cheap whiskey sat underneath the window, the contents mostly gone. A pack of Camels lay next to it. Jane decided he had to be the homeless man mentioned in the police report, the one both Patricia and Eddie had seen evidence of over the past few weeks.

Pulling back the blanket to see what, if anything, was underneath, Jane was surprised to find an expensive leather wallet sticking out from under the pillow. As she picked it up, an American Express card fell out. "Jeffrey Chapel," she whispered, reading the name on the front of the card. Inside she found Chapel's driver's license and the rest of his credit cards. Two twenty-dollar bills remained inside the flap pocket. Somehow, the man had managed to get his hands on Chapel's wallet. Did this constitute proof that Chapel's death was part of a robbery attempt—that Dove was innocent?

If the homeless man *had* committed the murder, he was taking a big risk by returning to the scene of his crime. It seemed more likely that he'd stumbled across the wallet sometime after the murder. If so, why not come back? Maybe he'd get lucky and find something else, something equally valuable. The building was normally empty at night. The man had undoubtedly cased the place and knew how to get in and out without being seen. By sitting across the street and observing, he could easily determine whether the cops were still watching the hotel. As for this morning, he was probably sleeping off a hangover and got scared when he heard Jane out in the hall. What else could he do but hightail it out the window before she could get a good look at him?

Leaving the wallet where she'd found it, she noted the room number—422—and then returned to the lobby to call the police. Patricia was still on the phone, still looking frustrated. Holding up five fingers, she waved at Jane from behind the desk in the small office.

Five more minutes, thought Jane. Well, the police could wait that long. As she crossed the lobby to one of the tall, narrow windows overlooking Third Avenue, she continued to think about the homeless guy. She wished she could've talked to him. Perhaps he'd been in the hotel when the murder occurred. If so, he might even have seen it happen, and that meant he might be able to point the finger at Andrew Dove, corroborate his guilt—or, just maybe, he'd point the finger at someone else. Jane's gut feeling told her that Chapel's murder was part of a complex series of events with a very specific desired outcome.

"Hey, Jane," said a voice from behind her.

Turning around, she saw that Eddie Flynn had just come through the front door. He looked windblown, his already ruddy cheeks raw from the cold. "What are you doing here?" he called.

She smiled. "Patricia brought me down to see the restaurant."

"She must be a mind reader." He was carrying a cardboard tube under one arm. "You may not believe this, but after I finished up a few things here, I was going to head over to the Lyme House to see you." He held the tube in front of him. "These are some of the preliminary plans. I take it you got a good look at the dump site?"

Jane smiled at his description of the hotel. "I did. And you're right. It's a mess."

Eddie unzipped his leather jacket. His expression remained confident. "Wait till you see what I'm proposing. I was hoping you'd take a look at these—you read blueprints, don't you?"

She nodded.

"Terrific. Then later tonight, what do you say we go over them? I don't mean to push you, but I need some feedback ASAP." He was his usual hale and hearty self.

"Sure, I'd be happy to look at them."

"What do you say I drop by the restaurant around eight?"

"Sounds fine."

He raked a hand through his ginger hair, then glanced over his shoulder into the office where Patricia was seated. Lowering his voice, he added, "Actually, I've got something personal I need to talk to you about. I'm in . . . kind of a bind."

Jane had no idea why he would want to confide in her. "I'm not sure what I can do."

"Just wait and hear me out," he said, stepping closer and handing her the tube.

Jane realized now that what she'd taken at first as Eddie's typical liveliness, was in reality nervous energy.

Before she could ask him what was going on, Patricia emerged from the back room. "I leave my office at Kastner Gardens for a few hours, and all hell breaks loose." She nodded to the tube. "What's that?"

"Kitchen plans," said Eddie with a broad smile. "Jane's going to look them over."

"Great. Hey, why don't we get together tonight, and you can tell me what you think. What do you say? My place? Eight o'clock?"

Jane glanced at Eddie.

"Give her a little more time, Patricia. I really want her to study what I've done."

"Okay, then . . . Sunday night. What do you say?" asked Patricia.

"Sounds fine to me."

"Maybe you can do that massage, wine, and hot-tub thing you proposed the other night," said Eddie, winking at Patricia. "If I thought you wouldn't drop-kick me through your front window for crashing the party, I might join you."

"Make it another night," she said, shooting him an amused look.

Returning his attention to Jane, he continued, "Don't hold back on your comments just because you think you'll hurt my feelings. I don't work like that. I want your honest opinion."

"You'll get it."

Stashing her cell phone in her shoulder bag, Patricia said, "Well, I've got to get back to the office before one of my employees poisons all the poinsettias."

Eddie laughed. "You do have some unusual problems."

"Don't I just." She slipped her arm through Jane's and walked her to the door.

Jane waved to Eddie over her shoulder. He obviously didn't want Patricia to know about their meeting tonight, which in turn only fueled her interest.

As they left the building, heading across the street to Patricia's car, Jane realized she hadn't called the police about the wallet. Now that she'd had some time to think about it, she was less inclined to report her discovery. The police had access to the building. She wasn't thwarting their investigation—she simply wasn't helping it along. Only time would tell if her reason for doing so proved valid.

Chapter 26

Since they were already downtown, Jane asked Patricia to drop her off at Linden Lofts instead of taking her back to the Lyme House. She'd catch a cab back to the restaurant later. It was still early, so she felt confident that Cordelia would be home. She wanted to check in and see how yesterday's Thanksgiving dinner had gone.

After riding the freight elevator up to the fifth floor, she knocked on Cordelia's door.

"It's open," shouted a weary voice.

When Jane entered, she found Cordelia lying on her overstuffed couch amidst a pile of satin pillows and the chaotic dregs of yesterday's party. In her paisley silk morning robes, she looked like some decadently plump pasha waiting for a cadre of voluptuous maidens to appear and feed her figs and dates.

Empty wine bottles, dirty dishes, and a myriad of glasses lay scattered around the loft. So did the Thanksgiving decorations—cardboard turkeys of various types and sizes, paper Pilgrim hats, and even a few toy muskets. Garish red, white, and blue streamers and dozens of matching balloons hung across the floor-to-ceiling windows, making downtown Minneapolis look like a tacky—though patriotic—amusement park.

"How thematic," said Jane, easing into a chair across from Cordelia. She set the tube of blueprints down next to her and then picked up one of the toy muskets.

"You missed a *grand* day," said Cordelia, lowering her voice and elongating the word. She lifted her arm and then let it drop with a thump onto her stomach. "I'm fried."

"Being thankful can really tire a person out. What time did you get to bed?"

"I think the last guest left around two."

"A.M.?"

"You have to ask?"

"Why so early?" Theatre folk were notorious for their late nights—especially Cordelia and her pals.

"If you must know, after we polished off that huge bird, we all got so sleepy we simply had no other choice but to make it an early night. But what a time we had! Janey, you really missed an *event*. Performance art fit for the National Gallery."

"That's why I stopped by. I want to hear all about it."

"Well," said Cordelia, fanning herself with a paper turkey, "before dinner, somebody was looking around my study and happened to find a stack of scripts for one of Oscar Wilde's plays. I mean, that's all it took. It started out as a joke, but before we knew it, we were *doing A Woman of No Importance*. Passing the scripts back and forth. We eventually made our way onstage." Again, she lifted her arm and pointed to the makeshift stage she'd had built at one end of her eighty-foot-long room. "It was an incredible hoot, Janey. I played Mrs. Arbuthnot, *of course*. Agnes took the part of Lord Illingworth. Denny played Lady Hunstanton. Drinks in hand, we went through three whole acts, flubbing our lines, falling over chairs laughing at how bad we were, and then we broke for dinner. By then, we needed sustenance. If I do say so myself, the food was extraordinary. Well, all except for the corn pudding, which I nearly incinerated, but nobody cared. The smoke only added to the evening's theatricality. When dinner was done, we were all pretty giddy, and that made our rendition of the fourth act even more pathetic—and hysterical. After we finished, we got seventeen curtain calls. Seventeen! That must be some kind of record."

"Who gave them to you?"

"We did! We just kept taking bows while we clapped and whistled. There were even a few catcalls for my performance—deserved, if I do say so myself. And then we retired to the living room for our pie, coffee, and brandy. When we were done eating, we sat around like seriously overpuffed blowfish, burping and nodding off, all the while trying to make the odd intelligent comment to add to the dying conversation. Eventually, we just gave up, and everyone left—tired, but magnificently entertained." Tilting her head toward Jane, she raised an eyebrow and asked, "And what did you do?"

Jane was stuck. She could hardly tell Cordelia she'd spent the day waiting to talk to Julia. Technically, that wasn't entirely true, although in retrospect, it was how it felt. She and Bean had gone for a couple of short walks. She'd dug out her car after Wednesday night's snowstorm. She'd also spent several hours sitting by the fire in her office, reading. Pretty dull stuff, by Cordelia's standards.

"You haven't answered my question, Janey."

"I'm thinking."

"The answer doesn't require thought."

"All answers require thought."

"All right. Then, what were you thinking *about?*"

"What happened on Wednesday night."

"Ah." Her nose twitched. "I smell a story."

"I think it's probably the rotting turkey carcass."

"Don't be rude."

Jane hesitated. "Julia called."

"I wondered when you'd finally hear from her. Where is she?"

"Santa Fe."

The eyebrow raised even further. "Let me guess. A secret turquoise expedition? No, no . . . she's searching for the ghost of Georgia O' Keeffe."

"I don't know what she's doing there."

Cordelia rolled over on her side and rested her head on the palm of her hand. "You never asked?"

"It's hard to remember. Our conversations move inexorably from one nonanswer to the next."

Blanche, one of Cordelia's more flamboyant cats, jumped up on the couch, nosed Cordelia's hand, and then flipped on her back and demanded to be stroked. Jane had never thought about it before, but Blanche and Cordelia were a lot alike. Both were exotic in a silent screen—star sort of way, and both were easily irritated and nervy—hedonists living in a world of dreary ascetics.

Jane watched the cat's eyes close in ecstasy. "She told me she didn't want to get into what's going on in her life right now. She thinks if she tells me, or if she returns to Minneapolis, it will put my life in danger."

"Oh now, *that's* welcome news."

Jane looked away. "But she promised to call every day—just to keep in touch, so I wouldn't worry. In return, I promised to stay away from anything to do with Jeffrey Chapel's homicide investigation."

"Thank you, Dr. Martinsen."

"I told her I had no interest in it, except that I thought she was involved—and by trying to find out what happened to Chapel, it made me feel as if I was getting closer to the truth behind all her evasions." Jane glanced down at a smashed Pilgrim hat resting next to her foot. "She promised she'd call me last night at six."

"And?"

She kicked the hat away. "She didn't."

Cordelia was silent for a few seconds. "She never even left a message?"

"Well," said Jane, looking glum. "I turned off the answering machine in my office to give me some extra time to get to the phone upstairs in the dining room. When I left the restaurant later in the evening, I forgot to turn it on. I haven't been back since."

"I see." She stopped scratching the cat and sat up. "Why do I sense that the name 'Patricia Kastner' will be mentioned momentarily?"

"I spent the night at her house."

"Jane, this isn't like you. You're starting to become predictable."

"I didn't sleep with her."

"I said predictable, not crazy."

She got up and walked over to the windows, gazing absently at the wintry downtown scene. "I don't form romantic attachments all that easily; you know that. These past few months have been very hard for me, and well . . . Maybe I'm just being a coward, but . . . I feel like I can't let it drag on any longer."

"What are you saying? That it's over between you two?"

Jane lowered her head. "I think it has to be."

She was silent for a few seconds. "You're the least cowardly person I've ever known, Janey. Maybe this decision is exactly what you need.

With Julia out of the way, you can get back to some semblance of a normal life."

"I didn't make the decision lightly."

"I know you didn't."

"But it still upsets me that I don't know what her big secret is. And, of course, I'm still worried about her."

"You're in a no-win situation."

"The only good thing is, I'm not bound by my part of our bargain anymore."

"You mean . . . staying out of the Chapel murder investigation?"

Jane turned around. "Get this. Andrew Dove was just arrested. The police think he did it, that he and Chapel were lovers. He was the one who took the calendars from Chapel's two offices."

"Back up a minute. Chapel and Dove were *lovers?*"

"That's the theory."

One of Cordelia's other cats, Melville, jumped up and draped himself around her shoulders. "Well, then. Case closed."

"Julia knew that priest who was murdered. Turns out he was the man who told Jeffrey Chapel to go see her."

"He did? Why?"

"Seems pretty clear to me. Julia's secret must have something to do with closeted gay men."

Cordelia drew Blanche into her arms, thinking it over.

"She continues to insist she doesn't know a thing about the murder, but I don't believe her."

"You think she's lying to you?"

"What's new in that?" As Jane said the words, she could tell she still resisted viewing it that way. "Or . . . maybe she knows something she doesn't realize is important—but something that could help the police."

"You don't think Dove did it?"

"I'm not sure. But I don't think the police have all the facts." She put the heel of her right hand to her forehead and pressed, hoping that she could force back the headache she felt coming on. It didn't help. The throbbing behind her eyes kept getting worse. This time, however, it wasn't part of last night's hangover. Instead, it was one of the nasty debilitating kind she'd been dealing with ever since the attack. Unless she was mistaken, she had an hour, maybe less, before the pain would force her to bed.

"You all right?" asked Cordelia. "Your cheeks look flushed."

"My head's starting to hurt."

"Do you have your pain medication with you?"

"No."

"How about some aspirin?"

"I've already taken some."

Cordelia's cordless phone gave a muted ring. Leaning over and rummaging around on the floor, she muttered, "Now where did I put it?" She located it under a couple of throw pillows. "Thorn here," she said, barking gruffly into the mouthpiece. After a second, she asked, "Who's calling?" She pushed the mute button. "It's Brenna Chapel. She called the Lyme House looking for you, and they gave her this number. Should I get rid of her?"

Jane held out her hand. "I'll take it." Clicking off the mute button, she said, "Hi. What's up?" She lowered herself into a chair.

"God, I'm glad I found you. Why the hell don't you have a cell phone?"

Not that it was any of her business, but Jane explained, "I can't stand the idea that I'd always be reachable. Sometimes I don't want to be reached."

"Must be good for business."

"I muddle by."

"I assume you've heard about my dad?"

"I have, and I'm sorry."

"Save your condolences. My father had nothing to do with Jeffrey's death."

She was her usual assertive self. "The police must have some reason, Brenna."

"They've got nothing but circumstantial evidence. As far as I'm concerned, it's harassment, plain and simple. They needed a scape-goat, and my father made an easy target. Arresting someone promi-nent is probably good for their public image. He isn't gay, Jane. And neither was my husband. If Jeffrey had the AIDS virus, he got it from a woman."

"Wait just a minute," said Jane, trying to get Brenna to slow down. "Your husband was HIV positive?"

Cordelia's eyes opened wide in surprise.

"The medical examiner's office ran a test from the blood sample taken during the autopsy. It came back positive."

"God, Brenna, I'm so sorry."

"They ran the same blood test on my dad last night. He insists it will come back negative. So . . . right there, that shoots their motive to bits."

Jane could have pointed out that it didn't matter if Andrew Dove *was* HIV positive, only that he thought he might be and that Chapel was the cause. "For his sake, I hope he doesn't have it. But what about you?"

"I'm fine."

"Did you have the test, too?"

"Not yet. I don't think I've got it."

"But you won't know for sure until you're tested."

"I can't think about that right now. Just listen, Jane. Dad talked to his lawyer last night. The man's in Switzerland, but as it turns out, it's moot. He explained that what my father needs is a criminal lawyer. He gave him a couple of referrals, all eminent local attorneys, but Dad wants the best. He wants Raymond Lawless."

So that was it. After trying to bribe her with drugs and women, and then threatening her, now he wanted a favor. Charming fellow. "You want me to call my father and ask him to represent your dad?"

"Could you? It would mean the world to me."

"I'm afraid he's out of town too."

"When will he be back?"

"Tomorrow, I think. Late morning."

Brenna groaned. "We need someone now! There's going to be an arraignment this afternoon. If Dad doesn't get out of that filthy cell, he's going to lose his mind. Someone needs to be in court to argue for him—just in case the D.A. wants to deny bail."

"Well—" She wasn't sure why she should even care. "Actually, my father took on a partner a few months ago. Her name is Elizabeth Piper. I've only met her once, but Dad thinks she's terrific. If she didn't know her way around a courtroom, he would never have brought her into his firm."

"I . . . don't know. It sort of feels like we're getting the second-string quarterback."

"Think about it. I'd be happy to give you her pager number, and you could call. Go ahead and use my name. Tell her you're a friend and that it's an emergency."

Silence. "Do you suppose your father would take over the case when he returns from his trip?"

"I can't say. You'd have to talk to him personally."

"Yes, but you could explain the situation—that my father is innocent. You could put in a good word for him."

"I could. But all I can do now is give you Piper's number."

Brenna hesitated. Finally, she said, "Okay. At least we'll have someone on board."

Jane quickly removed a card from her wallet and read the number out loud.

"Thanks. Say, while I've got you on the line, I was wondering . . . I made a mess of it the first time I talked with that friend of yours—Dr. Martinsen. But I'd like a second chance. Maybe if I try coming at her with a little less hostility, she might see how horrible this has been for me and open up about what Jeffrey told her before he died. There's even more at stake now."

"Sure, I understand."

"Have you heard from her recently? Do you know how I could get in touch?"

Jane hated lying, but she didn't feel she could tell her the truth. "Sorry."

"Damn." More silence. "Well, when she contacts you, will you tell her I really need to talk?"

"Of course."

After saying good-bye, Jane handed the phone back to Cordelia. "Chapel had the AIDS virus."

"I got that much. Think about it a minute, Janey. A gay priest told a closeted gay man to go see Julia. A doctor. I'm starting to see the light here."

"I am too." She rubbed her forehead. "I'd like to stay and talk this through, but my head is really starting to pound. I think I better get back to the restaurant."

"You can always stay here, you know. Take a nap. Let Auntie Cordelia feed you chicken soup."

Jane glanced around the messy apartment. "You've already got your hands full."

She sighed. "Have I ever told you about my slash-and-burn theory of housekeeping? I may even write a book about it someday. A thriller, of course."

Jane grinned. "Sounds like a best-seller."

202

"Yeah, especially if it's poorly written. Call me later, and let me know how you're doing."

After hugging Cordelia good-bye, Jane headed back to the elevator, careful not to jar her throbbing head. She pushed the down button, and a few seconds later, Rhonda Wellman, Julia's neighbor, drew up the wood grate separating them.

"Hey, Lawless. How's tricks?"

She stepped inside. "Okay, I guess. Did you have a good Thanksgiving?"

Rhonda pulled the grate back down, then hit the lobby button. "So so. Today's cleanup day." She nodded to the plastic garbage sacks resting next to her on the elevator floor. "Say, if you're looking for the good doctor, she's already gone. Left this morning at the crack of dawn."

Slowly, Jane turned to face her.

"She was on her way to the airport—I guess she had an early flight out. Hey, I really liked her new haircut. She looks real sexy with that short short hair. Not me. I gotta have lotsa hair, or I look like a turtle. Big shell—little head."

Jane was speechless.

"Something wrong?"

"No . . . no. Nothing."

"'Cause you look kinda funny."

"No, really. I'm fine. But . . . I mean . . . You say Julia was here?"

"I thought we already discussed that. I figured she came back to have Thanksgiving with you. Did you get together?"

"Ah, well—"

She cocked one eye. "You still having some memory lapses from that bump you took on the head?"

"Yes, I guess so."

"I mean, you knew she was staying at her loft, right? She arrived late last night."

"Sure. I guess I just got my times mixed up on when she was leaving."

"That's too bad, hon." Rhonda grabbed the handrail as the elevator rumbled to a stop.

"Did she say when she'd be back? Or where she was going?"

"Poor kid. You really are mixed-up this morning."

"I, ah . . . don't like to talk about it." She gave a weak smile.

"Hey, I understand. I was on Prozac for years. Screwed with my memory something awful. No, she never mentioned where she was going or when she was coming home."

Jane had to think fast. She knew Rhonda was in a hurry. "Look, do me a favor. If you see her again, will you call me? I know it sounds silly—"

"Well, yeah—you being sweethearts and all."

Jane fished a card out of her pocket. "But . . . will you do it? Will you call me at my restaurant if you see her again?"

Rhonda eyed the card as if it might be radioactive. Finally, plucking it from Jane's hand, she pressed it into the pocket of her heavy coat. "No problem. Now, I've got to hustle this garbage out to the Dumpster and then shoot over to the bar. I'm expecting a busy day today. Between you and me, people hate being cooped up with their relatives. When the bars reopen, that's when the real Thanksgiving begins." She winked, then hoisted the sacks and set off out the back door.

Chapter 27

"So, what did you think of the plans?" asked Eddie, twisting his coffee cup around in his hands.

Jane had offered him a drink, but he'd declined, saying he had a date later in the evening. They sat near the fire in the pub's back room. On the small stage in the main room, a Celtic band played an old Irish lullaby, one of Jane's favorites.

Before she answered his question, she took a sip from her glass. It was her second whiskey of the night, and wouldn't be her last. She'd spent the afternoon on the couch in her office, trying to survive her headache. By six, it was somewhat better, but the pain had killed her appetite and her concentration. Since the headache—and her life in general—had left her feeling generally depressed, alcohol seemed a quick solution. Sure, she knew that if she abused it, it was a potential minefield, but she felt she could handle it. After her first drink, she'd even felt good enough to spend some time in her office going over Eddie's blueprints. He'd redesigned the entire kitchen, using the space in some very clever ways. Still, she did have a few suggestions. She also wanted something from him, and knew she had a great excuse to get it.

"I like what you've done," said Jane. "The redesign is excellent. But I didn't see a list of the equipment you plan to buy."

"I'm still looking into that—getting the specs and prices."

"Well, a lot depends on your menu. I assume Patricia's given it some thought."

"She's talked to a couple of local chefs. Both have tons of ideas and are interested in our executive chef position, but she hasn't settled on one yet."

"It all takes time." Jane folded her hands around her drink. "You know, I'm sure you've already checked the codes for downtown Minneapolis, but you might want to consider installing a high-velocity discharge system—especially since the restaurant will be part of an apartment complex."

"I'll look into it. Thanks."

Jane ran a finger along the rim of her glass. "Actually, now that I've seen the blueprints, I guess I'd like to spend some time just walking around the space again. Unfortunately, I do my best thinking alone."

He laughed. "So do I."

"I don't suppose you'd be able to get me a key to the hotel?"

Eddie took out his key ring. "Done. I know Patricia wouldn't mind. And . . . well, commercial kitchens aren't my specialty, although, in the past few years, I've done more than a few." He removed a key and handed it to her. "I've got a couple extras back at my office. Feel free to use it whenever it fits into your schedule."

"Thanks," said Jane, placing it on the table and smiling. This was perfect. Just the break she'd hoped for. "I'll be able to give you more specific comments next week."

Eddie seemed pleased, but quickly shifted his attention to the fire in the hearth. "We don't have to talk about it anymore tonight. Like I said earlier, I've got something else I wanted to discuss with you. Something more . . . personal."

"Sure," she said, lifting the whiskey to her lips.

Before saying anything, he leaned in closer to the table. Whatever he was about to say, it was for Jane's ears only. "This may seem like an odd question, but I don't see any point in beating around the bush. Is someone trying to blackmail Brenna Chapel?"

Blinking back her surprise, Jane said, "Whatever gave you that idea?"

"A comment she made to you the other night. It was the same night I drove you home from Patricia's house and then stayed to have a drink here in the pub. Remember? She rushed into the back room and announced that she'd received another one of 'those' faxes."

Jane recalled it now. Eddie had been with her that night. "But . . . why would you assume she's being blackmailed?"

"Is she?"

"I'm not sure I should be discussing that with you."

"I knew it," he said, a note of triumph in his voice. He pulled a thick envelope out of his inner coat pocket, opened it, and withdrew a thin sheet of fax paper. "Did the fax look like this?"

Jane put on her reading glasses and skimmed the contents. The note looked just like the two sent to Brenna. And once again, it had been sent from the Haymaker Club. It was dated a week ago, the day after Jeffrey's death. In several terse sentences, it told Eddie that unless he wanted everyone in the community—and his place of employment—to know he was a faggot, he needed to leave twenty-five thousand dollars in unmarked bills in a Dumpster at the minimall on Forty-sixth and Nicollet. It gave him one week to get the cash together. Since it was the same location that Brenna had been directed to use, Jane assumed it had been sent by the same man. Handing the sheet back to him, she said, "You're gay?"

He nodded.

"Did you pay him?"

Once again, Eddie shifted his gaze back to the fire. After a few thoughtful seconds, he said, "No. But I did twice before—to the tune of thirty thousand dollars. That was two months ago. I thought I'd heard the last of him, but then a week ago, I got this one. Same thing. He wants more money. But this time, I don't have it. So I waited. I thought maybe he just liked torturing gay men. Two days ago, I got this in the mail." Again, he opened the envelope, taking out a series of Xeroxed photographs.

Even though the quality was poor, Jane could easily make out two men on a sleigh bed. The shot was taken from the foot of the bed, but their faces were clear enough for positive identification. "But you said—"

"I lied," said Eddie, his expression curiously impassive. "I didn't want you or anyone else to know." Pausing to return the photocopies to the envelope, he continued, "Jeffrey and I were lovers. We had

207

been for almost a year. I'm telling you this because I feel pretty sure I can trust you. Patricia swears you're as honest as the day is long. I trust her. She trusts you. And since you're a member of the tribe, you'd understand the pressure I'm under. I'm not making a mistake by telling you this, am I?"

She could hardly hide her astonishment, but she reacted quickly to put his mind at rest. "No. Of course not."

"Our conversation will go no farther than this table? You won't suddenly decide to have a heart-to-heart with Sgt. Duvik?"

She hated making spur-of-the-moment bargains, but knew he wouldn't talk unless he felt safe. And she wanted him to talk. "No. You've got my word. Whatever you tell me will be held in confidence."

"Good."

She gave him a moment and then asked, "So . . . does that mean everything you told me the other night was a lie?"

"Well, what I explained about my background was true. And the stuff I said about Brenna Chapel—that was all true too. She's a witch, Jane. She made Jeffrey's life hell."

Jane wasn't quite sure what was going on here. Why had Eddie chosen to confide in her? She decided to ask what seemed like the next logical question. "Was Jeffrey being blackmailed?"

Eddie gave a grim nod. "We'd both received the same kind of faxes—Jeffrey first, then me. Of course, Jeff was hit for more money. If you don't believe me, have someone check his bank account. You'll find he withdrew at least one hundred thousand dollars in the last month. You may think we were stupid, that we should have handled it some other way, but we couldn't involve the police, so we didn't know what else to do except pay the guy. We were both scared." Again, he looked down. "And now, it's starting all over again."

"Did Jeffrey know about the pictures?"

"I don't know. All I know is I didn't—until a few days ago." He squirmed in his chair. "See, everybody thinks I'm straight. You have to understand—the head architect at my firm is a total homophobe. A real dinosaur. He'd hit the ceiling if he found out about me. I've always kept my sexuality private, even before I went to work for Harris & Moss. What I do is nobody's business but my own. Even in college, that's the way I played it. Not that it matters anymore. If I don't pay the money, these photos will end up on Mr. Moss's desk. I'll be a star," he mugged, smiling with fake lightness, "in my own porno flick."

"You think you might lose your job?"

"For being gay? Of course not. Moss isn't stupid. It would be much more subtle—and law-abiding—than that. Try and understand, Jane. I'm comfortable there. I'm well paid, and I get the chance to learn from the best. It's the top architectural firm in the Midwest, and I have a specific niche I'm developing for them. I never would have met Patricia Kastner if I hadn't been connected with Harris & Moss. Can you see why I don't want to leave?"

This was hardly the time for a lecture on the virtues of coming out of the closet. Besides, Jane agreed with him. How he handled information about his private life was his own business. She also knew that hiding such an important part of your life always came with a big pricetag attached. The closet doubled quite nicely as a coffin. "What about Jeffrey?"

"What about him?"

"Were the two of you planning to stay together?"

"Oh, we weren't exclusive. I cared about him, but it wasn't a life commitment or anything like that. I'm sure he was sleeping with other guys. I know I was."

Jane tried not to sound disgusted when she asked the next question, but it was a struggle. "What about Brenna? Did Jeffrey ever plan to let her in on his secret?"

"A week before he died, he told me he'd decided to divorce her. He wanted the marriage annulled so she could marry again. For some reason, he felt a sense of loyalty to her. I can't imagine why, especially not after the way she treated him. See, Jeffrey'd known he was gay since he was a kid, but he fought it. All during the time he spent in the marines, he never acted on it. Not once. I can't imagine it myself, but I know Jeffrey, and I know he was telling me the truth. He hated that part of himself—and so when Brenna proposed marriage, he said yes. He really believed he could make it work. Thank God I never made that mistake."

Jane had heard the same story hundreds of times before, and yet it never ceased to sadden and frustrate her. "Those photos," she said. "They're pretty graphic."

"Yeah, there's no mistaking what we're doing."

"How do you suppose the blackmailer got them?"

"He must own a camera fitted with a lens that could take pictures without much light. I assume the shots were taken through my bed-room window. We always went to my house. A fortuitous crack in the shades maybe? All I can say is, if I could just get my hands on the bastard who took them, I'd—" He left the sentence unfinished.

Even after two whiskeys, Jane's mind started to race ahead, calculating what this new revelation might have to do with Jeffrey Chapel's murder. She decided to put the question to Eddie and see what he had to say. "Do you know if Jeffrey was sleeping with Andrew Dove?"

"Wouldn't surprise me. The guy's attractive. Kind of old, but then people have different tastes."

"So, you think the police are right? That he murdered Jeffrey?"

Eddie shrugged. "It's possible. Why not?"

"But . . . did it ever occur to you that the blackmailer could have done it?"

"The blackmailer? Why?"

"Maybe Jeffrey found out who he was and threatened to turn him over to the police."

"You think Dove is the blackmailer?"

"Anything's possible."

He shook his head. "I don't know. I guess I don't buy it. I mean, he's got plenty of money. What motive would he have?" Jane didn't have an answer.

After taking a sip of coffee, Eddie rested his hands on the table. "Look, one of the cops said to me the day after Jeff died that he was pretty certain Jeff's murderer had to be one of us—the people who were with him at the hotel the night before. I mean, that's a rather limited number of suspects. I didn't do it, and I know Patricia didn't, so that leaves only two people."

"Andrew Dove and Joe Patronelli."

"Exactly. I suppose Joe could have been blackmailing us, though again, I can't imagine why. But . . . then there's Brenna. She managed to sneak in without anyone noticing. Maybe if she did it, someone else could have too."

"Are you thinking of someone in particular?"

"Well." He looked down at his hands. "Jeffrey and I only had a couple of minutes alone that night. But he did say something about that friend of his—Loren Ives. They'd had a terrible fight right before he left the office. Jeffrey was really bothered by it. Have you ever met Loren?"

Jane shook her head.

"He and Jeffrey were pretty tight. They'd been friends forever. You know, I always kind of wondered about him."

"Wondered what?"

"Oh, I don't know. I guess I thought he liked Jeffrey more than he was willing to let on."

"Is Loren gay?"

"Apparently he insists he isn't."

"Do you think he could have met Jeffrey at the hotel that night?"

Eddie shrugged. "If Brenna could walk in completely unnoticed, so could Loren. So could anybody for that matter. But if it turns out Loren's the blackmailer, once again I don't know what his motive would be. I think he's pretty well-off financially."

"You think money is the only reason for the blackmail?"

"It's the most obvious one." Draining his coffee cup, he returned to his own problems. "I've got to do something to get that guy off my back. That's what I wanted to talk to you about. It seems pretty apparent that Brenna's confided in you. She must know by now Jeffrey was gay."

"I think she's still resisting the idea."

He shook his head. "I suppose I should cut her a little slack, huh? It probably came as quite a shock. I mean, I know Jeffrey would have told her himself—if he hadn't died. At one point after his death, I actually thought about talking to her myself, but I was in shock for the first few days. And then, later, I just figured it was better not to get involved."

Better for who? thought Jane, holding up her empty glass, motioning for the waiter to bring her another.

"So, I guess I was wondering what Brenna's going to do about the blackmailer?"

"Last I heard, she'd decided not to pay. She's going to call his bluff."

Eddie winced. "Not smart, lady! God, if she does that, my ass is cooked for sure."

"But why should she pay? With her father's arrest, her husband's HIV status—" Jane stopped. "You knew about that, didn't you? That Jeffrey was HIV positive?"

He gave a cautious nod. "I think he took some stupid chances. It was right at the beginning, before he really understood the scene."

"Well, the facts will eventually leak out. People can draw whatever conclusion they want, but I'd say that blackmailer is out of business."

"Yeah . . . but not when it comes to me."

Jane was completely fed up by a society that forced people to hide who they were just to make some people feel comfortable with their prejudices. Then again, she was also less than impressed with the callous way these two men had handled their personal lives. Nobody was going to come out of this smelling like a rose.

"What am I going to do?" demanded Eddie, directing the question not to Jane, but to the air around them. "I feel like my head's in a vise."

"Just out of curiosity," asked Jane, knowing she wasn't being as sympathetic as he might like, "do you know a priest named Michael Latimer?"

Eddie shook his head. "Should I?"

"No. No reason. He was a friend of Jeffrey's."

"Say, speaking of friends. That's the other thing I wanted to ask you. A couple of weeks before Jeffrey died, he told me about a woman—a doctor. Her name's Julia Martinsen. He was sure she could help him with his problem."

"You mean his HIV infection?"

He nodded.

"Are you HIV positive, Eddie?"

"I . . . I don't know." He smoothed a hand over the back of his hair, looking uncomfortable. "And I don't have a doctor I feel I can trust. I understand Dr. Martinsen's a friend of yours?"

"Who told you that?"

"Patricia. It's not a secret, is it?"

She shook her head.

"Then how can I get in touch with her?"

"I don't know."

"But you said you knew her."

Jane looked around, wondering how long it took to pour a simple whiskey. "She left town this morning. I don't know where she went or when she'll be back."

"Oh." He frowned. The frown deepened the more he thought about it. "Does she ever phone you? If she does, you could give her my name and ask her to call me—collect. I'd be happy to pay for the call."

He seemed awfully determined. "Surely she can't be the only doctor around who would keep your test results a secret."

"Yeah, I suppose you're right. But see . . . After Jeffrey talked to her, he seemed—I don't know—more calm. Less frightened."

"Maybe she told him to come out of the closet—to tell the truth."

"Easy for her to say," he mumbled. "You know, this may sound silly, but I just keep thinking that maybe somehow she knew who the blackmailer was. Maybe she told Jeffrey."

Jane's expression hardened. "How could she possibly know who the blackmailer was?"

"Oh, I don't know," he grumbled. "It's probably just wishful thinking." Now he looked really depressed. Resting his head on his hand, Eddie added, "To tell you the truth, for a few days, I even considered that this Martinsen woman might be part of the blackmail scheme. I suppose that's ridiculous. She's a doctor, after all. Why would she need the extra cash?"

Jane thought back to all the money Julia had spent fixing up her house on the lake. She'd spared no expense. The artwork alone could have bought and sold Jane's restaurant many times over. Even by a doctor's standards, Julia seemed awfully flush.

"You know," said Eddie, "if I'd never gotten involved with Jeffrey, I really believe none of this would have happened to me."

"Why do you say that?"

"Because he was such a high-profile guy. Someone was bound to figure out he was a closet case and take a shot at him. After all, he was a decorated marine. He did speaking gigs all over the country. He had money. Pilots are very sexy these days. Tom Cruise and all that. I just got caught in the crossfire."

"I suppose that's possible."

"I just have this feeling that if I talked to Dr. Martinsen, she might know something that could help me."

"Like who the blackmailer is?"

"Yeah, maybe."

"And maybe if you knew, you'd end up just like Jeffrey."

"Oh, crap. This just keeps getting worse. Why do I even try?"

"Look, if I hear from her, I'll let you know, okay? But don't hold your breath."

"I won't. Then again, she's my only hope, Jane. Unless you want to loan me twenty-five thousand dollars."

"Sorry.

His attempt at a smile was something less than successful. "Ask Patricia. She might be good for it."

Putting a finger to his lips, he whispered, "I don't want her to know a thing about this. It's my problem—and I want it to stay that way."

"Fine," said Jane. "Whatever you say." She turned at the touch of a hand on her shoulder. Looking up, she saw Felix, the night manager, standing over her.

"Jane, you've got a phone call. It sounds pretty urgent."

"Did you get a name?"

"He wouldn't give one. But he says he needs to talk to you right away."

"Okay. I'll take it in my office."

As Felix walked away, Eddie said, "It's about time I shove off. Really, thanks for your time. It's helped me a lot to finally get some of this off my chest."

Pushing away from the table, Jane stood, feeling an unwelcome numbness in her left leg. "Do me a favor. Let me know if you hear from the blackmailer again."

"Will do. Unless—" He hesitated.

"Unless what?"

"Well, unless somebody happens to find my body at the bottom of an abandoned elevator shaft." As he said the words, he grinned.

Jane wasn't terribly amused by his gallows humor. And in his eyes, she could see he wasn't either.

Chapter 28

Jane sat down behind her desk, opened her bottom desk drawer, took out a bottle and a glass, and poured her own whiskey. If the bar couldn't get their act together, she'd take care of it herself. Pushing the button under the blinking light, she picked up the phone and said, "This is Jane. Can I help you?"

"I sincerely hope so," said a precise male voice. "My name is Ives. Loren Ives."

She didn't recognize the voice, but she knew the name. "Yes, Mr. Ives. How can I help you?"

"I'll get right to the point. Your time is as important as mine. I need to speak with Dr. Julia Martinsen right away. Brenna Chapel tells me the two of you are friends. If you would kindly tell me where she is—give me a phone number where she can be reached."

"I'm sorry, but I can't do that."

"Why not?"

Jane was getting pretty sick of this. She wasn't Julia's appointment secretary. "Because I don't know where she is."

Silence. "What the hell's going on with that woman?" His voice was full of disgust. "I tried calling her practice up north several times. She never called me back. And nobody gives me a straight answer at that clinic of hers either. Has she gone into hiding?" He meant the words as a sarcastic exaggeration. Jane could hardly tell him he'd got it right.

"I can't say."

He grunted. "You can't say? How delicate of you, Ms. Lawless. You know, you may get a charge out of acting the two-bit diplomat, but you're not helping." After a few frustrated seconds, he added, "This is an *extreme* emergency. It's vital I speak with Dr. Martinsen right away."

"Why?"

"It's personal."

Wasn't everything? An awful lot of people seemed to be lining up to talk to Julia Martinsen. "I can't make her materialize out of thin air. If I hear from her, I'll give her your message."

"My phone number is in the book."

"I'll be sure to tell her that."

"The name is Ives." He spelled it.

"Yes, Mr. Ives. I've made a note right here on my desk calendar." She hadn't. "If you'd care to leave a further message—"

"No. Just that."

She should have engaged him in a longer conversation—used her innate cleverness to ferret out all his deepest, darkest secrets—but she didn't have the energy.

"Good-bye, Ms. Lawless."

Before she could say good-bye herself, Ives cut the connection. "Have a wonderful evening, you pedantic little pissant." She reached for her glass, taking a large swallow of the whiskey. Ives might be in a foul mood, but right about now, Jane was feeling no pain. Maybe she should make a list for Julia. She ticked the names off on the fingers of her right hand. Brenna wanted to talk to her. So did Eddie. And now Loren Ives insisted that Julia get in touch with him right away. Who would be the next to line up?

Before Jane could concoct an answer, her private line gave another ring. "The next applicant," she announced, picking up the phone and propping it between her chin and shoulder. "Jane Lawless here. The line's forming fast. Actually, I think we may do a drawing to see who gets to talk to Julia first."

216

"Excuse me?" said a man's voice.

She didn't much care who it was. "Who's this?" she asked abruptly.

"It's Leo Curtis calling from D.C. We talked the other night."

"Ah, yes. Leo. But you can't be part of the drawing. It wouldn't be fair." She picked up a pencil and began tapping it against the side of a cookbook.

"Have you been drinking?"

"Let's see." She glanced at the half-full glass. Her third.

"Yup, I'd say I have, not that it's any of your business."

His voice tightened. "Have you heard from Julia?"

"Do you realize, Leo, that that's the most often asked question in Minneapolis these days?"

"Maybe I should call back later."

Jane didn't want him to go just yet. "She phoned me on Wednesday night."

This elicited the desired effect. "Was she all right?"

"As far as I know. How come you're calling? I figured you'd said everything you had to say the other night." Which wasn't much, she could have added.

"Where was she when she called?"

"I thought Julia told you everything."

"Look, she was supposed to phone me last night and she didn't. I'm worried."

"Join the club."

"Do you know something, or don't you?"

"She apparently flew into the Twin Cities. I never saw her, but the woman who lives across the hall from her at Linden Lofts said she bumped into her this morning. Julia was just leaving for the airport."

"She flew to Minneapolis for one night?" He sounded skeptical.

"That's what I'm told."

"But why?"

"I have no idea."

"She wouldn't do that. She gave me her word."

"Did she? It's just an observation, you understand, Leo, but I find that Julia has a few credibility problems when it comes to keeping promises."

"It's not safe for her there."

"Well, I guess she's a big girl. She makes her own decisions."

217

"She came back to see *you.*" He made it sound like an accusation.

"If she did, we never connected. But whether she did or not, don't you think that's up to her?"

"No. Not with so much at stake. Don't you get it, Jane? Her life's in danger. If it weren't for you, none of this would be happening."

Jane was almost too stunned to speak. She dropped the pencil and switched the phone to her other ear. "Look, I've had just about enough—"

"If she'd left well enough alone, everything would be fine. But no. She had to turn her life upside down for you. *You* did this to her!"

"Hey, slow down, pal."

"You and your moralistic P.C. attitudes."

"My *what?* I don't have a clue what you're talking about."

"You just plain don't have a clue. If anything happens to her, I'm holding you responsible."

"Listen, you miserable bastard, if you'd care to enlighten me—" But before she could finish the sentence, he hung up.

"Damn," she shouted, slamming the receiver back on the hook. How could *she* be responsible for Julia's problems? She hadn't broken into Julia's house or her loft, looking for some nonexistent files. She hadn't made any of those anxious phone calls. She never once lied to Julia. As a matter of fact, she'd never told Julia to do anything! So where the hell did this creep get off accusing her of ruining Julia's life?

Storming out of her office, she returned to the pub.

As soon as she came through the door, one of the bartenders waved her over to the bar. "Did you ever get that Irish whiskey you ordered?" He pushed one across to her.

"Thanks." She'd left the other glass in her office. Easing onto a stool, she took several swallows, allowing the smooth, mellow taste to warm and calm her. For a few seconds, she toyed with the idea of calling Leo back, giving him an earful, but knew it would be an exercise in futility.

As the evening wore on and new drinks kept appearing in front of her, Jane's mood turned decidedly black. Even though she considered herself half-English, she was also the product of her midwestern upbringing. Once applied, *guilt* stuck like superglue to her dark Lutheran soul. Not that she was much of a Lutheran anymore, but guilt was a kind of homegrown, Minnesota virus. If you were even the smallest part Scandinavian, which she was, and caught the disease, you'd probably die of it.

By the shank of the evening, Jane had moved to a table in the back room. She didn't want to talk to anyone, and yet she didn't want to go back and sit behind her desk all alone. That should be some kind of warning bell, she thought to herself. When her life was on track, she liked being alone. Tonight, returning to her office felt like entering a prison cell.

"Jane?" said a voice from behind her.

When she turned to look, she realized how dizzy she was. She had no idea how many whiskeys she'd drunk over the past few hours. Probably too many.

"I'm going to close up now," said Felix. "It's after two. Everyone's gone except me."

As she tried to focus, she noticed now that the music had stopped and the pub was empty.

"Would you like me to leave the lights on?"

She had to think about it for a minute. "No. Just leave one on behind the bar."

"Sure thing. Do you . . . do you need any help getting back to your office?"

Jane shook her head. "Thanks, Felix. I'm fine."

He stared at her a moment and then said, "If you say so. I'll see you tomorrow."

As he switched off the lights, she didn't stir for several minutes. Finally, leaving the empty glass on the table, she ambled slowly back down the hall. Before going inside her office, she glanced up the back steps and heard Felix turn on the security system as he left the building. Feeling that the restaurant was secured for the night, she closed the door behind her.

Chapter 29

SATURDAY MORNING

   As Brenna pushed the key into the front door of her condo, she realized she was worn out, and yet her nervous energy was at an all-time high. After the arraignment yesterday afternoon, she'd spent the night at her father's home keeping him company. Thankfully, since yesterday had been a Friday, the banks were open late. She'd been able to arrange to pay the bail right away. As she was talking to the vice president of Northstar Savings and Loan—a personal friend—she'd received an unexpected shock.

   Hesitantly at first, the man had brought to her attention the fact that her husband had withdrawn a large sum of money from their joint account before his death. The withdrawals—fifty thousand dollars each—had been made exactly a month apart. Since it had been such a large amount, and Jeffrey had died under suspicious circumstances shortly thereafter, the bank officer felt she should know. He'd been wanting to call her with the information, but didn't quite know how to handle it, sensing that it was probably a matter of some delicacy. He explained that what she did with the information was now up to her. He had no intention of going to the police, though he assumed they would eventually come to him. He couldn't lie about the withdrawals; he simply thought Brenna should know about it before they did.

So. There it was. As far as she was concerned, this was proof positive that her husband was being blackmailed, and that he'd chosen to pay the blackmailer off rather than have details of his personal life made public. Did she need any more proof that he had something to hide? And yet, she couldn't help herself. She still resisted the idea that the man she'd known, the man she'd made love to for years, was gay. There had to be another explanation.

Hanging her coat up in the front closet, she entered the living room, but stopped suddenly when she detected the smell of fresh cigarette smoke. A second later, Loren walked out of the kitchen.

One hand rose to her chest in alarm. "You startled me!"

"Did I?" He seemed surprised by her reaction. "I'm sorry." He tapped some ash into the ashtray he was holding.

"I . . . I've been trying to get in touch with you for days. You haven't returned any of my phone calls."

"I've been busy, Brenna."

"No you haven't. You're still angry about our dinner date—the one I forgot. Why won't you understand? It was a mistake. I wasn't trying to hurt you. I wanted to apologize again, but you wouldn't let me." She glared at him, trying to decipher the look on his face. "You're not the only one with pressing personal problems, you know."

"I know." His gaze drifted away. "I'm ashamed of myself for treating you like that. I should have returned your calls."

She wasn't going to let him off the hook that easily. "How did you get in?"

"With a key. Don't you remember? You gave me one last Christmas when you and Jeffrey were away in Vermont. You wanted someone to water your plants."

She did remember. Somehow, the fact that he had one had never crossed her mind again.

"Do you want it back?"

"No. Yes. I don't know." She felt like a fool for being so indecisive.

"Brenna—" He took one last drag on his cigarette, then ground it out. "I didn't come here to talk about the other night. If you want

221

to associate with people like Joe Patronelli"—he said the name with distaste—"that's up to you."

She wasn't going to rise to Loren's bait. Not today. "Why *did* you come then?"

"First, let me say that I'm sorry about your father. I didn't hear the news until late last night."

"I'm sure you were devastated."

A shadow of a smile crossed his lips. "Okay, you got me there. I don't like him, but I know how much this mess is costing his daughter—and whether or not you believe me, I do care a great deal about you." He crossed to the couch and sat down. "Come and sit with me. Please?"

She stood her ground. For some reason, she felt wary of him today. "You still haven't told me why you're here."

"I need to talk to you. I don't like all this distance between us." He hesitated. "If you want me to say that I reacted stupidly the other night, that I jumped to erroneous conclusions—that it's all my fault— I will."

She could feel herself relenting. "No. I suppose I'm as much to blame as you are. This has been . . . a bad few days." She was beginning to crumble. She wanted to cry—wanted him to hold her.

"And I've made it worse, haven't I? You've got to believe me, Brenna. I'm so sorry. I care about you . . . more than you realize. Please, just come and sit down. There's something important I need to tell you, and I can't do it if you're halfway across the room." He tried a smile, though his eyes remained sad.

Brenna felt herself drawn to him, drawn to his genuine sorrow. He loved Jeffrey as much as she did. He understood.

As she sat down, he slipped one hand over hers. "I really am sorry."

"I know."

"But you don't, Brenna. There's so much you don't know. And God help me, I haven't the vaguest idea how to explain." A shiver crept down her spine.

"I've been keeping something from you. It was wrong of me. But I'm afraid that if I tell you the truth now, you're going to hate me. I could take anything but that."

She kept silent, waiting to see where this was heading.

"Promise you won't hate me, Brenna. Please, God, promise me

that much."

"You're scaring me." She pulled her hand away.

"I'm scared too." He ran his fingers through his thinning blond hair, then leaned forward, clamping his hands between his knees.

"Does it have to do with Jeffrey?"

He just stared at her, seemingly unable to speak. Finally, he gave a grudging nod. "Brenna, you've got to get an AIDS test—right away."

"Is that what you're worried about? That Jeffrey was HIV positive, and I didn't know? But I do, Loren. My father told me." Then, the significance of his silence hit her. "Did you know Jeffrey was HIV positive *before* he died?"

His gaze slowly dropped to the table in front of them. "I'm afraid so, yes."

"And you didn't tell me?"

He couldn't meet her eyes. "You remember that fight Jeff and I had in his office the afternoon of his death? You asked me about it a couple of days ago. The police asked me about it too. Well, I lied—to both of you. We weren't arguing about my impending financial demise. We were talking about his trip up north to visit that doctor. He'd been worried about his health for some time. He got the bad news several weeks ago, and he told me right away, but he made me promise to keep it to myself. He said he was going to talk to you about it, but it had to be the right moment—whatever that meant. The problem is, he kept dragging his feet. That day in his office, I completely lost it. I told him that his behavior had put your life at risk—and now he was too big a coward to tell you the truth. I said that I could kill him for what he'd done to you."

Brenna was speechless.

"He told me that it was impossible for you to have the virus because he hadn't slept with you since he started seeing . . . others."

"Other women?"

"No," he said, closing his eyes. "Other men."

There it was. She finally had her answer. Denials were no longer possible. "Who?" she demanded.

"I don't know."

"My father? He swears on a stack of Bibles that he isn't gay."

"Jeffrey never gave me their names. But . . . that afternoon, that's when he accused me of being in love with you myself. He said my feelings were clouding my better judgment. He promised he'd talk to you, but I was impatient. I was pushing him too hard. He had to handle this in his own time and in his own way."

Brenna watched him a moment. She couldn't help herself. Maybe it was off the subject, but she had to ask. "Are you in love with me, Loren?"

He shot to his feet. "I can't do this without a cigarette." Removing a pack from his pocket, he shook one free, lit it, then tossed the match in the ashtray.

"Answer my question."

Sitting down in a chair across from her, he seemed to need more distance now. "Yes," he said finally. "I've been in love with you ever since I first met you. I wasn't kidding when I told Jeffrey that if he hadn't decided to marry you, I would have asked you myself."

She was astonished. It had never occurred to her that Loren could have such deep feelings for her—or for anyone, for that matter, other than Jeffrey. Loren was such a buttoned-up, closed-off man. Sure, he'd been kind to her over the years, but she always assumed it was out of love for his best friend.

"I've embarrassed you," he said, drawing on the cigarette.

"No . . . I'm just . . . surprised."

"I understand entirely if you don't return my feelings."

"Dear God, Loren. My husband just died! Do you think I could tell you or any man—that I was in love with him?"

"I'm being clumsy. I'm saying all the wrong things."

"Just answer one question. Are you telling me you know for an absolute fact that Jeffrey was gay?"

Again, he nodded. "I'm sorry, Brenna. He made me promise never to say a word to you—to deny it if you ever asked—and like a moron, I agreed. I see now that I shouldn't have. The truth is, Jeffrey's been struggling with his sexuality ever since he was a kid. Of course, I knew about it. I think, when we were first getting to know each other, he thought I might be gay too. I mean, I looked the part far more than he did. Over the years, we both came to realize that it doesn't have anything to do with how someone looks. It's what's inside. If anyone tried to turn his back on his true sexuality, Jeffrey did."

"You actually believe he never acted on it . . . until recently?"

"I do. Jeffrey had steel for a backbone. Being a gay man—whatever that meant to him—didn't fit in with his life plan. When he met you, he really thought he'd found a way out. The problem was, he discovered

224

he was human after all. He could only keep a lid on something as powerful as his sexuality for so long—especially with more and more gay people coming out of the closet. I really believe that what he saw convinced him he could be a man—his kind of man—and still be gay. That revelation came as an epiphany."

"When he was growing up, he simply couldn't identify with the more queenly aspects of the crowd. Me, I wouldn't have had any trouble. But then, I was straight. It didn't really touch me—or, I should say, those people didn't represent me, so I could enjoy the outrageousness. The camp. Jeffrey, on the other hand, was only attracted to the football-jock types. I assumed it was all fairly psychologically convoluted—he needed some kind of reassurance or something, not that he ever acted on anything. Maybe, if he'd lived long enough, he would have come to terms with his feminine side. I believe strongly that all men have one, but that's my bias. Jeffrey and I used to argue about it all the time."

"When we roomed together in college, we'd have these marathon conversations about sex, girls, guys, life, love, personal integrity, God, whatever. I loved Jeffrey, Brenna. I've never revealed myself to another human being the way I did to him. In many ways, we were both outsiders, although Jeffrey passed for straight far better than I ever did. I was always the artistic geek, the butt of jokes—sometimes even gay slurs. But then, a lot of kids figured that since Jeff was my friend, I must be okay. Funny, huh? Only Jeff and I knew the truth. We understood each other's souls, and we trusted each other with that knowledge. I saw him suffer in ways you couldn't even imagine. But when he finally broke down and slept with a guy, he hurt you, and I couldn't abide that. He crossed a line. He knew he'd done it, and he also knew it was something I could never forgive him for."

Brenna just sat on the couch and let his words wash over her.

"So . . . is it true? Had you two stopped sleeping together?"

She gave a nod. "It was almost two years ago."

They sat in silence for several minutes, Loren finishing his cigarette and immediately lighting another, and Brenna just feeling numb.

Finally, in a low voice, Brenna said, "I guess the blackmailer was right."

Loren's head popped up. "Blackmailer? What blackmailer?"

"I've been getting faxes—blackmail notes. They said Jeffrey was gay, and that unless I agreed to pay money, information about his

225

private life would be made public."

Loren blew smoke out of the right side of his mouth. "Why didn't you tell me this before?"

"What good would it have done? What could you do?"

Taking another deep drag, he said, "Don't worry about it anymore, sweetheart. The cat's out of the bag now."

His use of the word "sweetheart" caused her to look up at him.

"Nobody's going to hurt you again, not as long as I'm around."

She knew he wanted her to be grateful, to appreciate his take-charge attitude, but the last thing she needed was another man's protection. As far as she was concerned, the price was too high.

"I still think you should have an HIV test run, just to be on the safe side. I could make an appointment with a doctor for sometime next week. What do you say? I'd be happy to drive you. Afterward, maybe we could have that dinner I promised."

All she really wanted was to be alone. She needed time to process everything she'd just learned. Then again, she couldn't just toss him out. An inner sense told her she needed to tread carefully. For one thing, he'd just said he was in love with her. Perhaps he felt that gave him certain rights. Not that it did. Or did it? She was so confused.

"Brenna? Are you all right?"

"Yes, I think so."

"You forgive me, don't you? For not telling you sooner about Jeffrey?"

"Sure." She said the word with little emotion. She could see that he was looking at her intently, trying to get a fix on her feelings. "I just . . . need a little time by myself, Loren. I have a lot to think about. My head is spinning."

"I understand." And yet he made no move to leave. "Maybe I should get you a drink?"

"God, no. That's the last thing I need."

"Sometimes it helps a person relax. I could stay. Fix you some lunch. We could . . . talk. You need to talk, Brenna. You can't bottle all this up inside you."

He had a point, she supposed. And he spoke so tenderly. She was about to give in when the phone rang.

"Want me to get that?" He headed immediately into the kitchen.

"All right," she said weakly, hearing him pick up the receiver. After a moment, she heard him say, "Who's calling?"

When he returned to the living room, his expression had hardened. "It's Joe Patronelli. He wants to talk to you. Should I get rid of him?"

"No, I'll take it," said Brenna. When Loren passed her the phone, she could see a deep scowl on his face. He also made no move to leave the kitchen so that she could have some privacy.

"Joe, hi. What can I do for you?" She fussed absently with the top button of her cashmere sweater.

"Hey, Brenna. I just wanted to tell you how sorry I was to hear about your dad. Is he still in jail?"

"No, he's back home. I would imagine right about now he's talking to his new attorney."

"That's good. Has he got good representation?"

"We hope so."

"Look, I'm sorry to bother you at such a bad time, but there's something I need to give you. It's . . . important. I don't think it can wait."

"What is it?"

"I have to see you in person to explain. How about tomorrow morning? I could drop by your condo."

"I thought you were going out of town for a game in Green Bay this weekend."

"The doc says I'm not 100 percent. He won't let me play. I could go, but it's too depressing to sit on the sidelines. Look, you'd be doing me a favor if we could get together for brunch or something. That way, the weekend won't seem so long."

"Sure, brunch sounds okay."

"I'll pick you up at ten."

"Fine."

After hanging up, she turned around. The expression on Loren's face was pure ice.

"What?" she said, demanding an answer to the look.

"Obviously, what I just said meant nothing to you."

"Loren, please."

"I thought you were through with him."

"I barely know him—how can I be through with him?"

"You're twisting my words."

Now *she* was angry. "*My* friends are *my* business. What bugs you so much about him anyway?"

227

"He's a jock. Jocks own the world."

"That's a load of bull, and you know it."

"Is it?" On his way through the living room, he grabbed his coat from one of the chairs and then leaned down and scooped up a cardboard box he'd set next to the door.

She followed him. "What's in the box?"

"Nothing that would interest you."

"Where are you going?"

"What do you care?"

"Loren, you're acting like a teenager. Of course I care about you. But I can't make a commitment to you—or anyone else for that matter. Not now."

"Spare me your rationalizations."

"I've never seen you so emotional. Or so . . . irrational."

He turned to face her. "I have feelings, Brenna. Deep feelings. And I have needs. My life's been nothing but chaos for months, and nobody gives a rip. Not even you. Why? Because you're too busy planning to have breakfast with Mr. Wonderful tomorrow morning. Well, you can tell him from me that I hope he chokes on his steak and eggs."

He slammed the door on his way out.

Several hours later, Brenna received another fax. This time, it was a photo of her husband naked with another man. She couldn't make out the other man's face, but Jeffrey's was unmistakable. The note that came with it said simply,

> So the world now knows your husband was a faggot. But do you want them to see the details in glorious living color? Think about it. I will be in touch.

Chapter 30

Jane pulled her car up next to the gate and stopped. It was just as Burl Hedges had said it would be. A tall, wrought-iron fence between two square pillars made from small rocks set in concrete. The spot was wooded, almost rustic. It could easily be the entrance to a summer camp or a tourist lodge, but in this case, it would no doubt open up onto a single dwelling close to the water. As she'd driven along Oaklawn Avenue looking for Hedges's house, she'd caught a glimpse of some of the other homes along Lake Minnetonka. Mansions were more like it. This was one of the richest suburbs in the metro area, mainly because of the beautiful lakeside setting and the proximity to the city. Though she couldn't see his house from the gated entrance, she assumed that the erstwhile financial director of the Haymaker Club lived in reasonably splendid surroundings.

Jane eased Julia's Audi up to the intercom. After she pushed a button, a man's voice answered, "Can I help you?"

"It's Jane Lawless. I'm here to see Mr. Hedges."

"Jane, hi. Burl here. You made good time. Okay, once I've opened the gate, drive straight ahead until you see a fork in the road. Take the right turn, and come on down toward the lake. You'll see the house on your left. Park anywhere in the drive."

"Thanks. I'll be there shortly." Moments later, the iron fence parted, and she drove through. As she sailed along the freshly plowed road looking for the turn, she opened a bottle of aspirin and popped a couple into her mouth. She washed them down with a cup of cold coffee she'd brought with her from the restaurant.

After last night's conversation with Leo, she'd drunk too much and ended up sleeping way too late. She was disgusted with herself when she woke, but since she had so many important matters to attend to today, she put the self-flagellation on hold, showered, dressed, and tried to eat something. As long as she kept popping aspirin, her headache seemed to be manageable.

She'd called Hedges after lunch, hoping that she could figure out a way to get him to talk to her. As soon as he heard her name, he jumped to the conclusion that she was an emissary from her famous father wanting to talk to him about the recent arrest of his old pal, Andrew Dove. Over the phone, his voice was a study in sorrow and regret. Poor Andy. Hedges had talked to him last night after he was released from jail. What a shame. And, sure, he'd be happy to help in any way he could. If Raymond Lawless needed a character witness for old Andy, Burl Hedges was his man. Since it suited her purposes, Jane let him continue to think that she was working on Dove's case for her father. In a way, perhaps she was. As long as she maintained the charade, Hedges would be friendly and cooperative.

Pulling up next to a gray Volvo, Jane slid out of her seat, locked the door, and then followed the cobbled walk up to the house. It was a fairly large two-story wood-and-stucco structure—sort of prairie style meets Swiss chalet—but with the pool and the boathouse, the private dock, the tennis court, and the incredible view of the lake, Jane assumed it was a multimillion-dollar estate.

She was about to knock on the front door when Hedges appeared, looking for all the world like George Burns in *Oh, God*. Hedges was thin, not terribly tall. His clothing was casual: blue knit sport shirt, navy blazer, gray slacks, and white loafers. More to the point, he seemed like the kind of old guy who, any minute, might break into song and a little soft shoe just for the hell of it. He motioned with his cigar for her to enter, and then led the way back to a four-season porch. He'd obviously been reading the morning paper. Sections were scattered all over the floor near an easy chair.

Joe Patronelli had been right. Hedges seemed to be a man in his late sixties or early seventies, though he still had a lively spring in his step. "Have a seat," he said, sitting down himself. "Excuse the mess. I can't seem to read the paper without making one. Would you like some coffee? A drink?"

"Thanks, no." She sat down on an old-fashioned fringed footstool, the farthest point in the room away from the cigar.

"So," said Hedges, "have you talked to Andy this morning?"

"No. My father will be handling the case. I'm just gathering information." She didn't add that the information was for her, not her dad. "We might as well get right down to business. I'm sure you're a busy man."

"Never too busy to entertain an attractive woman."

She smiled. "How long have you known Mr. Dove?"

He stuck the cigar back in his mouth and thought for a moment. "Well, I guess we met in sixty-nine. Can't remember who introduced us. We formed a business partnership for a while—built shopping malls in Wisconsin. That's how we got to be such good friends. Andy's a swell guy. Not that I ever trusted him at the poker table." He tapped some ash into a tall ashtray sitting next to his chair. It looked like the kind Jane had seen in old hotels.

"He cheats at cards?"

"That's off the record."

She nodded.

"He had nothing to do with that murder, Jane. You can quote me on that."

Thinking she should at least make a stab at looking official, she removed a notebook from the pocket of her pea coat. Clicking the top of her pen, she asked, "Did you know Jeffrey Chapel?"

"Sure. He was out here a couple of times. I give a lot of parties. Keeps me young." He winked. "Play your cards right, young lady, and you might get invited to one."

She tried to look interested. "Are you married, Mr. Hedges?"

"Call me Burl." He puffed on his stogie. "That's a leading question, if I'm not mistaken. Are you, Jane?"

She tried to keep her expression pleasant. "No."

"A shame. A beautiful woman like you going to waste."

"Oh, I'm not going to waste," she said, hoping he'd drop the

231

subject.

"That's good. Well, me, I took the plunge twice, but it didn't agree with my delicate constitution. Not like Andy. He was a one-woman man. When Sarah died, he said he'd never marry again, and he didn't."

Jane made a few scratches on the pad. "Back to Jeffrey Chapel. What did you think of him?"

Hedges shrugged. "He was an impressive guy. Very spit-and-polish. We never really talked much. Hard to believe he was a homo, but then what do I know about people today? I still live in the Dark Ages."

Right—when seventy-year-old men could make passes at women thirty years their junior and assume the women were flattered.

"By the way, that business about Andy being gay—it's just plain crap."

Jane nodded her understanding. "But, when Jeffrey took over your position as financial director at the club, wasn't there some kind of transition period when you showed him the ropes?"

"Andy pretty much took care of that. When I quit, I wanted to walk out the door and be done with it. I left and haven't looked back. I'm too old to work that hard. I want my remaining years to be stress-free."

"And working at the club was stressful?"

"It had its moments." He lifted the cigar from his lips and studied the tip.

"But it wasn't a fulltime job, was it, Mr. Hedges?"

"You were going to call me Burl."

"I'm sorry. Burl." She smiled. The last thing she wanted was to annoy him before she got to the question she'd really come to ask.

"You know, honey, you remind me some of your dad. He and I met a couple of times. Nothing criminal, you understand. Just socially." Again, he stuck the cigar back in his mouth. " 'Course, you're a hell of a lot prettier than him, pardon my French. But you got that same cagey Lawless smile and those eyes that . . . Well, let's just say I doubt either of you misses a trick."

"Thanks. I think."

"No, it's a compliment. Surround yourself with smart people, I always say. It never hurts business."

"Speaking of business, what's been your primary means of employment, Mr.—I mean, Burl?"

"Me? Hell, this and that. This and that. I got lucky, mostly. Made some good investments back in the eighties."

With what money? Jane wanted to ask. "Really. When did you start working as the financial director of the Haymaker Club?"

"Let's see." He blew smoke high into the air. "Must have been eighty-four. That's when Andy started it. He always wanted to do something for the little guy. He came up with the idea sitting right in my goddamn living room. Can you believe it? And now look at that club. It's a marvel. We did good work there, Jane. We've helped a ton of needy people."

Removing a sheet of paper from her pocket, she handed it across to him. "Do you recognize those names? Some are charities. Some I assume are private companies."

Hedges took a pair of reading glasses out of his pocket and put them on. Studying the page a moment, he smiled. "Sure. These are the most recent recipients of our charitable funds. Where'd you get this?"

"A man named Jim Nyvold faxed it to me."

"Yeah, old Jim. Good man."

"Did Andrew Dove ever say anything to you about the way Jeffrey Chapel was handling your old job?"

His expression grew more guarded. "He . . . said a few things. Not all that flattering."

"Like what?"

"Well, you know. Like the guy might be in over his head. He didn't really know what he was doing."

"Why would Dove put a man without sound financial qualifications in such a pivotal position?"

"Simple. He expected him to learn. To figure it out without a lot of hand-holding."

"Did Jeffrey ever come here asking for your assistance?"

"Yeah, maybe once or twice."

"Were you able to help him?"

Chewing on his cigar, Hedges replied, "I told him to go talk to Andy. If he had questions, Andy was the man to answer them."

Jane scratched a few more notes on her pad. "That list of charitable recipients—I wonder if you could help me there. My father would be very grateful if you could give us the names of the men or women who were your contacts in those organizations."

"My . . . contacts?"

"You know, the people you met with. The deal makers. It would save us a lot of time."

His demeanor had grown decidedly cautious. "Why do you need to know that?"

"More character references. Mr. Dove will need more than just you."

"Oh, right." He glanced down at the list again. "Gee, you know, my memory isn't what it used to be."

"You can't think of even one or two names?"

"Well." He scratched the side of his face. "There was Clement Nelson at Community Outreach. Good man. Very discrete. Then, let me think. Evelyn Villard. She's trustworthy," he said under his breath. "That's about all I can remember."

"I understand" said Jane, writing down the names. It wasn't much, but it was a start. "If you have the time, maybe you could consult your files and give me a call with a few more names. You did keep records, didn't you? Or did you leave them all at the club?"

"No, I took copies with me."

"Great." She smiled, trying not to look cagey.

"Yeah, I suppose I could look through my papers. In the meantime, why don't you ask Andy if he recalls some of the people we worked with. He's got a much better memory than I have."

"I'll be sure to do that." She closed the notepad, but didn't get up. "I've got one last question, Burl. It's an important one."

"Shoot."

"Do you know why Dove took Jeffrey Chapel's daily desk calendars?"

Clamping the cigar between his teeth, Hedges replied, "Beats the hell out of me, honey. It's certainly not something we've discussed. To tell the truth, sometimes Andy can be a real enigma. On the other hand, with Burl Hedges, what you see is what you get." He drew his arms wide. "A simple, honest, fun-loving man, a guy who thanks the Lord every day for the good luck he's had in his life."

Jane thanked him for his time.

After walking her to the front door, Hedges stood puffing on his stogie as Jane backed into the private road and drove away.

Chapter 31

Jane and Cordelia stood outside the front entrance to the Winter Garden Hotel, shivering in the cold night air. It was just after midnight. Sleet mixed with snow had started falling about an hour ago, turning the streets of downtown Minneapolis into a treacherous skating rink.

Surveying the building, Jane couldn't see a single light on inside. The hulking stone castle seemed eerily deserted in a downtown where, just a few blocks away, theatres and cabarets teemed with nightlife. Nothing could stop diehard Minnesotans from their Saturday night on the town. In Jane's case, however, she had a far different agenda in mind.

"I am *so* not into this," said Cordelia, blowing on her hands. She was wearing a black wool cape and matching tam, an outfit that made her look like a French bat. "I don't know how I let myself get talked into your little adventures."

"Well," said Jane, feeling for the key in her pocket, "sometimes I bribe you with food. Other times—"

"The question was rhetorical. I know what you said on the phone, but I can't see why we have to do this so late at night. I mean, *honestly*. Could you have picked a more dreary location? With a few well-placed klieg lights, this hotel could double for the House of Usher."

"I'll pass along your thoughts to Patricia."

"You do that."

Jane pressed the key into the lock. "The man we've come to find wouldn't hang around here during the day."

"Right. With our luck, he's probably asleep in his coffin."

"All I know is, the police report mentioned that someone—probably a street person—had been sleeping in the building. I found evidence to prove it yesterday when I was up on the fourth floor. I also found Jeffrey Chapel's wallet mixed in with some of the man's belongings."

"Which means *he* could have mugged Chapel, stabbed him with a screwdriver, and dumped his body down an elevator shaft. How utterly delightful that we're hoping to meet him in a dark building."

"I'd bet money he didn't do it," said Jane, pulling open the heavy door. Moving quietly inside, she removed two flashlights from her coat pockets, handing one to Cordelia. Shafts of weak light fell in crisscross patterns across the dirty granite floor.

"We've walked into a noir classic," whispered Cordelia. "I should have worn my shoulder pads and pumps."

Jane directed the beam of light first into Patricia's office and then let it wash over the lobby. "We won't know how the man got the wallet until we talk to him."

Cordelia followed Jane so closely she nearly bumped into her. "It's cold in here. And it smells like . . . like a rancid walnut."

"Keep it down, okay?" Aiming the beam at the stairs, Jane continued, "If that guy's upstairs, I don't want to scare him off."

"You know, Janey, we've already hit the top of my creep level. If I'm going to be terrified, I prefer sitting comfortably in a movie house where I can eat my popcorn and drink my five-gallon drum of Pepsi in peace. I mean, aren't you even a *little* frightened?"

Cordelia had no idea. The decision to go through with this tonight had been a struggle, won only after two stiff shots of whiskey. Jane had never lost her nerve quite this badly before. She was only standing here now because of pure stubbornness. And pure stubbornness, she'd concluded—after spending a good part of the evening staring at a bottle of Jim Beam—only took a person so far.

"Where are we going?" whispered Cordelia, stumbling along behind. "Actually, now that I think of it, I may have parked in a no-parking zone. Maybe I should go check—"

"This way," said Jane, ignoring Cordelia's nervous chatter.

They began their ascent. By the time they reached the fourth floor, Cordelia was puffing hard.

"We *must* have reached the gates of heaven by now," she whispered, leaning heavily against the balustrade. "I think I see St. Peter—no . . . no, wait. It's Bella Abzug!"

"Shhh," said Jane, putting a finger to her lips. She listened for a moment, but everything appeared to be quiet. The first order of business was to check out the room where she'd found the homeless man's bedding. If he was there, she hoped she could get him to talk to her. She'd brought a hundred dollars, thinking that the offer of some cash might get his attention quicker than anything else. "We've got to be as silent as possible," she whispered into Cordelia's ear.

"Being silent isn't part of my métier," Cordelia whispered back. Suddenly, she grabbed Jane's arm.

"What?"

"I thought I heard something."

Jane listened for a moment. "You're just jumpy."

"*Dah.*"

While attempting to drag Cordelia away from the steps, an idea occurred to Jane. Since the stairway was their only exit—or the only way someone could sneak up on them—she made a quick decision. "I want you to stay here."

"What? Why?"

"You can protect our flank."

"You make this sound like the invasion of Normandy."

"Just keep it down. It may take me a little while, so don't worry if I'm not back right away. And turn off your flashlight. That way, you'll be invisible to anyone coming up the stairs."

"I want to go home!"

"We will. This shouldn't take long." Jane failed to add that if she didn't find the man in the room, she intended to search the entire hotel.

"Why do I feel as if my entire life is flashing before my eyes?"

"Just relax and enjoy the show." Jane sounded more confident than she felt.

"But as soon as you move around the corner, I won't be able to see you."

"If I need you, I'll call."

"What if I need *you?*"

Patiently, Jane replied, "If you call, I'll come right back. But you better have a good reason."

"But if I'm supposed to stay quiet—"

"Cordelia!"

"Shhhh, Janey." She held a finger to her lips.

Taking a deep breath, Jane whispered, "You'll be fine."

"Famous last words."

Giving Cordelia's hand a reassuring squeeze, Jane moved around the corner and then headed down the central hallway. The air was so cold and dank, she felt as if she were entering an abandoned mine shaft. Most of the doors were shut. About halfway down the hall, she saw one that was open. It was close to the elevators, but on the other side of the hallway. Shining her light on the number, she saw that she'd found it. Room 422.

Easing carefully inside, she directed the beam of light across the interior. The pillow and the blanket were positioned exactly the way she'd left them. Walking quickly to the closet, she opened the door just to make sure no one was waiting to jump out at her. When she'd convinced herself that the room was empty, she knelt down next to the bedding to see if the wallet was still there.

It wasn't.

Okay, so now the big question was, had the man come back and taken it, or had someone else removed it?

Maybe, after she'd startled him yesterday morning, he'd decided it would be smarter to spend his nights somewhere else. But if he liked the Winter Garden, he might still be watching the building to see who came and went.

Jane had no idea if the police had staked out the place, but since she hadn't seen any squads drive by while she and Cordelia were outside, and no one appeared to be stationed inside, the cops obviously weren't all that interested in this fellow—or what he might have witnessed the night Jeffrey Chapel died. And that probably meant that they hadn't discovered the wallet, which would have linked him to the murder. Jane still didn't think he'd been involved, but she did wonder what he knew. For that reason alone, she had to find him.

Sitting down on the floor, Jane took out a business card and a pen, and scratched a note on the back of the card. "I need to talk to you," it began. "If you agree to meet me, I'll give you $100 for your time." She thought for a minute, then scratched out '$100' and wrote '$300' instead. What the hell? She wanted the guy to respond. She continued writing: "No cops. No strings. I just want to know what you saw the night Jeffrey Chapel died." She figured that, since he had the wallet, he knew Chapel's name. She signed her own name and tucked the card under the pillow. Next, she wrote a second card just like it. This time, she stuck it on the window ledge behind the curtain. Hopefully, he'd find one and take the bait.

Rising from the floor with some difficulty, she thought she heard a faint creak in the hallway. She stepped over to the door and pointed her flashlight in both directions, but saw nothing unusual. It was probably just her nerves, which were growing more frayed with each passing second. The idea of searching the entire hotel in the dark now seemed entirely too onerous. She'd had enough of playing detective tonight. She wanted to get away from here as fast as possible and back to the safety of her restaurant.

Taking one last look around, she started back down the hall toward Cordelia and the stairs. As she passed one of the closed doors, she heard another creak. It was a small sound, one that, under other circumstances, she would have ignored, but when she turned to look, the door suddenly split open. What happened next was a blur. Strong hands seized her around the waist and pulled her inside. Somehow, Jane dropped the flashlight, and the light died. In the darkness, she tried to squirm free, but stopped when she heard the click of a gun. The next thing she knew, a cold metal barrel was pressing against her cheek.

"Where's the doc?" came a whispered voice. The man ripped the stocking cap off her head and let her hair fall loosely around her shoulders.

"I don't know."

"Of course you know. You two are lovers."

"Not anymore."

He tightened his grip, pressing the gun barrel even deeper into the soft part of her cheek. "Do you think I care about your love life? Where is she!"

"I'm telling you the truth. I've had one phone call from her this week. She was in Florida."

"Florida? Fuck." He hesitated. "When will she be back?"

"I don't know that she's coming back."

"I don't believe you. She has her practice here. *You're* here."

She could smell his nervous sweat. "Why do you need to find her?"

"She has something I want."

"What? Her files?" And then it hit her. In that one moment, she saw it all. *"You're* the blackmailer. You want those files so that you can blackmail closeted gay men."

"Shut up."

It was so simple. Why hadn't she seen it before?

Her eyes had finally adjusted to what little light there was in the room. It wasn't much, but she was sure now that this was the man she'd seen in Julia's apartment. He was wearing the same heavy top-coat and the same ski mask.

"Tell me the truth!" he whispered. "I know you're planning to see her again."

"I have no plans at all."

"I don't believe you." He slapped her hard across the face.

The salty taste of blood filled her mouth. "I can't tell you what I don't know," she pleaded, feeling her left leg tremble and almost give way beneath her. Out in the hall, she could hear Cordelia's voice calling her name. God, he's going to kill us both, she thought.

Pressing his lips close to her ear, he said, "You give the doctor a message from me. I'm not giving up until I find her. She can't run far enough to get away from me."

Releasing Jane finally, he threw open the door and burst into the hall.

"Cordelia, he's got a gun!" It was all she could get out before she collapsed to the floor. For the next few seconds, she heard the sound of footsteps running away. Then, silence. She closed her eyes, and her body began to shake violently. She couldn't seem to stop it, no matter how hard she tried. After what seemed like an eternity, Cordelia came running into the room, shining the flashlight ahead of her.

Seeing Jane on the floor, she rushed to her side. "Janey, talk to me. Did he hurt you?"

Jane touched the cut on her lip. "Is he gone?" At least her voice was steady.

"I think so. I ducked into a room, and he ran past me down the stairs."

Willing herself to calm down, Jane tried to sit up. "He could still be in the building."

"What does he want?"

"Julia."

Cordelia brushed Jane's hair away from her face. "I wonder if he was here for the same reason you were. To find that homeless man."

"I don't know." Her mind felt scrambled. She couldn't think straight. "Help me up. We've got to get out of here."

"What if he's waiting for us downstairs?"

A wave of nausea hit her. Cordelia must have noticed it too because she tightened her grip.

"It's okay, Cordelia. I'll be fine."

"Sure you will."

"Just give me a minute." Thankfully, after a few seconds, the nausea seemed to subside. "I know another way out."

"If it involves ropes and pulleys, I'll take my chances with the front door."

Retrieving the flashlight, Jane limped back to the man's room. "There's a fire escape right outside this window."

"We're four stories off the ground!"

"I'm aware of that."

"I don't *do* heights, Janey."

"I'd suggest you make an exception." Opening the window, a gust of cold air hit her square in the face. "It's stopped sleeting."

"Thank you, Bella."

"But it looks like there's some ice on those rusted steps."

"Rusted?"

Jane climbed out the window, then reached back and helped Cordelia squeeze through the small opening. The stairs creaked menacingly under their combined weight, but after a tense few seconds, everything seemed to hold. Making sure her business card was still on the ledge, Jane shut the window behind them.

"I'm going to be sick," said Cordelia, covering her mouth with her hand.

"Don't look down."

"Next time I come along on one of your little excursions, I'm going to wear a parachute. And bring a barf bag."

"What if we visit a cave?"

"Bat repellent."

They were about halfway down. Jane hoped if she kept Cordelia talking, she wouldn't dwell on how high up they still were.

"Cordelia Thorn has limits, you know."

"Standards."

"That's right."

"Just hold on tight to the railing. We may have to jump the last twelve feet or so."

"What? Even the Flying Wallendas get a net! You know what, Janey? You owe me big time for this one. *Big time.*"

Chapter 32

By the time Cordelia dropped Jane back at the Lyme House, it was close to one-thirty. The restaurant and pub had already closed down for the night. She'd invited Cordelia to come in for a snack, mainly because she felt agitated and didn't want to be alone, but also because she wanted to unwind and talk over what had happened. Unfortunately, Cordelia had twisted her ankle during their death-defying leap to the sidewalk. She wanted to soak it—and herself—in a hot tub. As usual, she suggested that Jane stay at her loft for the night, but Jane declined. Before they said good night, Cordelia urged Jane to go straight to bed. In her mind, rest would solve a multitude of problems. In Jane's mind, however, a drink was a quicker fix.

After resetting the security system, she headed straight for the pub. Locating a nearly full bottle of Armagnac behind the counter, she carried it and a glass over to a table, took off her coat, and sat down. As she lifted her feet up on one of the chairs, she realized she'd started shivering again. The brandy would remedy that soon enough. Her lip stung from where the man had slapped her, but she knew the damage was minimal. All in all, she and Cordelia had made it through the night in pretty good shape, and for that she was grateful.

She did, however, foresee some potentially serious repercussions from tonight's visit to the Winter Garden. She'd never expected to run into the man who'd broken into Julia's house and loft—and more to the point, she was frightened by the fact that he knew her name. It didn't require an I.Q. much higher than a plant's to conclude that she was doing some private nosing around about Chapel's death—thus giving the man ample reason to come after her if he felt sufficiently threatened. The question was, after tonight, would he *feel* sufficiently threatened? In order to get to the bottom of Julia's secrets, Jane had put herself in the middle of a very dangerous mess. As much as she might want to turn her back on it all, she couldn't.

By the time the bottle of Armagnac was half empty, Jane had stopped trembling. After a mental review of what she already knew about Julia, a picture was beginning to form. Jane felt quite certain now that she knew what had been going on up there in northern Minnesota. Julia was right to think Jane wouldn't be overly impressed, though it was hardly the huge deal Julia and Leo had made it out to be. And yet, secrets and lies often led to more dangerous activities. No doubt, that's what had happened. Julia was involved in the Chapel murder, but perhaps not as directly as Jane had first suspected.

Tilting her head to the side, she closed her eyes and listened. For a second, she thought she'd heard a noise coming from the back of the restaurant. She was positive she was alone, so when the second sound came, more of a low bump this time, she shot to her feet. Her first thought was that the blackmailer had somehow managed to follow her and break into the building. She had to get to her office and find the gun she'd hidden in her desk.

Thankful that the interior of the Lyme House was imprinted on her brain, she shut off all the pub lights and then crept soundlessly down the long carpeted hallway toward her office. Taking hold of the knob, she eased it to the right and pushed the door open. The sight that met her eyes caused her to stop dead in her tracks.

Julia was sitting behind the desk, one dim light burning on the bookcase in back of her. Seeing Jane, she seemed surprised too—even a little embarrassed. "I fell asleep," she said, running a hand through her new—shorter—blond hair. "I'm sorry if I scared you."

"How—" She swallowed hard. "How did you get here?"

"My plane arrived around eleven, but it took some time to get

244

my baggage and rent a car. I actually made it to the restaurant by midnight, but your staff said you were out." She glanced at the clock on Jane's desk. "Lord, it's almost two. I had no idea."

Jane moved further into the room, but didn't sit down.

"The flight was a long one," continued Julia, "so I guess I was kind of tired. I sat down in your chair to read, but I must have dozed off." She was obviously nervous—talking too much, too fast. She tried a smile, then squinted into the darkness to get a better look at Jane's face. "Did you cut your lip?"

Absently, Jane touched a hand to the spot. "What are you doing here?"

"I came to talk to you. I made an important decision this morning, sweetheart. What I said the other night was a mistake. I've decided to tell you everything. That's why I jumped on the first flight back."

"Back from where?"

She folded her hands in front of her on the desk. "D.C."

"You went to see Leo."

"Yes, we saw each other. I'm sorry I missed calling you on Thursday night, Jane. I have a good reason."

"You always do."

Julia stared at her a moment, then looked down at one of her notebooks, examining it with faked interest. "I was going to call, but then I decided to come back instead. I couldn't stand not seeing your face when we talked. But I had to take a charter because it was such a spur-of-the-moment decision. We got stuck on the ground in Denver. It was Thanksgiving Day, and it was the usual mess. They wouldn't let any of us off the plane. And since it was a crummy, cut-rate airline, it was an old aircraft, and there wasn't a phone. There was no way I could call you at six, Jane. I'm really sorry. After we landed in the Twin Cities, I drove straight to the restaurant, but it was late. I figured you were pretty ticked at me, so you probably just took off." She paused. "Am I right? Did you leave? Were you angry?"

In a low voice, Jane responded, "Oh, I was far more than angry, Julia. I think that was the night I finally gave up on us for good."

They just stared at each other for several intense seconds.

Finally, Julia said, "I've made a mess of everything. I've got no one to blame but myself."

"Do you want me to disagree?"

"A small protest might be nice."

245

Jane walked a bit unsteadily over to a chair on the other side of the desk.

"Have . . . you been drinking?" asked Julia.

"What if I have?"

"I thought I explained to you. It's not safe to mix alcohol with painkillers."

"I'm not using the painkillers. They made me sick. Alcohol seems to be the only thing that helps. I feel better when I drink, so that's my preferred method of pain control."

"Emotional pain, too?"

"How wonderful that you think you understand me, Julia. No, I'm not drinking because of you. I had a rather. . stressful evening, so when I got back to the restaurant, I had a couple of brandies. Actually, there's no real need for you to be here. I know what you've been doing with your 'practice' up north. So whatever you came to tell me, it's unnecessary."

Julia blinked a couple of times. "Jane, look, I can see you think you've figured it out—"

"I have. Give me some credit."

"Oh, I give you lots of credit. I know you're good at unearthing secrets. That's why I'm here. I decided there was no real way to protect you because, whether or not I told you the truth, you'd find some way to get at it. And in so doing, you'd put yourself in danger."

"Tell me about it," she muttered.

"I want to," said Julia. "I've wanted to for a long time. But first, tell me what you think you know."

Jane gave a careless shrug. "It's pretty simple. Your practice consists of helping gay men who have the AIDS virus stay in the closet and at the same time get expert medical attention. Judging by the way you live, it seems they pay you pretty well for your services."

Julia just sat still and listened.

"That's why Chapel came to see you. A gay priest recommended you. Only problem is, that priest is dead. I assume there's some sort of network that knows about you, and the priest was part of that network. He undoubtedly told Chapel you could be trusted to keep his secret and that you knew your business. Problem was, somebody wanted Chapel dead. I think you know more about it than you're willing to admit."

"I don't, Jane. I swear it."

"Did Chapel tell you he was being blackmailed?"

Her eyes dropped to the top of the desk. "Yes."

Now they were getting somewhere. "Did he give you the blackmailer's name?"

She shook her head. "You have to understand, Jane. Jeffrey was in terrible emotional turmoil when he came to see me. An ex-lover of his, someone he'd slept with nearly a year and a half ago, came to him and told him he was HIV positive. He suggested that Jeffrey be tested. So that's what we did. The results came back positive. It was nowhere near full-blown AIDS, but he did have the virus. He was tied up in knots about what he should do. He knew he had to talk to his wife, but I think the fact that he was actually gay was finally sinking in—and it overwhelmed him. He'd spent his life as a marine, and they aren't exactly 'pro-fairy', as he put it. He spoke about that a lot—what the corps had meant to him. How much he valued the opportunity to serve his country. The only problem was, he'd been taught some very narrow ideas about what it meant to be a man. We talked about that for hours. I think, when he left that last time, that he'd pretty much made the decision to come out—to his wife, to his friends, and to his marine buddies. I felt sorry for him, Jane. Can you understand that? The pressure was almost too much for him to bear. He wasn't a coward. He was just dealing with a set of rules that told him he didn't deserve to take up space on the planet if he found himself attracted to another man."

"So you kept his secret."

"Yes."

"Just like you did for lots of other men. Those were the voices I heard on the phone, right? These men would come and stay with you; that's why you had that apartment all set up in the basement of your home. And the examination room—it was all part of the privacy provision. And because you thought I'd disapprove—that I wouldn't be able to cope with the idea that you were helping men stay in the closet—you finally decided to get out of the business entirely. The fallout was, these guys became hysterical because they thought their secrets would no longer be safe."

"Something like that."

"Exactly like that!"

"No, Jane. Not exactly."

Jane saw Julia's resistance as condescension. It infuriated her that

247

she would only admit partially to the truth. It also galled her that Julia felt she couldn't talk to her openly about what she was doing. For god's sake, what sorts of opinions did Julia think she held? Sure, she thought it was important for gays to stand up and be counted, but she also felt strongly that coming out was an individual decision—and a long, sometimes torturous process. And being HIV positive was just one thing more to keep in the closet—even if you were out about your sexuality. Jane had infinite compassion for people in that situation. They had the right to handle it any way they saw fit. "Why don't you tell me *exactly* what I'm missing?"

Julia didn't answer immediately. She seemed to be weighing something in her mind. Finally, she said, "Seven years ago, Leo came to me. It was summertime. I remember because we were sitting out on my veranda. I'd known for many years that he was gay, and I also knew he was in a committed relationship with a man high up in the Catholic Church. The night we talked, he was terribly upset. His friend was ill. He wanted me to examine him, run some tests. He never said the words, but I knew what he was afraid of. He thought his lover had AIDS. As you might well imagine, it was a very touchy situation. Leo had never even told me the man's name. When I finally met him, I could understand why. He was a national figure, Jane. The kind of person you'd see on the cover of *Time* or *Newsweek*."

"*Was?*"

"He died in late October—the same weekend you ended up in the hospital. I'd promised to come down and spend the weekend with you, but then Leo called and said his . . . friend was worse. They both ended up flying to Minnesota, intending to stay at my place in Grand Rapids until the man got better. He died the same night you were attacked. I knew he didn't have long to live, but you were so angry at me for lying to you. I couldn't blame you. I had to see you, talk to you face-to-face, and make you understand. When I got here, the paramedic van was already at your front door. I followed it to the hospital and found you in a coma. I was so torn. I felt terrible for leaving Leo alone, especially after I'd promised to stay with the two of them, but what could I do?"

Jane had no idea what had been going on behind the scenes that night. "Why couldn't you just tell me the truth?"

Julia shook her head. "I wanted to, but by then, there were so many lies, I didn't know where to start." She paused. "Remember the time I told you my uncle had died—"

"And I found out you'd been in Jamaica with Leo?"

"I was there with Leo, but also with his lover. He'd had a bad spell, and I'd flown down to care for him while he recovered. The whole reason I came to Minnesota and set up my practice in a small town was so I could work with these well-known men in the privacy of my home. Leo encouraged me all along the way. He told me I was performing a vital service. I believed I was. I'm a doctor, Jane, trained to help people, not to judge them. These men were all so frightened and desperate. At first they were mainly politicos—people Leo knew. Mostly decent guys, caught in the trap society laid for them. Occasionally, they were men whose faces would be recognized by a reasonably large section of the general public."

"They were all in the closet?"

"About their sexuality?" She nodded. "As my reputation became better known in certain discreet circles, others came to me. Actors. Religious figures. TV personalities. More politicians. At first, I just wanted to help, but the money was so good. I started to get drawn into some very uncomfortable situations."

"But, Julia, I would have understood. I wouldn't have interfered with your patient-client confidentiality. If you'd told me what you were doing, and not lied to me—or told me all those confusing half-truths—we might have had a chance."

Julia closed her eyes. "Maybe. But I'm not so sure. It certainly wouldn't have been the case if you'd known who some of these men were."

Jane didn't much like the sound of that. "What do you mean?"

Julia reflected a moment, then looked up. "A few of my patients were actually denouncing the gay community—loudly, actively. At the same time, they were sleeping with men—mostly male prostitutes. They were incredible hypocrites, Jane. And when they got in trouble, they came to me. I was supposed to keep their secret, minister to their crumbling bodies, and then ignore what they said and did publicly. I mean, I'd watch one of them on *Larry King*, or read about what another one had said in a newspaper or magazine, and I'd get sick inside."

"And yet you kept doing it."

"That's right, I did. These men trusted me—and paid me exceedingly well for my services and my silence. The longer I did it, the more patients I took on, the harder I could see it would be to get out. Not that I wanted to. I thought I'd found my medical niche. Some of these men are very powerful, Jane. Some were quite fascinating. Having a handsome Hollywood star sitting in your living room is heady stuff. The deal was, I was going to be their doctor. Period. They might come to me, or I'd go to them, but there were no provisions for my change of heart."

Julia fell silent. When she finally spoke again, her voice sounded less certain. "And then I met you. For a long time, I didn't see my work as a problem. Talk about magical thinking, right? I knew I was falling in love with you, but I figured I could handle it—even after I moved to Minnesota. But then everything began to go wrong. I couldn't talk to you about my life. And somehow, I found myself losing you. It was my worst nightmare. I could see it happening, but I couldn't stop it. That's when I knew I had to get out."

Jane's mouth felt dry; her heart was hammering. "So you informed your clients that you were closing down your practice." She nodded.

"And some of them got upset."

"Yes. You heard the phone calls. For the past eight days, I've been flying all over the country, talking to each one of them personally. I figured I owed them that much."

"And what about your files?"

"What about them?"

"You've got information that could destroy careers. Ruin lives."

She nodded. "That was one of their main concerns. It's why I had to see everyone in person. I've never been anything but the soul of dedication and discretion, Jane. They all know that. Still, they were understandably worried. It was my job to put those worries to rest. Not that it's been easy. I'm tired, Jane. More tired than I've ever been in my entire life. Some of these men have become my friends. It was . . . hard for me to let go."

For the first time tonight, Jane actually looked at the woman sitting across from her, and she was shocked by what she saw. Julia was normally such a self-possessed woman. Confident. Professionally polished. She had a fresh-faced, girl-next-door kind of beauty that even her long hours at the hospital couldn't dim. Yet at this moment, she appeared physically ragged, her clothes wrinkled, dark circles under her eyes. She *looked* like a woman who'd spent the last eight days on airplanes, living out of a suitcase, putting out fires wherever she found them. Jane hated herself for it, but she had an overpowering urge to take Julia in her arms and tell her everything would be okay, even though she felt no confidence in the sentiment herself. Instead, she fought to keep her emotions under control.

"In every way possible," continued Julia, leaning back in her chair, "I've put out the word that their secrets are safe. I've tried to set them up with other . . . discreet . . . doctors. For the most part, I believe I've succeeded."

"Even the sleazebags—the ones who are out there stirring up people's hatred?"

"Even them. As of this morning, I've talked to them all, tried to calm their fears. Generally, I believe I succeeded."

"You never told me where your files were."

"And I don't intend to. They're safe, Jane. That's all I can say. There's only one person I'm still worried about."

"The man who broke into your house and your loft."

"Exactly. The man searching for those files. He threatens everything I've worked for."

"Do you know who he is?"

Wearily, she shook her head. "But I do have a theory."

So do I, thought Jane. "Let's hear it."

"Well, I may be wrong, but I think he could be the same man who was blackmailing Jeffrey Chapel. You see, when Jeffrey first came to see me, he wasn't being blackmailed. That happened later. I'm not positive, but I think he may have told his future blackmailer about me, although I cautioned him not to give out my name or address. If I'm right, the blackmailer must have ferreted out the rest of the information on his own—and that makes me nervous. I don't like to think I'm that easy to find."

Jane thought of Chapel's missing briefcase with his daily planner inside—and also the appointment calendars in his offices, the kind of thing one might scratch a name and address on. Did that mean Andrew Dove really *was* behind everything? The police had proof positive that he'd taken the calendars. The daily planner hadn't been found yet, but it was probably only a matter of time. Then again, Jane thought she'd discovered another reason for Dove's interest in them, but perhaps she was wrong.

"Jeffrey told me that the man who was blackmailing him had done it many times before—always for the money. Jeffrey trusted the guy completely and couldn't believe it when it happened. Seems this blackmailer preyed on wealthy—or at least, well-off—closeted gay men. Somehow or other, he'd get proof that the guy was gay, and then bleed him for as long as he could. Jeffrey was really angry and also, I suspect, deeply hurt. I got the impression he cared about this person."

"And you think the blackmailer put it all together. He knew Jeffrey was seeing a doctor who specialized in helping rich, closeted HIV positive gay men. Men who, for a multitude of reasons, couldn't or wouldn't come out. And if he could just get his hands on your files, he'd have a gold mine at his fingertips."

"Exactly. Which is one reason I wanted to stay away from the Twin Cities. If he finds me, I don't think he'd hesitate to threaten my life to get what he wants. Unlike my patients, he's got nothing to lose. That's why I'm in danger every second I stay in this town."

For the first time, Jane realized the risk Julia was taking by coming back to talk to her. She felt her angry resolve starting to melt. "Do you think this blackmailer killed Chapel?"

"I'm sure of it. Jeffrey's plan was to turn him over to the police. During his last visit to my home, he said he didn't care what the man had on him anymore. He was done paying—and done hiding. The problem was, if he was dumb enough to tell the blackmailer the truth at the hotel that night, the guy probably jumped him. He had to get rid of Jeffrey to save his own life—and protect his illegal and highly profitable livelihood. By then, I'm sure the blackmailer had concluded that he had a pretty good shot at getting his hands on my files. Once he had them in his possession, he was set for the rest of his life. He could easily be a multimillionaire in a matter of weeks."

It all made perfect sense to Jane. The only question was, which man had committed the murder?

Julia pushed her chair back and stood. Walking around to the front of the desk, she sat down in a chair next to Jane. "So, now that you know the whole story, is there any way you can forgive me? I still care about you, Janey. I still want to be with you."

"You expect an answer tonight?"

"I was hoping for one. I've turned my whole life upside down just to prove how much I love you. But you've got to meet me halfway."

Jane could feel the old anger rising in her chest. It was just like Julia to think that because she'd offered a plausible explanation, Jane should forget everything and go on as if nothing had happened. All right, so maybe this time Julia knew it wasn't possible, but it seemed to Jane that she was still ringing her old bell and Jane was supposed to salivate on command. It wasn't going to be that easy. "Don't you see, Julia? The problem isn't that I disapprove of what you've done professionally. The real problem is, you never *once* trusted me enough to tell me the truth. If you had, we wouldn't have had this 'year of lies.'"

"You mean, you wouldn't have been upset about what I did for a living?"

"Of course, I might have been upset. Not about treating men who were in the closet. That's their choice. But if someone's closeted and at the same time actively speaking out against the gay community, fostering hate, I can't imagine anyone who wouldn't draw the line there. But Julia, we could have talked about it. There might have been a different way to handle all this. How can you ask me to trust you if you won't trust *me*? What are we supposed to base this great relationship of ours *on*? Do you think I'm so supercritical that I'd sit in judgment of you—that I'd condemn you without even trying to understand?"

Julia took hold of Jane's hand. "I don't know what I thought. I was just so afraid of losing you. I guess I felt you'd be repelled by what I've done. I know you respected my professional commitment. How could I tell you I was involved in something I knew was . . . at least partly loathsome? You'd think I'd sold out for the money."

"Did you?" Jane could see Julia was hurt by the question.

Julia withdrew her hand, suddenly out of patience. "All right. Are you happy? You hit a nerve. If I say it wasn't important, you'd know better."

"So where does that leave us? You obviously don't trust me. You think of me as hypercritical. Leo thinks I've ruined your life by forcing you to do something reckless and stupid. Maybe I'm wrong, but I'll bet part of you agrees with him."

"That's not true!"

"You better think about this a little more, Julia. I know I've got some thinking to do."

"Does that mean we might still have a chance?" Her expression grew eager. "Listen to me for a minute, Jane. I may have the perfect solution." She got up and grabbed her folder off the desk. Sitting back down, she opened it and drew out some airline tickets.

"What are those for?"

253

"Us." She handed one to Jane. "I want to get out of the country for a while—until things cool down here. And I want you to come with me."

Jane glanced at the ticket, looking for the destination. "Paris?"

"For a month. You need time to get your health back. We need time to work out our problems. This is a perfect chance for us, sweetheart. Have you ever been to Paris?"

Jane shook her head.

"Then I'll get to show it to you for the first time. It's so beautiful, especially at night. It hasn't exactly been *Splendor in the Grass* for us so far in our relationship, but this could be the start. All you have to do is meet me at Twin Cities International next Friday afternoon. I'll be waiting for you."

"And if I don't come?"

"I'm not even going to think about that. I'm just going to believe you'll be there."

"Julia, tell me something. If I'm so awful, so unworthy of your trust, why do you even care about me?"

"That's not how I feel. I know the kind of person you are. You're loyal, compassionate, and generous."

"You make me sound like a Saint Bernard."

"That's not what I meant! You've never been anything but patient and loving with me. But like anyone else, you've got principles you hold dear. I stepped all over some of them. I'm not blaming you for anything. I take full responsibility for what's gone wrong. To be honest, you put up with me far longer than I would ever have put up with you, if our situations had been reversed. That's because you really believed in us. You've taught me a lot, Jane, mainly about love and commitment. I still think we can find our way back to each other. You say you've got some thinking to do. Will you think about *that?*"

Forcing her voice to sound steady, she said, "I'll try."

"Good." Julia allowed herself a small smile. "That's good. I'll think too. And I'll see you on board that plane next Friday."

Jane felt as if she were being offered a carrot—an extremely appealing one, but a carrot nonetheless. She didn't much care for bribes. "So . . . when you leave here, where are you going?"

"I don't know. Probably a hotel for the night. Then back to D.C. for a few days."

"Back to Leo." Jane could hear the bitterness in her voice, and she knew it hurt Julia, but she couldn't stop herself.

"It's not like that, Jane. Leo and I are two different people. We don't always agree. When he told me what he said to you on the phone, I was furious."

"So was I," said Jane. "You can tell him from me that I think he's a horse's ass."

Julia's smile brightened. "It will be my pleasure."

"How will I get in touch with you?"

She hesitated. "I'll call."

By now, Jane's cynical reaction to Julia's standard reply was involuntary. "Right. You'll call."

"Jane, don't get mad. If you know where I'm staying, the blackmailer could get to you. I'd be surprised if he didn't know about our relationship. We never kept it a secret. He could force you to tell him what you know. Surely you understand why I can't allow that to happen. It would only put your life in greater danger."

"I'm so *sick* of this, Julia."

"I know you are, sweetheart. So am I."

"If that guy isn't found soon—"

"He will be."

"By the police? Unless it's Andrew Dove, I wouldn't bet the farm. And if it is Dove, he made bail yesterday and was released."

"That's not good."

"No, it's not. You know, Julia, you could help the police a lot if you'd talk to them."

"I can't. Surely you understand why. Something will work out. We just have to trust that it will. In the meantime, you've got to stay out of it. For both our sakes."

At this moment, Jane felt no particular compunction about lying to Julia. There was a certain symmetry in it that appealed to her. Or maybe it was just the brandy. Whatever the case, she didn't much care. "Sure. I'll be good."

"Are you telling me the truth?"

"Why would I lie?"

Jane walked Julia into the hallway. "I'll have to let you out; otherwise, the alarm will go off."

When they reached the back door, Julia put her hand on Jane's face and bent to kiss her.

Standing this close, Jane could smell the faint scent of the shampoo

Julia always used. For a moment, it made her ache for what they'd once had.

"Stay safe," whispered Julia, her lips brushing Jane's hair. "Stick close to the restaurant, and don't take any chances."

They held each other for a long moment, and then Julia left.

Chapter 33

Julia pulled her rented Lincoln out of the restaurant's parking lot and headed south along Penn Avenue toward Fiftieth. She wasn't sure where she'd stay for the night, but decided that something along the 494 strip, out near the airport, made the most sense. Opening the driver's side window for a moment to let a little fresh air into the car, she realized she'd put up a good front, but deep down, she had no confidence that Jane would join her on that plane to Paris. She'd screwed her life up royally and taken Jane along for the ride. When she got back to D.C. tomorrow, to the safety of Leo's apartment, she would sleep for days. With or without Jane, she felt the need to get out of the country. But just maybe, once Jane had given it some thought, she'd give Julia one last chance to set things right.

Jane had no perspective right now. Julia didn't either, but she did know one thing for sure: Jane wasn't well. She wasn't taking care of herself. Not that Julia was in any position to stick around and help her negotiate the local medical system. Jane should be in therapy—both the physical kind and the psychological kind—but true to form, she was trying to handle it all on her own.

The fact was, even though she was a strong, intelligent woman, someone with a great deal of personal integrity as well as her own brand of stubborn charm, Jane was also a deeply lonely person. It had taken Julia quite a while to figure that one out. Jane didn't talk much about her past, but the death of her mother at such a young age was a highly formative event. So was the death of her partner, Christine, after a solid ten-year relationship. Jane's past was dotted with significant people who'd disappeared, and no matter how hard she tried to escape it, loss—or perhaps more correctly, the *fear* of loss—had formed a great part of who she was. Whatever she did to fill up her life, whether it was the creation of a restaurant or the problems she occasionally helped her friends or acquaintances solve, it never quite satisfied some fundamental need. She'd put herself in dangerous positions before, but none had created the physical and emotional havoc that this recent head injury had. That, coupled with her other unresolved issues, made her a sitting duck for future problems.

The drinking Jane had been doing recently—and even before the attack—worried Julia a great deal. Cordelia had talked to Julia about it at some length, explaining how Jane had abused alcohol for a short time after Christine's death. Sure, she'd managed somehow to get back on track, but Cordelia was afraid that the tendency to abuse alcohol was still there, waiting just under the surface. It might be a quick way to anesthetize pain, thought Julia, but it was also a black hole waiting to suck her into a universe of darkness. She'd seen her own father fall into that bottomless pit, and she couldn't stand the thought that Jane might suffer the same fate. That's why she wanted Jane to come to Paris. Jane was always there for everyone in her life; now she had to let someone be there for her. Cordelia had helped her through the worst times after Christine's death, but Julia desperately wanted to be the person to help her now. The irony was, even though Julia had nothing to do with the attack, her crazy life was the cause of much of Jane's current stress. How could she "be there" for Jane when she was part of the problem?

As she continued to mull it all over, she glanced in the rearview mirror and saw what looked like the same dark minivan that had followed her around town last Sunday night—the night she was supposed to meet Jane at her loft. She came to a stop at Lyndale, then turned north, watching to see if it would follow.

Her pulse quickened as she realized it had.

All right, she told herself. It could be just a coincidence. There must be lots of dark minivans in the Twin Cities. Sailing along Lyndale for a mile or so, she turned finally onto West Thirty-sixth, driving down the hill toward Lake Calhoun. The minivan kept a respectable distance, but it was still there.

Now she was growing frightened.

What she feared most was getting caught by the blackmailer before she could slip out of town. She had to lose him—that was a given. But how? The streets were slippery from the drizzle and the light snow. Sudden turns could cause her to end up in a ditch or send her headfirst into a tree. The car was unfamiliar to her, but surely it was equipped with snow tires—or good all-season radials. Whatever the case, she was about to find out.

As Julia sped along Calhoun Boulevard, she made a sudden left onto Sheridan. Since it was late, there weren't many cars around. She skidded to the side, nearly hitting a parked Honda, but righted the Lincoln and kept on going. Checking her rearview mirror again, she saw that the minivan was still following.

Pressing the pedal to the metal, she fishtailed into an alley, then burst out onto a cross street where she turned left again, and then right into another alley. Looking for a deserted driveway, she slowed the car, finally easing up to a garage. Cutting the motor and the lights, she waited. She realized she was mere blocks from Jane's house now. If she could just make it there without being followed, she'd be safe. Since she had a key, she could spend the night and be gone in the morning without anyone being the wiser.

But for now, she had to sit tight and hope she'd given the minivan the slip.

Half an hour later, after seeing no one but a white-haired man walking a small dog, she turned the key in the ignition and eased the car back out onto one of the cross streets. She looked both ways, but everything seemed to be quiet.

Turning left, Julia made the three blocks to Jane's house in record time. She parked on a side street half a block away, just in case the blackmailer was still cruising the neighborhood looking for her car.

Carrying her purse and her briefcase, she moved cautiously down the alley and entered through the side gate. The house was completely dark, though the security light came on as she approached the screened porch. It felt spooky being here all alone, but as long as the heat was still on inside, she'd be fine.

Fitting the key into the lock, she pushed the door open, then stood on the back porch and peered into the darkness. The air coming from the kitchen smelled so familiar—a mixture of spices and drying summer herbs. She was about to switch on the light when she heard a noise behind her. Glancing around, she ducked as a man in a ski mask charged straight at her. She tried to dodge around him, but his right shoulder caught her in the stomach, sending her sprawling backward onto the kitchen floor. She let out a piercing scream, but stopped when she saw him pull a gun.

"Shut up," he growled.

Entering the kitchen, he switched on a small light over the stove, then shut and locked the back door.

"What do you want?" Julia demanded, her voice trembling.

"You, Doctor. Weren't you expecting me?" He stood over her, holding the gun almost casually. "I've found the witch—the hunt's over."

"You're . . . not making any sense."

"Sure I am. Witches were burned at the stake, right? Maybe I should look around for some nice, dry wood." He cocked the gun. "But first, we've got to have a little heart-to-heart."

Chapter 34

SUNDAY MORNING

Joe picked Brenna up at her condo shortly after ten. It was a dark, blustery, morning, and Brenna wasn't up for such a wintry day. She would much rather have stayed in bed or sat in front of a roaring fire with a cup of cocoa. But since she'd promised to have brunch with Joe, and she didn't like to break her promises, she'd put on her warmest sweater and wool slacks and prepared to brave the cold.

Ever since his phone call yesterday, she'd been wondering what he had to give her now. He'd already made her husband's briefcase materialize out of thin air, a fact that still concerned her. She'd passed it on to the police the next morning. Later that day, she'd heard from Sgt. Duvik that they'd questioned Joe about it at length. Duvik didn't really know what to make of his story. So far, the police had no way to disprove it, although Duvik was skeptical. As much as she'd grown to like Joe in the last few days, she was skeptical too.

"I made reservations at the Fountain Grill," said Joe, pulling off 1-94 onto the Fifth Avenue ramp. "Thought the art deco atmosphere might be fun."

"The Maxfield Plaza," said Brenna, her expression brightening. "I haven't been there in ages."

"My wife and I were married in the hotel's atrium—ten years ago tomorrow."

She glanced over at him. She was pretty sure he knew she was watching him, but he just stared straight ahead, making no show of emotion. "How is everything on that front?"

"I was served with divorce papers yesterday."

"I'm sorry, Joe. Really. That must be tough."

"Yeah. It is. But maybe it's for the best. At least our kids won't be in the middle of a war zone anymore."

Brenna sensed that he didn't want to talk about it, so she let the subject drop.

A block from the hotel, he pulled his Grand Cherokee over to the curb and shifted the engine into neutral.

"Why are we stopping?" she asked, glancing up at the St. Paul Cathedral on the hill.

"Remember? I have something I want to give you, but I don't want to do it in the restaurant. This is private. Just between you and me."

The muscles along her jawbone tightened. "All right."

He removed a white business envelope from the glove compartment and handed it to her. "Jeff gave this to me about a week before he died."

Hesitating, she took it, then turned it over. "It's sealed."

He nodded. "He said that if anything ever happened to him, I should take it to the police."

She sobered suddenly, her eyes narrowing. "Why did he give it to *you?*"

"I assume because he trusted me."

"But—" Her tone grew indignant. "He trusted you more than he trusted his wife?"

"I can't explain it, Brenna. I don't think you should be hurt."

But she was. "So why are you giving it to me now?"

"Because I don't want anything more to do with the police."

"But if you don't even know what's inside—"

He looked away.

He *did* know. The truth was written all over his face. He'd probably opened the letter, and then put it into another envelope. Or maybe

262

he'd steamed it open. In a way, she didn't blame him. Given the same set of circumstances, she might have done the same thing.

"You can do whatever you want with it. Just don't tell anyone where you got it."

Ripping it open, she drew out a single sheet of typing paper. On it were a bunch of names written in her husband's hand. "Who are these people?" she demanded, showing it to him. Every name but one was a man.

Joe shrugged. "No clue."

"You never heard of *any* of them before?"

"Nope. What about you?"

She read down the list. "I draw a complete blank."

"Are you going to give it to the police then?"

"I don't know."

"It's got to be important."

She folded the paper back up and returned it to the envelope. "Tell me exactly what my husband said when he gave it to you."

Joe leaned his head back and thought for a moment. "Well, it was after one of our racquetball games. We'd showered and dressed, but before we left the locker room, Jeff stopped me. He said something like, 'I've got this envelope I want to give you. Put it away. If anything ever happens to me, take it to the police.'" Again, he shrugged. "That was it."

"You didn't ask him what it was all about? Why he was giving it to you? I mean, did he seem frightened?"

"No. Not a bit. You know Jeff. He could be kind of cocky sometimes. He was grinning when he gave it to me. Said I'd probably never need to use it, but that he'd just feel better if someone else had a copy. I must have looked confused because he added that I didn't need to know anything more. As a matter of fact, it was better if I didn't. We left it at that."

Brenna nodded, trying to make sense of it. "Maybe it has something to do with his murder."

"I thought of that. It's possible."

"Then, why didn't you take it to the police right away?"

"I couldn't! If people knew we'd been buddies, they might think—" He left the sentence unfinished.

"Think what? That you're gay?"

"Exactly."

"But . . . Joe . . . Jeff's secret didn't come out until a few days ago. How could you possibly have known he was gay . . unless—"

Again, he turned his head away. After a long pause, he said, "I saw him with a guy once, Brenna. They weren't doing anything, but I just knew. I don't know how I did, but I did. I figured it might come out sooner or later, so when Jeff was murdered, I knew I had to distance myself from him."

"But . . . why?"

"Don't you get it?" he said, slamming his fist hard against the steering wheel. "I'm hanging onto my pro career by my fingernails. I'm getting old. Maybe too old to last another year. If word gets around that I'm a closet case, do you think I'd get any endorsements? How do you think a major network would feel about hiring a gay commentator? I'd be toast, Brenna. My whole future is up for grabs, and it could all be wiped out by something as stupid as innuendo. It's bad enough that the police asked me a whole bunch of personal questions yesterday—stuff about my sexuality. How the hell do you prove you *aren't* something? I mean, shit, I'm married. That should count for something." When he looked at Brenna, he winced. "Jeez, I'm sorry."

"It's okay. I know what you mean."

"I swear to you. Jeff and I were just friends."

The vehemence of his denial felt like an overreaction, but then Brenna wasn't in his shoes. He knew pro football; she didn't. If he wasn't a macho jock with pristine heterosexual credentials, then he was probably right: nobody connected to the game would touch him.

"I mean, do the cops want a list of the women I've slept with? I really don't want to come clean about that—especially now when my wife is looking for ammunition for the divorce hearing. This couldn't have come at a worse time." He wiped the back of his hand across his forehead. "Look at me. It's freezing cold outside, and I'm sweating." Glancing over at Brenna, his frustration turned instantly to concern. "God, I'm sorry. Your husband just died, and here I am spouting off that it's bad timing for *me*."

"I imagine Jeffrey thought it was bad timing for him, too."

They looked at each other. After a moment, they both almost smiled.

"I think that's what's known as black humor," said Joe. He squeezed her gloved hand. "I like you, Brenna. I don't mean to take my troubles out on you."

"You're not. It's just . . . we're both at an all-time low point in our lives. It's kind of hard to ignore."

"Yeah." He turned his attention to the parked car in front of them. "Look, let's make a deal. No more talk about our problems while we're having brunch. Think we can do it?"

"I'll give it my best shot."

Pulling the Jeep back into traffic, they continued on toward the Maxfield.

Chapter 35

In her entire life, Julia had never been so scared. She'd been tied up for hours, her mouth and eyes taped shut, cotton balls stuffed in her ears. She was totally cut off, with no real idea how much time had passed. More than once, her panic had been so intense that she'd nearly passed out from hyperventilation. She tried to control her breathing, counting breaths to calm down. She remembered the exercises she'd given her patients with panic and anxiety, but found that it was much easier said than done. If she ever got out of here, she'd be more sympathetic in the future.

Her captor had dragged her upstairs to Jane's third-floor apartment, the one she usually rented out. No one was living there now. He'd interrogated for what seemed like an eternity, demanding to know where she kept her files. When he realized he couldn't scare the information out of her, he'd beaten her with the butt of his gun. She could still feel the deep bruises on her shoulders and face. Only when she'd remembered a disk in her purse, telling him it was the list he was after, had he finally left her alone. He promised he'd be back once he'd looked at the contents. It was a threat, of course. He didn't trust her any more than she trusted him.

As she lay immobilized on the bare mattress, she couldn't imagine how she ended up this way. She'd been so careful last night—she was sure he was nowhere around. The only conclusion she could come to was that since they were in Jane's neighborhood and he probably knew about their relationship, he'd taken a chance on where she was headed. When she walked up to the back porch, he'd been waiting for her. But that meant he knew where Jane lived, and if that was the case, it wasn't a stretch to think he'd been following Jane too.

Feeling a fresh rush of panic, she struggled even harder against her bonds. Since no one knew where she was, nobody was going to crash heroically through the door to save her. Jane assumed she was winging her way back to D.C. Leo might worry, but he probably wouldn't call right away. It could be days before anyone realized she'd disappeared. It was a bitter truth, but she was alone. If she was going to get out of this alive, she only had herself to rely on.

Straining with all her might to break free of the strapping tape, she realized it was no use. The tape might as well have been iron chains.

The man in the ski mask had promised that if she gave him the information he wanted, he'd let her go. Maybe he would, but how could she betray so many confidences? Her only hope was to keep him talking, maybe send him on another wild-goose chase. Given a little more time, she might be able to figure out a way to free herself.

Feeling a sudden pressure against her shoulder, she froze, then tried to squirm away.

He was back.

A moment later, the tape was ripped off her mouth, and the cotton balls pulled from her ears.

"Very funny," he sneered.

She could feel him sit down on the bed next to her.

"I suppose you thought that was amusing—sending me home with downloads from a medical journal. Do you really think I'm interested in reading about gallbladders?"

His breath stunk of garlic and alcohol. He must have just eaten. "I . . . I guess I gave you the wrong disk. It was a mistake."

"Sure it was." He slapped her hard across the face.

"Please!" she pleaded, twisting her head away from the blow. "Think about what you're doing. You don't really want to hurt me."

He moved off the bed. "Just shut up."

She could hear him walking around. "At least . . . take the tape off my eyes so I can see."

The room fell silent.

Feeling the heat of his body near her again, the tape was ripped off her eyes. She struggled to focus in the bright light, realizing he was still wearing the ski mask, the heavy overcoat, and gloves. Tentatively, she asked, "Could I . . . have some water?"

"God, you want everything."

"Just some water." Her thirst was immense.

Strutting over to the small kitchenette, he took a glass from the cupboard and filled it from the tap. Returning to the bed, he set it on the nightstand, and then pulled her up against the back of the bedstead.

As he held the glass to her lips, she drank in big, noisy gulps. It was the sweetest liquid she'd ever tasted. "Thanks," she said after she'd emptied the glass.

He pulled a chair over to the bed and sat down. "What am I going to do with you?"

She didn't respond.

"Say, who's house is this again?"

Was he playing with her? "You know who owns it."

"Oh, yeah. Right. Your lover. Say her name, Doctor."

"Why?"

"Just say it!"

She hesitated. "Jane."

"Again."

"Jane!"

He smiled. "Is your real name Julia? Or is it Julianna, Julie—whatever."

"No, it's Julia." If he wanted to talk and not yell at her, she might as well cooperate. Besides, it might buy her some time.

"I thought I'd lost you last night," he continued, scratching his chest through his coat. "I figured you might suspect I was here, waiting for you."

"I didn't."

"Lucky for me. Where were you headed before you made the detour here? The airport?"

"To a motel. I was planning to leave town tomorrow."

"You mean today?"

Her eyes shifted to the windows. It was light outside. "Yes. Today."

"And I messed up your plans. Too bad. Well," he said, slapping his knees, "I guess we're going to be here for a while. By the way, that's the last drink of anything you're going to get from me. And don't expect any food."

She glared.

"I don't suppose you want to tell me where your files are? It could save us both a lot of trouble."

She looked away.

"Stubbornness is a dangerous trait. But I'm in a good mood this morning. I've just had a delicious breakfast. And I've got a foolproof plan."

Her head whipped around. "You think you can starve me into telling you what you want to know?"

"It's a thought."

Since she assumed she had nothing to lose, she said, "You killed Chapel, right?"

He shrugged. "If I did, it makes it even more likely that I might do the same to you."

Fear rippled through her body. "Who *are* you?"

He smiled. In a low voice, he responded, "I'm your worst nightmare, Julia. You have no idea the kind of pain I intend to cause you."

She felt herself begin to shiver. "I'm a doctor, for god's sake. I take my responsibility to my patients very seriously. I *can't* tell you what you want to know. Surely we can work out some kind of. . . deal."

"Like what?"

She had to think fast. "I've got lots of money. You can have it all. Everything. My property. My cars. My jewelry."

"It's not enough."

"I could get you more. I have friends."

"That's the point, Doctor. Your *friends*. We'll see how long you cling to your professional ethics, especially since we both know you're as corrupt as I am."

"That's not true! I was trying to help those men."

"For money." He lifted his feet up on the mattress. "The way I see it, once I have the names and medical information on the poor saps you've been treating, I'll be on easy street for the rest of my life. You could be too if you'd care to join me."

She turned her head away.

"Whatever, Doctor. You've still got time to change your mind."

He had this all thought out. "Are you gay?" she asked, still not looking at him.

"What's the difference?"

"It makes a difference to me."

He didn't respond for almost a minute. Finally, he said, "All right. Sure, I'm gay. That's how I find out who these men are. Once I do, I watch them. Get the goods on them, so to speak. Occasionally, I even get involved myself."

"And then comes the blackmail. God, that's so incredibly loathsome."

He jumped up, slapping her hard across the face. "You don't know me, Doctor. You don't know what I've been through—what I need. You think you're so morally superior. Well, you're not!"

She had to be careful. She didn't want to provoke another beating like last night's.

"You know, Julia, sometimes I think, when I finally get my hands on your records, that instead of blackmail, I'll go straight to the press and announce—anonymously of course—that I have the goods on a bunch of famous closet cases. I mean, just think about it. It would start a witch-hunt the likes of which we haven't seen in this country since the McCarthy days. The whole fucking nation would be scrambling to find the fairies in the woodpile—pardon the racist analogy."

He was laughing at her—at the whole world for that matter.

"Do you really hate gay people that much?" she asked.

"Hate gays? No. But I don't much care for hypocrites. In some circles, lady, if I outed your dirtbag patients, I'd be deified."

"You're a sick man."

"Mainly, I'm just greedy. So sue me." He laughed at his little joke.

She closed her eyes.

"Look, we aren't going to get anywhere arguing personal philosophies. And anyway, I've got something I want you to do for me. It will help pass the time."

"Until what?"

"You'll find out soon enough." Finding a serrated knife in one of the kitchen drawers, he cut the strapping tape off her hands. Then he took a book out of a paper sack he'd placed next to the bed and handed it to her. "Read to me, Julia. I'm just a kid at heart."

Was he insane?

"It's not a ploy. I've always loved being read to. Start with chapter one." He folded his arms over his chest and leaned back in his chair.

Julia glanced down at the thin volume. "This is nuts."

"It's not nice to insult your captor, Doctor. Come on, read." This time, his voice sounded more menacing.

She decided she had no choice but to play along. Positioning the book in front of her, she began, "Sally and Puff played in the rain. 'Look, Puff,' called Sally. 'I see Spot.'" She put the book down. "This is ridiculous."

"Read!"

"All right!" She cleared her throat, took a deep breath, and began again.

Chapter 36

Jane's Sunday morning was a rocky one. A wrong number woke her shortly after eight. Her "Minnesota Nice" gene wasn't operational on so little sleep, so she ended up shouting at the guy, telling him he was a self-consumed moron—or words to that effect. And as soon as her brain engaged—and she began thinking about Julia—it was all over. She knew she would never get back to sleep. She had a splitting headache from too much brandy, but she'd had a headache for so many weeks now that it just felt like more of same. After showering and dressing, and downing several aspirin, she went upstairs to see about some breakfast.

Continuing the cheerful morning cycle, she was met at the dining-room doors by an irate customer, furious that his brunch reservation hadn't been recorded. After taking care of that minor catastrophe, more problems descended. One thing led to another, and she was eventually trapped in the kitchen where she spent the next three hours dealing with various menu crises. Somehow during that time, she managed to wolf down a sandwich and a Sprite, but they seemed to just sit in her stomach, undigested. By two, she was exhausted, but too wired to go back to her office and lie down. That's when she received the SOS from Eddie Flynn. Standing by the reception desk in the lobby, she took the call.

"Jane, hi. Listen, I've got a favor to ask. You're planning to have dinner at Patricia's house tonight, right?"

She'd completely forgotten about it. "Yes, I was . . . I mean, I am."

"I know she wanted to go over those blueprints."

Jane had to switch gears. He was referring to the Winter Garden. "Yes, I've got them downstairs in my office."

"Great. So, here's the deal. I've been working on some new ideas since we last talked. I'd really like the two of you to look them over tonight. Only thing is, I'm expecting someone—you know, someone *special*—for dinner. As we speak, I'm up to my elbows in chicken stock and artichokes. I was wondering if you could stop by my place and pick up the newest set of drawings. See, the good part is, Patricia may have found another financial backer. It's not set in stone yet, but if it all works out, we've got to really move on these architectural changes." He paused. "What do you say? Could you come by?"

"Well . . . sure, I suppose." The idea of getting away from the restaurant just then really appealed to her.

"You're a lifesaver, Jane. Thanks. You've got the address?" As he repeated it, she copied it down on a piece of scratch paper.

"I'll see you soon, then?"

"In about an hour."

"Great. Bye."

Before leaving the restaurant, Jane phoned Cordelia. She thought perhaps she'd stop by her loft after she'd met with Eddie. She wanted to fill her in on everything Julia had said last night, maybe get a little advice—which Cordelia was always more than willing to give. When the answering machine picked up, Jane remembered that Cordelia was scheduled to be at the theatre all afternoon. That effectively nixed any thought of getting together.

By three, Jane was in St. Paul, heading east on Grand Avenue toward Eddie's row house. The afternoon was cold but clear, and the sky such an intense winter blue, it almost hurt her eyes. Since she was less than a mile from her childhood home, her thoughts turned briefly to her father and Marilyn. She wondered if they were back yet from their whirlwind trip to Hawaii. If she had to guess, she'd say that Brenna Chapel and her father were camped out on her dad's doorstep, waiting to pounce as soon as he got out of the cab. She probably hadn't done him any favors by getting him involved in the Chapel homicide. Not that there was much she could do about it now.

After finding a parking place on the street, she walked up the steep steps to Eddie's front door. She was using her cane again today. Last night's visit to the Winter Garden hadn't done her leg any good.

Eddie must have seen her coming because, before she could even ring the bell, the door opened. "Come in," he said, wiping his hands on a kitchen towel. He was wearing a chef's apron that said, "I'm beautiful *and* I can cook."

"Thanks," she said, moving inside. Even though the red brick exterior had seen better days, the interior was nothing short of turn-of-the-century elegance. Floral wallpaper. Tin ceilings. Gilt-edged oil paintings hanging on the walls. "You've got a real flair for interior design."

"Yeah, it's hard, gritty work, but somebody's gotta do it." He grinned. "Actually, it's taken me four years to get this place to look just right. Come on," he said, motioning for her to follow him up the stairs. "My study's on the second level. That's where I've got the plans I want to send back with you."

"From outside, the row house looks like it has three floors," commented Jane, taking the stairs a bit more slowly. She could smell something wonderful baking in the oven.

"Yeah. The third floor is a guest bedroom and a den. The master bedroom and my study are on the second. You can look around if you like. It might take me a minute to locate those drawings. I'm not the most organized person in the world."

Glancing into the bedroom, she saw an antique sleigh bed, the same one she'd first seen in the blackmail photos he'd shown her a few days ago. Along the far wall were three large windows facing the back of the house.

"I found it," called Eddie.

Jane took one last look at the bedroom, then turned and walked across the hall to the study. She found Eddie sitting behind a large drafting table. In that short time, his upbeat mood seemed to have withered.

"Something wrong?" she asked.

He crumpled up a piece of paper and tossed it in the trash. "Just more of the same."

"You seem upset."

"If I were you, Jane, I'd just take these floor plans and go."

But she couldn't. She was too curious. "What's happened?"

Eddie sighed, dropped the drawings on the table, and then leaned back in his chair and looked out the window. "If you really wanna know, it's our buddy, the friendly Haymaker Club blackmailer. I was supposed to pay him off last night, but I couldn't raise all the cash. I left three thousand dollars and a note that said I'd try to get the rest to him as soon as possible. I mean, as my good old dad used to say, you can't squeeze blood out of a turnip."

"And? Have you heard from him?"

"This morning." He nodded to the wastebasket. "I mean . . . maybe I'm wrong, but he's really getting testy—like somebody stepped on his forked tail or something."

"Can you be more specific?"

"Bottom line? If I don't get the money to him by Tuesday night, a letter and photos will be sent to my boss."

Jane had a feeling there was something more—something he wasn't telling her. "Is that it?"

"Isn't that enough? How the hell am I supposed to get my hands on twenty-two thousand dollars in two days?" He bit his lower lip, then seemed to deflate completely. "You won't believe this, but . . . I did the unthinkable, Jane. I called my father."

"To ask for a loan?"

"Yeah. I knew it was a long shot. First of all, we've never really gotten along. Second, he thinks *I'm* the rich one in the family. And third, I had no idea if he even had any savings."

"Does he?"

Eddie nodded. "But he said he needs some time to think about it. And in the meantime, that blackmailer is planning to roast my life over a spit. I mean, I feel like a total shit for asking my father for such a huge favor. But I'm good for it. I'd pay him back. Except, I'm not sure he believes me. I think, in some ways, he still sees me as fifteen years old."

"I'm sorry," said Jane. She wished she could offer more.

"God, if I could just find out who that blackmailer is, I'd tear him limb from limb—and I'd enjoy it." He looked up. "Say, you haven't

275

heard from that doctor friend of yours, have you? She may be my last hope."

Jane couldn't let anyone know Julia had come through town again. "No. Not yet."

"Damn," he mumbled. Getting down off his drafting stool, he handed her the papers. "It's hard to stay positive when your life's about to implode."

"Maybe the guy will do something stupid and get caught."

"I'm not holding my breath." He walked her back down to the front door and, after thanking her again for stopping by, unlocked the dead bolt and let her out.

Jane stood on the top step for a few seconds, breathing in the crisp afternoon air. If only there was something she could do to help. She felt sorry for Eddie, and frustrated that she hadn't made more progress on the Chapel homicide. Maybe, if she just got a little more sleep, her fatigued brain would have a better chance of putting the pieces together.

Returning to her car, she pulled back into traffic and continued down Grand Avenue thinking she'd catch the freeway in downtown St. Paul. As she passed the cathedral, a thought occurred to her. Glancing up the street where her father's law office was located, she was surprised to see his red BMW sitting outside the building. Thinking she should at least stop in and say hello, she eased the Audi in behind his car and switched off the motor. It wouldn't take long to say hi, give him a welcome-home hug, and get some brief details on the trip.

Her father's office was part of another St. Paul row house—in this case, a renovated 1890s brownstone. Using her cane to get her up the outside steps, she looked through the front window and saw her dad seated on the edge of the reception desk. He was facing away from the street, so he hadn't seen her arrive. Turning the shiny brass doorknob, she stepped quietly into the narrow foyer, instantly aware of several voices coming from the inner office. She listened for a second, not sure what she was walking in on.

Andrew Dove and his daughter were arguing. A moment later, her father interrupted. "You have to understand, Mr. Dove, if I'm going to represent you, you've got to tell me the absolute truth about why you took those calendars from your son-in-law's offices. It's critical to the state's case against you."

"But . . . what's the difference if he took some calendars?" asked

Brenna, sounding exasperated. "It's just circumstantial evidence. Nobody *saw* my father murder my husband."

"Make no mistake, Mrs. Chapel. Most people are convicted on circumstantial evidence alone. I need to know the truth if I'm going to defend you, Mr. Dove. I can't go into court with an argument based on half-answers. And I refuse to tolerate surprises."

Jane edged closer to the door. She wanted to listen, but she didn't want to be seen.

"All right," said Dove, clipping his words angrily. "I'll tell you. But first, let me assure you once again that I am not a homosexual. Even the idea of it makes me sick to my stomach."

"You've made that perfectly clear, Mr. Dove. Now, if you'd answer my question?"

Dove hesitated. "This is hard for me to talk about in front of my daughter. She knows nothing about it. I'm sorry, Brenna, but the truth is, before Jeffrey died, we were in the middle of some, shall we say, *rancorous* negotiations with the mechanic's union at Dove Airlines. I couldn't believe it at first, but it seems Jeffrey was on the side of the union. I mean, I couldn't fathom it. He was management—my right arm." His voice grew confidential. "I learned from several unimpeachable sources that he was meeting privately with top union officials. As president and CEO, I couldn't allow that, and yet it was an understandably delicate issue. After Brenna called and told me what had happened at the Winter Garden—that Jeffrey was dead—I saw my chance and went to his two offices to look around. I was devastated by his death, of course, but I'm a businessman, Counselor. I saw an opportunity, and I acted. To make a long story short, I found notations on his calendars—dates and times of meetings with various union leaders. I wanted to study the information at my leisure, so I took the calendars. It never occurred to me that they'd be missed."

"So, let me get this straight," said Raymond, sounding less than convinced. "You took your son-in-law's calendars to check up on his private dealings with the mechanic's union. Why didn't you just ask him outright?"

"I did!" Dove was indignant. "He refused to discuss it."

"You could have fired him."

"But I had no proof. Besides, Jeffrey had a great deal of support at Dove Airlines. People treated him like he was a celebrity. I couldn't just issue him a pink slip."

"So, if I asked you to produce the missing pages from your son-in-law's calendars, you could do that?" asked Raymond.

"Well—" Dove cleared his throat. "Sure. But . . . right off, I can't say I remember where I put them." Again, he cleared his throat. "Not that it matters anymore. Once the union leadership finds out he was a faggot, they'll probably dump his proposals on principle."

"Dad!" said Brenna, clearly outraged by the comment.

"I'm just calling a spade a spade," said Andrew. "People need to know what kind of man he really was."

In a patient voice, Raymond said, "You've lost me, Mr. Dove. Are you saying a gay man can't be a good man?"

"I leave it to you to form your own conclusions."

"You know, of course, that my daughter is gay. I happen to believe she's a very fine woman."

Jane wished she could see Dove's face.

After a moment, he said, "I meant no disrespect to your daughter, sir." His voice had lost some of its pomposity.

He was undoubtedly crossing his fingers behind his back. As far as Jane was concerned, Andrew Dove was an ignorant man. Not that his homophobia necessarily meant he'd murdered his son-in-law. On the other hand, it didn't exactly absolve him either.

Jane thought his explanation for taking the calendars had way too many holes in it. She assumed her father was already mentally picking it apart. On the other hand, she didn't buy the police's contention that Dove was gay and having an affair with his son-in-law. Perhaps in private, she could present her father with an alternate theory, one having to do with Dove's skimming of Haymaker Club funds. Once she found the proof she needed, it could easily turn out to be a highly potent motive for murder. Maybe it all fit together, with Dove being the connecting link. The Haymaker Club swindle. Chapel's death. The priest's death. Dove's homophobia. As for the blackmail, perhaps Dove's motive wasn't money after all, but hatred. Of course, it was still possible he had nothing to do with his son-in-law's death. And if that was the case, it meant the police had invested all their time and energy in convicting an innocent man, while a guilty one still roamed the streets.

Deciding she'd listened to enough of Andrew Dove's self-serving ramblings, she gave a couple of sharp raps on the wall, then rounded the corner into the office.

Seeing his daughter, Raymond jumped up. "Honey, this is a wonderful surprise." He crushed her against him, giving her a long hug.

With her father's arm still around her shoulders, Jane nodded to Andrew and Brenna. "I didn't mean to interrupt your meeting. I saw my dad's car outside and thought I'd welcome him home."

Raymond beamed at her. "I'm so glad you did. Say, what are you doing for dinner tonight? We've got a videotape of the islands that will knock your socks off."

It felt so good to have his strong, steady arm around her again. She wished she didn't have that date with Patricia. "I'd love to see it, but I've got some plans I can't break. Actually—" She glanced at her watch. She needed to run back to the restaurant and change clothes before dinner. "I can't stay. Maybe another night this week?"

"You're on, honey. Let me walk you to the door."

When they rounded the corner into the hallway, Raymond put a finger to his lips. He led her out to the front steps, shutting the door behind them. In a hushed voice, he said, "That Andrew Dove is a real piece of work."

"You don't think he's telling you the truth?"

"I'm not sure he knows how."

"Are you going to take the case?"

He hesitated. "Yes. But I'd like to get him to level with me first." He held Jane at arm's length, staring intently into her face. "Tell me something, honey. Is everything all right with you?"

"Me? Sure."

"You look worn out."

"I haven't been sleeping well."

"Any particular reason?"

She shrugged.

"You also look like you've lost more weight. Something's not right. You can't fool your old dad."

She tried a smile. "What could be wrong?"

"You tell me." When she didn't respond, he asked, "Does it have something to do with Julia?"

She looked away. "It's kind of a long story."

"And you've got to get going."

She nodded.

"All right. But I expect to see you at the house for dinner soon. Deal?"

279

She slipped her arms around him and held him tight. "Deal," she whispered, wiping a tear from her eye before he could see it. She didn't know why she was being so emotional.

As he backed up, he gave her another hard look. "You'd tell me if something were really wrong."

"Of course I would. I'm fine, Dad."

Brenna picked that moment to pop her head out the door. "Jane, could I talk to you for a sec before you go? It's important."

Raymond gave his daughter's arm a parting pat. "I'll see you soon?"

"You bet. Give my love to Marilyn."

"Will do."

After he was gone, Jane and Brenna walked across the street. Brenna seemed preoccupied. Even a little morose.

"What's up?" asked Jane, unlocking the car door.

"I, ah . . . well." She folded her arms protectively over her chest. It was cold out, and she hadn't put on her coat. "I had brunch this morning with Joe Patronelli. He gave me something. An envelope." She hesitated. "I can't make any sense of it." She quickly explained everything she knew about the envelope's contents; then she pulled it out of her purse and handed it over. "I want you to look at it. See what you think."

The sun had already set behind the cathedral's dome, so the late-afternoon light was fading fast. Still, Jane could make out the names on the page. When she came to Clement Nelson and Evelyn Villard, she stopped. Of course, she thought to herself. This was it! The proof she'd been looking for. Two of the names matched the ones Burl Hedges had given her. Before his death, Chapel had found out who Dove's contacts were at the individual charities.

"What?" demanded Brenna. "Do you know who these people are?"

Jane wasn't sure how much she should say. If she told Brenna the truth, the evidence her husband had been clever enough to leave behind might be destroyed. "I'm not sure," she said, handing the paper back to Brenna. "But here's what I think you should do. Give this list to my father. He can put it away for safekeeping—just in case it turns out to be important later. I wouldn't tell your dad about it; it would only upset him. Let my father look into it first. He has several private investigators that he works with. Who knows? They might be able to shed some light on it."

Brenna nodded and kept nodding. "That's a good idea. I'll do just that. Say, do you need any more money—you know, for your investigation?"

"I'm fine," said Jane. "You've been more than generous."

"Well, okay. Whatever you say. As long as you're comfortable with the arrangement." She looked across the street to the law office. "I better get back."

"You go," said Jane. "And good luck."

"Thanks. Even after everything that's happened, I still think my father is innocent. And now, with your father on board, we're in great legal hands."

Jane watched Brenna dash across the street. She looked more confident than she had when she'd first come outside. Jane felt awful for having to lie to her, but then she didn't have a choice. It wasn't her fault that Andrew Dove was a corporate swindler.

Chapter 37

Jane took the Minnehaha Parkway home. She needed time to think. In an effort to focus her mind, she switched on her favorite classical FM station, but instead of Bach or Mozart, Stravinsky's *Rite of Spring* was playing. Disgusted, she snapped the radio off and returned her thoughts to Jeffrey Chapel's list. Thankfully, it didn't include one very important name. Patricia Kastner was lucky her deal with Andrew Dove hadn't been finalized yet. If it had, she might have made Chapel's soon-to-be-famous top ten. The more Jane thought about it, the angrier she got. Why on earth would someone as smart and talented as Patricia take such a stupid risk?

Before she knew it, she was driving south on Bridwell toward Patricia's house. Darkness had finally settled over the city, though it was only a few minutes after five. Their dinner date wasn't for another couple of hours, but as far as Jane was concerned, this couldn't wait.

When Patricia opened the front door, Jane brushed past her and headed straight for the kitchen cupboard where she knew the liquor was kept. A drink was the quickest way to settle down, and right now she was into speed. She was sick of feeling out of control, her emotions raw and on edge. She knew that reading Patricia the riot act wouldn't get either of them anywhere, and yet that's what she felt like doing.

Standing in the kitchen doorway, Patricia folded her arms in front of her and watched Jane pour herself a drink. "A little early, isn't it?"

"That's a matter of opinion." She downed a brandy in several neat gulps.

"Jeez, Lawless. What happened to you?"

Jane turned to stare at her. "*You* happened to me."

"Me? What did I do?"

Leaning against the counter, she poured herself a second brandy, drinking this one almost as fast as the first.

"Hey, slow down, girlfriend. You're going to be under the table before I can get dinner on top of it."

"Cute."

"If you're just looking for a free drink—" She stopped, her amused expression fading. "Something's really wrong, isn't it?"

Jane shot her a hard look.

"What? Come on, tell me."

As soon as the alcohol hit her system, Jane could feel the welcome warmth spread through her stomach. She hadn't eaten much today, so the effect came quickly. After pouring herself another, she walked past Patricia into the dining room, sensing that with each step her body was growing lighter. Perhaps even more importantly, the pressure that had been building inside her head all day was beginning to ease.

"Do you want to sit on the couch?" asked Patricia. "You might want to sit down before you fall over."

Jane gave her a nasty look, then glanced at the dining room table. It was already set for dinner. White roses adorned the center, while two hurricane lamps cast a warm glow over the room. The finishing touch was a sexy jazz CD playing softly in the living room. Patricia had definitely been getting into the mood early. And now, here Jane was, about to blow this carefully orchestrated seduction scene to bits.

Taking another swallow of her drink, Jane said, "Why did you do it, Patricia? How could you be so stupid!"

"Stupid?" A hand rose to her hip.

"I'm talking about you and Andrew Dove. You made a deal with him to—to what? Give him some sort of kickback once you received the funds from the Haymaker Club?"

Patricia's expression sobered. "Who said anything about a

kickback?"

"A bribe, then? It was his idea, right? But you were only too glad to go along for the ride."

"I don't know what you're talking about."

"Sure you do. Dove did it all the time. He'd find a charitable organization or an entrepreneur he could corrupt; he'd use his formidable weight to insure a contribution from the club; and then, once it was a done deal, someone would slip him part of the money without anyone being the wiser."

"You do have a vivid imagination, Lawless."

"I didn't make this up."

"Really?" She straightened one of the salad forks. "What proof do you have?"

"Why do you think Jeffrey Chapel was against the restoration of the Winter Garden? It's a great idea. It's right up the club's philosophical alley. But he wouldn't go along with his father-in-law. Why? Because he'd discovered what dear old dad was up to. Bottom line— he was skimming money from club projects to line his own pockets. When the old financial director, Burl Hedges, was still on board, he was part of the swindle. They must have figured they'd covered their tracks. Either that, or they assumed Jeffrey was in so far over his head that he'd never figure out what was going on. But he did, Patricia. He was a much smarter man than they give him credit for. And if he hadn't died when he did, he would have blown the whistle on the whole operation. You could have gone to jail. That's what your insatiable love of *risk* would have gotten you."

Even in the candlelight, Jane could see Patricia's face had grown pale.

"So? Any thoughts on the subject?"

"What can I say?"

"Did I get it right? Did Dove come to you with a proposition?"

She conceded the point with a shrug. "But before you judge me too harshly, Jane, there's something you need to understand. That's how business works in the real world. You have to grease people's palms. You give something to get something. So what if Dove took a small cut of the funds? Great work still got done. Even you have to admit that."

Jane finished her third brandy, then set the glass down on the dining room table. "I can't believe you're defending him! What he was doing was illegal!"

"I realize that," she said, looking irritated.

"You do? Really? Did you ever sign any documents? Is there *any-thing* that ties you to his scam?"

"No."

Jane grabbed her roughly by the shoulders. "Are you telling me the truth?"

"Yes!" Her eyes flashed. "Why are you so worked up about this?"

"You asked about proof? Well, I saw some today. Before Jeffrey Chapel died, he was about to nail his father-in-law. For all I know, Dove murdered him because of it."

Patricia blinked. "What proof? What did you see?"

"A list of names. The contact people Dove dealt with at various organizations."

"Was my name on it?"

Jane shook her head.

Patricia just stared at her for a moment. All of a sudden, her face broke into a grin. "Well, there you have it. I'm home free."

"What's wrong with you? If this goes to trial, you still may be subpoenaed."

"Nobody can prove a thing. You said it yourself. And speaking of you, I still don't understand why you're so stoked about this. It's my problem."

"Because . . . because I don't like to think a friend of mine would make such an incredibly stupid decision."

"That's it? That's all?"

Jane couldn't believe how lightly Patricia was taking it. "Doesn't it bother you that you came mere inches from being arrested as an accessory to extortion?"

She shrugged. "I'd always have you in my corner."

"Don't be so sure."

Patricia put her hands on Jane's waist and drew her close. "You're my ace in the hole, Lawless. My knight in shining armor."

"Really."

Lowering her voice, she added, more seriously this time, "This is just a wild guess, you understand, but I'd say you've got deeper feelings for me than you've ever let on, even to yourself. That's why you blew in here tonight like a tropical storm. I think you're just a little bit in love with me."

Jane searched her eyes, not knowing what to say.

"Maybe we should test my theory."

After a long moment, Jane found herself saying, "Maybe we should."

They leaned closer. In the instant that their mouths met, all the obsessing Jane had done about Patricia and Julia, all of her insecurity, her excruciatingly devised logic, simply melted away. Her body surrendered with a shiver.

"Let's go upstairs," whispered Patricia. "I promise, I'll make this a night you'll never forget."

At exactly five minutes to midnight, the phone gave a shrill ring. Jane and Patricia had finally fallen asleep, entwined in each other's arms. Reaching a hand to answer it, Patricia said, "This better be good." She listened for a moment, turning on a bedside lamp. Handing the phone to Jane, she said. "It's for you. He won't give his name."

Jane rubbed the sleep out of her eyes. She felt momentarily light-headed from the brandy, but it seemed to pass. Disengaging herself from Patricia, she sat up against the pillows, running a hand through her tangled hair. "Hello?" she said, pulling a blanket up to cover herself.

"Is this—" There was a pause. "Jane Lawless?"

"Yes. Who's this?"

"It's Ernie. Ernie Taber. I'm the guy you left the message for."

She needed someone to jump-start her brain. "Message?"

"At the Winter Garden."

"Oh . . . sure." It had to be the homeless man. "How did you find me here?"

"I called the number on your card. Someone checked your schedule, and they said you'd be at this number. If you don't wanna talk now—"

"No, no. It's fine." Again, she rubbed her eyes. "Do you think we could meet sometime soon?"

"You got the money?"

She tried to remember how much she'd promised. "Yes. Three hundred, right?"

"Bingo. See, I was going to use Chapel's credit cards to buy me a bus ticket outta town, but then, after I left the wallet in the hotel room, someone stole 'em. Can you beat that? People today. They're animals."

"So when can we get together?"

"Tonight soon enough?"

"Where?"

"You know the old Stone Arch Bridge?"

"You mean, back of Washington Avenue, by the river?"

"I'll meet you in half an hour. I'm wearing jeans and a jeans jacket—and I got a ponytail."

They were the same clothes he'd had on the other day. Glancing sideways at Patricia, Jane could tell she was totally absorbed by the conversation.

"You must have been back to the Winter Garden; otherwise, you wouldn't have found my card."

"Shit, lady, I know twelve different ways in and out of that place. I been sleeping there for years. *When* I sleep. Sometimes I don't. See, I got a third eye right in the center of my forehead. I never close it. The other two I shut sometimes."

Jane decided not to pursue that. "Do you have anything important you can tell me?"

"You mean like—" He gave a deep, hacking cough, then continued, "Live every day like it was your last?"

Jane was beginning to wonder about his mental health. Even if he had seen something, he might not be a reliable source. Still, she had to find out. "That's, ah . . . good. But I mean specifically about Jeffrey Chapel—the night he died."

Patricia's eyebrows shot upward. "Who *is* this man?" she whispered.

"Yeah, I can talk about that too. I saw it. Bad karma. Really bad. But I gotta take a piss now. It's my nerves."

"What are you nervous about?"

"Meeting you. And . . . well, then there's the guy—the one following me."

"What guy?"

"*The* guy."

"You mean Chapel's murderer?"

"He says he wants to talk, but I don't trust him. He's not hard to lose. The police have been nosing around the Winter Garden too, but I keep outa sight. Street rats know lotsa tricks. I'm a royal rat. Did you know I was a royal rat? A buddy of mine told me that once."

"No," said Jane. "I didn't."

"I also designed all the uniforms for the postal service."

"Really." She tried to sound impressed.

"I gotta go." He cut the line.

Feeling a sense of defeat, Jane handed the phone back to Patricia. This guy was undoubtedly the only witness to Chapel's murder, and right now, she had no confidence that if she met with him, he'd have anything coherent to say. Looking over at Patricia, she said, "You're not going to like this."

"You have to leave."

She nodded.

"Will you come back?"

"I don't know. It may get kind of late."

"Then, I'm going with you."

"No. I want to meet with this man alone."

"Down by the river? And you think *I* take stupid risks?" Instead of arguing, Jane got up and started getting dressed. Patricia watched her from the bed. "I wish you'd stay." Sitting down next to her, Jane touched her fingertips lightly to Patricia's face, then cupped her hand under her chin and gave her a long, lingering kiss. "Don't worry. If not tonight, I'll be back soon."

"You better, Lawless. Or I'll come looking for you—with a gun."

"You own a gun?"

"It's a shotgun. I carry it in my purse."

Jane laughed. "This was a very special night."

"For me too."

"I guess we never had that dinner."

"I'll give you a rain check."

Kissing her one last time, Jane got up, found her coat and cane, and headed out into the hall and down the stairs. As she was about to leave through the front door, she thought she heard whispering upstairs. She stopped and turned around, moving back to the foot of the stairs. Sure enough, Patricia was talking softly to someone. The only explanation she could figure was that, as soon as she'd left the room, Patricia had made a phone call. Jane couldn't help but wonder who she was in such a hurry to talk to—and why.

Chapter 38

On the way to the Stone Arch Bridge, Jane stopped at an all-night grocery to pick up a flashlight and some batteries. The riverfront was slowly being restored and turned into a historic park, but wasn't completely gentrified yet. The Pillsbury A Mill, one of the area's dominant historic features, had nearly been destroyed by fire a while back and was currently being propped up by steel girders. For now, the mill and the area surrounding it were a wasteland. While some bike and pedestrian paths had been created along the banks of the Mississippi, the bridge was located in a part of town that wasn't entirely safe to visit after dark. The one thing the riverfront had going for it tonight was that it would be virtually deserted because of the cold weather.

Driving down the steep hill in front of the Army Corp of Engineers Visitor's Center, Jane parked her car near the chain-link fence. This close to the water, she was also within sight of St. Anthony Falls and the lock-and-dam system that allowed boats to navigate the upper Mississippi. The wind coming off the river was stiff, whipping her long hair across her face and making it difficult to see. She hadn't taken the time to pull her hair back into a bun, but wished she'd done so now. Raising the hood of her jacket, she stuffed her hair behind her, not caring that it was already hopelessly tangled.

Switching on her flashlight, she started down toward the arch closest to her. The structure was built in the 1800s, the graceful stone curves creating dark caverns underneath the bridge. The sound of rushing water filled Jane's ears, so much so that she couldn't hear as well as she might have liked.

Shining the light under the first arch, she saw matted brush, rocks, some snow, and melted water, but no man with a ponytail.

"Hello?" she called, taking a chance. "Ernie? It's Jane Lawless."

In response, she heard nothing but the roar of the falls.

She tried again, cupping her hand around her mouth and calling more loudly. "Ernie? It's Jane. Show me where you are."

This time, she noticed a flicker of light coming from an arch a good hundred feet closer to the river. Walking cautiously toward it, she shined her flashlight ahead of her. Sure enough, as she came nearer, she could see him. He was crouched behind a rusted metal drum.

"It's Jane," she called.

He waved her over.

As she approached, he emerged from his hiding place. He'd been warming his hands over a small fire. "You got the money?" he asked, stamping it out with his heavy boot.

She pulled the wad of bills from her back pocket and handed it over.

"It's not that I don't trust you." He stood still and counted it, then mashed it into his coat pocket. "Thanks."

"Now, tell me what you know about Jeffrey Chapel's murder."

"Oh, I know lots. They had a terrible argument."

"Can you describe the killer?"

He scratched his prickly beard. "Handsome, I guess. So was the guy who died."

That didn't get her very far. "Can you remember what his clothes looked like, or his hair color?"

"Well—" He squinted, trying to remember. "Now that you mention it—"

Before he could finish his sentence, a shot rang out.

Dropping to his knees, the old man clutched his chest. "God," he grunted, looking surprised, then horrified. "Shit."

A split second later, there was another shot. This one whizzed past

Jane's hand and caught Ernie in the neck. Blood spurted onto her clothing.

Realizing she had only moments to react, she dragged him behind the metal drum. He was like a stickman—all clothes and no real substance. She needed to determine where the shooter was, but she wasn't going to stick her head out and get it blown off.

Crouching in the ice, gravel, and melted snow, with the stench of rotting vegetation in her nostrils, she waited, holding Ernie in her arms as he groaned and whimpered. She tried to stop the bleeding in his neck by pressing her hand over the wound, but it was no use. "You're going to be okay," she reassured him, though she wasn't sure either of them would get out of this alive. She'd already turned off the flashlight. If she hadn't been shining it on him the whole time, he wouldn't have made such an easy target.

"It's *him*," said Ernie, coughing blood out of his mouth. "The *guy*."

She felt awful trying to wheedle information out of him at a time like this, but he might not last much longer. She had no way to stop the bleeding. Both of them were already covered with blood. "Ernie, listen to me. Can you describe him? The murderer."

His eyes closed.

She shook him. "Ernie. Try to stay with me. As soon as I know the shooter is gone, I'll get you some help. But you've got to help me now. Do you understand? I have to know who murdered Jeffrey Chapel."

He nodded.

"Can you answer my question?"

His eyes fluttered open, then closed again. Gripping her coat collar, he pulled her face close to his mouth. "Tell him . . . tell my buddy . . . I'm not a royal rat after all," he whispered. A second later, he made a low guttural sigh, then relaxed against her.

Jane checked for a pulse. Ernie was gone.

In an instant, she was up and screaming, "You killed him, you bastard! Are you happy? Do you want to kill me too? Here I am. Take your best shot!" She waited, her arms flung outward. When nothing happened, she yelled again, "Come on, you fucking coward. Show yourself. Let me see your face!"

Sinking slowly to her knees, she took Ernie in her arms again and began to rock him. "I'm sorry. I'm so sorry." She stroked his hair. Looking up at the stars she wailed, "For God's sake, somebody help us!" Under her breath, she cried, "I can't do this anymore. I can't."

Chapter 39

Julia was rushing as fast as she could. After she'd finished reading her captor several children's books and a hand-typed short story he claimed he'd written himself, she'd cupped her hands slightly as he stretched new strapping tape over them and around her hips. She hoped that the small space this created might give her some wiggle room, a chance—albeit small—to get out of her bonds. He'd also retaped her eyes. After he'd gone, she'd struggled for hours. Finally, feeling exhausted but elated, she pulled one hand free, then the other.

Next, she tried to remove the tape from her eyes. With her shoulder and arms still tightly bound, it was hard bending her body down to where her hands could be of some use. She was frustrated by the process, resting for short periods to keep her strength and her hope from waning completely. Without the use of her eyes, she wasn't sure she could remove the tape from her legs. Straining with all her might, she finally grasped the tape and yanked it off. Her ears and mouth could wait.

Resting for only a second, she attacked the tape around her ankles.

Again, since she didn't have her normal freedom of movement, the process was painstakingly slow, though she eventually found the end piece and started pulling. As she worked, she would glance up every now and then at the windows that faced Lake Harriet. The sunlight was the only clock she had. She'd never fully appreciated just how strong strapping tape was before—nor how quickly time could pass when you wanted it to stand still. It took her the better part of the afternoon to complete the task, but as light began to fade, she kicked her legs free. She had to massage her ankles and feet for a few minutes to bring some feeling back into them. As much as it was against every instinct inside her, she had to make haste slowly.

Swinging her legs over the edge of the bed, she gave her body a moment to adjust to the sitting position. Finally, bending forward, she attempted to get up. Like everything else, without the use of her arms, it was easier said than done. She didn't realize how badly her balance was off until she'd bounced her way to a standing position. She should have been more careful because, as she took a first step, she'd tilted sideways and started to fall. Without her arms to catch her, her head cracked against the side of the nightstand and her world went black.

When Julia finally awoke, the sun had set. Inside, a tiny night-light burned in the galley kitchen. Her head ached, but her vision seemed to be okay. Even if it wasn't, this was no time to worry about a concussion.

She twisted her body and pushed with her legs until her back was against the side of the bed, then took a deep breath and heaved herself up. This time, she was more careful. She waited until she felt her legs firmly underneath her before she took a step. So far, so good.

Inching her way slowly toward the kitchenette, all she could think about was finding some way to cut the tape off her arms. There was no telling how long she'd been knocked out—or when her captor would be back.

Bending slightly, she began to open drawers, looking for a scissors, a knife, anything sharp. In the last drawer next to the sink, she found the silverware. She grabbed the first serrated knife she saw, held it upward, and pushed the tip under the tape. She found that a sawing motion worked best. In less than a minute, she was free.

She ripped the tape from her mouth and pulled the cotton out of her ears. Realizing she didn't have a minute to spare, she grabbed her briefcase and purse and headed for the door leading to the outside stairway.

As she fumbled to open the lock, she heard a metallic click behind her. Whirling around, she saw that she was no longer alone.

"Amazing, Doctor," said the man in the ski mask. He was standing in the middle of the room, his feet apart, holding a gun with both hands. "I can't leave you alone for five minutes without you getting into trouble." The barrel was trained directly at her chest.

She froze. Her disappointment was so immense that she almost started to cry.

"I suggest you cooperate. That is, unless you want me to use this. I'm a very good shot, in case you were wondering. I practice at a local range twice a month."

"You wouldn't shoot me."

"I wouldn't *want* to shoot you, but I would. If you make it necessary.

She dropped everything she was holding.

"Good. Now, on the bed again, Doctor. Face down."

As she stepped carefully past him, she asked, "What are you going to do?"

"Just get on the bed and bring your hands around to your back."

Once she was lying prone, she saw that he'd brought another shopping bag with him. He set it down next to the nightstand.

"Lucky for me I'd already decided the strapping tape was a bad idea. It's all I had with me last night, but I brought something more useful tonight."

"What?" she asked, not really wanting to know.

"Handcuffs, Doctor. Did you know you can buy them at any army-navy surplus store?"

Julia felt the cold metal dig into her wrists. A second later, he'd cuffed one of her legs to the foot of the bed.

"There. Much easier." He dropped the keys on the night-stand, mere inches from her face.

She knew he did it to taunt her. No matter how close they were, there was no way she could reach them.

"I guess it's a good thing I decided to drop by. I happened to be down by the Stone Arch Bridge a short time ago getting some fresh air when I thought, yup, better go see how Doctor Julia is doing."

"Lucky me."

"Yes, actually it is. You don't want to miss the main event." He paused, then continued, "I brought you something, Doc."

She turned her head away.

"Oh, now, don't be like that. You're going to enjoy this."

He sat down next to her on the bed, tapping her lightly on the shoulder. "Aren't you curious what I've got in the bag?"

"No."

"Sure you are. Just take a look."

She didn't move.

"It won't hurt, I promise." He removed a heavy object and set it on the mattress. "Look at it, Julia. It's a tape recorder. Don't you want to know what's on it?"

Slowly, she turned her head back to face him.

"Here. Enjoy." He pushed the play button.

As she listened, she closed her eyes. "No," she groaned. She couldn't stand it any longer. Tears filled her eyes. "You can't do that."

"It's already done."

Chapter 40

Cordelia trudged down the hall to the door of her loft, did a small but tasteful pirouette, then shoved a key into her lock. As soon as she was inside, she heard the phone ringing.

"Hold your horses," she shouted, stomping into the kitchen. "I am in constant demand," she grumbled, checking the refrigerator for something to eat as she muttered a quick hello. Once she discovered who it was, her voice brightened. "Hey there, Neva. How's tricks?" Neva Moore was Cordelia's newest love. "Come on, don't get your bloomers in a twist. I thought we were supposed to get together *tomorrow* night. I had a long rehearsal at the theatre this afternoon, and I'm beat." She checked her watch. It was just after two in the morning. "I realize it's no longer afternoon, hon. The rehearsal stretched into the evening, and then some of the cast and I went out for a bite." She listened. "Yes, the Williams thing. I'm about to produce the definitive *Glass Menagerie*. It will be studied for years for it's subtlety and brilliance." Another pause. "Humility is boring, dearheart. Besides, it's not my fault you're working on that dreary piece at the Guthrie." Neva was a set designer. "If you recall, I asked you to come on board."

More silence. "Well, whatever. Money *is* important, but it's not everything. I'll talk to you more about *that* tomorrow night. Yes, your place. Eight o'clock. I'll be there. Oh, should I bring anything?" She listened again, then chuckled. "I can't wait. Yes, love you too. Bye."

Hanging up, she ducked her head back into the refrigerator and withdrew a package of sliced ham, a loaf of dark rye bread, mayo, mustard, a tomato, several slices of Wisconsin Baby Swiss, and some Boston Bibb, and set it all out on the counter. Dinner had been hours ago, and she needed sustenance if she was going to have enough energy to hit the sack. Otherwise, she might just waste away on the couch watching infomercials.

After assembling her sandwich, Cordelia sauntered into the living room and turned on her favorite mood light, a lava lamp she'd bought when she was sixteen. She nearly dropped the plate when she saw Jane sitting on the floor next to the couch, her legs and arms tucked up close to her body.

"Heavens, you nearly scared me to death." Her hand fluttered to her chest. "How long have you been sitting here in the dark?"

"I don't know."

Bending down to examine her more closely, she said, "What have you got all over you?"

Jane didn't respond. She didn't even look up.

"My God, it's blood! Are you hurt?"

She shook her head.

"Are you sure?"

"It's not my blood."

"Oh, that makes me feel *so* much better." She gave her a pained look. "What? You were out doing goat sacrifices?"

"A man died in my arms tonight, Cordelia. Ernie Taber. The homeless man."

She eased down next to her on the floor. The sandwich was definitely out of the question. Setting the plate on a table, she took Jane's hands in hers. "God, you're chilled to the bone."

"I . . . sat with him until the police came."

"Where did all this happen?"

She still hadn't looked at Cordelia. "Under the Stone Arch Bridge. About twelve-thirty."

"Janey, this is awful. We need to get those clothes off you right away."

She bowed her head. "I didn't know where else to go. I couldn't go back to the restaurant. I didn't want to go back to Patricia's."

"Patricia's," she repeated, raising an eyebrow. "You were there tonight?"

"She invited me for dinner."

"Was it good?"

"We never ate it."

Cordelia didn't like the sound of that. "And pray tell, what did you do to while away the hours?"

Jane looked up at her. "We slept together."

As far as Cordelia was concerned, the entire evening had been one huge disaster.

"I'm sorry," said Jane, lifting a glass to her lips. "I didn't want to wreck your evening, but when you weren't here, I didn't think you'd mind if I just came in and sat down for a while."

"What's that?" asked Cordelia, pointing to the glass.

"I don't know. Something you had in your cupboard."

Cordelia picked up the bottle. Ten-year-old scotch. "How much of it have you had?"

"Not enough."

She noticed now that Jane's voice sounded thick—and just a little slurred. "Janey, you've got to stop this."

Jane pressed her fingers to the pressure point between her eyes. "That's what I want too. For everything to stop."

"I'm talking about the booze."

"I don't need a lecture."

"Janey, listen to me. You're in trouble. You've got to get a grip. The alcohol will only make things worse."

"I need it. For now. Not forever. Don't make such a big deal out of it."

"But it *is* a big deal. Maybe you don't see it, but—"

"There's so much you don't know, Cordelia. So much I haven't told you." Taking another swallow, she added, "Sometimes life isn't a very good place to live."

Cordelia wasn't going to touch that. In Jane's current condition, it probably made sense—to her. "Okay, then tell me this. When the police came, did they call for paramedics?"

"God, those whirling lights gave me an instant headache, but they wouldn't turn them off. Cops must find them energizing."

"Then what happened?" coaxed Cordelia. Jane was moving in and out of the conversation. She couldn't seem to focus.

"What happened when?" asked Jane, looking confused.

"What happened after the police came?"

"Oh. I explained who the dead man was. One of the cops must have radioed for Sgt. Duvik. He showed up a few minutes later. I talked to him for a while."

"But what about you? Did anyone check *you* out?"

"I'm fine."

"Janey, you're driving me crazy," said Cordelia, examining her from head to toe. "Come on." She helped her get up. "You have to take a shower. Wash your hair. I think we should probably bag what you're wearing and toss it in the incinerator. You can use one of my pajama tops to sleep in. It'll be too big on you, but then you'll look devastatingly cute."

"That's always been my goal."

She walked Jane to the bedroom and began stripping off her clothes. "You're all wet."

Holding the scotch in front of her, Jane said, "We were hiding behind a metal drum, sitting in some melting snow—that was after the first shot, the one that hit him in the stomach."

Cordelia stopped. "You mean, you were *there* when he was attacked?"

"He was about to tell me who killed Jeffrey Chapel."

"Jane! You could have been killed." Suddenly angry, she yanked Jane's sweater off and then began unbuttoning her shirt.

"I wasn't the target, Cordelia."

"You were standing *close* to the target."

Her hand trembling, Jane finished the scotch. "You're my best friend, and—I know sometimes I try your patience, but—I love you very much."

"I prefer someone telling me that when they're sober."

"I have a great father, the best brother and sister-in-law in the world, and a career I adore."

"You're a lucky woman."

She stepped back, preventing Cordelia from unbuttoning the shirt any further. "If that's true, if I'm such a lucky woman .. then . . . why do I feel so lost?" She searched Cordelia's face for an answer.

"Janey, listen to me." She placed her hands on Jane's shoulders, noticing that her eyes were all puffy and red. "You just watched a man die. That wasn't easy. And even before that, your life has been nothing but chaos ever since you were attacked. Right *before* the attack, if you don't mind my saying so, you seemed to be headed for a train wreck in your love life. Relationships have always screwed with your emotions more than anything else. It's like there's you, and then there's this pink-and-orange flamingo with green legs and a yellow beak, and wherever you are, it's sitting in the corner."

"A flamingo?" She scrunched up her face, trying to make sense of it.

"Exactly. Your past. It's always with you. You're not made of iron, Janey. You're a human being. You can't just keep going as if nothing bad has happened. And you can't keep it all inside either. If you do, you'll go tilt."

"I think I've already gone tilt."

"Then, something's got to change. Do you hear me? You've got to stop drinking like this. You've done it before. It's got to cease right now. Tonight."

She nodded.

"Will you do it?"

Looking down at the empty glass on the nightstand, she whispered, "I'll try."

Chapter 41

MONDAY AFTERNOON

Rise and shine," said Cordelia, setting a tray on the coffee table next to the couch.

Jane was awake, but she hadn't opened her eyes yet. For the past half hour, she'd been listening to Cordelia putter in the kitchen, singing selected arias from *La Bohéme*. She assumed breakfast was on the way. Sitting up, she glanced at the food. "You know, there's something wrong with this picture."

"And what would that be?" asked Cordelia, fluffing Jane's pillow with uncharacteristic cheerfulness.

"I'm usually the one waking *you* up."

"Well then, next time, follow my example, and don't get me up at the crack of dawn."

"What time is it?"

She checked her watch. "Just after one."

"In the afternoon!"

"I thought I'd let you sleep in. You actually have a little color in your cheeks today, Janey. We're making progress." She lowered her ample frame onto the couch, scrunching backward until Jane's legs were pinned against the cushions. "I've already had breakfast," she said, spreading some kiwi jam on one of four buttered toast points. After taking a bite, she said, "Come on. Dig in."

"I guess I better—or there won't be anything left." As she picked up the fork, she realized she didn't have much of an appetite. Leaning back against the pillow, she said, "I'm sorry about last night."

"Don't be sorry you came here. You did the right thing. You just shouldn't have drunk half my bottle of scotch."

"I'll replace it."

"That's not the point, and you know it."

Jane took a deep breath, then let it out slowly. "Look, I feel awful about how I behaved. It won't happen again."

"It's not that simple."

"No, I know. But cut me some slack, okay? I had a pretty rough day yesterday."

"I agree. You've had a rough couple of months. That's why I think you should see a therapist. I'm here for you, Janey—always—but I'm not enough. And scotch won't make your problems go away."

"I realize that."

"Perhaps you should just stop drinking, period."

Jane didn't want to have this conversation right now. She didn't feel like starting the day off on such a negative note. "Your point is taken. I just think you're making too much of of it."

Cordelia shot her a frustrated look.

"Okay, maybe I have been drinking too much. I can stop that—it's not a problem. But I *would* have a problem with total abstinence. The fact is, this time next week, I could be in Paris."

Cordelia did a double take. "As in France?"

"Julia wants me to fly over with her. She plans to stay there a month."

Quickly spreading jam on another toast point, Cordelia said, "Give, dearheart. This is all news to me. Are you going?"

"I haven't decided yet."

She scrutinized Jane's face, then narrowed an eye. "Oh, I get it. It's because of your little tryst last night with Miss Teen U.S.A. Does Julia know about that?"

"She flew back to D.C. yesterday morning. And no, that's not the reason I wouldn't go."

"But—" She elbowed Jane in the ribs. "When the cat's away—"

"I hope you know me better than that."

"I thought I did. But at the moment, you seem to have one girl-friend too many. You usually have one girlfriend too few."

"I think I prefer it the old way." She took a bite of bacon, chewing it with little enthusiasm. "Anyway, I wasn't in any shape to get into this last night, but I wanted to explain—to fill you in on everything that's happened since Saturday night."

"It's Monday morning. How much could have happened?"

Jane began her story with Julia's surprise appearance. An hour later, as Cordelia finished the last of her breakfast, Jane completed what she was now referring to as "the epic saga."

"I'm glad your sense of humor has returned," said Cordelia, tapping a napkin to her lips.

"It comes and goes."

Tossing the napkin over the empty plate, Cordelia continued, "And everything you've told me is endlessly fascinating. But it still doesn't answer the burning question of the hour."

"Which is?"

"Will our heroine accept her erstwhile lover's offer of a month of sun and fun in gay Paree?"

Shaking her head, Jane said, "Thanks for the use of your couch and the breakfast, but I've got to get going."

"It *was* delicious, wasn't it?" As Jane struggled to disengage her legs, Cordelia put a hand on her arm to stop her from getting up. "There is one small problem."

"What's that?"

"We dumped all your clothes. Unless you want to arrive at the Lyme House looking like a waif wearing your big sister's hand-me-downs, this is going to take some thought." Eyeing Jane critically, Cordelia continued, "Actually, there is that one costume I brought home from the Grimby that might fit you. It was way too small for me."

"Costume?"

Cordelia grinned. "Lucky for you, I know right where it is."

It was nearing three-thirty by the time Jane got back to the restaurant. The idea that someone might actually recognize her was understandably embarrassing, but at least the costume fit. It was even pretty comfortable. There was a hat of sorts that kept her head out of the wintry wind, one that also covered her face. Now, if she could just sneak in without being seen.

Entering through the delivery door, she crept down the back steps, heading straight for her office. It was hard to maintain a low profile wearing a suit of armor—even a fake one—but she tried. The most annoying part was the scuffy, snappy, cheap sounds made by the tin scraping against the plastic. But so far, so good. Nobody seemed to be around.

Just as she was about to unlock her office, a deep voice bellowed, "Excuse me, sir. Can I help you?"

She turned to find one of the bartenders striding briskly toward her.

"You can't go in there. It's a private office."

"I know that, Barnaby," said Jane, realizing her voice sounded as if she were speaking from inside an old radio.

The man stopped and stared. "Jane?"

"If you tell anyone you saw me like this, you're fired."

He tried to hide his amusement. "Yes, my liege."

"You can go now. Oh, have someone in the kitchen bring me down a carafe of coffee. I've got a lot of work to do."

"Fighting dragons?"

She turned back to him. "You're treading on thin ice."

"Right." He stiffened, then saluted. "I go to mount the battlements, sire. Camelot shall never be taken by infidels!" He grinned, then hightailed it back down the hall to the pub.

"Camelot," she muttered, stepping into her office. The first order of business was to remove the suit. It was easier getting into it than it was out of it, mainly because Cordelia had been there to help. Finally, free of the thing, Jane sat down behind her desk and switched on a light, still wearing the fake chain mail. She wanted to check her messages.

The first one was from her father, asking her to call as soon as she got in. He had some questions about a list of names Brenna Chapel had given him. The second and third were business calls. Jane made notes of times and phone numbers so she could return them. Finally, she waited for the last message to play.

"Jane," came a familiar voice. "It's Julia."

Jane turned up the sound and gave the call her full attention.

"I didn't . . . leave town . . . after all. I'm . . . at your house. I didn't think you'd mind. I need to . . . talk to you. Can you come by soon? It's important. I love you. Bye."

Almost as a reflex, Jane opened her bottom desk drawer and removed a bottle of Jim Beam and a glass. This was an odd turn of events. The last they'd talked, Julia had been determined to get out of town as soon as possible. It seemed strange that she was still here— and even more strange that she'd decided to crash at Jane's house and not tell her until now.

Ignoring Cordelia's voice inside her head, Jane poured herself a drink, then rewound the message and listened to it again. Before she was finished, she'd replayed it six more times.

Finally, sitting back in her chair, she crossed her arms and stared at the bottle. She wanted that drink more than she cared to admit. After what had happened at the Stone Arch Bridge last night, she felt an almost irresistible need to tune out the world. Alcohol was a magic carpet. Once she got on, the ache in her head and leg, and the ache in her soul, would ease. And yet, after a long moment, she pushed the glass away. It was clear what she had to do tonight, and this time, Jim Beam couldn't help.

Chapter 42

As the late afternoon light faded over Linden Hills, Jane walked up the front steps of her house, painfully aware of the knot inside her stomach. She had no idea what tonight would bring, but in some important way, she knew this turn of events had brought her full circle. A dim light burned in the living room, but the rest of the house was dark. She stood for a moment on the landing, summoning her courage, then fit the key into the lock.

Once inside with the door closed behind her, she called, "Julia?" Her voice reverberated in the quiet house. She glanced into the living room, but nobody seemed to be around.

Standing motionless for a few seconds, she allowed the smell and the sight of the place to wash over her. Her most immediate fear was that the terror she'd experienced that last night—the night she was attacked—would return to paralyze her. This was a battle she knew she'd have to fight one of these days; she just never expected it would happen under these conditions.

And yet, the longer she waited and watched, the clearer it became that the ghosts of that evening were gone. It seemed completely normal to be back, standing in her front hall. She could almost hear her aunt in the kitchen, humming a gentle tune as she prepared dinner. Until this very minute, Jane hadn't fully realized how deeply she'd missed her home. She'd been disconnected from her life for months now. Wouldn't it be ironic if, in the end, she'd been afraid to reclaim the one thing that might have the power to ground her again? Thankfully, she'd made a decision, a pact with herself. She'd come to the conclusion that she'd been playing defense far too long. Tonight, she was going back on the offensive.

"Julia?" she called. "It's Jane. Where are you?"

She moved slowly through the living room, entering the rear hall. The study was on her left—the place where the attack had occurred. Since it appeared she had sometime, she decided to face that first.

Turning on the overhead light, she saw that someone, most likely Cordelia, had cleaned up the room. It was simply her study again. Julia's picture sat on the desk next to the lamp. The manuscript pages from the culinary memoir she'd begun late last summer were stacked neatly on top of the filing cabinet. Everything was as it should be. For an instant, she had an intense desire to sit down behind her desk and just spend some quiet time reflecting. But that wasn't possible.

Returning to the front hall, she headed quickly up the stairs to her bedroom. "Julia," she called again, stepping cautiously inside. She had to be around somewhere. Switching on a small night-light, Jane discovered another empty room. After inspecting the closets for signs of Julia's belongings and finding nothing, she sat down on the foot of the bed. Somehow, the memories just wouldn't stop coming. She recalled the many mornings she'd spent in this bed, just staring out the windows at the two magnificent oaks in the front yard. Up on the second floor, she could pretend she was deep in the woods, with no other houses around.

And that's when it struck her. The view! She'd completely missed it before. The more she thought about it, the more she realized *that* was the key. In a flash, Pandora's box burst open, and all the demons came rushing out. A picture was worth a thousand words, and what she'd seen was impossible. And if *that* was a lie . . .

A sudden noise shattered her concentration.

"Good evening, Jane," whispered a familiar voice. She twisted around.

The man in the ski mask moved out of the shadows and into the weak lamplight. "It's nice that you could join us."

Jane was surprised by her reaction. Her first response was fury. "How could you do it!"

He just stared at her.

"I trusted you. I empathized with you. I even liked you!" She should have put it together long before this, but she'd been too busy feeling sorry for herself. "You can take off the ski mask. I know who you are."

"You think so?"

"I'm slow, Eddie, but I'm not brain-dead."

He smiled. "I never thought you were. That's why I took so much care to keep track of what you were doing—and keep you in my corner." Removing the mask, he lifted a gun from his coat pocket. "Tell me, Jane, what did I do wrong?"

She rose, turning to face him. "You let me see your bedroom."

He shot her a questioning look.

"There's no way those blackmail photos you showed me could have been taken from the exterior window of your house. The angle was from the foot of the bed. The windows are on the other side of the room. I'd say either you took the photos with a camera on a tripod—a time-release with Chapel's permission—or you had a videotape going, with or without his knowledge."

"You *are* clever."

"Which means your whole story was a lie."

"A logical conclusion."

Her unblinking eyes held his. "You were blackmailing Jeffrey Chapel, and you murdered him because he planned to blow the whistle on your little scam."

"He threatened. I couldn't take any chances."

"Where's Julia?"

Eddie motioned her out of the room. "She's a little tied up at the moment, but she's waiting for you."

The amusement in his voice made her even angrier. "If you've hurt her—"

"If I hurt her, what?" He shoved her forward, then pushed her into the third-floor stairway. "Do you think I'm playing games? Why the hell do you think I went to such effort to get you here?"

"You put that phone message together, didn't you? You must have taped her voice."

"We're done playing twenty questions." As they reached the top of the stairs, he flipped on an overhead light.

Jane rushed to the bed, kneeling down next to Julia. She could see the unmistakable evidence of a beating. Hatred welled up inside her. "You fucking bastard!" she screamed at him.

"She's fine. Just a little banged up."

"Jane?" said Julia, her mouth dry and cracked. She struggled against her bonds. She was sitting up, each wrist handcuffed to one rung of the bedstead. Her ankles were taped together with strapping tape, and she was blindfolded. But she was alive. Jane had to be thankful for that.

"Jane, is that you?"

Touching Julia's golden hair, now matted with sweat, Jane pulled the cotton from her ears. "Yes, sweetheart, it's me." She fixed Eddie with a withering stare. "What do you want?"

"Remove the tape from her eyes."

Finally able to comprehend what was going on, Julia visually devoured Jane's face. "God," she rasped, swallowing hard. "I thought I'd never see you again."

Jane could read the terror in her eyes, and it twisted something deep inside her. Looking back at Eddie, she said. "You're after her files, right?"

"You get the door prize. Where are they?"

"How should I know?"

"Julia told you."

"I didn't!" insisted Julia, her voice a little stronger this time. "We've gone all through this. I never told her because I didn't want her involved."

"Oh, she's involved all right." He kicked Julia's briefcase out of his way as he strutted over to the windows to look outside. "And she's going to stay involved until you tell me what I want to know."

"Meaning what?" asked Jane.

"It's simple." He walked a little closer to the bed, his eyes focused on Julia. "I have the feeling you may never tell me what I want to know, Doctor. I've already caused you a great deal of pain, and you still won't cooperate. Since I can't exactly kill the golden goose, I decided to bring your lover here. Believe me, you won't like what I'm planning to do to her."

Fear rippled through Jane like burning acid. She watched in silence as he removed a switchblade from his pocket.

"I've murdered three people to get what I want. Maybe Jeffrey's death was hard, but the next two were a piece of cake."

"You wouldn't do that!" cried Julia, tugging frantically at her chains.

"Maybe not right away." The knife hissed as the blade shot open. "I thought I'd work on her face a little first."

"No!" shouted Julia. "Let her go, and I'll tell you whatever you want."

He smiled. "Tell me first, and we'll see."

"If you don't let her go, I won't tell you a thing."

"Fine." He closed the knife and pocketed it, then pulled a chair away from the windows. "Sit!" he ordered, glaring at Jane.

"Okay, okay! Just . . . leave her alone."

"It's no use, Julia." Jane hadn't moved from the side of the bed. "He's not going to let either one of us out of here alive."

"Is that true?" she asked, her expression growing even more terrified.

"I guess it's a chance you'll have to take."

Downstairs, the front doorbell rang.

"Leave it," ordered Eddie. "Whoever it is, they'll go away."

He sounded sure of himself, and yet Jane could read the indecision in his eyes. She knew this might be her only chance. Reacting quickly, she said, "If it's Evelyn Bratrude, she won't go away."

Looking suspicious, Eddie said, "And who the hell is Evelyn Bratrude?"

"My neighbor. She's been keeping an eye on the house while I've been gone. There shouldn't be any lights on at night. If someone doesn't go down and reassure her that everything's okay, she'll call the police. That was our deal."

"Oh, just fucking *great*," he snarled, running a hand through his ginger hair. "What am I supposed to do now?" He kicked a small table, sending it crashing into the wall, then looked out the window again. "You can't see the damn door from up here."

The bell sounded a second time. Then a third, and a fourth. Whoever was downstairs clearly wanted some action.

"Maybe it's not her," said Eddie.

"Maybe," agreed Jane. "But I don't think you want to take that chance. Look, why don't you let me go down and tell her I'm back home for good. I'll assure her that everything's fine and tell her I was just about to hit the sack."

"Oh, right. Like I believe you'd do that."

"No, I'm saying you'll come down with me. You can stand behind the door and listen to everything I say."

As he considered it, the bell rang again. Looking nervous and deeply frustrated, he said, "All right. But if you try anything, you're both dead. I don't want to hurt this woman, but I will. Understand?"

Jane nodded.

As they made their way back down the narrow third-floor stairway, Jane knew for a fact that the only person who *couldn't* be ringing the bell was Evelyn. She'd called her before driving over, explaining that she didn't want her to worry if she saw lights on in the house.

"Eddie?"

He pushed her forward with the barrel of the gun. "What?"

"Will you answer one question?"

"Why should I?"

"Is Patricia Kastner involved in any of this?"

"Jesus, no."

"Did she call you last night—tell you that I was planning to meet a man down by the river?"

His laugh was malicious. "Yeah, she phoned, but that wasn't the reason for the call."

"Then . . . why did it even come up?"

"You'd just left, and the bed was getting cold. She was pissed. She couldn't believe you'd run out on her just to go talk to some 'street dude,' as she put it."

That sounded like Patricia. "But . . . why did she call you, then?"

"To tell me that you'd found proof that Andrew Dove was taking kickbacks. She was relieved that our deal went sour. Come on," he said, pushing her toward the stairs, "keep moving." He followed directly behind as she made her slow descent.

The closer they got to the front door, the louder the music became.

"Does your neighbor often travel with a disco band?"

"Not usually." As she peered through the peephole, her mouth dropped open.

"Is it her?" asked Eddie.

311

She turned around, assuming she looked as surprised as she felt. "No . . . actually, it's another friend of mine. Cordelia Thorn."

The pounding strains of the Village People singing "Y.M.C.A." reverberated right through the wood.

"God, I feel like I'm in some hideous time warp," he muttered, mashing one hand against his ear. Pressing the gun into Jane's side, he said, "Get rid of her."

She pulled back the door, her mind racing. Before she could even utter a word, Cordelia burst into the room, eyes closed, emoting to the music.

Eddie scrambled backward into the darkness of the dining room and hid behind the arch.

"Cordelia!" shouted Jane, attempting to get her attention. "Turn that off."

"You should be in a party mood, Janey. You're back home! And see, no ghosts hiding in the closet. Where's Julia?" She did some Travolta moves into the living room.

"We . . . were hoping to have some private time," shouted Jane.

"You can have all the privacy you want after we eat the pizza."

"Pizza?" She glanced over her shoulder at Eddie. Even in the dark, she could see him draw a finger across his throat.

Grabbing the box and turning the music down, Jane was finally able to get Cordelia's full attention. "This isn't a good time."

"It's always a good time for pizza, Janey. Don't you listen to commercials? Go get Julia, and we'll ask her what she thinks."

"I, ah . . . can't."

Moving closer, Cordelia barely moved her lips. "Where is he?"

Jane flicked her eyes slightly sideways toward the dining room.

"Well," boomed Cordelia, rubbing her hands together. "Everything's all set. The pizza should be here any minute."

Jane had no idea what that was supposed to mean. "Look, kiddo." She put her arm around her friend's shoulders and walked her back to the front door. Every minute Cordelia stayed inside the house, her life was in danger. "I appreciate you coming by, but . . . this is kind of an important night for Julia and me. I wonder . . . would you mind giving us some time alone?"

Without missing a beat, Cordelia said, "Of course, Janey. Say no more. I am the personification of selflessness. The queen of the generous gesture."

Jane thought she was laying it on a bit thick, but was grateful she didn't put up a fight.

"I'll even let you keep the mood music."

"Gee, what a treat."

"The pizza should be here shortly. Enjoy."

As Jane said good-bye, she glanced outside, surveying the dark street for signs of the police. She couldn't help but wonder if Cordelia's sudden appearance meant there was some kind of trouble. Turning back to Eddie, she felt the tension in the room crank up a good ten notches.

Eddie stepped out of the shadows. "That was smart, Jane. Now, get back upstairs."

Before they'd reached the second-floor landing, the doorbell chimed again.

"The pizza?" said Jane. She really had no idea.

Eddie was clearly at the end of his rope. "Pay for the damn thing, and send the guy packing." He followed her back downstairs and moved to the side, out of sight.

When Jane opened the door, she found Sgt. Duvik standing outside.

"Evening," said the officer. "I wonder if I could have a word with you?"

But . . . this was all wrong, thought Jane. She felt herself begin to panic. Out of the corner of her eye, she could see that Eddie had raised the gun and was pointing it straight at her head.

"I ah . . ."

"It'll just take a second."

Eddie was shaking his head vehemently, his eyes telling her, *No! Get rid of him!*

"I'm sorry, but this isn't a very good time." She looked over the officer's shoulder, hoping to see reinforcements, but he seemed to be alone.

"Normally, I wouldn't bother you at your house, but I got this garbled phone message a few minutes ago from a woman named Thorn. Something about this address—I caught that much. And you. I may be wrong, but it sounded at one point like she was saying the name 'William Shatner' and then 'SWAT team.'" He laughed.

Jane laughed along with him, although at this moment, she felt more like strangling Cordelia. By now, the entire house should be

313

surrounded by police. Sharpshooters should be sitting in the trees. As it was, the only person who'd shown up was Duvik himself, and he was as confused as she was.

"Do you know someone named Thorn?"

"I, ah . . . I'm afraid so. And you're right," she added quickly. "It must have been a prank. I'm very sorry." She was torn. She desperately wanted him to stay, but she knew that if he came inside, they might both end up dead. On the other hand, if he left, she'd be alone with Eddie—with no help in sight.

"Maybe I better check out the house, just in case," said Duvik.

"No, really—"

"Can't hurt."

Before she could stop him, Eddie had spun away from the door and stood in the foyer, both hands holding the gun. "Get in here!" he ordered, his voice shaking with rage.

Duvik looked stunned.

"Now! Or I blow her away."

He stepped inside.

"Put your hands on the wall. Spread-eagle your legs."

"Calm down, son. Let's talk about this."

"Do it!"

Once Eddie had slammed the door and locked it, he turned his anger on Jane. "You think you're so fucking clever!" He shoved her back against the door, then hit her hard across the face with his gun.

The blow disoriented her, and she nearly fell.

"Take it easy," said Duvik. "You're upset. But we can work this out; I know we can."

His eyes fierce, Eddie shoved the barrel of the gun against Duvik's neck. At the same time, he removed the gun from the officer's shoulder holster. "This was all a setup!"

Jane watched him push the officer's gun inside his belt.

"You were the Trojan horse, huh, Jane? Clever. So clever, you're both going to die laughing."

"Listen to me, son," said Duvik, trying to sound soothing.

"Shut up!"

"I can get you anything you want. A car. A plane ticket. Money. Just name it."

"You don't get it," said Eddie. "I'm going to have *all* of that—and ten times more."

314

"Not unless you can get out of here."

"What's preventing me?"

Duvik looked around at him, obviously sizing up the younger man. "There's a woman across the street sitting in a car. I may be mistaken, but I think she knows what's going on in here. When I drove up, she waved at me."

It had to be Cordelia, thought Jane. In a situation like this, who else would wave?

"If something doesn't happen soon, my bet is she'll call for more police."

"Shut the fuck up!" shouted Eddie, staggering backward. "I need time to think." He sank down on the steps.

As he sat there, running his hand through his hair, Jane could see he was starting to sweat. His carefully made plans were all coming apart. Then again, her own plans hadn't exactly gone like clockwork.

"Cuff him," said Eddie suddenly, looking over at her.

"Pardon me?"

"What's so damn hard to understand? Take the cuffs off the guy's belt, pull his hands behind his back, and cuff him!"

She felt horrible doing it, but she didn't see that she had a choice. Once she was finished, she backed up and stood near the door.

Duvik turned around, eyeing Eddie warily. "What are you going to do?"

"You're right about one thing, asshole. We've got to get out of here."

"We?" repeated the officer.

"The doctor and I. And Jane, too, I suppose. I need her—for now." Thinking out loud, he added, "We can take Julia's rental car."

"But . . . what about the sergeant?" asked Jane.

"Yeah. What *about* him?" He wiped a nervous hand across his mouth. "Your friend Thorn never saw me, so I'm clean there."

"But she knows," said Jane, trying to bluff.

"No, she doesn't!" he shot back. "*You* didn't even know who I was until a few minutes ago. Stop playing with my head, Lawless. You're too fucking transparent!"

"So that leaves me," said Duvik, his eyes pressing into Eddie's.

"That leaves you."

"You could tie him up and leave him here," said Jane. "That would buy us some time."

315

"Us?" He grinned. "You're on my side now, huh?" The grin faded. "Problem is, you're forgetting about your friend outside. She's the reason we've got no damn time!"

"But . . . you can't just shoot him," said Jane. She watched Duvik's face go pale.

"Come on, son. We can work this out another way. I'll get a negotiator in here. You've always got choices."

Eddie shook his head. "You know who I am and what I did. You have to die."

"But Eddie!" pleaded Jane.

"Shut up! Everybody just shut the fuck up! Do you think I want to do this?" His eyes grew fever bright as he ordered Jane to back away.

"Have you ever executed a man before?" asked Duvik, struggling to keep his voice steady. "It's harder than you think."

Jane was frantic. She was too far away to jump him without getting shot herself. She could try arguing with him some more, but he was already close to the breaking point. He could snap without warning and take everyone in the house with him.

Eddie raised the gun. "Goodbye, Sergeant," he said, trying to hold his aim steady. "It's been real."

As he squeezed the trigger, Jane closed her eyes and turned away. She felt the shot like a physical blow to her own body. Two more shots rang out before it was over. She felt sick inside, and terrified for her own life, but she had to look. When she did, she was amazed to see Duvik still standing.

"Don't move," said the officer, his eyes fixed straight ahead.

Jane whirled around and saw Julia at the top of the stairs. She was holding a gun. Eddie lay crumpled on the steps, blood oozing from two wounds in his back and one in his head. It only took an instant for it all to sink in. Jane didn't know how Julia had managed to get free, or where she'd found the weapon, but she'd saved both their lives. "It's okay," said Jane to Duvik.

"I don't think so," he cautioned.

Julia pulled the trigger again, sending another bullet into Eddie's lifeless body.

"Julia, stop!" called Jane, jerking back. "He can't hurt you anymore.

"Get away!" demanded Julia. Her eyes looked out of focus, almost as if she were sleepwalking. "His hand moved. I saw it!"

Jane inched closer to the stairs. "He's dead, Julia. Put the gun down." That's when she saw Rhonda Wellman, Julia's neighbor, emerge from the shadows.

"Honey," said Rhonda, her voice patient and quiet, "it's all right now. You're safe."

Jane was confused. Why was *she* here? And how on earth did she get in?

"Give me the gun, Julia honey." Calmly, Rhonda walked up to her and held out her hand.

For an instant, Jane wasn't sure what Julia would do. She seemed torn. Confused. Her hand started to shake, but her eyes remained glued to the lifeless body. Finally, lowering the gun, she let Rhonda take it. Sinking to her knees, she clutched her stomach and started to sob.

"Unlock my wrists!" barked Duvik. "The keys are in my left coat pocket."

Jane wanted to run to Julia, but she knew she had to free the sergeant first.

"God, that's as close as I ever want to come," he muttered. Once his hands were free, he crouched down next to Eddie and felt for a pulse. Looking back up at Jane, he said, "You called it right. He's dead."

Jane sat on the couch with her arm around Julia, talking quietly to Cordelia and Rhonda who were seated on a bench next to the fireplace. Behind them in the foyer, Duvik took charge of the crime scene. The medical examiner had arrived in record time, but everything seemed to slow down now as videotape was taken and evidence gathered.

"Why did you have to leave Duvik such a garbled message?" asked Jane, looking baffled. "I thought we both knew what we were supposed to do."

After listening to the phone message from Julia over and over again, Jane finally recognized it for what it was: a setup. It was pretty apparent that someone had taped Julia's voice, then used snippets of her words to form the message. But it hadn't been done particularly well. Eddie must have been rushing. Then again, it had served a purpose. Jane knew that Julia was in terrible danger.

She'd called Cordelia immediately, explaining what had happened. She said she was on her way out the door, and that she wanted

Cordelia to call the cops right then, fill them in on the details, and ask them to get over to the house ASAP. She had faith that the police could figure out a way to get Julia away from her captor. Jane realized she was putting her own life in danger by responding to the message, but someone had to get inside the house and make sure Julia was okay. Since the message had been left last night, Jane assumed she had no time to spare. If nothing else, she hoped she could forestall any dire consequences until the police arrived.

"I left Duvik a clear and precise message," said Cordelia, her face puckered into a pout. "Can I help it if his phone is one of Alexander Graham Bell's original cell phones? I was in rather a dither myself, you know. I had to get over to the house to make sure *you* were okay."

"It's over now," said Julia, resting her head on Jane's shoulder. "Let's not argue."

Jane couldn't let it drop. "How did Rhonda get mixed up in all this?"

Cordelia raised a finger. "That was my idea. I needed backup."

"The Minneapolis police force wasn't enough?"

"I kept trying to reach Duvik, but all I got was that infernal recording telling me to leave a message. So, in utter exasperation, I called the fifth precinct and told the guy who answered what was going down, but . . . I don't know. Maybe I did sound a bit . . . exercised. I think he thought I was some sort of nutcase. He said they'd send a squad car around to check it out, but I got the sense it wasn't going to be a priority."

"You were annoyed, so he became testy, so you got snooty—"

Cordelia held up her hand. "Let's just say, it wasn't my finest hour."

"Cordelia! Our lives were at stake!"

"I know! That's why I brought Rhonda with me." Jane failed to see the connection.

"See, after I ran into her in the hall and told her what had happened, she offered to come with me and bring her gun. Hell, I thought, why not?" She bent forward, lowering her voice to a more conspiratorial level. "Okay, so when we got here, we waited for a few minutes hoping the police would show, but when they didn't, we both started getting nervous. We followed the lights going on in the house—until you hit the third floor. I figured that's where you'd all gathered. And that's when we worked out our plan. See, I rang the front doorbell.

That brought you and whoever was holding Julia hostage downstairs. I didn't think he'd let you come alone. I wondered if maybe you wouldn't all come down. But I figured that if I really laid on the bell, he couldn't just blow it off."

"Thanks to my quick thinking, he didn't."

"That's right, Janey. Take all the credit."

"Finish your story, Cordelia."

"Okay, so I grab the boom box from the trunk of my car, slip in a CD, and while I'm making a racket downstairs, Rhonda sneaks up the back steps to the third floor without being seen or heard. She checks out what's happening inside."

Rhonda picked up the story from there. "Cordelia had given me her key. When I looked in the window, I saw Julia on the bed. I waited for a good five minutes, but when I didn't see anyone coming or going, I unlocked the door and crept inside. The keys to the handcuffs were on the nightstand, so I had her free in no time. As soon as she saw my gun, she grabbed it and headed downstairs. I didn't feel all that confident about letting her go, so I followed—at a distance—and well, the rest is history."

Jane shook her head. "Amazing." It wasn't a compliment.

"Yeah, it was, wasn't it?" said Cordelia, a proud smile on her face.

"Sorry to interrupt," said Sgt. Duvik. He was in his element now, issuing orders and taking charge of the investigation. Sitting down on the couch next to Julia, he said, "How are you doing?"

She pulled away from Jane and sat up. "Better. Thanks."

"The doctor who checked you out said you were going to be fine." He took a notepad out of his pocket and flipped it open. "I'm sorry, but I have to get a statement." Glancing around, he added, "From all of you. But right now"—he returned his attention to Julia—"if you could just answer a couple of quick questions. I know this is bad timing, but I'll make it brief. When you're feeling better—tomorrow maybe—you need to come down to the station for a more formal taped interview."

"Of course." She tried to straighten her blouse and slacks, but they still looked crumpled.

"All right. I understand you're a doctor. Is that correct?"

"Yes."

"You have a practice up in northern Minnesota?"

"The Earlton—Grand Rapids area."

319

He scratched something down on his pad. "So, why was Mr. Flynn holding you hostage?"

Julia looked meaningfully at Jane, then back at the detective. "Well, he knew that Jeffrey Chapel had been a patient of mine."

"You were treating Mr. Chapel for the AIDS virus?"

"That's right. Eddie was afraid that Jeffrey had told me he was being blackmailed."

"Because he was gay?"

She nodded.

"Had he?"

"Yes, but I had no idea who was doing it. Jeffrey never said, and I never asked. When Jeffrey was murdered, I guess I just assumed the blackmailer had done it."

"And when Eddie took you hostage, he admitted all of this to you? That he had indeed murdered Mr. Chapel?"

"Eventually, yes."

Duvik scratched a few more notes.

"I flew back into town to see Jane on Saturday night," continued Julia.

"Where were you before that?"

"Los Angeles. My practice extends all over the country. Anyway, Eddie must have been watching the restaurant. He knew that Jane and I have a personal relationship. When I left, he must have followed me. I was headed to a motel, but I changed my mind and decided to stay at Jane's house until the next morning when I had a flight out of town. When I got to the back door, he jumped me. Tied me up. He wanted me to tell him everything I knew. For some reason, he assumed Jeffrey had given me information on the other people Eddie had blackmailed. Apparently, he'd been blackmailing closeted gay men for many years. I'm not a psychologist, you understand, but the man showed clear signs of paranoia. He wouldn't believe me when I assured him I knew nothing. He thought I'd even confided the information to Jane—and perhaps to others. Without telling me, he taped my voice, then used parts of the tape to make a phone message, one he left on Jane's answering machine. When she showed up here, he was going to beat the truth out of her—or torture her to get the truth out of me. I don't know what would have happened if—" She swallowed hard, then looked away.

Cordelia waved at the sergeant to get his attention. "You're, ah, not planning to arrest her for—you know—causing that body out there to become dead?"

"No," said Duvik, lightly touching Julia's hand. "She saved my life. What she did was not only heroic, but completely justified." As he got up, he said, "That's enough for now. But tomorrow, I'd like to see you all down at the station."

"Sure," said Jane. She watched him return to the knot of people in the front hall.

Once they were alone again, Julia moved back closer to Jane.

"I'd say you sidestepped the real issues very adroitly," said Jane, stroking Julia's arm. "Especially for someone in your condition."

"You know, this may not make any sense, but I feel better than I have in months." She snuggled even closer. "An inner sense told me I wouldn't get through this without something awful happening. Now that it has, I feel like it's finally over."

"You hope."

"Hope is a very powerful emotion, Jane. And yes, I have a lot of hopes."

Catching her drift, Cordelia smiled. "I understand the two of you are going to Paris at the end of the week."

"If everything is squared away with the police by then," said Julia, "that's the plan."

"*Is* that the plan?" asked Cordelia, raising her eyebrows inquiringly.

Julia looked up. "You're coming, aren't you?"

Jane didn't like being put on the spot. Even now, after everything that had happened, she still hadn't decided what she'd do.

"I'm not sure," she said, realizing her indecision hurt Julia terribly.

Taking Jane's hand in hers, Julia said, "I'll be on that plane next Friday. I assume you still have the ticket I gave you?"

She nodded.

"Then, all I can do is hope you'll join me. You will think about it?"

Jane put her arm around Julia and drew her close. "I doubt I'll be thinking about anything else."

Chapter 43

WEDNESDAY MORNING

When Brenna answered the door of her condo, she assumed it would be her father. After the death of Eddie Flynn on Monday night, it hadn't taken long for the news to reach them. Her father was finally off the hook for her husband's murder, no thanks to Sgt. Duvik and his myopic theories. However, some equally distressing information was beginning to surface about a scheme her father had participated in to bilk the Haymaker Club of millions.

Feeling disgusted by the whole situation, Brenna decided she no longer had the energy to watch her father throw his life away. She knew his constant wheeling and dealing might get him in trouble one day—and that day seemed to have arrived. Right now, she had her own messy life to come to terms with; she couldn't take on his as well. Not that she planned to abandon him, but she wasn't going to hold his hand anymore either. She assumed he'd come by this morning for a little TLC.

She was wrong. When she finally drew back the door, she found Loren Ives standing in the hallway. He was holding the same cardboard box he'd brought with him the other day.

"I thought we weren't speaking," she said, not even trying to be nice.

He took a deep breath. "I'm sorry, Brenna. I was a fool. I repent in dust and ashes. I should never have reacted the way I did about your brunch date with Knute Rockne."

She could tell he was trying hard, but he couldn't help himself. He had to slip in a little sarcasm just to show he hadn't entirely lost his edge. "Haven't we played this scene before?" she asked.

"You have a perfect right to see anyone you want."

"Damn right I do."

He hesitated. "May I come in? I don't have much time."

"And why would that be?"

"My accountant and I have an appointment with an IRS agent in less than an hour. Next time you see me, I may be wearing stripes and dragging around a ball and chain."

"They don't make prisoners wear striped clothing anymore."

"A tasteful prison system. My heart is all aflutter."

She cracked a smile. "All right, come in."

Once he'd removed his coat, he perched on the couch, placing the box on his knees.

"Would you like a cup of coffee?"

"Thanks, no. I've come to say my piece . . . and then leave."

She sat down next to him. "I'm listening."

"This is on the order of a prepared speech, Brenna, so don't interrupt." After clearing his throat, Loren continued, "My dear friend Jeffrey Chapel made many mistakes in his life for which he should be duly condemned. But then, so have I. The worst one was keeping Jeffrey's secret from you. By doing so, I not only allowed Jeffrey to hurt you, but I hurt you myself. I've been furious at Jeffrey for a long time, but I think I'm finally willing to take a more patient look at what he did. His intentions were honorable; he simply couldn't become something he wasn't. Unfortunately, he thought he could, and that's the real tragedy. If anyone was strong and determined, it was your husband. And yet, in the end, even he couldn't pull a straight rabbit out of a gay hat. He failed all of us, but most importantly, I believe he failed himself." He paused for a second, shifted in his seat, and then went on. "I'm just beginning to see how I failed *him*. Here," he said, handing her the box.

"What is it?" She opened the cover and looked in.

"It's Jeffrey," said Loren. "Or as much of him as I'm able to pass on to you. These are his diaries and journals. Some he kept in college; some he wrote when he was a marine. He always saw to it that they were well hidden. When the notebooks were full, he'd mail them to me for safekeeping. I felt I owed him his privacy, so I never read them. That is, until last Saturday. I give them to you as a peace offering. I've behaved like a proprietary ass, and I know it. Perhaps, after you've read them, you'll understand a little more what it was like to be Jeffrey Chapel. It's all in there. A gay man's life. In so many ways, it truly tears me up inside. He was a creature of his time, Brenna. When he was growing up, everyone told him he was sick and sinful just for being who he was. I wish to God he could have grown up twenty years later. He might have had a chance at a more normal life—and every bit as importantly, he might not have hurt you. You see, I can't let go of the notion that he was a truly noble soul. He was my friend. We were the repository of each other's histories. We grew up together. All I can say is, I loved him, but I wish I could have understood him more, and judged him less."

Brenna removed the top notebook. It was dated 1968.

"All I ask is one favor," continued Loren. "When you're done reading these, I'd like to talk to you." Lowering his head, he added, "I know you may never have the same kind of feelings for me you had for Jeffrey. I'm not much of a catch, I realize that. But, we'll always have Jeffrey's memory in common. Maybe, in a way, that means we're related. I don't want to lose you, Brenna. I *can't* lose you both."

She could see him struggling not to cry. Taking hold of his hand, she said, "Of course, we'll talk."

"I'll call you. Even if we have to speak to each other through a wire cage, or on a prison phone like the one Jimmy Cagney used in—"

"Someone in this room tends to melodrama. And it's not me."

He smiled. "Will you keep your fingers crossed?"

"Always."

Together they got up and crossed to the door. After they said their good-byes, Loren bent and kissed her very lightly on the lips.

Watching him walk down the long hall, Brenna couldn't help but wonder what their future would bring. "Thanks again for the note-books," she called, wishing he could have stayed longer.

As the elevator doors closed in front of him, he gave her a thumbs-up and a hopeful smile.

Chapter 44

FRIDAY AFTERNOON

Jane switched off the light in the kitchen and then crossed through the dining room into the foyer where her suitcase rested next to the front hall closet. By now, Julia was probably at the airport waiting for her. As the time to leave approached, Jane sat down for a moment on the stairs, pressing her hands between her knees and wondering if she'd made the right decision.

Amazing as it seemed, she still wasn't sure. From her standpoint, there was a lot at stake, and she'd wanted to take her time—to consider all the ramifications—before deciding on a course of action. She didn't really know what Julia expected of her, but in a way, that wasn't important anymore. Jane had to do what was best for her. Not just for her future, but for her health.

Cordelia had made her opinion crystal clear. She felt strongly that if Jane didn't go to Paris, she'd regret it. Perhaps not right away, but later, when she realized she hadn't truly given Julia a fair chance. Cordelia's one hard-and-fast personal rule was to live her life in such a way that when she got to the end of it, she wouldn't have regrets. "Never stifle honest emotion," she'd told Jane on the phone. "And don't be afraid to take a few chances. What was it that Kurt Vonnegut said? 'Unexpected invitations are dancing lessons from God.'"

Patricia Kastner had a very different take on the situation. Jane hadn't really asked for her opinion, but she'd given it anyway. She told Jane in no uncertain terms that if she followed Julia to France, it would be nothing short of pathetic. "When you're playing a game you can't win, it's best to cut your losses and get the hell out." Typical of Patricia to see life as a game, but then, like Cordelia, she had a point.

Jane's father had given her no advice at all. He'd merely called last night to wish her a good trip, just in case she was planning to go. He said the issues were complex, but whatever decision she made, he'd support her. All he really wanted was for her to get her health—and her life—back on track. If that meant spending the month with Julia, fine. If it meant staying home or ending the relationship, it was her call.

And so, Jane had been left alone to come to a decision. She knew the time was drawing near. If she didn't leave soon, the plane would take off without her.

Standing, she took one last look around her house. "What's it gonna be?" she whispered, staring at the suitcase.

Until her plane was called for boarding, Julia sat in the passenger lounge, watching the huge jets land and take off. Every few minutes, she'd glance down the long red concourse, searching for a sign of Jane. So far, Julia was still alone, though she couldn't believe she'd stay that way much longer.

She hadn't seen or talked to Jane since Wednesday afternoon, the day she'd bumped into her down at city hall. They'd both agreed to give each other some time apart. Julia had moved back to her downtown loft, and from what Jane had said, she was still staying at the restaurant, though she planned to return to her house on Wednesday night. Initially, Julia didn't much like the sound of that. Jane seemed so upbeat about moving back home that it made Julia wonder if she would want to leave so soon to go on an extended vacation. But then, who could turn down an all-expense-paid trip to Paris, especially when the two of them desperately needed time to work out their problems? Julia didn't want to push, but she did ask Jane if she'd made a decision.

326

All she got was, "I don't know yet. But I will by Friday." Jane was typically warm and full of concern about Julia's health, especially after the beating she had taken last weekend, but beyond that, Julia couldn't get a fix on how she was feeling.

Picking up her carry-on bag, Julia looked over her shoulder one last time, then handed the ticket to the flight attendant and moved on down the narrow hallway to the door of the plane. Once seated—in first class, a luxury she wanted to share with Jane—she ordered some white wine and settled in. There was still a good half hour before the doors would be shut and the plane would be readied for takeoff.

Taking a medical journal out of her bag, she perused a few articles, but couldn't get interested in any of them. Perhaps she was more anxious than she thought. She took a couple of sips of wine, then looked around the cabin. The seats were filling up fast.

This particular flight was headed to Montreal. From there, they'd board another, larger jet and fly straight to Orly. Closing her eyes, Julia let her thoughts drift to the romantic scenarios she'd created for the two of them. Strolling along the Left Bank. Visiting the Louvre. Eating something wonderful in an out-of-the-way bistro. In no time, Jane would take on her old healthy glow. They'd resolve their differences—perhaps slowly—but it would come. And most importantly, they'd be together—in every sense of the word. Julia had so much she wanted to tell Jane. It would be a glorious time, one they would remember always.

"Please make sure your seats are in an upright position and your tray tables put away," came a voice over the loudspeaker.

Julia looked up, and instantly her heart started to pound. There she was, standing behind a group of people loaded down with carry-on luggage, taking their sweet time about getting on. Julia stood in her seat, ready to greet her, but stopped just as she was about to call her name. She squinted to get a better view. No, it wasn't Jane after all, but a woman who looked very much like her.

Julia felt her spirits sink as she sat back down. Only a few more minutes remained. Feeling at a complete loss, she scrutinized her watch, willing the time to stop. Could it be that Jane really wasn't coming? She glanced up at the door again, her eyes fixed on the empty hallway just outside the hatch. The head flight attendant seemed to be getting ready to close it up. She was talking to the pilot, motioning to several of the other attendants. Surely they could wait another couple of minutes.

"Miss," said Julia, waving to get her attention.

The flight attendant walked over. "May I help you?" Her accent was decidedly French.

"My traveling companion isn't here yet. How much time do we have?"

"We'll be shutting the door shortly."

"But . . . I'm sure she's coming."

"What's her name?"

"Lawless. Jane Lawless."

"I'll have her paged," she said, walking back to the front of the cabin and disappearing into the galley.

Julia counted the seconds until she returned.

"I'm sorry, madam, but your friend doesn't answer the page. I can only assume she isn't in the airport."

Julia returned her gaze to the door. There was still no sign of her.

"I'm afraid we can't hold the plane, madam. Perhaps your friend will be on another flight?"

Julia nodded her thanks, knowing there wouldn't be another flight. Jane had given her answer. It was probably the one Julia deserved, and yet she couldn't believe it. Jane had always forgiven her before. The hope of their reconciliation was what had kept her going for months now. Without it, what did she have? Her medical practice was in shambles. She'd alienated Leo. And the one true love of her life had rejected her.

As the plane backed out of the gate and was directed toward the runway, she turned her face to the window, tears streaming down her cheeks. She didn't even try to wipe them away. It was all her fault, she might as well wallow in it. And yet . . . it shouldn't have ended this way. It mustn't end this way.

Feeling the power of the engines build, she leaned back as the plane moved forward—slowly at first, but picking up speed until the jets roared in her ears. In a matter of seconds, the ground fell away. The plane banked toward the north, and Julia caught sight of the city she loved. "Good-bye, Jane," she said, leaning her head against the small window. Closing her eyes, she whispered, "I'll be back."

328

Publications from
Bella Books, Inc.
Women. Books. Even Better Together.

P.O. Box 10543
Tallahassee, FL 32302
Phone: 800-729-4992
www.bellabooks.com

THE GRASS WIDOW by Nanci Little. Aidan Blackstone is nineteen, unmarried and pregnant, and has no reason to think that the year 1876 won't be her last. Joss Bodett has lost her family but desperately clings to their land. A richly told story of frontier survival that picks up with the generation of women where Patience and Sarah left off.
978-1-59493-189-5 $12.95

SMOKEY O by Celia Cohen. Insult "Mac" MacDonnell and insult the entire Delaware Blue Diamond team. Smokey O'Neill has just insulted Mac, and then finds she's been traded to Delaware. The games are not limited to the baseball field!
978-1-59493-198-7 $12.95

WICKED GAMES by Ellen Hart. Never have mysteries and secrets been closer to home in this eighth installment of this award-winning lesbian mystery series. Jane Lawless's neighbors bring puzzles and peril—and that's just the beginning.
978-1-59493-185-7 $14.95

NOT EVERY RIVER by Robbi McCoy. It's the hottest city in the U.S., and it's not just the weather that's heating up. For Kim and Randi are forced to question everything they thought they knew about themselves before they can risk their fiery hearts on the biggest gamble of all.
978-1-59493-182-6 $14.95

HOUSE OF CARDS by Nat Burns. Cards are played, but the game is gossip. Kaylen Strauder has never wanted it to be about her. But the time is fast-approaching when she must decide which she needs more: her community or Eda Byrne.
978-1-59493-203-8 $14.95

RETURN TO ISIS by Jean Stewart. The award-winning Isis sci-fi series features Jean Stewart's vision of a committed colony of women dedicated to preserving their way of life, even after the apocalypse. Mysteries have been forgotten, but survival depends on remembering. Book one in series.
978-1-59493-193-2 $12.95

1ST IMPRESSIONS by Kate Calloway. Rookie PI Cassidy James has her first case. Her investigation into the murder of Erica Trinidad's uncle isn't welcomed by the local sheriff, especially since the delicious, seductive Erica is their prime suspect. 1st in series. Author's augmented and expanded edition.
978-1-59493-192-5 $12.95

BEACON OF LOVE by Ann Roberts. Twenty-five years after their families put an end to a relationship that hadn't even begun, Stephanie returns to Oregon to find many things have changed . . . except her feelings for Paula.
978-1-59493-180-2 $14.95

ABOVE TEMPTATION by Karin Kallmaker. It's supposed to be like any other case, except this time they're chasing one of their own. As fraud investigators Tamara Sterling and Kip Barrett try to catch a thief, they realize they can have anything they want—except each other.
978-1-59493-179-6 $14.95

AN EMERGENCE OF GREEN by Katherine V. Forrest. Carolyn had no idea her new neighbor jumped the fence to enjoy her swimming pool. The discovery leads to choices she never anticipated in an intense, sensual story of discovery and risk, consequences and triumph. Originally released in 1986.
?78-1-59493-217-5 $14.95